THE EMPEROR'S REVENGE

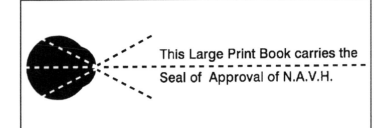

This Large Print Book carries the
Seal of Approval of N.A.V.H.

AN *Oregon* FILES ADVENTURE

THE EMPEROR'S REVENGE

CLIVE CUSSLER
AND BOYD MORRISON

LARGE PRINT PRESS
A part of Gale, Cengage Learning

GALE
CENGAGE Learning·

Farmington Hills, Mich • San Francisco • New York • Waterville, Maine
Meriden, Conn • Mason, Ohio • Chicago

GALE
CENGAGE Learning

LIBRARY OF CONGRESS CATALOGING-IN-PUBLICATION DATA

Names: Cussler, Clive, author. | Morrison, Boyd, 1967- author.
Title: The Emperor's revenge / Clive Cussler and Boyd Morrison.
Description: Large print edition. | Waterville, Maine : Wheeler Publishing, 2016. | Series: A novel of the Oregon files | Series: Wheeler Publishing large print hardcover
Identifiers: LCCN 2016016587 | ISBN 9781410489975 (hardback) | ISBN 1410489973 (hardcover)
Subjects: LCSH: Large type books. | BISAC: FICTION / Action & Adventure. | GSAFD: Suspense fiction. | Adventure fiction.
Classification: LCC PS3553.U75 E47 2016b | DDC 813/.54—dc23
LC record available at https://lccn.loc.gov/2016016587

ISBN 13: 978-1-59413-974-1 (pbk.)
ISBN 10: 1-59413-974-1 (pbk.)

Published in 2017 by arrangement with G. P. Putnam's Sons, an imprint of Penguin Publishing Group, a division of Penguin Random House LLC

Printed in Mexico
1 2 3 4 5 6 7 21 20 19 18 17

THE EMPEROR'S
REVENGE

PROLOGUE

ST. HELENA
APRIL 28, 1821

Lieutenant Pierre Delacroix cursed himself for his overconfidence. He had taken a huge risk by sailing into the predawn twilight, hoping to get just a few miles closer to the rocky cliffs on the north side of St. Helena before sunup. A British frigate, one of the eleven guarding the remote island, appeared around the coast and turned in their direction. If his submarine were caught on the surface in broad daylight, the mission to free Napoleon Bonaparte from exile would be over before it began.

Delacroix lowered his spyglass and called down through the hatch. "Prepare to dive the boat!"

Three men quickly lowered the sail in the gusting wind. With the bright sun at his back, Delacroix took one last look at the approaching frigate before ducking below and closing the copper hatch. His nostrils flared at the rank odor of fifteen men packed together inside the cramped quarters.

"Did they spot us?" asked Yves Beaumont, a frown creasing his forehead. Though he kept his voice calm, his eyes flicked incessantly toward the closed portal, betraying his anxiety. The experienced alpinist had nonchalantly stood on ledges at heights that would cause normal men to faint in fear, but the idea of submerging inside the confines of a hollow metal and wooden tube terrified him.

Delacroix had no such claustrophobia, one reason why he was the perfect man to lead the mission on the world's first operational submarine.

"We'll know if they've seen us soon enough, Monsieur Beaumont."

They'd also soon know if the sub would be able to withstand submerging in the open ocean. It had been built based on designs American engineer Robert Fulton had used to demonstrate the concept of submarine warfare to Napoleon's naval staff. Delacroix named his fifty-foot-long update *Stingray*.

Since casting off from the schooner that had towed the technically advanced vessel within sixty miles of St. Helena's shores, the *Stingray* had sailed under cover of darkness. So far, the voyage had been uneventful, and the copper-clad oaken hull remained watertight.

Now it was time to find out if the harbor dive tests that the *Stingray* had passed with flying colors were matched by her performance under the high seas.

"All hatches sealed, Lieutenant," said Ensign Villeneuve, Delacroix's second-in-command. "The snorkel is closed and tight."

"Ready on the ballast pumps."

The sub's two engineers prepared to work the manual pumps that would force water into the empty tanks. The rest of the twelve-man crew was in position to operate the crank that would turn the propeller at the rear, while Delacroix held the stick that controlled the rudder. Beaumont and their second passenger, who wore a black mask at all times to keep his identity secret, pressed themselves against the hull to stay out of the way.

With a deep breath as if he were preparing to plunge into the ocean himself, Delacroix said, "Dive the boat."

The engineers cranked the pumps, and in a few minutes water began to break against the two windows in the *Stingray*'s viewing tower. The wood of the vessel creaked as it adjusted to the pressure pushing against it on all sides.

"It's not natural to be in a boat underwater," he heard one crewman murmur, but a sharp glance from Delacroix silenced him.

He waited until the external line attached to a float indicated they were submerged twenty feet below the surface, then said, "Hold here."

The engineers stopped pumping. The *Stingray* held steady and the creaking ceased.

Now all they could do was wait. Except for an occasional cough from the crewmen, the *Stingray*'s interior was eerily quiet. Even the reassuring sound of water lapping against the hull was gone.

By now, the sun had fully risen, providing enough light through the inch-thick windows in the observation tower under the water so that a lantern was no longer needed to illuminate the sub's interior. They should now be able to remain underwater for six hours before needing to either extend the snorkel tubes or surface for air.

Two hours into their vigil, a shadow passed over them. Delacroix, squinting through the window, could just make out the hull of the frigate not a hundred feet away, her sails shading the sub from the sun.

All movement inside the submarine stopped as the crew waited for an attack, looking up at the ceiling as if they could see through it to the threat above.

Delacroix's eyes were glued on the frigate for any clue that it was tacking in their direction. Instead, its course stayed straight and true. In a few minutes, it was out of view. Out of extreme caution, Delacroix waited another three hours before ordering the snorkel to be extended.

With their air supply renewed, they remained submerged until darkness fell. The *Stingray* surfaced to a night illuminated by a half-moon. Delacroix was pleased to see that no lights were visible.

He turned his gaze to the jagged cliff of Black Point close by. The northern face rose five hundred feet above the sea. He'd been training for months with the mountaineer Beaumont, but seeing the rocky crag in person made him doubt the mission for the first time.

Beaumont joined him in the hatch and nodded as he viewed the steep cliff.

"Can we climb it?" Delacroix asked.

"Oui," Beaumont replied. "It's not the Matterhorn. And it will be easier to climb than Mont Blanc, which I've ascended three times."

Instead of this covert infiltration, Delacroix would have preferred a full-on invasion of the island, but he would have needed three dozen warships and ten thousand men to have any chance at success. The garrison of twenty-eight hundred soldiers and five hundred cannon protecting a single prisoner twelve hundred miles from the nearest land made Napoleon Bonaparte the most well-guarded person in world history. It probably would have been easier to abduct the King of England.

The crew tumbled out onto the deck, inhaling the fresh air. They lowered cork bumpers around the edges of the *Stingray* to keep it from being dashed on the outcroppings and dropped the anchor.

Delacroix looped a large coil of high-strength fishing line over his shoulder, and Beaumont did the same. They hooked a safety line between them. More than a thousand feet of rope was piled on the deck, along with a contraption that looked like a child's swing.

With a nod, Beaumont stepped onto the nearest rock and began climbing. When he was ten feet up, Delacroix followed. They methodically climbed the cliff face, detouring when they needed to avoid a particularly sheer part. Beaumont proceeded with seemingly little effort, pausing only to give De-lacroix some rest. Just once did Delacroix slip, but the safety line prevented him from plummeting to his death.

Normally, Beaumont would take forty minutes to climb five hundred feet on his own, but Delacroix's inexperienced pace meant that the ascent took more than an hour.

When they reached the top of the cliff, Beaumont hammered an iron bolt and ring into the rock. He then attached a pulley, tied both coils of fishing line together, and looped the line over the pulley before anchoring it with a metal weight painted bright yellow. He tossed it far over the side to make sure it would extend all the way down to the water next to the sub. Delacroix spotted no ships on the horizon, so he waved a small flag to signal the crewmen to hook up the rope to the line.

When they received a signal in return that the rope was attached, he and Beaumont hauled up the fishing line over the pulley. The heavy rope snaked up the cliff. When it reached the top, they signaled again.

With two hundred pounds of the masked man muscle added to the weight of the rope, progress was agonizingly slow. After ten minutes of backbreaking labor, Beaumont held the rope fast while Delacroix heaved the masked man over the edge and helped him out of the wooden swing contraption, called a bosun's chair. A separate board was lashed behind for Delacroix to stand on while it was being lowered later in the evening.

"Doesn't he ever talk?" Beaumont asked, pointing a thumb at the masked man.

"He's paid not to," Delacroix said. "Just like you were paid to bring me up here. Now your job is done, and I thank you."

"So who is he?"

"You'll never know," Delacroix said, and jabbed a stiletto into Beaumont's neck. The alpinist went rigid, his eyes staring in confusion and disbelief. He slumped slowly to the ground.

Delacroix shoved twenty pounds of stones into the pack on Beaumont's back. Using his foot, he nudged the mountaineer's corpse over the cliff at an angle to avoid hitting the submarine below. The crewmen would see the tumbling body and the splash, and Delacroix would tell them that Beaumont had slipped and fallen. Now there was one less witness to worry about.

"Come," Delacroix said to the masked man as they began their arduous three-mile trek inland. Delacroix's companion followed dutifully behind without a word. Barren rock slowly gave way to lowland scrub brush and then thick forest.

By midnight, they reached the edge of the Longwood estate, the sprawling manor house where Napoleon was being held prisoner. It was in the dreariest part of the island, miles from Jamestown, the only port. The isolation was intended to be part of the defeated emperor's punishment, but it also played into Delacroix's plan. Because it was so inaccessible, the guards were lax and let Napoleon roam wherever he wanted as long as he did not head toward town.

The sole road to Jamestown lay on the opposite side of the estate, as did the main guard shack and barracks. The guards didn't even bother with a random patrol of the grounds, a carefully tended garden comprising a mix of native gumwoods and English hardwoods.

Using the trees as cover, Delacroix and the masked man were able to reach the house without raising an alarm. Delacroix had memorized the floor plan and guided them to the nearest door.

At this late hour, the house was still and dark. Delacroix navigated noiselessly through the halls until they reached the bedroom they were looking for. Delacroix eased the door open and crept inside, followed by the masked man. He instructed the man to remove his mask, then struck a match to light the bedside lamp.

The occupant of the bed stirred at the sudden light.

"We've come for you, Your Majesty," Delacroix said.

With a start, Napoleon Bonaparte sat up in bed. He was prepared to shout for assistance when he saw Delacroix's companion.

He could have been Napoleon's twin brother. Same balding head, same diminutive height, same Roman nose. Even though Delacroix had been expecting this moment, the sight of them together still took his breath away.

Napoleon squinted at his doppelganger and said, "Robeaud?"

"It is I, Your Majesty," the double said in a pitch-perfect imitation of the emperor's cadences.

François Robeaud had served for many years as Napoleon's duplicate, appearing at events when the emperor chose not to and allowing Napoleon to stay out of harm's way when he feared an assassination attempt. His existence had been known only to a select few, and it had taken years for

Delacroix to track him down in debtors' prison, where Robeaud had been incarcerated ever since his benefactor had been captured by the English.

"Who are you?" Napoleon demanded, turning to Delacroix, who saluted smartly. His heart pounded at meeting the military mastermind who had conquered a continent.

"Lieutenant Pierre Delacroix, Your Majesty. I served under Commodore Maistral aboard the *Neptune* during the Battle of Trafalgar." The *Neptune* was one of the few ships to escape the decisive naval engagement that made Lord Nelson a hero to the British.

Napoleon narrowed his eyes at the mention of one of his country's worst defeats. "What is the meaning of this intrusion?"

"I mean to spirit you away from this island, Your Majesty. I have a fleet of eighty warships waiting for your command back in France."

"Then why did you not attack the island to free me?"

"Because the officers will follow only your orders. They will not risk fighting the Royal Navy unless they know you've been liberated."

He stared at Robeaud. "And Monsieur

Robeaud? Why bring him to this godforsaken island?"

Delacroix nodded at Robeaud, who took a flask from his cloak. He unscrewed the cap, looked at the opening for a few long seconds, and downed its contents.

Delacroix took the flask and tucked it in his coat. "Not only did Robeaud volunteer to take your place, he agreed to swallow that arsenic in return for money to settle his family's debts. He will be dead in a matter of days, but his family will be well off for the rest of their lives. The physicians that the English recently sent to take your personal doctor's place do not know you well enough to recognize an impostor."

Napoleon slowly nodded in appreciation of Delacroix's tactical acumen. "Very good, Lieutenant. I see that you learned well from my example. If the British knew I had escaped, the squadron of ships guarding St. Helena would chase us down before we got thirty miles out to sea."

"Exactly, Your Majesty. Now we must go."

"Go where? How are we to escape?"

"I have a submarine waiting at Black Point."

Napoleon's eyes widened. "You mean Fulton's strange vessel actually works?"

"Come with me and I'll show you."

Robeaud donned the nightclothes and got into bed while Napoleon dressed in one of the military uniforms that the British had allowed him to keep.

"I insist on retreating with the honor of a soldier," he said. Napoleon picked up a book by the bedside. He tore several pages from it, tucked them in his tunic, and replaced the book. The cover read *L'Odyssée,* with Greek letters below the title. Homer's *Odyssey.*

When Delacroix gave him a puzzled look, Napoleon said, "The pages have sentimental value to me."

They snuck out of the estate the same way Delacroix and Robeaud had entered. Napoleon was in poorer health than his replacement, so the journey back to the coast took longer. They reached the cliff top with only a couple of hours until sunrise.

Delacroix tossed one end of the rope over the side so that the submarine crew could catch it, then readied the bosun's chair. When Napoleon saw how he was to be lowered to the water, he initially refused. Delacroix reminded him that the bosun's chair was the way officers were hoisted onto naval vessels while they were at sea, which quelled the emperor's objections.

He took a seat in the chair while Delacroix

19

stood on the operator's board behind him and held on to the rope to steady them. When Delacroix signaled with three quick tugs on the rope, the crewmen below started playing the rope out that wrapped around the pulley at the top of the cliff. Napoleon sat erect, trying to retain as much dignity as possible in such an awkward position.

With only an hour remaining before dawn, Napoleon and Delacroix alighted on the deck of the submarine. The crewmen hauled the rest of the rope down as they stared with mouths agape at the legendary leader. When the rope was reeled in, all that would remain of their escape would be the inconspicuous bolt and pulley at the cliff top.

They shoved away from the cliff and retrieved the cork fenders. They would sail as far from the coast as they could before daylight and then submerge.

"Congratulations on your success, Lieutenant," Napoleon said. "You will be highly decorated for this daring raid. Now, when we rendezvous with our frigate, I expect we will make straight for our fleet to —"

Delacroix shook his head. "There is no fleet."

The statement was met with a look of disbelief. "No fleet? But you told me we had eighty ships at our disposal."

"I said that so you would come with me willingly. This is a secret mission. No one must know you've escaped. Ever."

"You expect me to skulk away like a thief in the night, leaving an impostor in my place? No! How am I to retake my rightful position as emperor? I must announce my illustrious return to power. I refuse to flee my prison like some common criminal."

"You no longer have any choice in the matter."

Napoleon slammed his fist against the submarine's conning tower. "Lieutenant Delacroix, I demand to know what your intentions are for my rescue!"

"You misunderstand, Your Majesty," Delacroix said, and nodded to a sailor holding a set of iron shackles. "We did not come to this desolate place to rescue you. We came to kidnap you."

ONE

ALGERIA
PRESENT DAY

Towering dunes and rocky crags stretched as far as the eye could see, baked by the harsh midday sun. The IL-76 cargo plane, now three hours out of Cairo, had been flying a zigzag pattern across the Sahara according to instructions.

Tiny Gunderson turned in his pilot's seat and blinked in confusion when he saw Juan Cabrillo standing behind him.

Normally, Juan sported short blond hair, blue eyes, and a tan complexion like the native Californian he was, but today he was disguised as an Arab native, with dyed black hair, brown contact lenses, skin darkened even further by makeup, and a prosthetic nose to alter his appearance.

"For a moment, I thought you were one of our other passengers," Tiny said.

"They're busy down in the hold, checking

their gear," Juan replied. "They look a little nervous. A couple of them have never sky-dived before."

"Well, they picked a doozy of a place to learn. I haven't seen so much as a road for the last thirty minutes."

"They want to make sure no one beats us to their target."

"Fat chance of that happening. We're nearing the latest checkpoint. I'm going to need the next set of coordinates."

"Then my timing is impeccable," Juan said. "Our client just gave me this. He said it's the drop location." He handed Tiny a piece of paper with a set of GPS coordinates. Tiny plugged the new numbers into the Russian jet's autopilot computer, and the four-engine plane began banking in that direction.

"We should be on-site in ten minutes," he said. "I'll open the rear door two minutes before the drop."

Juan nodded. "What's our fuel status?"

"No problem. I've got eight more hours of flight time."

"Remember," Juan said, "they won't leave the landing zone until you're out of sight, so hightail it as soon as we're away."

"Like I've been bit in the butt, Chairman. Have a good fall."

Juan smiled. "Keep in touch." He left the cockpit and took the stairs down into the cavernous hold.

Four pallets occupied the center of the hold. Three dune buggies were packed nose to tail, their parachutes piled on top and their rip cords attached to the plane so they would be triggered automatically when dropped.

The dune buggies were Scorpion desert patrol vehicles sold as surplus by the Saudi Army, with their armaments removed, of course. It had taken a day to refit them with the .50 caliber M2 Browning machine gun and 40mm Mk 19 grenade launcher that were usually mounted on the chassis. Now they could take on anything, short of a tank, and, according to their clients, the weapons weren't going to be just for show.

The fourth pallet, the same size as the dune buggies, was still under wraps at the front of the hold. It wouldn't be joining them on this drop.

Juan strode toward the six men gathered near the rear door. All of them were elite soldiers of the Saharan Islamic Caliphate, a terrorist organization hoping to build a fundamentalist state that would span the entire width of North Africa.

The leader of this particular group, a

brutal Egyptian named Mahmoud Nazari, who was suspected of several attacks on tourist groups, had made it known that he was trying to gain access to weapons of mass destruction that would aid in his goal to become the ruling caliph. The NSA had intercepted a conversation between him and his benefactors in Saudi Arabia that he needed funds to make an incursion into Algeria, where he could obtain such weapons.

Although the type of weapon was never specified in the call, the threat was taken seriously, and the Corporation had been tapped to take on the mission to discover what Nazari was looking for.

Juan stopped in front of the group. Nazari, a thin man with a heavy beard and dead eyes, showed no emotion whatsoever. He said in Arabic, "How long until our jump?"

"Less than ten minutes," Juan replied with flawless Saudi Arabian inflection. He also spoke Russian and Spanish fluently in various accents, but he'd never been able to master Arabic in any other dialect, so his backstory sold him as a jihadist from Riyadh.

Given the atrocities Nazari was thought to have committed, Juan got a bad taste in his mouth every time he had to talk to the terrorist. When Nazari bragged about slicing off an infidel civilian's hands during one of his attacks, Juan nearly threw him out of the plane's door without a parachute, but the mission to find the WMDs was too important to indulge his urge.

"How far do we have to drive once we land?" Juan continued.

"You'll know when I tell you. Now, complete your preparations." Juan hadn't been expecting an answer, but he would have seemed suspicious if he weren't curious about the mission.

"Yes, sir," Juan said, forcing himself to say the words with a convincing tone of feigned respect. He pointed at the warning light above their heads. "That will flash red when the rear door opens. Stay behind the yellow line on the floor if you don't want to get sucked out. The light will change to amber a minute before the jump, then green to signal the jump. The pallets will go first, then us. Understand?"

"We went over this in the preflight briefing," Nazari said with clear disdain. "We're not simpletons." His men, who busily rechecked their harnesses and static lines, didn't seem bothered by the reminder.

"Of course," Juan replied. "I didn't mean to offend. I'll see you on the ground."

Juan left them and headed to the front of the cargo deck. The only reason he cared if they made it to the ground intact was so they could lead him to the target. It had been a challenge to get them to trust him to the degree they had, which was why this operation hadn't been tasked to U.S. Special Forces. As good as they were, infiltration wasn't their specialty, and the CIA had their own limitations.

Juan had created the Corporation to do work the U.S. government couldn't engage in directly. Plausible deniability was the rule. His stint as an agent in the CIA had made it clear that there were plenty of those types of operations needing to be carried out through the Corporation. Juan had offered to take on the risks, for which he and those in his employ had been well compensated. Side jobs supplemented their income when work from the CIA was scarce, but Juan never took on a job that he didn't feel was in the best interests of America.

This mission certainly fit the bill.

It had taken weeks of secret meetings to gain Nazari's trust enough to be hired for the mission. He required a clandestine insertion into the southern Algerian desert, fifty miles of rough terrain from the nearest settlement or oasis. The dune buggies had only enough fuel to get them from the drop to the target and then back to civilization, which was one of the reasons for the aerial insertion. The other was because they weren't supposed to be on Algerian soil. The *Oregon* was already positioned at the port of Algiers to smuggle them out of the country. Tiny Gunderson, the Corporation's fixed-wing pilot, would return the chartered IL-76 to its owners at the end of the mission. Originally, the operation was to take place three days from now, but Nazari had suddenly shortened the time line for unknown reasons.

Juan found Eddie Seng verifying that the pallet tie-downs for the dune buggies were tight. As lean and sinewy as an Olympic gymnast, Eddie was another veteran of the CIA and the Corporation's chief of shore operations. Though he was fluent in Mandarin, he didn't know any Arabic, so he hadn't mixed with Nazari and his crew. Juan told them that Eddie was a freedom fighter from Indonesia, the most populous Muslim country in the world. Luckily, they hadn't recognized that Eddie was actually of Chinese descent.

"How are our friends doing?" Eddie asked, and smiled when he saw one of them wrestling with the line that would pull his rip cord. "Some of them look a little green."

"I just hope they hold it together until they jump," Juan said, shrugging into his parachute rig. "Tiny will have a fit if they toss their cookies and he has to clean up the mess before he returns the plane. Are we set?"

"Everything checks out. We're good to go."

"Where's Linc?"

"Just took one last trip to the head," said a basso voice behind Juan. He turned to see Franklin Lincoln, carrying his chute in one hand and two AK-47 assault rifles in the other as if they were toys. The gargantuan African American, with a head as smooth as a cue ball, handed Juan an AK-47, one of his least favorite weapons. He took it reluctantly.

"Don't blame me, Chairman," Linc said. As a former Navy SEAL, he would have much rather been carrying a more state-of-the-art weapon, too. "Remember, we're trying to fit in." Linc's cover was that he was a Nigerian who had joined the struggle to fight the Western infidels.

Intel said that it was unlikely that Nazari and his men spoke any English. Juan had told Nazari that he, Eddie, and Linc had only English as a common language, since they were supposed to be from Saudi Arabia, Indonesia, and Nigeria. Still, Juan kept his voice low when he could, just in case the intel was wrong.

"Doesn't mean I have to like it," Juan said. He secured the rifle to his pack.

"Any word yet on what our target is?" Eddie asked.

"Nada. Nazari's not the sharing type. I'm not even sure his men know." Juan tapped his watch, and voices suddenly popped into his earpiece. He could hear Nazari as clearly as if he were standing next to the terrorist. So far, the minuscule microphone transmitter that Juan had installed in the liner of his harness hadn't yielded any strong intel.

"But they have done everything we've required," Juan could hear one of the soldiers telling Nazari.

"I don't care," Nazari said. "We can't take that chance. Once they realize what we've dug up, they may change their minds about —"

At that moment, the rear door lowered, letting in a blast of air that garbled the sound so much that Juan could only catch a few snippets of the remaining conversation.

Juan, Eddie, and Linc didn't waste any time finishing the drop prep. Everything was ready when the amber light flashed.

A minute to the drop.

31

"We're going to have to keep on our toes once we reach the target and recover whatever it is they're looking for," Juan said, his eye on Nazari at the other end of the hold. "I'm pretty sure I just heard that that's when our client plans to kill us."

Linc smirked. "Lovely."

Then the green light blazed, the dune buggy pallets neatly slid out the back one after the other, and Juan led the jump out over the desert waiting a mile below.

Two

MONACO

Henri Munier would never admit to a soul that he couldn't stand motor sports, not when he was the president of a bank in a country with the world's most famous auto race. Many of his biggest clients were Formula series drivers who lived in Monaco to take advantage of its reputation as a tax-free haven. They would be appalled to learn that he thought their sport was obnoxious and boring.

He couldn't help cringing as he drove his new customized Tesla electric SUV past the Monaco Grand Prix turn known as La Rascasse. The morning race of Formula 3.5 cars was nearing its end, the sleek race cars' high-pitched engines whining as they rounded the corner and revved to full speed. The SUV's windows did little to block out the incessant shriek.

And it would only get worse. The main

Formula 1 event, featuring the most advanced race cars on earth, would take place later in the afternoon. The race was one of the few Grand Prix events run on city streets, and Munier hated the disruption to Monte Carlo traffic, for the six weeks before and the three weeks after, as the course was constructed and then taken down.

He had no intention of attending the race and getting stuck feigning interest in it for two hours. As he did every year, he took the opportunity to accept an invitation to one of the lavish parties thrown on the multitude of mega-yachts squeezed into the harbor, many of them with a perfect view of the racecourse. He'd sent his wife and two daughters to sunbathe on the beach in Antibes so he could enjoy the weekend by himself.

This year, he'd scored the most sought-after invitation in town. One of the largest yachts in the world, the *Achilles,* had tied up along the harbor's longest berth, and the decadent bashes visible on her decks had been the talk of the city all week. The host, Maxim Antonovich, had sent a gilded invitation for Munier to be his guest, and the banker suspected the reclusive billionaire wanted to talk about stashing a substantial portion of his holdings in Credit

Condamine. Perhaps he was even considering becoming a citizen.

Munier wouldn't mind combining a little business with his pleasure.

He stopped at the end of the pier closest to the *Achilles* and stared at the massive vessel. Even though Munier was accustomed to the trappings of wealth, it was like no other yacht on the water.

At 400 feet, she wasn't as long as the largest mega-yachts, but her width was unsurpassed. The main body of the superstructure sat astride gigantic twin hulls, which would give the ship impressive stability even in heavy seas. The interior space had to be double that of other similar-length yachts, and two huge pools and a hot tub on the top deck were the settings for many of the parties. The rear deck had room enough not only for a helicopter landing pad but for a hangar as well.

The bone-white yacht had been built in secrecy, so many of the features were only rumors, but it was thought to have a submarine and a defense system to ward off rocket-wielding pirates. Munier wouldn't be surprised if it did. Ever since the luxury yacht *Tiara* had been boarded off the coast of Corsica in 2008 and robbed of a quarter million in cash, yacht owners had been going to greater and greater lengths to protect their vessels.

When he got out of the car, a light breeze ruffled Munier's pima cotton shirt and silk slacks as he walked toward the *Achilles*'s gangplank, where he was greeted by a lovely young blond woman flanked by two huge men in suits guarding the entry from passersby. Dressed demurely in tailored trousers and vest that nonetheless showed off her slim figure, she glanced at the tablet computer she held before addressing him in perfect English.

"Mr. Munier," she said with a glowing smile, "my name is Ivana Semova, Mr. Antonovich's personal secretary. Welcome to the *Achilles*."

He shook her hand and said, "I'm thrilled to receive the invitation. His reputation as a generous host is well known. Will I have a chance to meet him while I'm aboard so I can thank him in person?"

"As a matter of fact, Mr. Antonovich has requested your presence in the forward drawing room. If you'll follow me . . ."

She led him up the gangplank and then a series of stairs to the main outdoor deck. Dozens of bathing beauties in skimpy bikinis cavorted with men of all ages and physiques, some in the pool, some on plush chaise longues. Thumping electronic dance music, only slightly more tolerable than the race car engines' whines, blasted from speakers hidden throughout the deck.

When they went inside and the thick doors closed behind them, the music was instantly muted to a barely audible hum. The clip of Ivana's Louboutins was occasionally deadened when they whispered across Persian rugs.

"Here we are," Ivana said as they entered another elegantly appointed room, this one with a huge mahogany desk at the far end. The high-backed chair behind it was facing away from Munier so that he couldn't see its occupant.

He thought that this must be Antonovich's way of making a dramatic introduction. He'd only seen grainy photos of the reclusive billionaire, who was in his sixties, with a paunch, thick salt-and-pepper curls, and a port-wine birthmark on his left cheek that was the shape of a scimitar. Antonovich had made his money the old-fashioned way: he'd bought up many of the most valuable mineral deposits in the Caucasus Mountains when they were privatized. Since making his fortune, he'd supposedly channeled funds into political operations that opposed the Kremlin, leading to a paranoid lifestyle.

Munier waited for the billionaire to reveal his presence.

Nothing happened.

Ivana tapped on her phone, paying no attention to the awkward silence.

Munier cleared his throat. "Will Mr. Antonovich be joining us soon?"

"Just a moment," she replied, but Munier didn't know if that meant he'd be there in a moment or that she needed a moment. At the bank, Munier would be the one to keep people waiting, but here he remained quiet despite his growing annoyance at the delay. If nothing else, he wanted to go out and join in the revelry.

A door at the far end whisked open and a short, muscular man stalked in, accompanied by two others, an Indian and a pale man with ginger hair, both of them athletically built. The diminutive leader had a stippling of close-shaved black hair that was balding in spots. His nose looked as if it had been broken in a couple of fights, his thin lips turned down in a tight frown, and he had a burn scar that started below his left ear and disappeared beneath the collar of his shirt. Despite his brutish appearance, charisma seemed to flow from him in waves.

He came to a stop in front of Munier and appraised him without saying a word.

Munier decided he'd be the one to break the ice. "Mr. Antonovich, what a pleasure it is —"

The man barked a laugh that ended abruptly.

"I'm not Antonovich. My name is Sergey Golov, the captain of this vessel." His accent wasn't thick, but it was definitely Slavic. "Have a seat, Munier. We have some things to discuss."

Though he was confused, Munier did as asked. He expected to be offered a cocktail, but none seemed to be forthcoming.

He glanced at the still-turned chair and then at Ivana, whose smile had vanished. "I was under the impression that Mr. Antonovich would be here."

She shook her head.

"Antonovich isn't coming," Golov said. "I asked you here."

Munier grinned halfheartedly. "I appreciate you inviting me to the party. Is there something I can do for you?"

Golov chuckled and took a seat across from Munier, leaning his elbows on his knees. The Indian and the redheaded man stood behind him, stone-faced.

"A party . . . Right," Golov said. "Yes, I invited you to a party, but it's not the kind you think."

39

Munier adjusted his seating position, suddenly uncomfortable with the situation. "What do you mean?"

"Mine is more like a raiding party."

"I'm sorry?"

"You're going to help me rob your bank. Today."

Munier blinked several times, trying to make sense of what he just heard. Then a smile tickled the corner of his mouth. "You're joking, right? This is some kind of gag. Did Georges Petrie put you up to this?" Petrie, the vice president of the Credit Condamine, was known for his elaborate pranks.

"No joke, Munier," Golov said, all traces of his smile gone. "Do we look like fun-loving people to you?"

Munier's heart hammered against his sternum. "I suppose not."

"You see, the biometric locks in your bank can only be opened by you."

Petrie's fingerprints and retinal signature could be used as well, but Munier didn't correct him.

"And, of course," Golov continued, "they'll only work while you're living and breathing. Chopped-off fingers and plucked eyeballs only work in the movies. We know the latest readers sense active blood flow."

"Why should I help you?"

"I will kill you right now if you don't." To emphasize his point, his men drew pistols from their jackets and held them casually at their sides.

Munier tried to gulp, but he discovered that his mouth had dried up. "So, I help you and then you let me go free?"

"You're not a stupid man, Munier. You've seen our faces. It couldn't be helped because of what we're planning. We can't leave witnesses, so I think it's clear you're not going to make it out of this alive."

"Then . . . Then what possible reason could I have to do what you say?"

Golov nodded at Ivana and she glided over with the tablet. She tapped several times and then turned the screen to Munier.

He gasped when he saw the image.

There were his wife and two daughters, playing on the beach, making sand castles.

"Show him," Ivana said into her phone.

The image shifted so that Munier could see the pistol that the cameraman was holding.

Munier had the urge to scream a warning to his family through the screen, but Ivana took the tablet back before he could.

"You're a monster," Munier could barely utter to Golov. He looked at each of them.

41

"All of you are monsters."

"Believe me," Golov said. "We didn't want it to come to this. Still, I've done worse."

A desperate thought seized Munier. "Georges Petrie! You can take Petrie! He can get you in. Just don't hurt my family." His throat caught in a sob. "I swear I won't tell anyone."

"No. You're our only option."

"But Petrie —"

"Unfortunately, we already tried him," Golov said. He nodded at the Indian, who went over to the desk chair and spun it around.

Until that point, Munier had held out hope that there would be some way out of this, that he could come up with a solution. But now he knew he had no choice but to do what they said.

It wasn't Maxim Antonovich that had been hiding in the chair, as he'd thought. Staring back at him were the unseeing eyes of Georges Petrie, his tanned forehead marred by a bullet hole.

THREE

ALGERIA

As he descended, Juan could see more clearly the rock outcroppings that jutted from the giant sand dunes at irregular intervals and he hoped that none of the dune buggies had made a hard landing on any of them. Since there were nine men and only three seats on each buggy, a bent frame or broken axle would leave at least three of them stranded in one of the harshest environments on the planet.

Juan knew who would draw the short straws, if it came to that. Nazari wouldn't hesitate to leave them behind, especially since he seemed to have his own way out of Algeria if he planned to kill Juan, Eddie, and Linc.

Juan floated down right next to his team, but the untrained Egyptians had landed all over the place in heaps.

With his chute cast aside, Juan climbed

the nearest dune to survey the location. The sun was scorching. His headscarf kept a little of the heat at bay, and he was happy to have the latest lightweight ballistic fabric sewn into his clothes instead of the Kevlar body armor that soldiers lugged around.

"There are the Scorpions," he said, pointing at the desert patrol vehicles that had landed in a line in the adjacent dune valley. "Get ours detached from the chutes and pallet."

"What about you?" Eddie asked.

Juan saw Nazari closing on two other Egyptians to their left. One of the men was lying on the ground, writhing in pain.

"I'm going to see what happened to him. Come pick me up when you get the Scorpion ready."

Juan walked carefully down the slope to keep from starting a mini-avalanche. The loose, fine-grained sand made for slow going, and driving over it would be tricky.

He reached the injured man at the same time as Nazari. He was one of the inexperienced jumpers. His face was contorted in agony.

The man attending to him turned to Nazari and said, "His lower leg is broken. He landed on that rock and his leg buckled." He nodded to an outcropping beside them, although the unnatural angle of the man's shin made the explanation unnecessary.

Juan felt a familiar twinge at seeing the gruesome injury. He had lost his own leg below the knee in a battle with a Chinese gunboat. He'd grown accustomed to the prosthetic limb he wore, so much so that Nazari would never suspect he wasn't a two-legged man, but the phantom pain of the missing leg never fully subsided.

Juan bent down to examine the damage. Then he looked at Nazari. "Both the tibia and fibula have snapped. We'll have to set it and then fashion a splint. He won't be able to walk on it, so he'll either need help or we'll have to get him some kind of crutch."

"You're sure?" Nazari asked.

"I'm not a doctor, but I've seen this kind of injury before."

Nazari nodded. Without another word, he drew his pistol and put two rounds into the man's head.

Juan leaped to his feet and stared at Nazari and the 9mm SIG Sauer in his hand.

"We don't have time for all that," Nazari said calmly. "He would just be a hindrance."

The other man jumped up, and it seemed as if he were about to make a big mistake by taking a step toward Nazari.

"He's now a martyr," Nazari said to his

soldier. "As we all eventually will be. We couldn't take him with us, and leaving him here to die of thirst would be cruel. Get our Scorpion prepared to go. As I said, we don't have much time."

The soldier stepped back, took one last look at his comrade, and ran toward the buggies.

"He doesn't understand like you and I do," Nazari said to Juan. "I can see it in you. We're both alike."

Juan nearly shuddered at the thought. "How is that?"

"We both are willing to do what it takes to accomplish the mission."

Before Juan could respond to the insult that Nazari meant as a compliment, Eddie and Linc arrived in Scorpion 1, with Eddie driving and Linc on the .50 caliber in back. The 200-horsepower engine growled as it pulled up next to him. The only thing that distinguished it from the other dune buggies was the small "1" stenciled on the side.

Eddie looked at the corpse and said, "What happened?"

"Our client was just showing me his resolve," Juan said. Nazari's eyes didn't betray any understanding, but they regarded him coolly.

Juan climbed into the front passenger seat

behind the 40mm grenade launcher and donned the helmet Eddie handed to him.

Scorpion 2 showed up a few moments later and Nazari got in.

When the third dune buggy was ready, Nazari led the way, peering down at a GPS unit as they drove up and over dunes and around the bigger rocks.

Nazari had ensured they would be far from the drop zone when they reached their destination. Thirty minutes into their drive, Juan spotted the glint of sun on metal in the distance, shimmering in the heat rising off the sand.

"Is that a mirage?" he asked. The helmet-mounted communication system linked Juan to Eddie and Linc only.

Linc, who was higher in his seat in the back, said, "I don't think so, but I can't make out what it is."

Nazari must have seen it as well because his Scorpion adjusted course and accelerated toward it.

"Must be our target," Juan responded.

Eddie goosed the throttle to keep pace. When they got within four hundred yards of the object, its shape became apparent.

It was the bright aluminum tail of an airplane. Although it showed signs of weathering, it seemed to be in decent condition.

Juan suspected that it had been buried by the shifting sands and was only recently uncovered by a storm. Wandering nomads loyal to Nazari's cause must have reported it.

"That looks like it's been here a while," Juan said.

The tail section was big enough to be part of a medium-sized passenger plane, but Juan could soon make out a new detail.

Not only did the rear part of the fuselage have no windows but it sported the familiar Stars and Bars roundel of the United States Air Force.

"That's either a cargo jet or bomber," Juan said. He squinted at the tail. The black numbers stenciled on it were faded but still visible.

52-534

"Linc?"

"I'm on it," Linc replied. He surreptitiously checked a database about WMDs he'd downloaded to his handheld tablet computer and plugged in the number to see if it matched any known missing planes.

Less than ten seconds later, Linc said, "I got it. Serial number 52-534 is a B-47 strategic bomber that went missing in 1956 on a transatlantic flight to Morocco. It was part of a four-plane formation that was supposed to rendezvous with a tanker for refueling, but when they came out of some heavy overcast, this one was missing."

"They must have had some kind of equipment malfunction and gone off course," Eddie said.

Juan assumed he now knew why Nazari had hired them to come all this way, but then he tilted his head in thought. The B-47 was designed to carry ten-thousand-pound thermonuclear weapons over the Soviet Union. But if this plane had gone down in a controlled enough manner to take it hundreds of miles off course and come to rest relatively intact, the pilot must have jettisoned that heavy load before attempting his landing. Even if he hadn't, this expedition didn't have the equipment to carry such a tremendous load, and no one on Nazari's team had the expertise to dismantle a nuclear bomb. It couldn't be what they were after.

"Was it declared a Broken Arrow?" Juan asked, using the term for a missing nuclear device.

"Yes," Linc said as they pulled to a stop next to the tail. He stuffed the tablet back into his bag. "They searched for it for weeks. Even called in the British Navy and

French Foreign Legion to look for it."

"What was it carrying?" Juan asked as he saw Nazari climb out of Scorpion 2, a malevolent smile breaking the Egyptian's stoic demeanor for the first time. "Something portable, right?"

He turned to see Linc flip up his helmet's visor and nod grimly. "The plane was transporting atomic bomb components to a base in Europe. Sitting about fifty feet away from us, somewhere under that sand, are two plutonium nuclear weapon cores."

FOUR

MONACO

With most of the city's thirty-five thousand residents at the Grand Prix racecourse, the Boulevard de Belgique, only a few blocks away, was nearly deserted. On a normal Sunday, this Monte Carlo district, where Credit Condamine's bank headquarters was located, would be teeming with tourists, but most of them were at the race. Sergey Golov was satisfied to see that they wouldn't have to contend with many witnesses, just as they'd planned.

Henri Munier's Tesla SUV stopped at the gate to the underground parking garage, and Golov slid Munier's identity card into the reader. The hardened steel gate cranked up, and Golov steered the vehicle to the bank president's private parking spot.

He switched off the SUV and nodded to Ivana Semova in the passenger seat. She connected her laptop to the car's data port and began typing on the keyboard. Although she had introduced herself to Munier as Antonovich's assistant, in reality she was the billionaire's computer expert. The Kiev native had ditched her hacker lifestyle — breaking into American retail databases and designing viruses that could worm into secure financial systems — to help Antonovich protect his own companies from people just like her. Her work had been so stellar that he'd asked her to lead the team that designed the state-of-the-art digital control architecture on his yacht. He'd paid handsomely for her services, and she was worth every penny.

After a minute, she said, "Reprogramming complete."

"That's my girl," Golov said. He turned in his seat to face Munier, who was sandwiched between O'Connor and Sirkal, Antonovich's most trusted security operatives.

Rahul Sirkal had gained combat experience in the Indian military during the Kashmir conflict before joining the intelligence service, then retired five years ago to build a private security business. Though Antonovich was Russian, he had traveled the world extensively, so he didn't limit himself to hiring from Russia alone. He'd come across Sirkal during a particularly troublesome negotiation with his Bangalore subsidiary and was so impressed that he hired the Indian to head up his own security team.

Seamus O'Connor, a florid Irishman and a veteran of the Irish Republican Army, was Sirkal's weapons expert who didn't mind getting his hands dirty when the need arose. He was the brawler to complement Sirkal's technical approach.

Sitting between them, Munier looked decidedly apprehensive.

"I want to remind you that we will be watching and listening at all times," Golov said to Munier.

Ivana turned the laptop's screen toward him to show her and Golov, as seen from the wide-angle lapel camera on Munier's jacket.

Munier nodded. "I understand."

"If we lose the signal for more than three seconds, or we don't see your hands in the frame for a similar amount of time, we will assume that you are attempting to reveal our involvement. Not only will we detonate the tiny explosive in the camera but your family will suffer before they die."

"I said I understand." Munier glanced around the parking lot. "And the guards inside? What are you going to do to them, once you're in?"

"What do you think?"

"I . . . I can't . . ."

"You can if you want your wife and children to live."

Munier composed himself and nodded again.

"You have five minutes," Golov said.

Munier got out and went to the elevator.

Ivana had the ultra-light laptop propped on her knees. The image coming from the lapel camera was clear, and they could distinctly hear Munier's ragged breathing.

"Don't hyperventilate," Golov said into his microphone. "You're supposed to look natural. Don't leave the elevator until you compose yourself."

"All right," Munier replied, and his breathing slowed enough so that he no longer sounded like he was about to pass out from nervousness.

The elevator dinged, and Munier walked into the bank's lobby. He was met by a uniformed guard, coming out of the security office.

The guard spoke to him in French. Ivana, who was fluent in four languages, translated for Golov.

"Munier called him André. He's surprised to see Munier there."

"He doesn't look too happy about it, either," Golov said.

"He was probably about to watch the race and is embarrassed he missed the arrival of Munier's car in the garage. He doesn't seem suspicious."

Munier spoke again. The guard nodded and ducked into the security office next to the lobby.

"He went to get another guard named François. Munier told him that his driver was having a problem with the car and needed their help."

Golov smiled. "He's good at following a script."

The plan was going exactly as he'd drawn it up. Golov's command before Antonovich hired him to captain the *Achilles* was a Ukrainian frigate named the *Poltava.* He'd been trained by the Soviet Navy before the breakup of the USSR and then transferred to the newly christened navy of his native Ukraine. He'd become one of Ukraine's preeminent naval strategists and was about to be recommended for a star in the admiralty. Then the Crimea crisis occurred. Russia annexed the entire peninsula and took over the Ukraine naval base at Sevastopol. Many of Ukraine's best ships were seized, including the *Poltava.*

Golov had been reprimanded for letting his ship be confiscated, instead of sailing it out before the Russians could take it, and his career was effectively over.

An ex-pat Russian, Antonovich found a kindred spirit in Golov. Both of them despised the current leadership in Moscow. Antonovich had needed someone with Golov's skills to command a yacht with the *Achilles*'s unique capabilities, so it had been a perfect match.

Now Golov was able to apply his planning skills to even more interesting work.

The two guards returned from the security office, never questioning the bank president's request for them to leave their post and accompany him to the garage.

Golov and the three others exited the SUV and took positions on either side of the elevator. Sirkal and O'Connor had their Glock pistols leveled.

The elevator dinged when it arrived at garage level, and Munier led the guards out. When they were clear of the door, Golov said, *"Bonjour."*

As the guards turned toward the voice, Sirkal shot André twice in the chest, then François.

Munier sobbed at the sight of them collapsing.

"Your family or them," Golov reminded him.

O'Connor and Sirkal made sure the two guards were dead, then dragged their bodies to the back of the SUV and dumped them inside. Sirkal tossed the Glock in as well.

Golov nodded in satisfaction. "Let's go."

O'Connor shoved Munier into the elevator and they rode up to the lobby. The elevator camera had a good shot of all of them, but it wouldn't matter now that the guards were no longer monitoring it.

Munier's lavish office was at the rear of the marble lobby. Once they were inside, Ivana took a seat in his chair at the computer terminal.

"Thumb, please," she said.

Munier sighed and put his thumb on the reader.

"Password."

He typed it in, then leaned close to the desk. His right hand casually dropped to its surface.

"Don't even think about pressing the silent alarm," Golov said when he noticed Munier's fingers edging under the desk. "Your family would be dead before the police could arrive."

Munier snatched his hand away as if the desk were on fire.

"I wasn't," he said unconvincingly.

"I'm sure."

With the computer system now wide open thanks to Munier's biometric access, Sirkal and O'Connor pulled him back.

"This is pointless," Munier said. "The vault is on a time lock until nine o'clock tomorrow morning, and that computer doesn't even control it. I can't open it no matter what you do to me or how much you threaten my family."

"We don't want your money," Golov said.

Munier looked at him bewildered. "You don't?" Comprehension dawned on him. "You're going to transfer our depositors' funds?"

"You are so very close. We needed a hard connection to your internal servers. After hackers repeatedly gained access to bank servers, security at every bank, including yours, was stepped up, and firewalls became impossible to breach from outside. But we're not here to transfer money."

"If you're not stealing money, then why kill all these people and take such a big risk?"

Golov considered telling Munier the entire plan just to show how clever he was, but that would be bragging. Golov preferred to let his work speak for itself. Munier would never know the whole story, but the depositors would know soon enough.

"Your bank's shareholders are going to have a very bad day tomorrow" was all he would say.

After ten minutes, Ivana announced, "The virus is uploaded and operating. It should be done in a few hours. I have to say it's some of my best work."

While humility was one of Golov's traits, Ivana, like most hackers, was an incorrigible show-off.

"Excellent," he said. "Then let's take care of the cameras."

She logged out, and they all went into the security guards' observation room. She rapidly found the files she wanted and deleted everything except the segment showing Munier talking to André and then leading both guards to the garage.

With the videos edited, they went back to Munier's office.

"Well, we're almost done here," Golov said, and turned to Ivana. "Are we ready?"

She nodded. "Everything is set up. The car is waiting outside."

"I suppose this is when you kill me," Munier said, sounding resigned to his fate.

"Not exactly," Golov said. "We have other plans for you."

"But you promised that my family —"
Munier protested.

Golov put up his hands to calm him.
"You've done what I asked and your family
will remain unharmed. But it's not going to
be that easy for you, Mr. Munier. You have
one more job to do."

To Munier's shock, Golov walked past
him, reached under the desk, and pressed
the button to trip the silent alarm.

FIVE

ALGERIA

"I found a body!"

The shout came from one of Nazari's men. They'd been digging at the side of the plane for a half hour, trying to find a way into the bomb bay. The bomb bay was directly under the wing roots, which they'd revealed early in the dig.

They had also uncovered the canopy, and none of the three officers who'd been aboard the plane were inside. It was likely all three had survived the crash. A dead man would have been left in his seat while the others waited outside for rescue.

When the Egyptian made his discovery, everyone else stopped digging and rushed to see what he'd found.

Only the head was visible. Even though it had been there nearly sixty years, the mummified features were plainly visible. The skin was stretched and dried, exposing the teeth and empty eye sockets in a gruesome expression. Hair still covered the head.

It was the obvious place for them to find remains. Anyone who'd stayed with the aircraft instead of wandering into the desert would have taken refuge in the shade of the immense wing, which had been sheared off fifteen feet from the fuselage but still provided protection from the intense midday sun.

They all scooped sand away from the corpse to uncover a green U.S. Air Force flight suit. The bars on his shoulder indicated he was a captain. The patch underneath read *369th Bomb Squadron.* The name on the man's chest patch was *Robert Hodgin.*

Further digging revealed the mummified corpse was still holding a logbook. Nazari removed it roughly from the desiccated hand, flipped through it, and tossed it to Juan.

"Translate that."

The logbook indicated that Hodgin was the aircraft commander. All of the entries leading up to March 10, 1956, were standard status reports about fuel, heading, and aircraft condition.

On March 11, Hodgin's script suddenly became the less confident scrawl of a man in desperate straits. While Juan translated into Arabic, Eddie and Linc read the English over his shoulder. The date and precise military time preceded each entry.

March 11, 0905: Ten minutes before rendezvous for midair refueling, aircraft suffered a catastrophic malfunction when struck by lightning during descent through clouds. Navigation and communication systems knocked out by electrical surge. Hydraulics still functional, but control panel magnetized by the lightning strike. Compass useless. Thought we had turned west toward Morocco but realize now that we had headed south. When fuel ran out, there was enough moonlight for a controlled descent in desert.

Captain Gordon Insley, our navigator, and my copilot, Second Lieutenant Ronald Kurtz, were both uninjured in the crash. I must have torn something in my knee, making it impossible for me to walk for very long. Our emergency beacon was also damaged by the lightning. None of us can pinpoint our location. We will wait for rescue here.

March 12, 0813: Our emergency rations

are limited. Only enough water for two days, and that's stretching it. Now I know why we took that survival course, but the Montana wilderness was never this hot. To stave off boredom while we wait, I had Insley and Kurtz check to see the status of our cargo. The carrying cases for the nuclear cores are still intact and the seals tight. No chance of a leak. At least we won't die of radiation poisoning.

The scrawl of Hodgin's writing was getting increasingly shaky. Juan continued to translate.

March 12, 2128: As hot as it is in the daytime, it's even colder at night. None of us expected that in the Sahara. We have our flight jackets, and when the wind becomes merciless, we get back under cover of the canopy. But sleeping only happens in the twilight of dawn and sundown when the temp is mild. Sand is everywhere.

March 13, 1053: Our eyes are starting to get bad. Hard to write. Blisters all over our faces from the wind and sun. Wearing helmets helps.

Where are you guys? We keep looking for signs of an air search, but we haven't seen a thing. We have our flares ready.

March 14, 1134: It seems clear that rescue isn't coming. I've sent Insley and Kurtz to look for help, heading due north. Hopefully, they'll run across a road or town. If they keep walking long enough, we know they'll hit the Mediterranean, but how far is that?

March 14, 1945: I thought I knew what it felt like to be alone, but I was wrong. Now I know.

March 15, 0717: I've been out of water for ten hours now. I gave most of my supply to Insley and Kurtz for their journey. Food is gone, too, not that I could eat. My mouth is as dry as this sand.

Even though it's only been a day, I have to assume they won't be coming back. At least, not in time. I hope they make it.

March 16, 0856: So thirsty. Don't know if I can make it through another day. Tell my wife and boys I love them.

March 17, 1129: So thirsty.

"That's it," Juan said, smoothly pocketing the logbook. He could only imagine the pain, desperation, and loneliness Hodgin must have gone through. Who knows how far Insley and Kurtz got before they succumbed to the elements.

Nazari didn't seem moved at all by Hodgin's suffering. "Now we know that the cases are still intact. Keep digging so we can get into the bomb bay." He checked his satellite phone, then gestured at two men. "Come with me."

Juan looked at Eddie and Linc, then back at Nazari. "Where are you going?"

"Why is that your business?"

"Well, we've just found out that we're going to be digging out nuclear weapon cores. I just wanted to know if there are any other surprises you haven't shared with us."

Nazari stroked his beard in thought before speaking. "Al-Qaeda in the Islamic Maghreb wants this recovery as much as we do. They also know the location of this airplane and crossed over the Algerian border from Libya yesterday. We don't know the size of their force, but they should be coming from the east. I'm going to that escarpment to scout for any signs that they are getting close."

He pointed at a bluff about three miles away.

"We should all go," Juan said, "in case we need to engage them."

"No. You five keep digging."

Juan was protesting for the sake of appearances. In reality, he liked the improved balance of forces. It would be him, Linc, and Eddie against Nazari's remaining two soldiers.

With his two men, Nazari walked toward a Scorpion, the number 3 dune buggy that was parked closest to the B-47. But instead of getting into the passenger seat, he hopped up into the top seat behind the .50 caliber machine gun. He swung the barrel so that it was pointed at Juan and racked the bolt.

"Drop your weapons!" Nazari yelled.

Juan exchanged surprised glances with Eddie.

Linc looked coiled to go on the attack. "I'm pretty sure I don't need a translation to know what he just said."

Juan put up his hands. "What are you doing?"

Nazari didn't blink. "I said drop them."

Juan nodded, and they did as they were told. Linc reluctantly unslung the AK-47 from his back, and Juan and Eddie unslung theirs slowly and threw them to the ground. Nazari's men grabbed the guns and backed up, piling them on the hood of Scorpion 3.

"Now that you know what we've come for," Nazari said as he gestured for one of his soldiers to take his place at the machine gun, "you might get it into your heads to sell the nuclear cores for yourself." He jumped down as another of his men climbed up and took position behind the .50 caliber M2.

"If you don't trust us," Juan said, "why did you hire us?"

"Because you had the only means to get us here before the Libyans. And since I need to go see if they are anywhere close, I can't leave you with three-to-two odds. As I mentioned, you seem to be a man who will do what it takes to get the mission done."

"Your mission is the same as my mission." Both the truth and a lie, depending on how you parsed the phrase.

"Maybe. But I can't take that chance when we're so close. If you keep digging, I'll let you live. If you try anything, Hasim is to kill you without hesitation." He glanced at the man on the machine gun, who nodded, and then turned back to Juan. "Do you understand?"

Juan backed up and picked up one of the shovels. "Of course." Eddie and Linc followed his lead and lifted two more shovels.

They started digging, joined by Nazari's other soldier. Hasim stayed at his post behind the machine gun, his hands resting on the vertical spade grips, his thumb on the trigger.

Nazari and the other two soldiers got in Scorpion 1.

"I hate to point this out," Eddie said, "but Nazari is taking our ride."

"I noticed," Juan said as he shoveled sand. "We'll deal with that when we need to."

The driver started the engine and took off, flinging sand behind the fat tires. In another minute, they were over the next dune and out of sight.

As they dug, Juan nodded his head in a rhythm only he could hear. After five minutes, he seemed to point and give instructions in English to Eddie and Linc about where to dig so that their captors wouldn't realize they were having a conversation.

"We'll give Nazari fifteen minutes to reach the escarpment and dismount," he said. "That's when we'll make our move. Linc, you take out our digging companion. Eddie and I will rush the machine gun."

Linc nodded and started digging in the spot that Juan had pointed to. "Do you think that'll give us enough time to recover the nuclear cases?"

"Did you figure out Hodgin's code?" Eddie asked.

Juan nodded in response to both questions. In his translation to Nazari, he'd left out one key note that Hodgin had recorded in his logbook. Linc and Eddie didn't give any sign that Juan had skipped it, and he had committed the passage to memory.

> March 15, 1429: If the Soviets are searching for us as well, they might find us before the Americans. I couldn't leave the cases for them to find, so I buried them. Hard work, with no water and a bum leg. You'll find them straight on from the Jimmy Durante for the number of blue paces in my suede shoes.

Hodgin knew that no Russian would recognize the American references. Jimmy Durante was a famous comedian and singer of the era known by the nickname "The Schnozzola" for his bulbous nose. Hodgin had buried the cases straight in front of the plane's nose.

The number of paces to count off referred to Elvis Presley's hit "Blue Suede Shoes." Juan had played the song back in his head while he was digging and counted twenty-one mentions of the word *blue.* If he was right, twenty-one paces out was where they should dig.

"I'm glad you knew the song," Linc said. "I'm more of a Marvin Gaye fan."

"If it had been a Beatles song, I would have been all over it," Eddie chimed in.

"That would have been about ten years too late," Juan said. "Be ready for my signal."

He waited another ten minutes to be sure Nazari was at the farthest point in his trek. The timing would be close, depending on how far down the cases had been buried. Given Hodgin's feeble condition at the time, he couldn't have dug very deep. They had to hope the same storm that exposed the aircraft hadn't heaped more sand over the spot.

Juan speared his shovel into the sand and leaned back to stretch. He took the canteen from his belt and conspicuously drained it. He shook it out looking for more, then turned and started walking toward the Scorpion.

Hasim, the soldier at the machine gun, straightened at the movement toward him.

"Where are you going?" he demanded.

"To get more water."

"Keep digging."

Juan kept moving toward the dune buggy

71

only forty feet away. "I'm thirsty."

"I don't care. You'll get water when Nazari gets back."

Thirty-five feet. The AK-47s were still lying on the hood of Scorpion 3.

"Stop! I will kill you and your men if you don't."

Juan picked up his pace. Thirty feet now.

The M2's sight was squarely on Juan's chest.

"Stop!"

Juan broke into a run.

Hasim didn't shout again. He thumbed the trigger and let loose a deafening barrage of .50 caliber shells.

Six

Credit Condamine's gate opened and the Tesla SUV barreled out of the dark garage into the sunny street as police cars skidded to a stop in response to the bank's silent alarm. The first policemen were barely able to get out and draw their firearms before the SUV clipped their car, the Tesla's motor whining in an eerily quiet hum that belied its quickness. Both officers had just enough time to clearly identify Henri Munier, screaming incoherently behind the wheel.

From the tiny camera and microphone mounted on the dashboard, Golov could see and hear that Munier was actually yelling for their help, but the startled policemen must have assumed the bank president was shouting for them to get out of the way as he fled the scene of a crime.

Golov hadn't told him to scream, but he figured that Munier would. The scenario

73

was playing out perfectly.

The SUV was already equipped with a camera built into the front bumper, so Ivana had routed the feed through a transmitter that broadcast to the display Golov was watching. He controlled the Tesla's steering, accelerator, and brakes using a modified Xbox controller connected to the laptop.

While Golov steered Munier's SUV from the passenger seat of their car, Sirkal drove them sedately in the opposite direction toward the *Achilles.* They were already blocks from the bank, and with the security recordings of them erased, the police would have no idea they were involved.

Munier's wrists were lashed to the steering wheel with plastic ties. He wasn't driving the Tesla. The wheel's input had been disengaged from the signal going to the front wheels, so turning it did nothing. The accelerator and brake pedals had been similarly disabled. Munier had no choice but to go along for the ride.

The SUV's acceleration was faster than everything on the road except expensive sports cars. Certainly nothing in the Monaco police fleet could match it. By using the reconfigured backup camera to monitor the pursuit, Golov kept the chasing police cars in view. He wanted to make sure there would be no doubt that Munier had remained in the vehicle until the end.

The Tesla rocketed down the street, sirens wailing behind it. The few cars that were on the road either didn't see the approaching car or simply didn't react and continued to block the way. Instead of heading into opposing traffic and risking a wreck, Golov drove it onto the sidewalk, sending pedestrians diving out of the way.

He was disappointed there was no fruit cart to upend, like he'd seen in countless American movies, and he had to satisfy himself with smashing through an outdoor bistro. Tables and chairs went flying in all directions.

Golov was sure the chase was being recorded on police dashboard cams and various street and security cameras. When the video was pored over in the aftermath, the obvious conclusion would be Munier had accidentally tripped the alarm during his crime and then tried to escape when he realized his mistake.

Of course, people had seen him board the *Achilles,* but that would be understood as a crude attempt to provide himself an alibi. The discovery of Georges Petrie shot to death in his condominium with the same

Glock that was now in the back of the SUV would be the final piece of evidence against Munier.

There was still one last thing to eliminate and he was currently sitting in the Tesla's driver's seat.

Merely crashing the SUV wouldn't do. Golov had something more spectacular in mind.

He steered the SUV around the next corner and accelerated toward his destination. He could see the Formula 1 racetrack two blocks ahead.

The Grand Prix course was laid out on city streets, some of them so narrow that the race cars could not pass each other. Barriers were erected along the track edges as a safety measure not only for the drivers but to keep out other vehicles.

However, the track had a few spots that could be opened to let fire trucks and ambulances enter and exit the track. Golov knew where the closest of those was.

The weak point was near the famous hairpin turn by the Fairmont Hotel.

"What's the race status?" Golov asked Ivana, who was monitoring the Grand Prix from her seat in the back next to O'Connor.

"They threw the yellow caution flag two minutes ago. There was a crash near La Rascasse. The safety car is just passing the casino."

Golov smiled. Even better than he'd hoped.

The Tesla sped up as it approached the temporary gate that allowed access to the emergency entrance. The policemen guarding the gate put up their hands to stop the vehicle, then saw the chasing police cars round the corner behind it. They didn't have time to draw their weapons before the SUV smashed through the barrier and swerved through the entrance to the track.

About half the Formula 1 race cars following the safety car had passed the entrance already. Even the caution pace was still faster than freeway speeds. Golov could only imagine the look on the nearest driver's face when he saw an SUV rush onto the track in front of him.

The driver yanked the wheel of his race car to the right to avoid the Tesla, careening into the wall in the process. Debris from the car's carbon fiber body went flying in all directions. Three other cars behind it were caught in the ensuing crash.

Golov accelerated and began to pass the race cars ahead of the SUV. He had always been a race fan and driving the Monaco Grand Prix track during the actual race was a dream come true, even if he was doing the driving virtually. It was as if he were playing the most realistic video game ever devised.

"The special effects are so lifelike," he muttered, and then chuckled to himself when no one else in the sedan responded.

Most of the Formula 1 drivers moved over to give him a wide berth. But at a narrow point, Golov scraped the wall as he tried to get past a car. The front bumper of the heavy SUV hit the wing of the race car, spun the car around, and slammed it into the opposing wall.

It came to rest backward on the track, and one of the pursuing police cars hit the front of the car like a ramp. The police vehicle flipped into the air and finished the job of blocking the track. Golov's pursuers could no longer continue the chase.

He braked for the hairpin, which was so tight that even the most advanced race cars in the world had to take it at thirty miles per hour. He could almost hear the squeal of the tires competing with Munier's shrieking.

The next curve led into the track's most unusual feature, a thousand-foot-long tunnel. The safety car, a Mercedes sports car with yellow lights flashing on its roof, paced the two leading race cars into the gloomy entrance. The driver seemed to be speeding up, trying to stay ahead of the crazy man behind him.

This was the fastest part of the racecourse, with Formula 1 cars typically reaching a top speed of one hundred and sixty miles per hour. The safety car was pushing a hundred. Despite his effort, the Tesla gained on them.

They exited the tunnel, and Golov slammed on the brakes heading into the kink in the track, called a chicane, and then onto the part of the track that abutted the harbor. Large grandstands were built along the next ninety-degree corner, and fabulous yachts were packed, gunwale to gunwale, to allow their passengers to watch the race from the comfort of their lavish surroundings.

Golov caught up to the tail end of the three-car convoy as they reached pit road. The cars ahead continued to rocket along the course, but Golov didn't follow them. He flicked the car to the right and sped down pit road at a speed far higher than the limit for the race cars.

He took aim at one of the open garages next to the road. Pit teams scattered like minnows in front of a shark. Munier's eyes widened in terror.

"No!" was all he could cry out before the SUV plunged into the garage at over a hundred miles an hour and struck a fuel rig. A flash of white engulfed the screen and then it went dead.

Golov switched to the live feed from the television cameras covering the race. A ball of fire erupted out of the garage. Several of the helmeted pit crew ran out of the building, the exterior of their fire-retardant suits aflame. Surely others inside hadn't been so lucky.

The highly reactive lithium in the batteries along the SUV's chassis would now be burning ferociously, ignited by the fuel explosion. Little would be left of Munier's corpse except his teeth for dental identification. The plastic ties cuffing him to the wheel would be vapor, and the bodies of the two guards in the back would be charred beyond recognition. Evidence of the electronic tampering would also be destroyed.

The sedan rolled to a gentle stop at the dock where the *Achilles* was tied up.

"Well done, everyone," Golov said as they got out. "The champagne tonight is on me."

"Shall I shut down the party now, Captain?" Sirkal asked.

Golov looked up at the guests who were

gathered along the railing, watching the black smoke rise from the racetrack. Many of them were taking photos or videos with their phones. Few of them had put their drinks down.

"Not just yet," Golov said. "We don't want to seem too eager to get them off the ship. But with the tragic events of today, I don't think anyone will be in the mood to continue the festivities for much longer. Make the ship ready to sail in an hour. I'm sure Mr. Antonovich wouldn't want to stay here any longer than he needs to. I want to be south of Majorca by tomorrow morning."

"Yes, sir." Sirkal left with O'Connor to make preparations.

Golov put his arm around Ivana's shoulder and took in the dazzling orange flames that continued to engulf the garage. "There's no turning back now, Ivana. We're going to carry this through to the end, and I think we're off to a wonderful start." He turned to her and beamed with pride. "Excellent work, my dear."

She smiled back at him. "Thank you, Father."

Seven

ALGERIA

Hasim was shocked as Juan continued to run through what seemed like a hail of rounds that should have torn him to shreds. Instead, noise and empty ejected shell cases were the only product of his efforts. He screamed in disbelief when he realized the machine gun was loaded with blanks.

He released the trigger and reached for the assault rifle slung across his back. He brought it to bear, but not in time.

Juan had already covered the distance to the Scorpion. He grabbed one of the AK-47s and fired three shots into Hasim's chest. The Egyptian fell back and slumped against the seat, blood streaming down his shirt.

Juan wheeled around, ready to take out the second soldier if needed, but he could see Linc hunched over the man, who was sprawled on the ground with the hilt of a combat knife jutting from his chest.

Eddie was right behind Juan and grabbed the two other AK-47s.

"It's good Hasim didn't use the grenade launcher. He might have taken your head off."

Juan shrugged. "I would have come up with something. At least there are two more down. Now it's three of them and three of us. The odds are even."

"That's a generous assessment," Linc said as he approached them, wiping his knife on the headscarf he'd removed. He put it back in the scabbard and took the extra AK-47 from Eddie. "Are you forgetting that Nazari now has the only armed Scorpion?"

Juan had suspected some kind of double cross from the very beginning of the mission, which was why they'd loaded live ammo only into their Scorpion, the one marked discreetly with a "1." Eddie had made sure to claim it first when they landed, intending to take Nazari and his men captive once they had the WMDs in hand, but his sudden departure had put a kink in that plan.

Juan checked his watch. Certainly Nazari had heard the shots. He might think that they'd been killed as ordered, but the distinctive sound of the AK-47 following the M2 could have given him doubts.

Nazari would return as quickly as he could in the fully armed Scorpion.

Juan said, "We need to dig out those cases pronto."

They counted off twenty-one paces from the nose of the plane according to Hodgin's "Blue Suede Shoes" code. Putting their backs into it, they scoured a hole up to Juan's waist in less than five minutes. If it had been dirt, they never would have reached the depth they needed to in time, but the fine sand was easy to toss aside.

Two minutes later, Linc's shovel clanged on something hard. They attacked the ground and quickly unearthed two aluminum cases. The yellow and black radiation hazard symbol hadn't lost any of its menace in sixty years of burial.

Linc and Juan each picked up a lead-lined case by its handle, while Eddie ran to get the Scorpion that didn't have a dead body in it.

"It must have taken Hodgin forever to drag these out here with a torn-up leg."

"You have to admire the guy," Juan replied. "Dedicated to the end."

Eddie skidded to a stop next to them in Scorpion 2 and pointed into the distance. "By the way Nazari's Scorpion is tearing over those dunes, I'd say he figured out that we didn't follow his command to dig or die."

The desert patrol vehicle jumped over the crest of a dune, and Juan caught a glimpse of Nazari, yelling at his driver.

He and Linc bungeed the cases to the Scorpion's frame and got in, Linc on the impotent machine gun and Juan in the passenger seat behind the grenade launcher. They donned their helmets as Eddie took off.

Moments later, the first grenades landed where they'd just been parked.

"Are they nuts?" Linc yelled over the comm system. "If they rip open one of those cases, we're all toast!"

"Either they're not thinking clearly or they don't care," Eddie offered.

"I don't think it's a good idea to stop and point out their poor judgment to them," Juan said. He pulled his pant leg up, opened his combat prosthesis, and removed a tiny transmitter. He clicked the button and said, "Head for those cliffs."

"You got it," Eddie said, and steered toward a wall of rock five miles away.

Grenades rained down behind them, churning the sand into clouds of dust. Every time they were provided with a smoke screen of sand, Eddie veered to one side or the other to throw off any subsequent shots.

The zigzagging was slowing them down, while Nazari came at them on a direct path.

"Any ideas?" Eddie said.

Juan scanned the horizon for any obstacles to put between them. One feature stood out.

A dust trail rose from the surface, and it was approaching.

It had to be the Libyans. Nazari hadn't been hightailing it back just because of the gunfire. He had seen the competing terrorists coming their way.

"We've got more company," Juan said, and pointed at the plume of dust only a few miles to their right.

"Well, that's just great," Linc said.

"It is. Eddie, bring us in closer to them."

Eddie turned to look at Juan, confusion in his eyes turning to understanding. "You want to start a fight?"

"Exactly."

Over the next dune, Eddie yanked the wheel to the right, heading directly for the Libyans.

"You're going to have to time this just right," Juan said.

"I'm all about trajectories and timing."

"If there's going to be a math quiz on this," Linc said, "count me out."

Nazari and his men continued to pound away with machine gun and grenade fire. A few shots splashed them with sand, but, so far, they'd been lucky.

Over the next crest, Juan could see ten pickup trucks on huge tires. Men in the back of each were carrying assault rifles and RPGs. Two of them had mounted machine guns like the ones on the Scorpions.

"How are the odds looking now?" Linc said with a rueful chuckle.

"I'll bet on Eddie's driving any day," Juan said.

"Good," Eddie said. "Because you need to hang on."

Just before he got to the top of the next dune, Eddie wrenched the wheel around ninety degrees. Juan brought the grenade launcher to bear on Nazari's Scorpion as it came over the dune behind them.

Juan pulled the trigger on the launcher, sending a stream of inert grenades flying. Since he'd anticipated where the Scorpion would appear, several of the grenades hit the driver, knocking him back in his seat. He slumped down, and the dune buggy nearly tipped over before Nazari could grab the wheel and right it.

Eddie accelerated away as Nazari shoved the unconscious driver out of the vehicle and took his place.

Juan waved to him, goading Nazari to follow. This distracted him from the impending danger. Nazari gave chase as his machine gunner sprayed bullets.

"Anybody hit?" Juan asked.

"Not me," Eddie replied.

"I'm fine," Linc said, "but our ride isn't. They plugged the fuel tank."

Eddie glanced down at the gauge. "We're losing gas fast."

Juan looked at the looming cliffs ahead. "How long?"

"It's going to be close."

Juan swiveled in his seat. Nazari was so intent on closing the distance that he didn't notice one of the pickups come over the dune right next to him. His machine gunner turned the weapon on the new enemy, slicing the truck apart with the .50 caliber rounds at point-blank range. The driver turned too quickly on the slope and the truck rolled, sending the surviving men tumbling.

The rest of the Libyan assault force hurtled over the dune. Nazari had to make a choice to flee or face his enemy. Seeing that he had little chance of escaping, he flashed one last sneer at Juan and chose to turn and fight.

Juan watched as Nazari leaped into the seat with the grenade launcher. He put up a good battle, blowing away three more of the pickups in rapid succession. But the numbers weren't in his favor.

The pickups had him surrounded. One of the four RPGs shot toward the Scorpion and made contact. Nazari disappeared in a massive explosion as the grenades detonated.

"Scratch a whole bunch more terrorists," Linc said.

"That still leaves six truckfuls of them," Eddie said.

Juan turned back to the front. "And they're not waiting around to see who they killed. All of them are headed our way."

The cliffs rising before them went on for miles in either direction. Even if they had gas, they'd be hemmed in by the natural barrier.

To punctuate the problem, an RPG blew up about a quarter mile behind them.

"If they're trying to convince us to slow down," Linc said, "it's having the opposite effect."

A roar slowly grew louder and overcame the engine noise of the Scorpion. It was approaching fast from the rear. Juan turned his head to see the IL-76 coming in low over the pursuing Libyans.

"Tiny got my message," Juan said.

Tiny had been circling out of visual range as a backup in case Juan called him in an emergency. A radio transmitter had been secreted in Scorpion 1, which Nazari had commandeered. But Juan never put all his eggs in one basket and had a microtransmitter inserted into his combat leg prosthesis. It was so small that the only information it could transmit was their location. When Juan activated it, Tiny understood his services were needed and homed in on them.

As the cargo jet overflew them, one of the Libyans took a potshot with his RPG. The rocket tore through the sky, and only Tiny's quick reflexes prevented it from hitting one of the engines. He rolled right and the unguided rocket sailed past within a few feet of the wing.

"You think he got *that* message?" Eddie asked.

"I hope so," Juan said.

The jet made a wide turn and then flew in a straight line perpendicular to their path about a mile ahead, far out of range of the RPGs. The rear cargo ramp lowered. When the IL-76 got to a point almost dead ahead, a pallet slid out the back. The chute opened immediately, and the object floated to the ground in front of them.

"That man can fly!" Linc yelled, and waved at the departing plane. Without a landing strip, there wasn't anything more Tiny could do besides radio their position back to the *Oregon*.

Not that it would make a difference. Further help would arrive far too late.

Eddie aimed for the pallet, its chute ruffling in the breeze like a flag that beckoned them to a safe haven.

A hundred yards from the pallet, the Scorpion's engine sputtered.

"Told you it would be close," Eddie said.

The engine finally died fifty yards from their destination. They all jumped out and sliced through the cargo bungees with knives to free the cases holding the nuclear weapon cores. As before, Eddie ran ahead to unpack their gear while Juan and Linc lugged the heavy containers.

The growl of the pickups grew ominously close, but Juan didn't dare take a second to look. The cliffs towered over them, and Juan was concentrating on calculating how much distance they'd need.

By now, Eddie had the cover off the pallet, exposing another dune buggy. But this one was different from the Scorpions.

It had a large, four-bladed propeller on the back, like one found on an Everglades airboat. The vehicle was based on a French design called the Pegasus. Max Hanley, the Corporation's chief engineer, had enlarged it to carry three people instead of two, saving weight by building the frame out of carbon fiber tubing. He dubbed it the *Daedalus* after the mythical father of Icarus.

They heaved the cases in the storage area and got in. This time, Juan took the driver's seat.

"I don't think there's enough room between here and the cliff," Eddie said.

"I agree," Juan said, and gunned the engine. He raced forward, turning the vehicle toward the Libyans.

As he accelerated, Linc and Eddie fired at the approaching convoy, hoping to slow them at least a little.

Juan spun the *Daedalus* in a U-turn and floored it. When it hit sixty miles an hour, he flipped the safety switch on the dashboard and punched the red button underneath.

A parasail was released from the rear of the *Daedalus* and unfurled behind them. It caught air and began to rise. When it was nearly overhead, Juan felt the vehicle's wheels leave the ground, and they were airborne.

The *Daedalus* rose briskly. Three RPGs

detonated on the cliffs as they flew past, the operators unwisely aiming at the small dune buggy instead of the enormous blue para-sail above them. Juan glanced up and saw a few rifle rounds perforate the sail, but it didn't rip, and there was no effect on its performance.

Juan was more concerned with getting over the looming cliffs. He pulled back on the steering column without stalling the craft. It didn't exactly have the agility of a hummingbird. The *Daedalus* could fly about as well as a seaplane could swim.

Circling around for another pass would bring them in range of the RPGs again, but if they slammed into the cliff face at the vehicle's top speed of seventy miles per hour, this would be a very short trip.

"Chairman . . ." Eddie said, the worry in his voice obvious.

The rocks were at eye level. Eddie was right to be worried. The lead cases weighed them down more than they'd expected. They weren't going to make it.

Juan pulled back even farther, risking the stall. The *Daedalus* nosed up and the wheels cleared the cliff with no more than a foot to spare.

He eased the wheel forward and the tires kissed the ground momentarily as the *Dae-*

dalus stalled and then took to the air again as the parasail refilled.

The Libyans disappeared from view.

"I think I'll leave the flying to Tiny next time," Juan said with a sigh of relief.

"Would it sound bad if I agreed with you, Chairman?" Linc asked.

"I second that," Eddie said. He activated the onboard radio.

"You out there, Tiny?" Juan said.

"Loud and clear, Chairman," he replied. "Glad to see you sailed over the cliffs. Looked like a close one. Everyone all right?"

"No injuries, thanks to you. Your aim was impeccable."

"I nearly didn't make it out myself."

"We saw that. We're on our way to a town called El Menia. We'll land there and gas up. We should be back to the *Oregon* late this evening. Have Max let the Algerian Army know that they've got some Libyan intruders at the coordinates where you made the last drop."

"Did you make any recoveries?"

"We found the packages we were looking for. Tell Max that Langston Overholt should get ready to make a deposit to Credit Condamine with a lot of fluffy zeroes."

"There may be a problem with that," Tiny said, all humor gone from his voice.

"Why?"

"Because Credit Condamine was robbed today during the Monaco Grand Prix. Max said it's a big mess."

The Corporation held its assets in several banks around the world, but Credit Condamine was one of its biggest deposits, mainly because of Monaco's status as a tax haven.

Eddie and Linc knew just as well as Juan did what the implications were.

"You're kidding," Linc said.

Eddie looked at Juan with a raised eyebrow. "This doesn't sound good."

Juan shook his head in disgust. "How much did they get?"

"All of it," Tiny said. "All our money in that account is gone."

EIGHT

ALGIERS

Curious stares from dockworkers greeted the odd-looking *Daedalus* when it arrived at the port, with the evening sun nearing the horizon. Juan was too concerned about the theft of Corporation funds to care. The old rust bucket tied to the dock may have been the ugliest ship in the harbor, but Juan was happy to see the *Oregon* again.

To say the 560-foot-long cargo freighter had seen better days was like saying Chernobyl had had a slight accident. The ship looked as if it might sink within minutes of setting sail. The peeling green paint was the color of something a seasick sailor might produce in heavy swells. Rust patches that dotted the hull were so pronounced, they seemed to be mere days from becoming holes.

The upper segment was even worse. Gaps in the bent railing were spanned by chains and bailing wire. The ship was equipped with five cranes, but three of them were in such disrepair that they were obviously useless. The single funnel was caked with soot. Barrels, both upright and overturned, and piles of trash littered the deck. The filthy white superstructure aft of amidships sported windows that were so etched, they looked as if they'd been cleaned with steel wool. One pane of glass was missing and replaced by a moldy piece of plywood.

"Home sweet home," Linc said, echoing Juan's thoughts.

The *Daedalus* was hauled up by one of the operational cranes and lowered into the hold.

They made their way up the gangplank and separated once they were on board. Eddie and Linc went to secure the *Daedalus* and its radioactive cargo, and Juan entered a companionway toward the crew area.

Buzzing fluorescent lights blinked overhead, providing dim illumination for the grimy bare metal walls and chipped linoleum floor. He passed the captain's quarters, the pungent odor coming from it as overwhelming as ever. The interior was so sparsely furnished and dingy that it would have made a Third World interrogation chamber seem like a palace by comparison.

Juan reached a utility closet and opened it to find mops, brooms, and other cleaning supplies that had gathered dust from disuse. He closed the door behind him and turned the knobs on the slop sink in a practiced pattern, and, with a click, the back wall slid open, revealing lush carpeting and mahogany walls in a hallway lit by recessed lighting befitting a five-star hotel.

Juan went inside and the wall closed behind him, the buzzing of the fluorescents and the foul smell vanishing instantly. Paintings by impressionist masters lined the halls, which safeguarded some of the Corporation's resources in assets that were stowed aboard the *Oregon.*

Selling them would be a last resort, but he was glad he had them as a backup, especially after hearing that a major portion of the Corporation's cash reserve was now gone.

The biggest asset the Corporation owned was the *Oregon* itself. When Juan had created his brainchild for carrying out U.S. government operations off the books, his first task had been to find a ship appropriate for the job. After a long search, he found photos of an 11,000-ton lumber carrier destined for the scrapyard. The old freighter had performed well over a couple of decades hauling timber to Asia from the Pacific

Northwest, but she had become too slow and obsolete to be profitable. She was so plain and unassuming that Juan knew she would be perfect for his purposes.

Although three breaker yards had bid against him, she was still far cheaper than a new ship. He took the junker to a covered dry dock in Vladivostok, where she spent six months getting a radical keel-to-deck overhaul, care of a friendly and corrupt Russian admiral who knew a good business opportunity when he saw it.

When the *Oregon* emerged from her refit, she actually looked worse than she had when she went in. But that only served the anonymity that Juan had desired.

It was underneath the skin where all the real work had been done. Stabilizing fins were added, and the frame was stiffened and fortified to withstand the stresses that would be placed on it by its cutting-edge power plant.

Her old diesels were gone, replaced by revolutionary new magnetohydrodynamic engines. Only a few vessels had ever been equipped with them. Four pulse jets were powered by supercooled magnets that stripped free electrons from seawater to produce practically unlimited electricity. Two thrust-vectored drive tubes focused the power, making the *Oregon* the fastest and most maneuverable ship in the world for her size.

Fiber optics and wiring throughout the ship allowed it to be upgraded on a regular basis with all of the latest technology and electronics, including high-definition closed-circuit cameras, encrypted satellite communications, centralized ship operations, and military-grade radar and sonar. A mighty IBM Vulcan supercomputer powered the *Oregon*'s network.

Her defensive and offensive capabilities were equally potent. Attacks could be carried out using Exocet antiship missiles and twin tubes that launched Russian-made Type 53-65 torpedoes, which had recently replaced its TEST-71s.

The ship's vast array of guns were cleverly hidden by retractable hull plates. At the bow was a 120mm cannon like the one on an M1A1 Abrams main battle tank. For defense against small vessels, missiles, and aircraft, the *Oregon* was armed with three General Electric 20mm Gatling guns, a Metal Storm electronically fired multibarreled-salvo array, and vertical launchers for surface-to-air missiles. A batch of remote-controlled .30 caliber machine guns could pop out of the deck oil barrels to repel boarders.

An MD 520N helicopter stored in the aftmost hold could be raised into position for takeoff on a hydraulic platform, while her two submarines could conduct covert missions by launching from the keel, where two huge underwater panels opened into a cavernous space in the center of the ship called the moon pool. At the waterline were the concealed doors of a boat garage that housed small craft, such as Zodiacs and a SEAL assault boat.

Should the need arise, as it sometimes did, the *Oregon* had a fully staffed medical bay with a sterile operating theater. The Magic Shop was the onboard facility where all of their made-to-order equipment, uniforms, disguises, and false identifications were created.

To attract a crew of the best and brightest in their fields, the accommodations were some of the most luxurious afloat. Chefs trained at the Cordon Bleu prepared gourmet meals made from the freshest ingredients. One of the ballast tanks doubled as a Carrara marble–lined Olympic-length swimming pool, in addition to the full-sized Jacuzzi and sauna.

Juan entered his cabin and office. Crew members were given generous allowances to decorate their quarters as they liked. Juan had recently updated his to a more sleek modern style. The feature he enjoyed most was the wall-mounted, 4K super-high-def LED screen that stretched the length of the cabin. Most of the time, like now, it showed the feed from an external camera. With the ships and harbor defined in crisp detail under the beautiful sunset, the illusion of a window was uncanny.

He called Max and Linda to come to his cabin in twenty minutes. After removing the fake nose and taking a quick shower to wash the grit off and the dye out of his hair, he changed into jeans and a linen shirt. As soon as he was dressed, there was a light knock on his door. He opened it to see Maurice, the chief steward, dressed in his impeccable suit and tie as usual. His left arm had a white linen napkin draped over it and held a covered silver tray. His timing was so spot-on that Juan sometimes wondered whether the dour Englishman had a camera in Juan's cabin.

"Good evening, Captain," Maurice said in his plummy British accent. As a veteran of the Royal Navy, Maurice insisted on using the nautical honorific rather than "Chairman," which was what the rest of the crew called him as the head of the Corporation.

Juan waved him in and Maurice set the tray on his small dining table. Beneath the cover were a marinated rib eye, green beans, and potatoes O'Brien. Maurice poured steaming coffee from a china pot into one of the three cups. He even knew Linda and Max would be joining him.

"Thank you, Maurice. I hope you had a better day than I did."

"That somewhat depends on whether we really did lose all of our money." In addition to being the best steward on the high seas, Maurice had a nose for information. If Juan wanted the latest gossip on what was going on behind the scenes on the *Oregon,* Maurice was the first place he turned.

"That's what I'm going to find out," Juan said as he savored the Kenyan brew.

"I know you will, Captain."

He slipped out of the room like a wraith a moment before Linda and Max appeared in the doorway.

"Come in," Juan said. "Pour yourselves some coffee. Did you already eat?"

Max Hanley had been the first person Juan hired for the Corporation and its second-in-command as president. A former Vietnam War Swift Boat commander, Max was also the ship's chief engineer and had helped design the *Oregon,* so he considered it his baby. Not only was he in charge of running the ship when Juan wasn't on board but he was also Juan's best friend. Though he was in his sixties, with gray licking at the red curls circling his balding head, Max seemed to have the attitude of a much younger man and was as cantankerous as ever.

"Chef fed me well tonight," Max said.

"Well, I figured *you* ate," Juan teased, looking pointedly at Max's stomach. "I was asking Linda."

"Are you kidding?" Max said. "She wolfed down more than I did."

Juan raised an eyebrow. "I find that hard to believe."

Linda Ross, the Corporation's vice president of operations and third-in-command, was as lovely as a wood elf and about as small. Her cute, upturned nose and high-pitched, girlish voice might have kept her from getting promotions when she served in the Navy on an Aegis cruiser and as a Pentagon staffer, but Juan brought her on because she had no trouble putting that voice to use when she was barking out commands during battle. She'd earned the entire crew's respect for her skill and discipline. But now that she was out of the military, she took advantage of the less stringent rules and frequently changed the color of her hair. Today, it was a vibrant silver, cut in a shaggy bob.

"Believe it," she said, putting her hands on her hips. "I was starving."

"Me, too," Juan replied, taking a seat. "I hope you don't mind if I eat while you fill me in. Tell me what happened."

Linda and Max sat as well. Max sipped his coffee while Linda explained the events of the afternoon.

"Hali is a big Formula 1 fan, so he was keeping an eye on the race and saw the whole thing in real time." Hali Kasim was their Lebanese American communications officer. "By the way, he said Langston Overholt will be calling in a few minutes. As far as they can tell, the Credit Condamine president, Henri Munier, sabotaged his own bank and then went on a rampage. He crashed through a barrier and destroyed several race cars before smashing into a pit garage and setting off a fuel tank. They're still cleaning it up, but the latest news is seven dead and dozens injured. I'll show you."

She tapped on her phone and the screen on Juan's wall suddenly flickered to a view of the Monaco Grand Prix. They watched the recordings of the frenzy of destruction from multiple angles as Linda shared more of the details.

Juan shook his head. "It doesn't make sense. I met the guy once and he seemed as mild-mannered as you'd expect a bank president to be. Do the police have a motive?"

"Not that we know of," Max said, "but the investigation is just getting under way."

"And what about our account? The message I got was that our money is gone. Don't you mean 'stolen'?"

Linda gave him a grim look. She and Juan shared the duties of keeping track of the Corporation's finances. "The problem is that we don't know. It looks as if Munier somehow disabled the accounts. The money could still be locked in there somewhere, the money might have been transferred, or he could have done something else to destroy the accounts. I've been putting together our files here, but even if we prove what was in there, it could take months for the money to be accessible again."

Juan didn't like the sound of that. Cash flow was always an imperative for the Corporation. Running a ship this size wasn't cheap. The outlay for the latest operation had been substantial: weapons, chartering the cargo jet, buying and modifying the

Scorpions and the *Daedalus.* A bonus was due for finding the WMDs, but it wouldn't tide them over for long.

The Corporation was run like a partnership, with each crew member getting a share of the profits, which also meant that they would share in any losses. They were paid extremely well for the hardships and hazards they endured, but their income and retirement savings depended on a healthy and financially solvent Corporation. They needed to find out what happened in the bank attack and get their money back.

Juan's phone rang. It was Langston Overholt IV, Juan's former boss at the CIA and the person most responsible for encouraging him to found the Corporation. He put it on speaker.

"Juan here, Lang," he said. "I've got you on speaker with Linda Ross and Max Hanley."

"I hear you have some good news for me," said the octogenarian in a gravelly voice.

"We recovered two cases from a B-47, serial number 52-534. Each of them contains a nuclear weapon core."

"Are they still intact?"

"The cases are a little worse for wear, but no leakage that we could detect."

"And Nazari?"

"Dead, along with his soldiers. We also got a few Libyan terrorists who came to the party."

"Excellent work as usual," Overholt said. There was some clicking of a keyboard on the line. "There's a U.S. destroyer in your region, the *Bainbridge*. Can we set a rendezvous tonight to make the transfer?"

"Yes," Juan replied. "How about near Sicily? We're headed in that direction anyway."

"Right. I know about your problem resulting from the bank heist in Monaco."

Linda spoke. "We've already changed all of our accounts and passwords in case any of them were compromised in the incident. I've forwarded you our new information for payment."

"Yes, I received it. Your fee will be sent by wire transfer once we have the cases. In fact, your situation with Credit Condamine has national security implications for us as well. That's why I want you to team up with an analyst we have embedded with Interpol. She's a forensic accountant based in Paris who's been authorized to investigate the incident on our behalf. Since you're intimately affected by the results and have expertise that might help her, I thought it would be a good match." There was a slight

108

hesitation before he continued. "Her name is Gretchen Wagner."

Juan's fork stopped halfway to his mouth, a green bean dangling in midair. He put the fork down and sat back, his eyes looking into the unfocused distance.

"Gretchen Wagner?" he said.

"Is that going to be a problem?" Overholt asked.

Juan composed himself after a second and said, "No. No problem at all. Linda and I will head to Monaco to meet her, once we get the cases squared away."

"Good. I'll have the Navy contact the *Bainbridge*'s captain. I'll send you the co-ordinates in a few hours. And we've begun negotiations with the Algerian government to retrieve the remains of the Air Force pilot and search for the others. I'm sure their families will be grateful for your discovery."

He hung up.

Linda stared at Juan for a moment, but when she saw that further explanation wasn't coming, she stood. "I'll go make the arrangements to cast off and set course for the rendezvous."

"Thanks, Linda," Juan said. "Let's book a flight out of Palermo to Monaco."

"Got it." She closed the door behind her.

Juan pushed his plate away, no longer

hungry. He rose and made a motion to follow Linda out.

Max got up, too. "Where are you going?"

Juan opened the door. "To make sure those cases aren't spreading radiation all over my ship." He knew his voice sounded a bit more terse than usual, but he couldn't help it.

"Wait a minute," Max said, catching up to him in the hallway, all but blocking the way. "This Gretchen Wagner — it sounded like you knew the name. Do you two have a history together?"

"You might say that."

"Why? How do you know her?"

"Well, for three weeks, she was my wife."

Juan gave Max an inscrutable grin and left him standing in the cabin passageway, mouth agape.

NINE

SOUTH OF MAJORCA

With a storm fast approaching, Cobus Visser didn't want to stay out on the deck of the containership *Narwhal* any longer than he had to. He and Gustaaf Bodeker had been tasked with checking every single reefer unit connection to make sure they were secure enough to weather the morning squall. If the refrigerated containers lost power during the storm, the vegetables inside would rot before they could reach port in Malta.

As the lowest-ranking members of the twelve-man crew, Visser and Bodeker had been assigned this tedious and undesirable task. Lanky, twenty-year-old Visser was the newest addition, and while he didn't mind the warmer waters of the Mediterranean, he didn't understand why they'd been sent so far from their home port of Rotterdam. Normally, this small feeder cargo vessel was limited to short trips in the North Sea, distributing loads from Dijkstra Shipping's giant containerships that carried goods from ports in Asia. But without explanation from the captain, the *Narwhal* had been suddenly diverted on the long trip to Malta, an island country located between Italy and Libya, which had caused much speculation among the crew.

"Why do you think the captain won't tell us what we're picking up in Malta?" Visser asked Bodeker, who was inspecting the connections on their thirtieth reefer unit. The former speed skater, with thighs the size of beef slabs, seemed irked by the discussion, but Visser didn't care.

"We're paid to go where the captain takes us and where the owner tells us to go," Bodeker replied. "Why does it matter what we carry? All of the containers look the same anyway."

"Yes, but we've always been told before. We know these reefers hold tomatoes, peppers, and cucumbers. The rest of the containers are filled with computer parts to be recycled in China. I saw the bill of lading. But the cargo master told me we are picking up only one container in Malta. Don't you think that's strange?"

"No more strange than being sent to the

Mediterranean in the first place."

"That's another thing!" Visser went on excitedly. "We've been shuttling back and forth between Rotterdam, Oslo, and Bergen for the last three months, and then, out of nowhere, we're going a thousand miles in the other direction to pick up a single container?"

"So?"

"Well, it's weird. Do you want to know what I think?"

"Not really," Bodeker said.

Visser ignored him. "I think we're on a classified mission for the Dutch government. We're picking up cargo that they don't want anyone to know about."

Bodeker rolled his eyes. "You *would* think that. Don't you ever get tired of all these conspiracy theories?"

"And I suppose you think the government tells us about everything they do."

"I didn't say that. But don't you think it's more reasonable that the company has some time-sensitive cargo to bring back to Rotterdam and we're simply the only ship that was available?"

"Come on, Bodeker," Visser said. "That's just failure of imagination. And boring."

"Your *pestering* is getting boring. Let's finish this job and get back inside."

Visser waved his hand in disgust. He stretched and looked out to sea, surprised to see a bone-white ship passing by in the other direction no more than a mile off the port bow. He'd never seen a design like it.

He tapped Bodeker on the shoulder. "What do you think that is? It can't be a navy ship."

Bodeker straightened in annoyance and then looked curiously at the vessel. "I'd say it's a yacht."

"You're kidding. That thing is huge!" The sleek vessel had to be 400 feet long, a hundred feet longer than their own cargo ship. "It's got to be a cruise ship, although I've never seen one that had a twin-hull configuration. It's too far away to make out the name."

"It doesn't have enough portals or balconies for a cruise ship."

Before they realized it, she was even with the *Narwhal,* racing past as if she were a cigarette boat.

Bodeker furrowed his brow. "How is that possible?"

"What do you mean?" Visser asked.

"If I didn't know better, I'd say she was doing fifty knots."

Visser squinted at the odd ship. Without a reference point, it was difficult for him to tell speed at sea.

"Are you sure it's not just an optical illusion?"

Bodeker blinked twice. "Must be," he muttered.

The yacht turned smartly and sped away on a perpendicular course.

Bodeker shrugged. "You'll soon learn that you see all kinds of strange things on the ocean, Visser."

He went back to work, and Visser followed him as they moved toward the bow, but the younger man couldn't take his eyes off the bizarre vessel until it was no more than a dot disappearing into the gathering storm clouds.

Then a bright light flashed above the yacht.

"Looks like it got hit by lightning," Visser said.

"Then let's get out of the weather as quick as we can," Bodeker replied.

Visser nodded, his eyes on the aft superstructure, where the dry and warm crew quarters were. He spotted the captain on the top-level bridge, watching the approaching storm with his binoculars. "Okay, but when we eat lunch, I'm going to ask the captain what —"

His next words were drowned out by a

massive explosion on the *Narwhal*'s bridge. The windows burst outward, and a section of the roof panel, along with the antennas, flew into the air. Fire and smoke belched from the remains. Bodeker and Visser were thrown to the deck.

"What the hell happened?" Bodeker yelled.

Visser felt himself shaking uncontrollably. "It just blew up."

A moment later, an enormous boom nearly deafened them, like a gigantic thunderclap from a lightning strike right next to them.

"Heaven help us!" Visser screamed, terror gripping him.

Bodeker could only shake his head, the whites of his eyes huge.

Then another explosion took out the lower part of the superstructure. Every crewman inside had to be dead. The blast was followed a few seconds later by a second thunderclap.

A third explosion in front of the superstructure blasted six of the forty-foot containers off the starboard side of the ship like they were aluminum cans. The explosion after that impacted the hull at the waterline, throwing a geyser into the air.

Visser and Bodeker watched the carnage

in silent awe, frozen in place. It was clear that they were under attack, but from where? Sabotage was the first thought that came to Visser's mind. Someone had planted explosives all over the ship.

Explosions and thunderclaps came in rapid succession, each getting closer to the bow where they were standing.

Visser and Bodeker looked at each other. They realized there was no choice. The lifeboats were destroyed, and they didn't even have time to find life jackets.

By unspoken agreement, they both leaped overboard.

Visser surfaced and panicked when he didn't spot his crewmate in the churning waves. He swiveled around until he saw Bodeker twenty feet away, swimming for his life. Visser didn't need to be told to do the same.

Visser lost count of the explosions and didn't stop to turn around. Bodeker was the first to halt, and he treaded water while he looked back.

Visser was almost more terrified by Bodeker's stricken look than by the prospect of seeing the damage. He forced himself to turn and face what had become of the *Narwhal.*

He gagged when he saw the remains of

his home at sea. The tidy ship had been reduced to a ruin, the *Narwhal*'s red and black hull transformed into battered metal. Its stern was already underwater. They watched without a word as the ship's bow pointed straight up into the sky and then slipped beneath the waves. The refrigerated containers bobbed on the surface until they drifted from view.

Visser cried, the tears stinging even more than the salt water. Bodeker linked arms with him, and they helped each other keep their heads above the waves, but with a storm coming their chances were slim. The cold water sapped their strength with each passing minute.

An hour later, Visser was exhausted and about to give up in despair despite Bodeker's staunch faith that they could make it. But when he saw an approaching ship in the distance, he began to believe.

They both shouted for joy and waved their arms as the ship neared. It was another container vessel about the same size and shape as their own sunken ship. It even had the same red and black livery.

As it got closer, the similarities became even more apparent, down to the same types of cargo containers Visser had watched being loaded in Rotterdam.

Then an icy hand gripped his stomach when he read the name on the bow.

"No," he said, sputtering salt water. "No, it can't be!"

The white lettering said *Narwhal.*

It was as if his own ship had never sunk.

Visser assumed he was hallucinating, but the look on Bodeker's face made it clear that he saw the same thing. Although they couldn't make sense of the vision, they desperately screamed and waved their hands as much as they could without going under themselves.

The ship got within five hundred feet of them, but it showed no signs of slowing, and Visser couldn't see a single face in the bridge windows. It sailed on, implacable. The crew were either ignorant or uncaring, leaving him and Bodeker alone in the mounting waves without another ship on the horizon.

TEN

NICE, FRANCE

The midnight transfer of the nuclear cases from the *Oregon* to the Navy destroyer *Bainbridge* went off without a hitch. After almost sixty years, the atomic weapon cores would be headed back to Norfolk, and a Broken Arrow nuclear event could be scratched off the list.

Once the handoff was complete, Juan ordered the *Oregon* to make a dash to Palermo, where they caught a midmorning flight to Nice, the Côte d'Azur airport that served the principality of Monaco. Thirty minutes after landing, four of them were in a rental car, taking the winding coast road for the short drive. In addition to Linda Ross, Juan had decided to bring two other crew members along with him, Mark Murphy and Eric Stone, the Corporation's resident computer experts and research specialists. If their money was still in Credit

120

Condamine's computers somewhere, he wanted his own people on the job to find it.

Murph and Stoney were in their twenties, making them two of the youngest crew on the *Oregon*. They spent much of their downtime together, playing video games and complaining about the pitfalls of trying to date over the Internet. Their latest pastime during R & R was racing around on Jetlev-Flyers, water-powered packs that they'd somehow convinced Max to buy as a complement to the ship's Jet Skis. Although Murph and Eric stuck with each other like conjoined twins separated at birth, their appearance and demeanor couldn't have been more different.

Murph, the only Corporation employee who had never served in the military or intelligence services, had graduated from MIT with a Ph.D. at the age most kids were getting their first jobs out of college. He went on to use his incomparable computer and mathematics skills as a top weapons designer for a U.S. Navy contractor until he'd been recruited by the Corporation. His appearance would make him fit right in at a comic book convention, with uncombed dark hair, wispy chin stubble, and a scrawny frame typically clad in a T-shirt from his enormous collection. His idea of dressing up for the mission had been to put on a black jacket over a T-shirt that read *Give me ambiguity or give me something else.* Not only was he a whiz with anything electronic, he also served as the *Oregon*'s weapons officer.

Unlike Murph, Annapolis graduate Eric Stone had been a naval officer in research and development, which is where he'd first met Murph, brought together by their rare technical acumen. Although he was no longer in uniform, Eric preferred to dress in crisp white button-down shirts and chino slacks, adding a blue blazer to the ensemble for today. He chose to wear glasses instead of contacts over his soft brown eyes, and his short hair looked as if it were parted with a straightedge. Despite little experience on the high seas during his stint in the Navy, he had honed his skills as a helmsman to the point that he was the *Oregon*'s best ship driver other than Juan himself.

Overholt had made some phone calls during the night, which resulted in the four of them being brought onto the case under the guise of private insurance investigators assisting Interpol. Kevin Nixon, the *Oregon*'s special effects and prop master, provided them with flawless fake IDs crafted in the ship's Magic Shop.

Murph, who sat next to Eric in the back-seat, was grimacing at his ID. "I still think it was you who got Kevin to change my undercover name."

Eric could barely contain a smirk. "You don't like Christopher Bacon?"

"You mean Christopher *Paul* Bacon."

Juan, who hadn't heard the full name until now, looked at Linda and chuckled. She laughed and shrugged her shoulders as if to say *Don't blame me.*

Juan glanced in the rearview mirror. "Your name is Chris P. Bacon?"

Murph groaned and nodded, then pointed a thumb at Eric. "And *his* name is Colt B. Patton. He might as well have called himself Hombre T. Rockpuncher."

Eric put up his hands. "I swear I didn't have anything to do with it."

"Right," Murph grumbled as he put the ID away.

"I don't know," Linda said. "I think your name sizzles." The three of them laughed, and Juan spotted the corner of Murph's mouth turn up in a reluctant smile. He was proud that his crew could keep their sense of humor intact even in the face of losing a good portion of their savings. Facing adversity head-on instead of hanging their heads in despair was what they did best.

They arrived at Credit Condamine to find police cars swarming the block. Juan got out, flashed his ID, and asked an officer who was in charge. He was directed to a trim man in his fifties, arguing with a striking raven-haired woman. Heated French words were flying back and forth so quickly that neither of them noticed Juan's approach.

The man was the chief detective, judging from the badge sticking out of his pocket. Graying at the temples and sporting a slim mustache, he kept shaking his head like it was attached to a paint mixer. He was the shorter of the two and had to look up at the woman as he spoke.

The tall woman had a few more lines around her eyes than Juan remembered, but otherwise Gretchen Wagner looked exactly the same as she did when they had served in the CIA together. Wearing a tailored Armani suit, she still had a lithe, athletic figure sculpted by a daily routine of martial arts. Light makeup dusted her high cheekbones, and her sparkling green eyes had lost none of their fire. Even though she had a face that would stand out at a fashion show, Juan admired the fact that she wouldn't think twice about cloaking it in the grubby likeness of a homeless person when the mission called for it. She was all about getting the job done, and the chief detective was, apparently, finding that out the hard way.

"Excuse me," Juan said, interrupting their repartee. "I am looking for Gretchen Wagner."

They stopped speaking, and Juan and Gretchen held each other's eyes for a few moments. She kept her face expressionless, and he couldn't tell if that was for his benefit or the detective's.

The detective sneered at Juan as if he'd been handed a used handkerchief.

"This is he?" the detective asked Gretchen, jutting his index finger at Juan.

She nodded. "Blake Charles, from Columbia Mutual Insurance, this is Chief Inspector Rivard of Monaco's Sûreté Publique. I was just explaining to the inspector that you are to be given full cooperation during this investigation at Interpol's request."

Rivard didn't offer his hand but spent a good amount of time inspecting Juan's identification. He sniffed disdainfully when he couldn't find anything amiss. "My government may be able to order me to give you access, but I don't have to like it."

"As you are aware, Inspector, this security breach affects bank customers from dozens of countries," Gretchen said with a steely cadence. "If you have a problem including them in the investigation, I can contact your commissioner for more guidance."

Rivard's nostrils flared in fury. This would probably be the biggest case he'd ever get in the sleepy principality and jeopardizing his position as the lead inspector by protesting a decision from his superiors wasn't going to get him off to a good start.

"Fine," he said finally. "But you brief them. And if I find that they are hindering or obstructing the investigation in any way, they will be gone." He stormed off, shouting at some uniformed officers for letting gawkers get too close.

"For some reason," Juan said, "I get the feeling that he has some objection to us being here."

Gretchen gave him a faint smile. "Yes, he shouldn't keep his emotions bottled up like that."

Juan could tell that she had the urge to give him a hug, but she merely shook his hand with a strong grip. The skin was smooth on the back of her hand but calloused on her palm. Two of her knuckles were bruised.

"Still throwing people around the karate mat?" he asked.

She rubbed her hand. "I've moved on to Krav Maga. I find it relaxes me." Juan had never heard that benefit of the lethal Israeli self-defense system, a combination of street-fighting tactics and skills from boxing, wrestling, and numerous types of martial arts.

"White-collar crime does seem to be getting deadlier," Juan said, looking pointedly at the bank.

"Seven dead, including the bank president. It's the first time I've worked on something like this. Most of my job entails tracking fraudulent transactions from the comfort of my office in Paris."

"Do you miss the field?" Juan asked.

"Sometimes."

"Why'd you leave ops?"

Gretchen huffed a derisive breath. "My identity was outed by an idiot congressman, which is a redundant description of him, I know. Ironically, he was on the intelligence subcommittee and blabbed about my covert status to a mistress who happened to be a Russian agent. My career in fieldwork was over after that."

"Sorry. I didn't know."

She shrugged. "It was after you left. If it had happened during our marriage, you probably would have been caught in the mess, too."

Juan surreptitiously glanced at her left

hand and didn't see a ring, but that didn't necessarily mean anything. He then said, "It's good to see you again."

She gave him a cockeyed smile. "Is it?"

He hesitated a bit too long. Before he could respond, she looked over his shoulder. "Is that your team?"

He followed her gaze and saw that Linda, Murph, and Eric were watching him intently. Linda must have filled the team in on the conversation with Overholt the previous night, but he didn't know whether Max had told them anything further. He waved them over.

Juan introduced them using their fake names. Because Rivard was still watching, Gretchen made a show of checking their IDs.

She snickered when she read Mark Murphy's card. "Are you the lean and smoky variety?" she said, handing it back.

Murph turned red and glowered at Eric, who chewed his lip to keep from laughing.

"So you must be Eggs?" she said, indicating Eric, who gave her a quizzical look. She pointed at his ID. "You know, Colt *Benedict* Patton?"

Murph snatched it away, letting out a huge guffaw when he read it. "As in eggs Benedict?" It was Eric who blushed this time. They both turned to Linda.

She grinned at them coyly. "Guilty. I thought we needed to lighten the mood." She turned to Gretchen. "Have your computer techs found out anything?"

"Not much so far," Gretchen said. "The virus that was installed is so complex that they're stumped at how to pull up any of the files at all."

Juan nodded at Murph and Eric. "Why don't you see if you can give them a hand?" The two of them took a last look at Gretchen and went through the bank's front entrance.

"I'd like to take a look at the Grand Prix garage explosion and fire," Linda said. "I'll see if I can spot anything that might have been missed." She had watched the TV recording of the car chase and crash repeatedly during the flight to Nice.

"Good," Juan said. "Gretchen and I will go over the video from inside the bank. Let's get together for lunch in two hours to go over our findings."

Linda went back to the car and drove off toward the harbor, leaving Juan and Gretchen alone again.

"Come on," she said, and led him toward the security office.

As they walked, Juan said, "Gretchen,

where's our money?"

"As far as we know, it's still in the bank. It's simply frozen. We've detected no unusual transactions from this location since the virus was installed. Besides, it would have been nearly impossible to transfer the money without authorization from the depositors because of two-factor authentication. Someone from your side would have needed to give permission for any transactions."

"So we haven't lost our money —"

She held up a hand. "I can't promise the accounts are still intact until I can look at the data, and they're currently locked up. Let's hope Bacon and Eggs have more success opening up the computers than Monaco's finest."

When they reached the security office, she pulled up the video of Henri Munier stepping off the elevator into the bank lobby.

Juan gave Gretchen a questioning look. "Is this the first video we have of him? Nothing from the garage?"

She nodded. "Except for a couple of minutes, it's all been wiped clean."

On the video, Munier spent a minute talking to the guard, who then walked off and reappeared a moment later with the second guard. They all entered the elevator, and the video ended. There was no audio.

"Why would he miss these two minutes?" Juan wondered aloud.

"Rivard thinks Munier was being careless or that the alarm was tripped before he could finish erasing the videos."

"Munier is sophisticated enough to plan all this out, plant a computer virus, and kill three men, but he forgets to erase his own face?"

"I didn't say I agreed."

"How did the alarm go off?"

"Rivard thinks one of the guards did it before he died. They carried remote activators in case of a robbery."

"And what's Munier's motive?"

"Embezzlement is the first thought in cases like this," Gretchen said. "He could have been covering his tracks but then got caught and had no other options."

"What do *you* think?"

She tilted her head at the screen. "Take another look at the video."

Juan watched it three more times before he saw it.

Munier moved his lips twice while the guard was away, like a whisper. At first, Juan thought he was speaking to himself, but it seemed too deliberate, on third glance, as if he were responding to something being said to him.

Juan looked back at Gretchen. "Someone's talking to him. He could be wearing an earpiece that we can't see."

"That's my thought. Rivard thinks he hired a hacker to build the computer virus for him, but I think someone forced him to do this. I've studied Munier's dossier and he was a family man, made a lot of money, and didn't have a gambling problem."

"Some people think they never have enough money."

"True," Gretchen said, "but he wasn't the violent type. Assassinating three men, including his vice president? No, Munier is the type to take his chances with a lawyer, not try to cover his tracks with this killing spree. Believe me, I've seen plenty of bankers get away with crimes you'd think would send them to prison for years."

"But that doesn't explain why he made a mad getaway from the police and killed himself when he got cornered."

With no more answers from the video, they went down to the garage.

They spent an hour trying to reenact how Munier might have killed two guards and stuffed them into the back of his vehicle. They concluded the middle-aged banker could have accomplished it, but it would have been a physically draining experience.

"Where was he before he came to the bank?" Juan asked.

"Many witnesses saw him get on a yacht called the *Achilles* to attend a party during the Grand Prix. Rivard concluded that was intended to be Munier's alibi."

"No one saw him leave?"

"If anyone did, they haven't come forward yet."

"I'd like to talk to the crew."

"You can't," Gretchen said. "The *Achilles* is gone, along with a dozen other yachts. Few of them wanted to stick around after the Grand Prix was called off."

"Without witnesses, it'll be impossible to retrace his steps and find out if anyone was coercing him."

"The police are talking to his wife, but she seems to be as shocked as everyone else."

"Maybe Linda will be able to shed some light on the situation when she gets back."

Juan's phone rang. It was Eric.

"Did you find something?" Juan answered.

"You could say that," Eric said with excitement. "It's a message from the hacker."

ELEVEN

Just as Juan and Gretchen reached the bank lobby on their way to Munier's office, Linda walked through the front door with a grim look on her face.

"Bad?" Juan said.

"The entire garage was gutted," Linda said. "Munier hit a fuel tank dead-on. He was driving an electric car, and the lithium-ion batteries ignited and cooked it good. The bodies were ash and bones, one in the driver's seat and two in the trunk. They had already been taken to the morgue, but the car was still there."

"Did you see anything that stood out?" Juan told her about their suspicion that Munier was being coerced.

Linda thought about it and then her eyes lit up. "I talked to the crime scene investigators and they did mention one odd detail. There was an extra cell phone in the car."

"You mean one of the men inside had two

cell phones on him?" Gretchen asked.

"No, they found the cell phone on the floor of the front seat, like it had fallen there. It seemed to have some plastic residue melted onto it. They thought it might have been in a bag, but I got a gander at it. It looked to me like the plastic from a zip tie was wrapped around it."

Gretchen gave her a puzzled look. "You mean the phone was lashed to something?"

Juan nodded slowly. "Makes sense. If they were using the camera in a cell phone to observe the interior of the car, they'd have to attach it to the dashboard somehow. It would also allow them to talk to Munier and tell him what to do."

"It's odd he would commit suicide in such a public and gruesome way just because someone ordered him to," Gretchen said.

"It gets stranger," Linda said. "They found some of the same residue melted onto the face of Munier's watch and on the steering wheel."

Juan paced as he imagined how someone might force the bank president to install the virus. Then he stopped and said, "Could his hands have been tied to the steering wheel?"

"Sure," Linda said. "But why?"

"It doesn't seem possible," Gretchen said to Juan. "He wouldn't be able to make a full rotation of the wheel with his hands lashed to it. From the look of the TV feed, he was making violent turns that would have required free hands."

"This might sound crazy," Juan said, "but what if he wasn't driving? The Tesla is drive-by-wire. It could have been programmed to be remotely driven."

Linda snapped her fingers. "Just like the PIG."

"Right."

"The PIG?" Gretchen asked.

"We have our own remote-controlled truck," Linda said. "Powered Investigator Ground. It was damaged in a recent mission, but the remote control system worked beautifully. I'll go take a closer look at the TV feed from his car chase. If we're lucky, maybe someone got a high-def video of Munier's hands on the wheel."

"Good idea. We're heading to the bank president's office. Apparently, whoever wrote the virus that Munier installed has left a message for us."

"Can't wait to hear that," Linda said, and she was gone.

They arrived at Munier's office to see Eric and Murph excitedly talking with a woman in her twenties, a cute blonde wearing horn-rimmed glasses and her hair in a pixie cut.

She was at the computer's keyboard, and Murph and Eric were hunched over her on either side, pointing at the screen. The three of them chattered in dense computer jargon, little of which Juan understood.

"Sounds like you two have made a new friend," he said.

After Juan and Gretchen identified themselves, Murph and Eric stepped on each other's words to introduce the seated woman to them.

"This is Marie Marceau," Murph said at the same time that Eric blurted out, "She's the Sûreté's top computer analyst."

"Let's take it one at a time," Gretchen said, obviously amused at their infatuation.

"Pleased to meet you," Marie said in a silky French accent. "We were stuck . . . *I* was stuck about how to break in to the computer system. The virus is a very unusual design that has us locked out. But then Chris and Colt had some fantastic ideas about how to approach the problem."

"She really just needed a little push in the right direction," Eric gushed.

Murph jumped in. "Marie was already on the right track. She would have figured it out soon enough —"

"Okay, okay," Juan said with a gesture of surrender. "You all make a great team and were able to get into the system — got it. You said there was a message?"

"What message?" Rivard said as he burst through the door, breathless, as if he'd run three blocks. "Marie, what is this?"

"*Ah bon,* you got my text."

"It just said that you had a breakthrough and to come at once. Now I find you telling these consultants information before you tell me?" He eyed Juan and Gretchen with contempt.

"I haven't told them anything yet," Marie said in exasperation. No doubt Rivard was unpopular with his staff. "They arrived only a moment before you did."

Rivard was partly mollified and collected himself. "Well, go on. Tell us what you've found."

"I think my new friends are being generous. I wouldn't have gotten this far without them. But, together, we were able to override the code that had us completely locked out of the system. When we did, a message popped up on the screen. Here it is. 'To the winner go the spoils, you computer genius, so congratulations! It's impressive that there's someone out there worthy of this message. All other hackers may be inferior to you, but don't bother trying to crack my code. It's 4096-bit encryption, so you'd need about a hundred years to break it.' "

"Is that true?" Rivard demanded.

"Not at all," Murph said.

"Good. Then how long will it take?"

Murph and Eric looked at each other and shrugged.

"Maybe ten years," Eric said.

Rivard looked like he'd blow an artery. "What?"

"A hundred years assumes using current technology. But with computer power doubling every eighteen months, we should be able to solve a cryptographic problem like this in ten years."

"Maybe even five," Murph suggested.

Juan didn't know if they were being serious or just yanking the imperious Rivard's chain. "Keep reading," he said.

"Don't think you have that long, either," Marie continued. "Every day counts and you've got ten left. All of the backups and banks connected to Credit Condamine are infected now. Upon reaching the time limit, if our forthcoming demands aren't met, you'll see the economy of Europe plunged into a chaos that will make you long for the good old days of the Great Depression."

The room quieted at that line.

"Can they really do that?" Juan asked Gretchen.

She shook her head. "I don't know. Without being able to see exactly what they've done to the software, it may be impossible to tell. But this bank is connected tightly with many other European banks. Perhaps they found some way of corrupting the transfer files."

"There's one final part," Marie said, and kept reading.

"Go ahead and comb through the code looking for this time bomb, if you dare, but eventually you'll have to cough up the dough to us. Heaven help you if you don't. One more major bank will suffer a catastrophic system failure in five days as a signal that we're not lying. We'll be in touch."

"We're obviously dealing with at least one highly skilled hacker here," Murph said. "This is top-of-the-line work. And we likely won't be able to dig down farther without some kind of access key."

"For all we know," Eric said, "digging farther may even activate the time bomb that they're talking about."

Rivard didn't seem worried by the threat. "You all are fools. Don't you see? Munier planted this."

"What do you mean?" Gretchen asked.

"He knew that we would bring in analysts to check out the system, once he reported the break-in, and the guards were found dead, wherever he dumped them. This message was intended to throw the suspicion off him."

"A bank president didn't create this virus himself. It's possible that the hacker had his own agenda and wrote this message without Munier's knowledge."

"There's another possibility," Juan said. "We think Munier might have been coerced into planting the virus, that he was framed to make it look like he was trying to cover up an embezzlement scheme."

"That's absurd," Rivard said. "If someone went to the trouble of framing Munier, why would they give themselves away by planting a message?"

That was actually a good question, and Juan thought there were several possible answers.

"The hackers might have thought we wouldn't crack their code so quickly. Or they wanted us to read it so we'd think Munier was a willing accomplice."

Rivard gave him a skeptical look. " 'They'?"

"The message refers to 'our demands.' We have to assume larger forces are behind this."

"I think we should take the threat seriously," Gretchen said.

Rivard took a breath and wiped his brow. "And we will. We take all threats seriously. Thank you for your help in uncovering this message. But we need to concentrate our resources on investigating the most likely possibilities first. If you want to focus your investigation in a different direction, by all means go ahead."

Gretchen began to object but was rebuffed.

As a cringing Marie looked at them apologetically, Rivard kept talking. "I will not send us on a course that makes the Sûreté Publique look ridiculous and causes an unwarranted economic panic. I will let Interpol decide if they want to issue a warning to the banking community based on this flimsy evidence, but that warning will not be coming from us. If, and when, we find more data to support your theory, I will gladly take that path. Until then, leave us to do our work. I spoke to the commissioner on the way over and he agrees. I will inform you of our findings as they become available."

Juan knew a firm dismissal when he heard it. They would have to continue their part of the investigation on their own. But if Rivard was wrong and the threat in the message was real, they had only ten days to prevent the world from suffering a disastrous financial meltdown.

TWELVE

WEST OF GIBRALTAR

Lars Dijkstra punched the END button on his phone in frustration.

"Still no answer," he said. He seethed as he watched the Spanish countryside pass beneath them on their way into the British territory of Gibraltar. Their Gulfstream was on its final approach.

Lars's brother, Oskar, had his head buried in his laptop. "Satellite shows a storm front in the vicinity of the *Narwhal.* That's probably why we're not able to reach the captain."

"But we haven't heard from him in hours." He poured himself a glass of akvavit.

"Relax. You worry too much."

Lars downed half the glass. "Why do you think I'm drinking?" He fidgeted in his seat as he stared at the phone, willing it to ring. Oskar had always been the calm half of the duo heading up the Dijkstra shipping and manufacturing empire, the operational genius to Lars's abilities as a dealmaker and strategic thinker.

"I don't like this sudden change of plans. I want to know how long Captain Peters thinks it will take him to get from Malta to Algeciras, once he picks up the cargo." The reason for their last-minute flight to Gibraltar was to make preparations for the *Narwhal*'s arrival at Algeciras, the large Spanish container port across Gibraltar Bay from the British territory.

"According to the ship's specifications and engine rating, he should be able to make the trip from Malta in three and a half days."

"Three and a half days?"

Oskar shrugged. "Time wasn't a factor when we thought the *Narwhal* would be returning to Rotterdam."

"We should have picked a faster ship," Lars muttered.

"Well, it's too late now," Oskar said. "We're committed."

"You're sure we can't ship the column by air?"

"The container is loaded and ready at the docks. If we take the column out to put it on an airplane, we risk exposure where we can't control the situation. Better to get the cargo to Algeciras, where we can examine it in our own facility."

"And our man in Malta is fully briefed?"

Oskar nodded. "He knows the *Narwhal* is coming. The container is scheduled to be loaded the night before the auction."

"Does he know what the container holds?"

"No. Nobody but you and I know the significance of what's in it."

"Once we have time to study the column and discover the meaning of its inscriptions, we will be that much closer to finding the treasure. Then we will own Maxim Antonovich." He swallowed the rest of the akvavit and poured another. "What about the diary? Do we have any idea who's bidding against us for it?"

"There's no way to know," Oskar replied, "but the price will be exorbitant."

The column inside the shipping container was only half of the puzzle they were trying to solve. The other half was called *Napoleon's Diary* — actually, a Greek copy of Homer's *Odyssey* that Napoleon had kept with him until his death on St. Helena. Napoleon had made margin notes in the book and it was those notes that held the secret they were after. The diary was one of the star attractions of the auction because it had been considered a myth until the contents of the collection were revealed.

Some speculated that a British guard or one of the doctors had stolen it as a souvenir when Napoleon died.

There was no doubt about its authenticity. Independent experts confirmed that the margin notes were in Napoleon's handwriting.

The auction was being held at the Maltese Oceanic Museum, which was acting as the representative for the anonymous collector offering the biggest trove of Napoleonic artifacts that had ever come up for sale. The auction would commence in four days, and, on the night before, a gala showing was to take place where potential bidders could inspect the items up close. It was expected to attract some of the wealthiest people in the world who wanted this one chance to see the pieces before they disappeared into the hands of other private collectors.

The Jaffa Column, as it was known, had been stored outside the warehouse where all the other artifacts were being held. The stone relic dated to Roman times, with edicts chiseled in Latin, Greek, and Hebrew, and had vanished during Napoleon's invasion of Syria. Many speculated that it had been destroyed in the war and considered it lost until it suddenly reappeared in the collection. Made of white granite and weighing over thirty tons, it had been deemed too hard to sell because of its size, so it had been donated to the museum. Lars and Oskar had hired a team to pick up the column, in a nondescript container, under the pretense of transporting it to the museum. Instead, they detoured the container to the dock. Since the column wasn't going to be studied by the museum staff until after the auction, it wouldn't be missed until that time. By then, it would already be loaded onto the *Narwhal* and headed for Algeciras.

Because of its notoriety, *Napoleon's Diary* was much more closely guarded, so buying it was their only recourse. Once they finished in Algeciras, Lars and Oskar would attend the gala in Malta to make sure the diary was what they expected and then a representative would do the bidding for them the next day. They had no intention of letting anyone else buy the diary.

"We have to win that auction," Lars said. "What do you think the top bid will be?"

Oskar paused to think. "The auction house put a range of five hundred thousand to a million euros, but I think we have to be prepared to go over two million to get it."

Lars took another swallow of his akvavit and leaned his head back. "We're sinking a lot of money into this venture. And you

148

should be more worried about our necks than you seem to be."

"I have seven men on our security force waiting for us when we arrive."

"Good. Because if certain people found out what we're looking for, they'd kill us in an instant."

"The reward is worth the risk," Oskar said, though there was a hint of doubt in his voice.

"I hope you're right," Lars said, and finished his drink.

The pilot announced over the intercom that they were ten minutes from landing.

"Come on, David!" the coach yelled. "You can kick the ball better than that."

David Kincaid, whose father had recently been transferred with his family to Gibraltar, knew he wasn't making a good impression on his new teammates. David liked to blame his lack of focus on the distraction of having the secondary school football field abutting not only the bustling Gibraltar marina but also the runway for the territory's international airport. But he knew putting his poor play on the blast of the jet engines and sounding of yacht horns was merely an excuse.

He moved to the back of the line to wait

his turn for the next shot at the goal, determined to prove his worth and make striker on the team. He focused on the sky and imagined himself kicking the winning score.

Almost immediately, his concentration was broken by yet another plane coming in for a landing. All of his teammates were so used to the din that they paid it no attention. This was a small jet, one of those private planes that celebrities and rich people used. But there was something different about it.

One of its wings was glowing red. It grew brighter by the second, like an electric burner on a stove heating up.

To no one in particular, David said, "Hey, does that —" He stopped speaking when he saw what happened next.

The plane was a quarter mile from the end of the runway when its right wing burst into flames. Fire streamed from fuel gushing out of the tank. The plane yawed to its right, no longer aimed at the runway, and began to tumble out of control.

It was headed straight for them.

"Run!" David yelled, and pointed at the onrushing plane.

Curses and screams were drowned out as the jet's twin engines were boosted to full throttle in a vain attempt by the pilot to regain altitude.

In a panic, David dashed toward the marina, running out onto the short dock and jumping into the water, as the plane passed overhead and exploded in a fireball, raining flaming debris all over the field where they had just been practicing. Fragments of white-hot metal fell into the water around David.

He surfaced to see blazing wreckage strewn across the football pitch. Certainly no one aboard could have survived such a horrific crash.

David swirled around in the water to see if any of his teammates had gotten the same idea. But he must have been the only one to seek refuge in the harbor. He couldn't spot anyone else.

The only movement he could see was the smooth motion of an unusual-looking yacht cruising out of the harbor.

The name on its side read *Achilles.*

THIRTEEN

"Where are you from, Gretchen?" Linda asked over lunch.

"All over, actually," Gretchen replied as she grazed on a grilled chicken salad. "Both my parents were in the foreign service, my mother as an interpreter and my father as a diplomat. I spent my childhood in Paris, Berlin, Moscow, Tel Aviv, and about a dozen other places."

"One reason she's fluent in so many foreign languages," Juan said. "What are you up to, five?"

"Seven. French, Russian, German, Spanish, Italian, Greek, and Arabic."

"Impressive," Linda said. "The Chairman knows only three."

"Except her Russian accent sounds like she was taught by Chekov on *Star Trek,*" Juan said.

Gretchen shot back, "And his Arabic makes him sound like he's auditioning to be a member of the Saudi royal family."

Everyone at the table laughed. After effectively being shut out of the investigation, the five of them — Juan, Gretchen, Linda, Murph, and Eric — had found an empty outdoor café where they could get a late lunch and brainstorm what to do next now that they'd seemed to hit a dead end.

"Was calling Juan 'Chairman' instead of 'Captain' his idea or yours?" Gretchen asked anyone but Juan.

From the look on their faces, Juan could see that they were wondering whether she was cleared to know about the *Oregon,* so he interjected, "Overholt has fully briefed her about us. She's got a top secret clearance."

With that, the hesitation vanished. Eric was the first to speak. "It happened organically. We all think of ourselves as partners in the Corporation, so it just made sense."

"Do you call it the Corporation for anonymity?"

"Partly," Linda said. "But it also doesn't make sense to give it a specific name when it's called something different wherever we have our assets."

"Assets that are now depleted because of this hacker who's taunting us," Juan said. "If we really have just ten days left before a global financial catastrophe, how would they do it?"

Gretchen put her fork down and sat back as she considered the possibilities. "They could have planted a virus that would lock down trading at the major banks. That would cause the markets to crash. Or they could wipe out the computer data where the assets are held, causing a banking panic. There would be a run on the banks, and interest rates would go through the roof. Lending would effectively be brought to a halt. International trade would go into the dumpster. We're talking food and gas shortages and massive unemployment."

"The question is, who would benefit from that kind of carnage?"

"Short sellers, for one. They bet that stock prices go down and that they can make a killing when markets take a dive. Or it could be commodity owners. The price of gold would probably skyrocket because of its reputation as a safe haven, and those holding a good chunk of it could then buy distressed properties for dirt cheap prices."

"Or it could be terrorists who simply want to cause grief in Western countries," Linda said. "Or anarchists opposed to world trade and big business."

"So it's someone who's either greedy or

vengeful," Murph said. "That doesn't narrow it down a whole lot."

"All we know is that it's someone with extremely advanced computer skills," Eric said. "I wouldn't put it past them to be able to do some heavy damage to the financial system."

Linda looked as frustrated by the lack of a lead as Juan felt. "So we just wait until a bank goes belly up and they make their demands?" she said. "There's got to be something else we can do."

"The video that you found of Munier in the car during the chase wasn't definitive enough for us to prove that he was being coerced," Juan said. "Even if he was, without knowing more about the hacker, we have no clue who's behind this."

"I've informed Washington about the threat," Gretchen said. "They're sending out a generic warning to banks, but no one can take any useful preventive measures, not without more specific info about how to spot the virus or which banks might be targeted. We'll have to get lucky to identify the bank mentioned in the message before it's attacked in five days."

"Or hope whoever is behind this makes a mistake before then," Linda said.

Gretchen shrugged. "You say Po*tay*to, I

155

say Po*tah*to. It'll still be luck on our part."

Murph suddenly got a faraway look on his face. After a few moments, he victoriously yelled, "Potato chips!" and yanked the phone from his pocket.

"What are you talking about?" Eric asked him, as confused as the rest of them by Murph's strange outburst.

"I'm pulling up the photo I took of the warning the hacker left. Remember Minecraft?"

Eric thought about it for a moment and then the same dawning look of excitement crossed his face. "You're right! We missed that." He started scribbling on his napkin.

Juan spoke for the rest of them, who were still dumbfounded by the exchange. "Would you mind sharing your blinding insight?"

"Remember in the message when the hacker was daring us to break the code?" Murph said. He read from his phone. "Go ahead and comb through the code looking for this time bomb, if you dare, but eventually you'll have to cough up the dough to us." He tapped on his screen and went quiet.

Juan was still puzzled. "What has that got to do with potato chips?"

"And what's 'Minecraft'?" Gretchen asked.

Eric showed Linda, Gretchen, and Juan

what he'd written on his napkin.

Ghoughpteighbteau tchoghs!

"What is that?" Linda said after she tried sounding out the phrase. "Klingon?"

Eric shook his head. "Minecraft is a very popular video game. Whenever you fire it up, it shows a splash screen with a phrase on it. It rotates through a bunch of different phrases, and this is one of them. You know what it says?"

They all shook their heads.

"Potato chips!" Murph cried out, and then went back to working on the phone.

"No, it doesn't," Gretchen said.

"Actually, it does," Eric said, "but it uses a nontraditional spelling taken from odd pronunciations in English." He scribbled again and showed them a new word.

Ghoti.

"You might have seen this one."

Juan nodded, getting it now. "That spells out *fish.* Pronounced like the *gh* in *tough, o* in *women,* and *ti* in *nation.*"

"And *Ghoughpteighbteau tchoghs!* spells out *potato chips* in the same way," Eric said, and wrote down the equivalents.

Hiccou*gh.* Th*ough.* P*tarmigan.* W*eigh.* De*bt.* Bur*eau.* Pi*tch.* W*omen.* Hiccou*ghs.*

"When you said, 'po*tay*to/po*tah*to,' " Murph said to Gretchen, "it made me think

157

of that Minecraft phrase. I knew a hacker of this skill level wouldn't leave out a signature. Reputation is everything to them. They want people to know who was responsible for an epic hack."

"I'm still missing something," Linda said.

Murph read the sentence again. " 'Go ahead and comb through the code looking for this time bomb if you dare, but eventually you'll have to cough up the dough to us.' The hacker was leaving us a clue. It's in the different pronunciations of the same letter combinations: *comb* versus *bomb,* *through* versus *cough* and *dough.* He wasn't just being cute."

"I know you're leading us somewhere with this," Juan said. "What's the punch line?"

Murph showed his screen to Eric, who nodded and said, "The hacker used an acrostic code. Normally, they're easy to detect. You take the first letter of each sentence or the first letter of every third word, or some other variation, to spell out a message." He scribbled on his napkin yet again.

"But this hacker was more subtle," Murph said. "He used an acrostic that was itself encoded. The code is spelled out by the first letter of each sentence. I've iterated through a bunch of different pronunciations and this is the only one that makes sense."

Eric passed the napkin around with a new gibberish word above plain English words.

Tiaideaughow.

Na*tion*. Pl*aid*. Bur*eau*. Tou*gh*. L*ow*.

Juan sounded out the pronunciation in his head, then looked up at Murph. "Shadow-foe?"

Murph nodded. "He's notorious in the elite hacker community. ShadowFoe came up with some of the nastiest worms and viruses to hit major companies. No one knows who he is, but he's considered the cream of the crop."

Gretchen seemed stunned by the information. "Oh no."

"You know who it is, don't you?" Juan said.

She swallowed. "Interpol received an anonymous tip last week, but we didn't think it was credible. It gave the location where ShadowFoe is operating from and said he was planning to release a new virus that would attack banks."

"Why wasn't it taken seriously?"

"Because it came with a picture. A twenty-eight-year-old Albanian named Erion Kula. He'd been on our radar already because of some credit card database hacks, but we knew him by the handle Whyvern, not ShadowFoe. We figured that one of his competitors was trying to frame him by falsely identifying him."

"Where is he?"

"The tip said he's working from Vlorë Castle on the Albanian coast."

"Then we go get ShadowFoe and persuade him to give us back our money," Juan said. "I'll call Max and tell him to prepare to set sail for Albania as soon as we get back to Palermo."

"I'm coming with you," Gretchen said. "You may need someone who's an accounting expert to sort out whether he's giving you good information."

Juan paused for a moment as he thought about the implications of having her aboard the *Oregon* and then realized she was right. She could prove helpful, both for her financial expertise and her connections to Interpol and the CIA.

"All right," he said. "I'll have Max set up some quarters for you."

"Thanks. But there's one other thing you should know, another reason we thought the information wasn't credible."

"What's that?"

"We thought whoever sent the tip was trying to lure us into a trap. If we had sent in Interpol agents, there could have been a nasty scene."

"Because of the Albanian government?"

Gretchen shook her head. "Vlorë Castle was built by the Venetians in the fifteenth century and refurbished five years ago by its owner, a businessman named Dalmat Simaku. He's also thought to be one of the biggest crime bosses in the Albanian Mafia."

FOURTEEN

Juan had the *Oregon* sail the minute they stepped on board in Palermo. Slowing only to pass through the Strait of Messina between Sicily and the Italian mainland, they pushed forty-five knots the entire way and made the three-hundred-and-fifty-mile trip to Albania in less than eight hours.

By the next morning, the *Oregon* was holding station in the Adriatic Sea ten miles from Vlorë Castle, which clung to the end of a rocky peninsula studded with low shrubs and wild olive trees. The terrain reminded Juan of the California chaparral near Santa Barbara. The castle had been built as a fortress, guarding the entrance to a natural harbor, where an Albanian Coast Guard station now stood five miles away on the other side of the peninsula from the *Oregon.* Vlorë had a commanding view from its perch on the rugged coast, its thick stone walls rising fifty feet above the water.

Openings in the rim were spaced to allow cannons and archers to fire from protected positions, both toward the sea and at the gravel road that led up to an iron gate sealing the entrance. Instead of a single structure, the castle was more like a wall surrounding a village of ten stone buildings scattered around a central yard. The broad wall had a walkway down the middle to allow for patrols of two or three men, side by side, who could look over the stone battlements at the ocean on one side and the central courtyard on the other. Round twin towers flanked the front gate, where the road ended.

Juan had a detailed view of the castle courtesy of a drone, circling far above and using its high-definition camera. He was watching the feed on his cabin's wall screen while he poured coffee that Maurice had brought him. So far, the only movement he'd seen was four guards, who lazily patrolled the grounds.

He answered a knock at his cabin door. "Come in."

Max Hanley entered with Gretchen, who was carrying her own cup of coffee.

"Good," Juan said as he took a sip from his cup, "you found the mess hall."

"More like five-star dining room," she said

in wonder. "Private work is treating you all well."

Max regarded him with a raised eyebrow.

"What?" Juan asked. "I know that look and it makes me worried."

"Gretchen told me something *very* interesting on the walk from the mess hall," he said with obvious enjoyment.

"I was telling him about our mission to Moscow," she said. "No classified details, of course. Just that you and I were married for three weeks during the operation."

"You left out that little bit," Max said to Juan. "That it was for a mission."

Gretchen looked from Max to Juan in surprise and then laughed. "You mean you thought the two of us were married for real?"

"*Someone* wasn't very clear on that."

Juan nonchalantly took another sip of coffee and with a smile said, "Did I forget to mention that part?"

"Yes, you did."

"We were both married at the time to other people, but the operation called for a couple, so Juan and I were tapped for the job. Mr. Gabriel Jackson and his wife, Naomi."

They had never worked together again until now, and Juan was still wary about how the past might affect the present mission.

"Just when you think you know a guy . . ." Max said with a sly grin.

"Maybe he's had other wives that even *I* don't know about," Gretchen said.

Juan shook his head. "Just two." To change the subject, he said, "Why don't I show you the op center and get this show on the road."

Gretchen held his eyes for a moment, then said, "Lead the way."

They left Juan's cabin and walked down the corridor to the *Oregon*'s Operations Center, the command hub buried deep in the ship's center where it was protected by the armored hull. Gretchen gaped as she entered.

A giant view screen at the front of the room displayed the same overhead camera feed of Vlorë Castle that had been piped into Juan's cabin. As opposed to the bright daylight of the morning sun outside, the charcoal-colored op center was bathed in a soft blue glow from the latest computer monitors that were at every workstation. With touch screen displays, slick control systems, and sound-deadening rubber floors, the high-tech facility would have been beyond the starship *Enterprise*.

Gretchen walked right over to the rotating chair that sat on a pedestal in the middle of the room.

"This must be your position," she said to Juan.

"We call it the Kirk Chair," Max said. "Controls in the armrests let Juan operate nearly every aspect of the *Oregon,* if needed, including driving the ship."

"With the expert crew that I have," Juan said, "that's rarely necessary."

He gave her a tour of the different stations, starting with Eric Stone at the helm and Mark Murphy at the weapons station. Linda controlled radar and sonar, and Max took up his position at engineering and propulsion.

"And this is Hali Kasim," Juan said, introducing the slim Lebanese American wearing a headset. "He's our communications officer. This is Gretchen Wagner, on loan from Interpol and the CIA."

"Oh, do you speak Arabic?" she asked.

"Not a lick," Hali said. "Born and raised in Philadelphia. My parents believed in immersing me in American culture. Sure would come in handy sometimes if I did."

"I'd be happy to give you some lessons if we have time."

"We might be a little busy for that if your

166

intel pans out," Juan said.

He moved on to the last workstation, where a strikingly handsome man wearing a generous mustache and a cowboy hat casually thumbed a pair of joysticks that were maneuvering the unmanned aerial vehicle above the castle.

"Here we have George Adams, our resident helicopter and UAV pilot," Juan said. "Don't bother telling him how good-looking he is. He already knows."

He shook her hand. "Call me Gomez."

"Gomez Adams?" Gretchen said. "As in the Addams Family?"

He grinned and winked at her. "That's what I get for going out with a woman who looked like Morticia. She's gone, but the nickname stuck."

"What's our status?" Juan asked him.

"The Wasps have about an hour on station before their batteries are drained," Gomez said, referring to the foot-long drone that was circling above the castle. The gimballed camera on its underside had a three-hundred-and-sixty-degree field of view. "I'm rotating them out every hour to recharge so that we have eyes on the castle at all times."

"Any chance they've been seen?"

"I doubt it. I've got them flying about a mile above. No way they're loud enough to

167

be heard from that distance. I'm recording the whole time so that we can look back if we need to."

Juan peered up at the screen. One of the buildings in the castle's central yard had the long and narrow look of a barracks, with a satellite dish and microwave antennas mounted on the roof. Five large cars were parked near the gates, indicating that there could be twenty or more people in the compound.

"Any movement?" Juan had been watching for only the last ten minutes.

"About a half hour ago, we saw two men come out of that multistory main building with the smoke coming out of the chimney," Gomez said, referring to the structure at the opposite end of the yard from the front gate. "They were carrying what looked like trays to that barracks-style building in the center with all of the electronic gear. They went inside, and, two minutes later, two different men came out with empty trays."

"Changing of the guard?" Gretchen said.

"Could be. None of them matched the photos you provided of Erion Kula or Dalmat Simaku." Gomez was referring to the hacker Whyvern and the Mafia boss. While the live feed continued, Gomez played back an earlier recording in a corner of the screen. It was footage of men walking to and from the barracks. All of them were in their twenties or thirties, dressed casually in light jackets and jeans. The full trays held food and drinks.

"I'd guess they're low-level soldiers," Juan said.

Gretchen edged toward the screen. "Yeah, but who were they bringing the meals to?"

"That might be where Whyvern is working."

"Looks like there are at least a few more of them, by the amount of food they brought in."

"Assuming we get confirmation that he's there, let's go over the plan for bringing him out."

After calling in Linc and Eddie to join them in the op center, they spent the next three hours plotting out their strategy for abducting Whyvern, knowing that time was of the essence if the hacker's threat was real. Juan was impressed to see that Gretchen hadn't lost any of her tactical skill when she proposed some truly inspired wrinkles.

Gomez interrupted their discussion to note that three cars were approaching the front of the castle.

The gates were opened to allow a black Mercedes to drive into the castle interior, followed by two black SUVs. A pair of hulking bodyguards got out of the Mercedes and opened both rear doors while eight other men dismounted from the SUVs.

Two men stepped out of the Mercedes's rear, one older and one younger.

"Zoom in," Juan said.

The older man was dressed in a two-piece silk suit that softly reflected the afternoon sun. He was wearing sunglasses and had long, wispy gray hair.

"Can we bring up the picture of Simaku?" Gretchen asked.

Juan nodded and instantly a picture of the same man appeared, this one taken by a long lens on a city street.

"That's him," she said.

The younger man was shoved forward by the bodyguard and stumbled, nearly falling to the ground. He was dressed in a T-shirt and dungarees, his hair was tied in a ponytail, and he had a scraggly beard.

Before anyone asked, a picture of Erion Kula appeared on the screen. In the photo, he was clean-shaven, and his hair drooped down to the shoulders, but it was clearly the same person being manhandled in the castle.

"Seems like Whyvern isn't there voluntarily," Juan said.

"Maybe Credit Condamine wasn't enough for him," Murph said. "Could be that he stole the Mafia's money, too."

Max shook his head in amazement at the thought. "That's never a smart move."

The hacker was practically dragged to the barracks and pushed inside. Simaku talked to the bodyguards for a few moments and then walked with the rest of the soldiers to the main building. The bodyguards disappeared inside the barracks.

"We need to capture Erion Kula before Simaku does anything to him," Juan said. "At midnight, we go in and get Whyvern."

FIFTEEN

Pavel Mitkin's teeth chattered as Rahul Sirkal strapped lead diving weights to his ankles. The terrified engineer couldn't move because Seamus O'Connor held him down by the shoulders, and his hands were tied behind his back. Mitkin shivered in the wind coursing over the aft deck of the *Achilles* as it sped east toward Malta.

Nearly the entire crew of fifty had gathered to observe his punishment. Only Maxim Antonovich and the bridge officer were missing and both were likely watching on the closed-circuit TV system. The crew Mitkin could see from his supine position were the men and women on the balcony above. Their expressions ranged from anger to open curiosity to unrestrained excitement about what was about to take place. Some of them murmured to one another in hushed voices while a few jeered at him. Though his lip quivered, Mitkin held back the tears that threatened to stream out.

When the twenty pounds of weights had been secured to his legs, and another ten pounds had been placed around his waist, he was hoisted to his feet. Sergey Golov slowly approached him, appraising the job that Sirkal had done before looking Mitkin in the eyes. The captain shook his head in disappointment, then turned to address the crew. His daughter Ivana stood behind him with her arms crossed.

"We are supposed to be a team," Golov said in English, the common language of the multinational crew. "We are supposed to support each other, protect each other, even die for each other, if it comes to that. By going on this journey together, we have made that commitment."

Golov pointed at Mitkin. "But this man has betrayed us."

Catcalls rained down on Mitkin until Golov held up his hands to silence them.

"Not only is he a deserter, but Pavel Mitkin is guilty of the most heinous crime at sea: mutiny. When he was caught, he tried to convince other members of this crew to rise up against the senior officers and overthrow our command of this vessel. Of course, the rest of you are loyal crew members and refused to take part. For his crime,

Mitkin must be punished."

Mitkin couldn't hold his tongue any longer.

"Don't you all see what's going on?" he cried out. "The captain is leading us all down a terrible path. He'll get us all killed! Think of what Mr. Antonovich —"

Sirkal quieted him with a vicious backhand slap across the face. Mitkin's knees buckled, but O'Connor kept him upright, with fingers digging into Mitkin's scrawny biceps so hard that his hands were going numb.

Mitkin knew that Golov could have simply shot him in the head and dumped his body overboard after he'd been found slithering over the side during their layover in Gibraltar. But a public punishment was needed to show the crew what would happen to them if they had similar thoughts of betrayal. Mitkin had noticed that several crew members hesitated to restrain him when he had made his panicked plea to be let go. So had Golov. A demonstration of the captain's authority was required.

"If there is anyone here who wishes to speak in Mitkin's defense," Golov said, "do so now."

Mitkin scanned the crowd with a flash of hope, but it was dashed when his eyes settled on the *Achilles*'s chief engineer. The old sea dog sneered at him in disgust. No one uttered a word.

The fact that he was branded a traitor and mutineer by his fellow crew finally became real and the irony of the situation overwhelmed him.

He laughed, a chuckle that grew into a hearty belly shaker.

Golov cocked his head at Mitkin before speaking. "You see? He finds your loyalty amusing. He thinks you're fools."

Mitkin had realized that he couldn't trust the other crew members, so he'd planned his escape while setting in motion the keys to exposing Golov's plot.

Simply pointing the authorities toward the *Achilles* and its captain not only would have been discovered by Golov and Ivana but it would also have implicated him as a participant in the conspiracy. He'd been going for a more subtle tactic that would reveal their scheme while enabling his flight to freedom.

But all his plans came to naught when he was spotted shimmying down a rope as the yacht had been departing Gibraltar. He'd plotted everything down to the second, so it had been pure bad luck when the third mate had been wandering the deck and saw him, alerting the security team to retrieve him.

Now Mitkin would pay for that bad timing with his life.

Golov walked toward him and stopped so that he was face-to-face with Mitkin.

"Pavel Mitkin," Golov said, "you have been found guilty of treason and mutiny, both capital offenses. Your sentence will now be carried out." Golov looked at Sirkal. "Extend the plank."

Sirkal raised a section of the railing and pressed a button next to him. A diving board, normally used for water activities during anchorage, swung out from the deck. The ten-foot-long fiberglass plank extended over the water and locked into place.

Golov nodded to O'Connor, who shoved Mitkin toward his fate. Mitkin considered pleading with the captain, but he knew his appeals for mercy would fall on deaf ears. Even the lone remaining secret he'd been hoping to use as a bargaining chip wouldn't save him now.

"Walk," Golov commanded. Many of the crew joined in a chant.

"Walk! Walk! Walk!"

Mitkin took a breath and shuffled forward, his legs gaining strength from the realization that he had one last bit of control over his tormentors: his actions hadn't all been in vain.

He stepped onto the diving board and inched his way forward, goaded by a long fishing gaff thrust at him by O'Connor.

The wind nearly knocked him off several times, but the rock-solid stability of the twin hulls kept the yacht from rolling and throwing him over the side. When he reached the end of the board, Mitkin carefully turned to face the crew, the board bouncing under his weight. He looked at Ivana, then Golov.

Mitkin summoned up all the courage he could muster and spoke in a trembling but clear voice. "You think you've defeated me. You haven't. Because you don't know everything I've done."

O'Connor was about to jab Mitkin with the gaff, but Golov stopped him. "What do you mean?"

Mitkin smiled ruefully at Ivana. "You think you were so clever with your little Easter egg about ShadowFoe. You just couldn't keep from bragging. Well, Interpol will soon find out all about ShadowFoe. I couldn't lead them to you, but your online nemesis Whyvern might."

Golov looked at Ivana in confusion and alarm. She avoided his gaze in embarrassment. Golov whipped around and stared at Mitkin in fury.

"Go get him!" he yelled.

O'Connor stepped onto the diving board and edged his way toward Mitkin. The board dipped farther toward the ocean, threatening to spill both of them over the side.

Mitkin didn't harbor any hopes that they would free him because of this new information. They would torture him until he confessed everything and then kill him afterward.

He wasn't going to let that happen.

Mitkin smiled, expelled what breath he had, and fell backward off the diving board. His last view of Golov was of the captain screaming to get him back.

Mitkin hit the water and plunged beneath the surface. He fought the good fight against the terror of drowning, but the desperation to breathe quickly overpowered him and he took in a lungful of seawater. With the weights dragging him down toward the ocean floor two thousand feet below, the light above quickly dwindled to twilight and then darkness.

Sixteen

Eddie Seng nudged the bow of the Rigid-Hulled Inflatable Boat, or RHIB, onto the narrow beach a half mile up the peninsula from Vlorë Castle. It scuffed the sand with a sound barely louder than the nearly silent electric motor that he was using instead of the powerful twin outboard diesels that could push the RHIB over fifty knots. The boat was specifically designed for use by Special Forces around the world and allowed Eddie, Franklin Lincoln, and Mike Trono to remain unseen and unheard from the castle.

With heavy cloud cover blotting out the crescent moon, the midnight landing was so dark that the three of them wore night vision goggles. Eddie shut off the motor while Linc and Trono anchored the RHIB to a rock. Dressed all in black, they were difficult to see even with the goggles. Without a word, they grabbed their packs and weapons and crept up a switchback path, worn into the side of the hill, leading up to the road.

At the top, Eddie peered over the edge. Pocked asphalt stretched to the castle a half mile in one direction and to a small town five miles the other way, where the peninsula jutted from the mainland. Potent spotlights around the castle gate and easy sight lines from the battlements made a land approach suicide. But visibility from those lights ended a quarter mile away from them, so Eddie was confident they'd go undetected.

No cars were in sight.

"Clear," Eddie said quietly into his throat mic pressing against his neck.

Eddie and Linc took up prone positions, Eddie aiming his M4 assault rifle toward the castle and Linc facing the town. Eddie nodded at Trono, who raced across the road and started climbing the telephone pole. Using crampons attached to his boots and a belt slung around the wooden pole, he scurried up as easily as a squirrel.

"Look at him go," Linc said. "Those fly-boys love heading for the sky."

Mike Trono, slender of build and with fine brown hair peeking out from under his wool hat, had served in the Air Force as a para-rescue jumper, and then raced powerboats to get his adrenaline fix, before joining the Corporation. Being one of the few non–Navy veterans on board the *Oregon* made him the frequent target of ribbing.

" 'Aim high' is our motto," Trono said into his mic as he hoisted himself up. "Linc, what's the Navy motto? Oh, right, it doesn't have an official one."

"Don't need it," Linc said. "That's how much more awesome we are than the Air Force."

That got a small chuckle from Trono, who was now at the top of the pole.

"I see power, telephone, and fiber-optic lines," he said.

"The fiber-optic line gives them a fast Internet connection for their hacking activities."

"Not for much longer," Trono said. "Planting the C-4."

After a few minutes, Trono announced that the charges were in place and climbed back down. He took up watch while Linc jogged a hundred yards in the direction of town to lay low-reflection spike strips across the road.

Eddie took out his binoculars and trained them on the Albanian Coast Guard base at the end of the harbor next to town. There were two patrol craft tied to the dock, but no large cutter. Eddie couldn't see any movement.

When Linc was done, he jogged back, and the three of them crouched down along the side of the road.

Eddie keyed his encrypted shore-to-ship radio.

"Welcome Wagon here," he said to Hali, who was manning communications on the other end in the *Oregon*'s op center. "The reception committee is all set. Let the Chairman know he can start the party."

The Nomad 1000 submarine hovered in its spot next to the castle, submerged at periscope depth. Already in his drysuit, Juan stood behind Max, who was piloting the sub. The view from the periscope's remote camera showed no one on the wall, looking down at them.

"Hali tells me that Eddie and his team are in place and set," Max said.

Juan checked his watch. "Right on schedule."

"Eddie is a stickler for punctuality." Max turned to look at Juan with a serious expression. "After you're away, I'd like to hang around. Just in case. Linda doesn't need me." Linda was back on the *Oregon* in command of the ship.

"I need you to get back to the *Oregon* and stow Nomad. Once we nab Whyvern, we'll have to get out of here pronto, and Nomad's built for comfort, not speed."

The sixty-five-foot-long Nomad could dive to a depth of one thousand feet and had an onboard air lock, perfect for clandestine insertions like the one they were about to attempt. She looked like a miniaturized version of a nuclear sub, with a polycarbonate nose, where Max sat, and robotic claws jutting from the chin. Including a pilot and copilot, she had room for up to ten people.

Juan slapped Max on the shoulder and went into the passenger compartment. Gretchen, Murph, and MacD Lawless were making their final preparations.

Gretchen and Murph were on the mission for their expertise in finance and computers, while MacD was along for his skills as a former U.S. Army Ranger. *MacD* was short for his middle name, MacDougal, which he liked marginally better than his first name, Marion. Muscular and blessed with a face of a heartthrob — though his features were now covered with black greasepaint like the others — he gave Gomez Adams a close race in the good-looks department.

As he pulled on his drysuit over the same black combat gear they all wore, MacD unleashed his syrupy Louisiana drawl on Murph. "Ah know these guys like their funny names, but what in the world does *Whyvern* mean?"

"A *wyvern* is a type of dragon," Murph replied. "It has two forelegs, and a snake's body, and probably came from the —"

"Ah know what a *wyvern* is, but why is this guy called Whyvern. He got no legs?" Then MacD saw Juan pulling his drysuit over his combat leg and winced at the question.

Juan smiled. "Don't worry, MacD. I'm sure Whyvern makes do fine with just a tail."

Gretchen chuckled at that. She knew about his missing leg. Not only had she been amazed that she hadn't noticed any difference in his gait, but she'd been fascinated by the hidden compartments in the titanium-reinforced prosthesis, which had room for a .45 caliber ACP Colt Defender, a ceramic knife, and a wad of plastic explosive and a detonator no bigger than a deck of cards. A single .44 caliber slug could be fired from the heel.

"Remember," Juan said, mainly for the benefit of Gretchen, who wasn't accustomed to their routines and coordination, "this is a quick snatch-and-go, so we'll avoid engaging Simaku's men, unless it's absolutely necessary. Eddie's ready at the post-extraction rendezvous, so let's get going."

The plan was to get into the castle silently, abduct Erion Kula, and go out through the front gate using one of Simaku's own cars, dropping spike strips behind them. The sharp prongs would puncture the tires of any pursuing cars, giving them time to escape with Eddie's team on the RHIB.

Juan opened the air lock hatch and gestured for Gretchen to enter. "Ladies first."

"Chivalrous as always," she said, and climbed inside the cramped confines.

Juan squeezed in with her, holding his helmet so that he wouldn't have to clamp it onto his suit until the last possible moment. The drysuits were clumsy, but they would keep their clothes from getting soaked. Wetsuits would leave telltale trails of water during their infiltration.

With their bodies pressed together and facing eye to eye, the awkwardness came back. Juan could tell Gretchen felt it as well, but both of them were too professional to say anything. They had a job to do.

Juan reached for the valve that would flood the air lock. "Ready? This is your last chance to bail out if you're having second thoughts."

She tilted her head at him as if to say

Really? and clamped the helmet to her suit. "Do it."

Juan opened the valve and water rose from the floor. The drysuit kept the cold at bay. He attached his own helmet while watching Gretchen. She had her eyes closed in a meditative state, and he could feel a slight press of her body with each deep breath she inhaled.

Juan shook his head and focused on the mission. When the readout indicated that the pressure was equalized with the water outside, he opened the hatch. He swam up, and pulled the packs behind him, before helping Gretchen out. They crouched on the deck of the sub, the ocean surface just ten feet above them, as they waited for Murph and MacD to complete the same process.

When everyone was out and the sub was sealed again, they swam for the cliff face, which plunged down from the castle into the water like a rocky wall. There was just enough room to pull themselves onto a small ledge they'd identified in their reconnaissance. No one on the wall would see anything amiss unless they happened to be looking straight down.

They quickly stripped off their drysuits, and Juan shoved them into a container that was attached to a nylon line leading back to the sub. The rest of them retrieved their equipment and weapons from the drybags.

"Our feet are dry," Juan said to Max over the comm link. "Reel it in."

"Starting the winch," Max replied. "See you soon."

The container slipped into the water and was pulled back to the sub. No sense in leaving the expensive drysuits behind.

MacD withdrew a crossbow from his pack and loaded it with a rubberized three-pronged hook connected to a rope that disappeared into the bag. He nodded at Juan.

Juan keyed the radio linked to his throat mic. "Do you read me, Hali?"

"Loud and clear, Chairman."

"We're in position."

"Roger. Gomez spotted you from the drone as soon as you climbed out of the water. Pretty eerie."

"I bet. Any guards up above?"

"They just finished their quarter-hour sweep. You have fourteen minutes until the next one. No one is in sight on the wall."

"Good. Keep us posted if you spot anyone."

"Absolutely."

Juan looked at MacD. "Let's make like Spider-Man."

MacD grinned and shouldered the crossbow. With a press of the trigger, the hook arced silently up over the battlement, trailing a rope ladder behind it. MacD slung the crossbow over his back and pulled the ladder down until the rubberized hook was firmly snagged on the wall above.

"We're good to go," he said.

Gretchen stepped forward and flashed a smile. "Ladies first again?"

Juan shook his head and put his head through the sling of his silenced MP5 submachine gun. "This time, you're second." He insisted on being first in and last out on a mission whenever possible.

He tested the rope ladder and found that it could hold his weight. A glance at his watch told him that there were thirteen minutes left before the next security patrol.

That is, if the guards kept to their regular schedule.

Juan put his foot into the lowest ladder rung and began to climb.

SEVENTEEN

Linda pointed at the upper right quadrant of the main view screen from the command seat. Eric was at the helm, Hali at his communications station, and Gomez focused on the drone controls. The *Oregon* was five miles south of the castle, all her lights out so that she wouldn't be seen.

"Two guards are coming around the top of the wall counterclockwise," Linda said to Juan. Hali had put him on speaker so she could communicate directly with him.

Gomez was coordinating three drones that gave the op center a comprehensive view of the castle from the air. Instead of the winged drone he'd flown this morning, these were quadcopter drones that could hover in position. They had to fly closer to the castle for good sight lines, but the darkness concealed them. Gimballed cameras hanging from them could zoom in with high-definition visible light mode or could be switched to infrared and night vision modes.

One of the cameras showed two men making their sweep around the rim of the castle wall on the side opposite from Juan and his team. They walked lazily and smoked cigarettes, displaying little of the discipline that Linda had demanded of her crew in the Navy and expected, without a thought, on the *Oregon.*

Linda watched as Juan and his team crabbed along the top of the ten-foot-wide wall. They disappeared into the closest gate tower before the approaching guards could turn the corner and spot them.

A minute later, Juan's voice came over the radio. "We've got two men manning the gatehouse. They're about as bored as the two guards on the wall. They didn't notice us sneak by. We'll hold up outside behind one of the SUVs until you give us the all clear."

Juan and the others hustled out of a ground-level door into the center yard. They gathered behind the largest SUV, out of the predicted path of the two guards who were coming down from their wall patrol.

The guards appeared a few moments later in the courtyard and ambled toward the main building and past the hiding team.

They seemed to be idly chatting, suspecting nothing strange. Finally, they went inside. Linda noted the time and reset the clock for another fifteen minutes.

"You're clear," she said. "No one else is outside."

Juan pointed at the front gate, and MacD raced toward it to plant C-4 charges so they could blow a hole in it to allow their escape by car. Juan and Gretchen darted among the vehicles, slapping smaller plastic explosive bundles into the wheel wells. Murph went over to Simaku's Mercedes and pulled the door handle. It popped open.

"Nailed it," he said. "Nobody locks the doors inside a castle."

He climbed inside and turned off the dome light. The plan was for him to program a blank electronic key fob with the onboard diagnostics system used by Mercedes mechanics. The *Oregon*'s Magic Shop had a full set of tools for hacking into the cars of all the major manufacturers.

After a minute, he closed the door quietly and said, "We've got wheels."

They all converged back at the SUV.

Linda made one last check of the castle grounds and then had Gomez switch to infrared to make sure she hadn't missed anyone. A warm body would have appeared as a bright white figure. All three drone images were dark.

"You're all alone," she said.

"Copy."

Juan and the others sprinted to the barracks's only door, which was set into the narrow end facing away from the gates. They pressed themselves against the wall, Juan and Gretchen on one side of the door and MacD and Murph on the other side.

Juan put his hand on the door handle and said, "The door's thick, but I can hear laughter. We're going in."

"Good hunting," Linda said.

Juan pushed the door open and dashed inside.

Juan had his MP5 up to his shoulder as soon as he crossed the threshold. The four of them entered so fast that the three men sitting at a card table barely had time to look up and stare into the deadly end of three submachine guns and a crossbow. The guards were confused momentarily, perhaps thinking it was a joke by their fellow mafiosi. All three were lanky, sported greasy slicked-back hair and five o'clock shadows, and wore dark T-shirts under leather jackets. They didn't move.

Gretchen closed the door behind them.

The sparsely furnished room held little more than the table, four wooden chairs, and a coffeepot on an end table. Two bare bulbs hung overhead. The table was littered with coffee cups, playing cards, and euro bills.

"You speak English?" Juan asked.

Two of them looked at the third guard, who had a dusting of gray in his stubble. That had to be the senior guard. He shook his head slowly, a glint of malice in his eyes.

"No English," he replied.

"That's okay," Juan said. "We'll use Albanian."

Murph took out a mini-tablet and spoke into it. "Raise your hands." The tablet instantly interpreted and spoke in a mechanical Albanian dialect. The three guards obviously understood because their hands went up in the air.

Juan pointed at the leader. "Tell him to very slowly remove that Glock under his left armpit with his left hand, butt first. Keep an eye on him, MacD."

"Ah ain't blinkin'," MacD replied.

The tablet translated and the lead guard nodded. He moved his left hand as ordered and reached into his jacket. He withdrew the Glock with two fingers.

Then he did something stupid.

He flipped the semiautomatic pistol around in his hand in a lightning-quick maneuver. Too bad for him, MacD was faster.

The crossbow bolt went through the guard's eye before he could bring the pistol all the way around to fire. His brain snapped off so suddenly that the pistol flew out of his hand as it was coming around and smacked into the wall. The guard teetered forward and slammed into the table, where he lay motionless. The end of the crossbow bolt protruding from his skull knocked a few of the bills off the table and they fluttered to the floor.

His companions hadn't taken his cue and still had their hands in the air. They gawked at the dead man until Murph repeated the command to remove their guns slowly.

MacD nonchalantly reloaded his crossbow while the other guards followed the translated commands to the letter and offered no resistance. In three minutes, they were gagged and hogtied on the floor. A search of the guards produced a ring of keys from the dead one's pocket.

The drone surveillance hadn't shown any more guards enter or leave the building, but they couldn't be sure, so Juan took up the same stance at the only other door in the room. He tried the handle, but it was locked. He quietly inserted keys until he found one that fit.

Juan pushed the door open and saw a dank, empty hallway running the length of the building. Doors, each with a small barred opening set into it at eye level, were spaced at regular intervals on either side.

It looked like a prison.

While MacD stayed in the anteroom to guard the front door, Juan, Gretchen, and Murph checked the rooms. Juan went to the first door and peered through its barred portal. Sitting on a cot was Erion Kula — Whyvern — staring back at him. The room was bare except for a cot, a bucket, and a tray with a plate licked clean. No computer equipment at all. Kula stood and backed up when he realized it wasn't the guard he'd been expecting.

He said something in Albanian.

"I know you speak English," Juan said.

Kula gave him a confused look. "Who are you?" His accent was thick, but his diction was perfect.

"I'm here to find out what you did with our money."

"I don't understand."

"I think you do."

Juan found the key for Kula's door and

was about to open it when Murph, who was two doors down, said, "I found the computer room. Two of the latest Lenovo desktops. Four twenty-five-inch monitors. High-speed Ethernet cables. A couple of printers. Another chair behind the workstation. Looks like he was observed while he worked."

"This is about Credit Condamine, isn't it?" Kula said.

"I knew you could help us," Juan said with a sardonic grin.

"No, no! You have to get me out of here. Simaku knows you're coming!"

"What are you talking about?"

Before Kula could say more, Gretchen called out, "Juan! Come here quick!"

She was standing in front of the last door, her eyes wide as she stared through its portal.

Both Juan and Murph ran down the hall to Gretchen, whose face had drained of color. Juan looked into the room and his stomach twisted in fury when he saw its occupants.

A matronly woman in her fifties sat with her back against the far wall, a look of hopelessness on her face. Her gray hair was held back by a headband, but wisps of it coiled around her face. Her sweater was ragged and her pants had holes in the knees. She mumbled softly in Albanian as if she were praying.

Curled up next to her, dressed in soiled and torn clothing, were four children no older than ten.

Eddie heard the sound first. He'd been watching the castle, but the thrum of engines was coming from behind him.

He turned. "That sounds like a car."

Linc nodded.

"More than one," Trono said.

Headlights rose over a hill three miles distant. They were coming fast.

"They're expecting company after midnight?" Linc said. "I don't think so."

"We've been made," Trono said.

Eddie keyed his radio. "Welcome Wagon here. Is the Chairman on his way?"

"Not imminently," Hali replied.

"Then we have a problem," Eddie said. "Because in about three minutes, we're going to have guests. And by the way they're hightailing it here, I have a feeling that they won't be happy to see us."

Linda was about to relay the info to Juan when Eric gestured at the big screen.

"We've got movement," he said.

197

The door on the main building opened and men poured out, fanning across the yard. Linda recognized Simaku's long gray hair. He waved a pistol at the barracks where Juan and his team were. Men with assault rifles took up positions around the door.

"Chairman, do you read me?"

"I'm here."

"Don't go out the front door. Simaku's got nine men aiming AK-47s at it. Is there another way out?"

"Not at the moment," Juan said. "But we have another issue. It looks like we're going to have too many to fit in the car, so we can't make it to the RHIB."

Linda was perplexed. "Who else do you have?"

"Long story . . . Is Max there?"

"He just returned with Nomad. He's on his way up from the moon pool."

"Good. Tell him we need our backup escape route. And cut the castle lights. You're going to be our eyes."

"Aye, Chairman." She turned to Hali. "Tell Eddie to kill the power. Gomez, switch to night vision."

Just as Gomez made the transition, the castle was plunged into darkness.

EIGHTEEN

With the lights out, Juan and the rest of his team turned on their flashlights instead of activating their night vision goggles. Juan unlocked the cell holding the woman and children and told Murph to bring Erion Kula in to translate. He entered the cell with the gun slung behind his back, his hands raised, and the warmest smile he could muster given his seething anger at their captors. When they shrank back from him, he couldn't blame them. A large armed man in black camouflage had to be frightening.

Gretchen came to his rescue. She removed her stocking cap and shook out her hair as she approached them with a smile of her own. The sight of a friendly woman seemed to put them more at ease. She knelt next to them and tenderly caressed the hair of the oldest girl while the woman regarded them warily.

"They're filthy and underfed," Gretchen

said, "but I don't see any injuries except for the woman's bruises." Her neck and arms were dotted with black and blue marks.

When Kula stepped into the doorway, a look of confusion at being summoned switched instantly to relief. He rushed over to the children, who leaped toward him.

"Baba! Baba!" they cried as they hugged him tightly. Juan didn't need a translation to realize that Kula was the children's father.

While Kula comforted them in Albanian, Murph said, "Well, I didn't see that coming."

Kula looked up at Juan. "These are my children and aunt. I thought they were still in Tirana. I had no idea Simaku brought them here. He told me he was holding —"

Juan put up his hand. "We'll get the story later. Right now, we need to figure out an exit strategy. Linda, what's the situation outside?"

"Simaku and his men were about to breach the door when the power went out," she said in his earpiece. "They backed off when that happened, and some of them returned to the main building, I assume to look for some portable lights."

"That gives us another minute at best." Juan peered out of the small barred outer window and confirmed that this room was

200

the closest to the guard tower they'd descended. Only the parked cars stood between him and the tower. The window was also on the opposite side of the building from the mass of gunmen waiting to assault the barracks.

"You have to help us," Kula pleaded. "Simaku will surely kill us all now. Please take us with you."

The Mercedes was temptingly close, but no way were ten of them going to fit inside. They needed to go to Max's backup plan.

"No one's getting left behind," Juan said to Kula. "Linda, tell Max to launch the cargo drone. I want it on the wall in two minutes. Have Eddie meet us in the RHIB on the west side."

"Aye, Chairman. Max says it's already in the air. The *Oregon* is five miles away and heading toward you at flank speed."

"We're also going to need help getting to the tower. Have Gomez prepare his air raid. We're going out the back door. All of us." He nodded at Murph, who went to the wall and began pulling gear from his bag.

"What back door?" Kula asked in confusion. "The only door is at the front of the building . . ." His voice trailed off when he saw Murph slapping plastic explosive bundles against the stones. He didn't need to be told to hustle the children into the hallway. His aunt no longer eyed them with suspicion. She calmly herded the kids out the door with him.

"You really think we can do this with a bunch of kids in tow?" Gretchen whispered to Juan.

"I really do," Juan said confidently, although his training hadn't exactly prepared him for shepherding a flock of grade school children through a gun battle. But Juan agreed with Kula that worse would happen if they stayed here.

"Charges are set," Murph said as he stood.

The three of them went into the hallway, where they met MacD, coming from his post in the anteroom. He gaped at the six hostages.

"Someone running a school in here?"

"Meet Erion Kula's family," Juan said. "Now, get your goggles on and snuff your lights. Kula, tell your family that we're heading for the tower, but you're not to move until Gretchen here says to."

Kula nodded and spoke to his family in Albanian as they extinguished their flashlights. Two of the children cried out, but he and his aunt soothed them.

Juan checked to make sure Murph was set with the detonator. "We're ready here,

Linda," he radioed. "Buzz Simaku with Gomez's hornets."

With the targets identified on the op center's main viewer by red crosshairs, Linda nodded to Gomez. He pressed a button and three tiny drones were released from beneath the three observation drones hovering above the castle. The hornets were so small — only six inches in diameter — that they disappeared from view in moments.

Max, who was now manning his engineering station, had specially designed the hornet drones for remote attacks. They had only enough battery power for a short-duration flight, but they made up for a lack of range with the stingers they wielded. Each hornet carried six ounces of Composition B, the same explosive used in American M67 hand grenades.

The hornets weren't flown manually. Once a target was selected, each hornet was directed by its carrier drone to its destination.

All three were heading straight for Simaku's men outside the barracks door, with one specifically aimed at the men returning with lights and another centered on Simaku. A range finder on the view screen counted down the distance to target for each hornet.

When the hornets were seconds from hitting, Linda radioed to Juan, "Now!"

The back wall of the barracks blew out, showering the cars with stones and shattering windshields and windows.

At the sound of the explosion, an alert bodyguard launched himself at Simaku and knocked him to the ground just as the hornets hit. The view screen bloomed with three white flashes of destruction. Men and body parts went flying in all directions. Linda estimated that they'd taken out at least a third of Simaku's men in that strike, which was the only one coming. They were now out of hornets.

She didn't need to tell Juan to move. She could see him and MacD emerge through the blasted opening in the barracks with their night vision goggles on. Two mafiosi who hadn't been killed in the explosions went down under Juan and MacD's covering fire as eight more people stumbled through the blasthole and out of the barracks.

Linda recognized Gretchen and Murph, but she tilted her head in astonishment at what she saw on the view screen.

"Are those kids?" Max said, incredulous.

"I don't think they're hobbits," Gomez replied.

Linda spotted movement by one of the towers at the castle's entrance. "Chairman, you've got two men coming out of the nearest tower. They're both carrying rifles."

They must have been the men manning the gate controls. With the children behind the cover of the cars, Juan and MacD circled around and flanked the gunmen, who were focused on the chaos at the barracks entrance. Juan and MacD popped up from behind the Mercedes and each took out one of the men with a single shot.

Simaku's men were quickly regrouping and were about to close in, now that they had picked up the remaining undamaged lights. Even though his forces were thinned, he still had at least twenty men at his disposal, more than enough to wipe out Juan's team.

Juan herded his gaggle toward the tower, providing cover fire, along with MacD, as they went. The children screamed in terror but followed their father's instructions to come with him. Though the aunt cringed at the gunfire, she remained stoic. When they reached the tower, MacD ducked inside. When they got the all clear from him, they followed him in.

Simaku split his men, sending half of them to follow Juan toward the tower, while he and the other half disappeared through a door in the wall near the main building.

"It looks like Simaku's trying to trap you in a pincer movement," Linda told Juan. "Stay low once you reach the top of the wall."

"Affirmative," Juan said. "Let me know when his men are by the cars."

The men approached the cars cautiously, intending to use them as cover. Linda smiled grimly. Irony.

"Hit it," she said.

A second later, the C-4 charges attached to the cars blew up one after the other. Linda was satisfied to see that most of the bad guys were taken out at the same time. The few who were still able to move spent their next moments extinguishing their flaming clothes.

With eight fiery cars illuminating the castle, lighting was no longer a problem.

Juan came out of the gate tower onto the top of the wall.

"You're clear for the moment," Linda said. The rest of them exited the tower and joined him.

"Where's the cargo drone?" Juan asked.

Linda turned to Gomez, who was piloting the drone using his own screen.

"About to touch down, Chairman," he said.

The cargo drone entered the view screen, backlit by the auto bonfire below. The drone was much larger than the observation quadcopters, with double the number of propellers but half the lifting power of the *Oregon*'s helicopter. Although it couldn't carry passengers, it was tailor-made for delivering gear to inhospitable and dangerous locations.

It touched down atop the wall that Juan and the team had scaled from the sea. It stayed there for just a second and released its load, a container the size of a steamer trunk, before it rose back into the air.

Simaku and his men reached the top of the wall at the far end of the compound in time to see the cargo drone taking off. They unleashed a torrent of fire in its direction.

"I'm taking hits!" Gomez yelled.

"Get it back to the *Oregon,* if possible," Linda said, "but keep those observation drones on station."

Juan poked his head over the ocean-side wall and said, "Eddie isn't here yet. Tell him we're ready for our water taxi. Where are you?"

Linda checked the *Oregon*'s position. "Less than four miles out."

"Get here as soon as you can. We might need our own cover fire once we get in the water."

"Understood," she said, and looked at Max. "How much reserve do we have left in the engines?"

"I can give you a bit more juice, but we won't be able to maintain it for long without damaging them."

She turned to Eric, who was at the helm. "Mr. Stone, push it to the limit."

"Aye, ma'am," Eric replied, and the *Oregon* trembled as the output of her magneto-hydrodynamic engines churned over the redline.

Eddie knew they were late getting the RHIB back into the water, but they'd been busy. The spike strips had stopped the first two police cars to cross them. A truck behind the cars had swerved in time to avoid blowing out its tires and stopped to disgorge a dozen officers in full tactical gear. The officers were about to remove the strips when he, Linc, and Trono had opened fire to pin them down and stop them from reaching the castle.

Simaku's backup might be late to the party, but the corrupt police were returning fire in disturbing quantity, if not accuracy.

Eddie knew the Chairman didn't have time for his team to get stuck in a prolonged gun battle.

"Smoke grenades out," Eddie ordered.

The three of them pulled the pins on their grenades and tossed them onto the road. The thick gray smoke obscured the vehicles' headlights, creating an eerie fog punctuated by sporadic gunfire now that the police couldn't see what they were shooting at.

"Come on," Eddie said, and they left their ditch to scramble down the slope to the boat.

By the time they reached the rocks, the police had stopped firing altogether. Only their own heavy breathing and deadened footfalls pierced the misty silence.

Linc leaped onto the RHIB and took the helm, ready to start the engine the second the boat was in the water. Eddie took one side of the bow and Trono took the other to push it out. With a single heave, the boat slid into the sea.

Linc started the engine, and Eddie boosted Trono aboard. Trono reached down to help Eddie up but let go abruptly and emptied the rest of his magazine into someone on shore. The few rounds that the attacker was able to get off merely sliced into the water around them.

Trono yanked Eddie over the gunwale, who then took position next to him to repel any other assaults.

"I owe you one," Eddie said.

"Are you kidding?" Trono replied. "I completely missed him."

"You were supposed to. The Chairman wanted us to avoid killing cops, even crooked ones."

Trono gave him a knowing grin. "Oh, right. I guess you do owe me."

Linc wheeled the RHIB around to race toward the castle, and they were out of sight before any other policemen got a chance to practice their sharpshooting.

"We're trapped!" Erion Kula shouted. Simaku's men were exchanging fire with Juan, MacD, and Gretchen as they crept along the top of the castle wall walkway. It was only a matter of time before Simaku could get into position to rush them. "How are we supposed to get out of here?"

"That is a good question," Juan said between shots. "Murph, would you like to show him the answer?"

Murph, who had pulled the top off the container that the cargo drone had deposited, nodded and said, "With pleasure."

He pushed it over to the edge of the wall,

quickly clamped the container to the stone with a hammer and pitons, and then pulled its rip cord. A rush of gas began to inflate the contents of the container. In seconds, a yellow bag ballooned up and over the side of the wall.

The fabric continued to inflate until it was clear what the object was: an emergency slide, like the ones used to evacuate airplanes. Max had acquired it over a year before, not knowing what kind of escape they might use it for. Now they finally had a chance to put it to the test.

Ten seconds later, the slide was fully deployed. Murph looked over the edge.

"The end's in the water," he said.

"And Eddie?" Juan asked.

"I can hear the RHIB. Should be here in less than a minute."

"Then it's time to go."

At that moment, the door to the tower burst open and two Mafia soldiers ran out. The children and Kula's aunt shrieked and ran away from them and right into Juan and MacD's line of sight, preventing them from firing on the men. Gretchen was the only one with a clear shot.

She took one down before he could fire, but the second was able to get off a three-round burst before she put two bullets in his chest. Then she sank to the ground and grasped her right thigh.

Juan left MacD to continue the fight with Simaku's men and raced toward her. "Murph, check on Kula's family!"

"We're okay," Kula called back. "They're just frightened."

Juan knelt down next to Gretchen, whose jaw was clenched in obvious pain. Blood oozed between the fingers clutching her leg.

"How bad?" Juan asked.

"You mean my reaction time?" she said through gritted teeth. "Apparently, rusty."

Juan removed a strap from the slide container and prepared to wrap it around her leg. "I'd say it's not bad for a desk jockey. We need to keep your blood loss to a minimum until we can get back to the *Oregon*. This will hurt a bit."

"So did getting shot. Do it."

He pulled it tight, eliciting little more than a guttural groan from Gretchen. She was still as tough as he remembered. He pulled her to her knees.

"Chairman, we need to go now!" Murph yelled. "Two of the rounds hit the slide. It's starting to deflate."

"Kula, you first with one of the kids," Juan said.

"We can't!" Kula protested.

212

"You want to stay up here?"

"But they can't swim!"

"Doesn't matter," Juan said. "We can. Murph, take one of the kids and go."

Murph picked up the oldest child and launched himself onto the slide, enveloping the boy in his arms, while Juan and the rest of them kept Simaku and his men pinned down.

Kula followed with another child, then Kula's aunt with a third, and finally Gretchen took the hand of the last one, a girl no older than eight. Juan helped Gretchen get on the slide, as she winced through the pain, and watched them sail down the rapidly deflating slide. It wouldn't be able to hold a person's weight for long.

Simaku's quickly approaching men made the decision for Juan. He and MacD emptied the rest of their magazines in that direction, threw the guns down, and dived onto the slide, Juan going last. Rounds ripped into the slide's fabric behind him. Air whooshed out of ragged holes.

Juan had no way to slow himself, so he tucked his arms by his sides and hoped that his ride wouldn't end up on the rocks. At the bottom, his boots plunged into the cold water of the Adriatic Sea. He surfaced to see the RHIB approaching the splashing group of adults and kids.

He looked up at the castle. The half-moon had risen, though it remained partially hidden by the clouds, providing meager illumination of the scene. The slide had completely deflated and rested against the stone wall like a crashed hot air balloon. On the battlements above, Simaku looked down at him with a wicked smile on his face. To either side, Mafia goons had their assault rifles ready to fire. Now Juan knew what it was like to be the fish in the barrel.

Simaku raised his hand, preparing to give the order to take them out, and all Juan could do was watch.

The Mafia leader never got to say another word. The battlement blew apart without warning, taking Simaku and his men with it. No one could have survived the explosion, as pieces of stone fell into the water around Juan. The remnants of the evacuation slide fluttered to the ground.

A few seconds later came the report of the *Oregon*'s 120mm cannon. Linda had closed the distance enough to get within the gun's two-and-a-half-mile range and must have seen their predicament from the observation drones.

Eddie, Linc, and Trono arrived and scooped up the children first before pulling up the rest of the group. Linc yanked Juan into the boat with a single tug. Trono and Eddie were busy wrapping survival blankets around the children.

"You all right?" Linc said.

"One casualty," Juan said. "Gretchen took one in the leg. Have Hux get the medical team ready to dig it out."

"Aye, Chairman. We need to get out of here anyway. There's an Albanian Coast Guard patrol boat headed our way." He spun the wheel to head back to the *Oregon* and gunned the engine while radioing in that the ship should expect visitors.

"What are you going to do with us?" Kula sputtered through the water still streaming from his hair.

"We'll take you back to our ship and get your kids cleaned up and fed while we have a chat with you. I have a lot of questions about your involvement with the Credit Condamine attack."

"That wasn't me. ShadowFoe was the one behind it."

"Interpol thinks *you're* ShadowFoe."

"That's what she wanted you to think."

"She?"

"I've never met her, of course," Kula said, "but I think ShadowFoe is a woman. And I'm going to help you find her."

NINETEEN

By the time the coast guard arrived at Vlorë Castle, Erion Kula and his family were aboard the *Oregon,* the RHIB was stowed, and the ship had hightailed it out of the area. After making sure Kula's children and aunt were given fresh clothes and a hot meal, Juan went down to the infirmary to check on Gretchen's injury.

Julia Huxley, the ship's Navy-trained chief medical officer, was applying a dressing to Gretchen's thigh when he arrived in the sick bay. Despite having just attended to Gretchen's bloody leg, Julia's customary white lab coat remained spotless as it draped over her voluptuous curves. Her ponytail bobbed as she finished taping the gauze.

"How are you?" Juan asked Gretchen.

"Annoyed with myself. Ten years in the service and I never got shot."

"Could have been worse. Has she been a good patient?" Juan asked Julia.

Julia smiled. "Could have been worse. She's a tough one. Refused morphine, so I stuck her with a local anesthetic. The bullet hit the quadriceps, a lateral through and through. Luckily, the round didn't tumble, so there was no serious damage, although it's going to hurt like a mother when the anesthetic wears off."

"Can she walk?"

"I wouldn't recommend running any marathons for a few weeks, but she should be hobbling around just fine in a day or so."

"A day or so?" Gretchen said. "I'm not waiting here that long. We have to interrogate Whyvern." When she sat up, the cut-open flap of her pant leg flopped to the side. She looked down at her exposed leg and said, "Maybe I should get changed first."

"Already took care of it," Juan said, handing her a clean change of clothes and shoes that he had fetched from her cabin. She took them and ducked behind the curtain.

"How did the kids look to you?" Juan asked Julia as he waited. She had checked them over before tending to Gretchen's wound.

"Malnourished and scared, but they shouldn't have any lasting physical effects. The aunt looks pretty haggard and bruised, but she refused an examination. I'd like to

217

string up whoever did this to them."

"Don't worry. Their captors got the worst of it. They won't be bothering anyone again."

Julia glanced at the curtain and lowered her voice. "So this is the missus, huh?"

"*Fake* missus. I had a real missus at the time we were partnered up."

"Oh" was all Julia said, though her raised eyebrow invited more info that Juan wasn't about to share.

"I'm ready," Gretchen said as she pulled back the curtain. Her leg gave way suddenly, and Juan rushed over to keep her from toppling onto the floor. He put his arm around her waist while she leaned a hand on his shoulder.

"Thanks for the patch job, Doc," Gretchen said.

Julia stuck a bottle of pills in her hand. "Take one of these if the pain gets too bad."

As they exited, Juan caught Julia giving him a knowing smile.

By the time they reached the wardroom where Murph and MacD were watching over Kula, Gretchen needed to steady herself with her hand lightly on Juan's arm. She eased into a chair opposite Kula, while Juan remained standing.

"I want to thank you again for saving my

children and aunt," Kula said. "But I must ask what you are going to do with us now."

"Your family is being well taken care of," Juan said. "After you tell us what we want to know, we'll let you all go. *If*, that is, we're convinced you aren't ShadowFoe. Do you have other family back in Albania?"

"No. But I have cousins who immigrated to Greece, on the island of Corfu. We would be safe there."

Knowing that Max was listening to the conversation and would already be changing course for Corfu, Juan said, "Now, you said you know how we can find this hacker?"

Kula shifted uncomfortably in his chair. "What I said was that I'd help you find her. The problem is that I don't actually know who she is."

"What makes you think ShadowFoe is a woman?" Gretchen asked. "Have you seen her?"

"Well, no. I don't know what she looks like. I only know her through our online communications."

"Then ShadowFoe could be a sixty-year-old man, for all you know," Murph said. "Or a teenager emailing you from his parents' basement."

"That is true," Kula said. "I don't know for sure. But the way she words things in her emails is more like the women I work with than the men. I can't put my finger on it better than that. But I do know that she is the best coder I've ever worked with."

"So you *did* work with her," Juan said.

"For five years. We started by trading viruses and Trojan horses that we'd written. Then we moved up to ransomware."

When Juan glanced at Murph for an explanation, he said, "It's malware that's installed when a user clicks on an infected link or opens an app from a spam email. The installed app then locks up your computer, and the only way to get it unlocked is to pay the creator a ransom to receive the password. If you don't pay, your PC becomes a brick. Bye-bye, data."

Kula shrugged, seemingly both proud of his ability and embarrassed by his deeds. "It was good money. If people weren't so gullible, we wouldn't make anything. Their idea of computer security is a joke."

"I'm sure you taught them a valuable lesson," Juan said sarcastically. "Why were you in an Albanian mobster's castle?"

"I got . . . uh . . . too curious, let's say, about a new project ShadowFoe wanted me to work on. She found out and didn't like it. *Really* didn't like it, as a matter of fact. So she told Simaku that I was stealing from him and sent him false evidence of the theft. I'm sure she hoped he would have me killed. Instead, he took my children and forced me to work for him. When she found out I was still alive, she must have pinned the Credit Condamine attack on me."

"The project you got curious about was the bank heist?"

Kula shook his head. "That was just the first part of the full operation. The endgame is much bigger than a simple bank theft."

MacD chafed at that. "Simple? She and the people she's working with wiped out half the Monaco Grand Prix to cover their tracks."

"And do you think they would have gone to all that trouble for the money in a single bank? Believe me, there are less risky ways to break into computers and steal."

Juan took a seat on the table. "What are they planning?"

"I don't know."

"You know *something* or ShadowFoe wouldn't have gone after you."

"I'm sure she thought I discovered more than I did. All I got were bits and pieces, really."

"You just couldn't help yourself," Murph said with a knowing shake of his head. "You broke into her computer system, didn't you?"

Kula nodded. "The things she was asking me for were so bizarre that I wanted to find out more. I had no idea she was so ruthless or I never would have looked."

"What did you find?" Juan asked. "What was she asking you for?"

"She wanted me to write a program for her that would let her change the settings on industrial protective relays. They're the microprocessors that control circuit breakers. When a protective relay detects an overload condition, it trips the breakers to prevent damage to an electrical circuit."

"Why would she want that?"

"That was exactly my question. We're not talking about the kind of breaker that would keep a shorted hair dryer from causing your lights to pop out. She was aiming at huge power station breakers that could take out a city grid. I gave her some info about the breaker control software, but I didn't end up writing the code. My ethics may be questionable, but even I know taking out a power system of that size gets whole countries after you."

"And asking her what she was doing wasn't an option," Gretchen said.

"Of course not. So I backtracked her IP

address. It was spoofed very well, but I had discovered some of her favorite methods when I was working with her in the past. But when I found her computer and hacked in, she had only a few files on it that weren't encrypted. Most of them were irrelevant, but I found an obscure folder buried down deep. It was marked *Dynamo Op Res.*"

"*Op Res* could mean 'operation research,' " Murph said. "Was *Dynamo* the code word they were using for the operation?"

Kula shrugged. "She never told me they had a name for it."

"What was in the files?" Juan asked.

"It was bizarre. There were notes about Napoleon's invasion of Russia in 1812 and a subsequent search for his treasure."

"What treasure?" Gretchen asked.

"According to the files I found, Napoleon attacked Russia in the summer of 1812 with one of the biggest armies ever assembled until that point, over six hundred and fifty thousand men."

Juan nodded. "Yes, and it ended up being one of the greatest military disasters in history. Russia pioneered the scorched-earth tactic, leaving nothing for Napoleon's army to forage. He retreated from Moscow in December, during a particularly brutal winter, and crossed back over the Russian border with fewer than thirty thousand soldiers."

"But what most people don't realize," Kula continued, "was that Napoleon looted everything he could along the way. The Russians weren't able to take all their valuables with them when they fled in front of Napoleon's army, and the fires were concentrated on the food stores and lodging. When *Le Général* reached Moscow, much of it was still intact, including the Kremlin. It is thought that the French acquired two hundred wagonloads of gold, gems, antique weapons, and other valuables."

"What happened to it?" Murph asked.

"No one knows. When Napoleon began the retreat, he took the treasure with him, but they were losing horses at a staggering rate due to the cold and hunger. Two hundred thousand horses are estimated to have died. Many of the soldiers ate them or cut them open and crawled into their bellies for warmth. Because of the shortage of horses, Napoleon had to abandon the treasure along the way. The amount of gold alone could be worth hundreds of millions of dollars. Some think he sunk the entire treasure in a lake, but no one's been able to find it in two hundred years."

Gretchen shook her head in disbelief. "What does this have to do with a bank heist and shutting down electrical systems?"

"Most of the files in the folder were unreadable, but I found mentions of banking system encryption algorithms and utility maps of Europe. There's definitely some kind of connection. I also found the PDF of a letter from a French naval lieutenant named Pierre Delacroix. It was secretly sent to a French businessman after Napoleon supposedly died."

Juan narrowed his eyes at Kula. "What do you mean 'supposedly'?"

"I don't speak French, so my online translation may have been spotty. But it seems that the businessman hired Delacroix to abduct Napoleon from St. Helena in order to help him find the treasure. According to Delacroix, the abduction was a success."

"Wait a minute," MacD interjected. "Ah've been to Les Invalides in Paris. That's where Napoleon is buried. He died on St. Helena, in 1821."

"That's the year the letter is dated," Kula said. "They supposedly carried him away on a submarine called the *Stingray.*"

MacD laughed. "Oh, come on! A submarine? Mah kid could come up with a better story than that."

"I thought the same thing. But *Smithsonian* magazine had an article about real plans for such a rescue by some of his most fanatical followers. Now it looks like someone actually went through with it."

Murph, who was tapping on his tablet, said, "He's right. I just found the article. The sub was based on one designed by Robert Fulton, the same guy who invented the steamboat. He demonstrated it for Napoleon's navy, but they thought it wasn't practical even though the test was a success. Fulton's sub was called the *Nautilus.*"

"Did this Delacroix find the treasure?" Juan asked Kula.

"The letter didn't say. The reason Delacroix wrote it was because Napoleon had some demands before he would lead them to the treasure. The emperor also implied that he left behind clues to its whereabouts on St. Helena to suggest that someone else might find it first. He had been planning to smuggle the information off the island so that the treasure could be found by his loyalists and fund his triumphant rescue."

"What were the clues?"

"He wouldn't reveal them, but Delacroix suspected that they may have been in a book he left behind. Napoleon ripped some pages from it before they escaped, but the information on those pages seemed to be incomplete."

"What book?"

"Homer's *Odyssey*. It's also called *Napoleon's Diary*. ShadowFoe was intent on getting it in the hope that it would lead them to the treasure."

"And she might," Murph said, looking at his tablet. "It's being auctioned off in Malta in two days."

Gretchen put up her hands. "Just stop. Let me get this straight. ShadowFoe and her cronies broke into Credit Condamine and threatened to take down the banking system, while at the same time asking you for help in causing some kind of electrical outage. And all of that is related in some unknown way to finding Napoleon's lost Russian treasure using a diary the emperor left behind after he was supposedly kidnapped from exile without anyone realizing it?"

Kula gave her a halfhearted grin. "I did mention it was bizarre."

Gretchen pounded a fist on the table and pointed a finger at Kula. "I think you're making all of this up to get out of being put in prison for helping them plan the bank heist."

"I swear it's the truth! I can prove it!"

"How?"

"I couldn't copy the files, but I took screenshots and uploaded them to a private file-sharing site." He rattled off the URL and password to Murph, who put the information into his tablet.

"Got it," he said. "The files are all here. I see the letter, but I don't read French."

Gretchen reached for the tablet, and Murph handed it over. She took a few minutes to read it and looked up with an astonished expression when she was finished. "If this document is authentic, Kula is telling the truth."

Juan shared her surprise, but he also felt the same confusion about the links between such strange events. "It still doesn't explain how everything fits together. We need to track down ShadowFoe. Can you do it?"

"You know everything I do now," Kula said. "They want *Napoleon's Diary* badly. I think that's your best chance of finding her."

Juan shook his head. "The auction is still two days away. I don't want to wait. You said you traced her computer. Where was it?"

"At sea."

"ShadowFoe was on a ship?"

Kula nodded. "Somewhere in the Mediterranean. I don't know what type or the name of it. But I did find a coded reference to a refitting the ship had undergone recently that leads me to think she may be Russian, possibly in the military."

"Why?"

"Because it was done at the Primorskiy Kray Naval Base near Vladivostok."

Juan felt a chill in his stomach. He slowly stood up and turned to MacD. "You and Murph take Kula to his kids. I don't think this guy is ShadowFoe. We'll drop him off in Corfu as promised." He turned back to Kula. "We'll inform Interpol to meet you there."

Kula protested, "But I've helped you —"

"And we appreciate it. If what you've told us proves useful, we'll recommend that you be shown leniency."

"Who knows?" Gretchen said. "If you play your cards right, Interpol might even offer you a job. It's better to recruit hackers than fight them."

That seemed to mollify Kula. MacD blindfolded him for the walk through the secret parts of the ship and left with Murph.

Gretchen frowned at Juan. "What's the matter? You look like you've just seen a zombie."

"More like a clone. ShadowFoe must have

some powerful allies."

"What are you talking about?"

Juan took a seat opposite her. "The Primorskiy Kray Naval Base is known for outfitting ships with the latest weapons technology. Nationality isn't a barrier. They sell to the highest bidders."

"How do you know that?"

"Because that's where we refitted the *Oregon.*"

TWENTY

MALTA

When Sergey Golov left Antonovich's cabin aboard the *Achilles,* he found Ivana waiting for him outside in the corridor, her fingers dancing across her tablet. She was dressed in a sleek, knee-length skirt and a silk blouse instead of the jeans and sweatshirt she preferred when she was at the computer writing code.

"How is he?" she asked without looking up.

Golov was amused. His daughter seldom asked about anyone's health besides his. "Why should you care?" She fell into lock-step with him as they walked toward the aft deck.

"I ask purely from a business standpoint. We'll need our employer coherent when the time comes."

"He's responding to the medication as the doctor expected. Nothing to worry about."

"Good. I mean, what is he? A hundred and fifty?"

"Sixty-eight."

"Might as well be," she mumbled.

Golov smiled. He didn't need to ask her if she thought her old man was over the hill for being in his late forties.

"There was an incident at the Maltese Oceanic Museum yesterday," Ivana said. "Did you hear?"

"Yes, some kind of attack. We'll find out more about that soon enough. What did you find out about Whyvern?"

"Not good. According to police reports, there was a gun battle at Simaku's castle last night. The Mafia leader was killed, along with more than half his men."

"And Erion Kula?"

"He wasn't included in the report, so we have to assume he got away."

"Do they know who conducted the assault?"

Ivana shook her head. "No one on the strike team was listed as a casualty, and none of them were captured. But the report does indicate that it was a highly sophisticated two-pronged attack. Apparently, they escaped by boat before the coast guard could get there."

"So we're not dealing with amateurs."

"It sounds like these were top-of-the-line pros."

Golov had mixed feelings about that. He liked to test himself by going up against the best, but he also saw the appeal of a resounding victory against an overmatched opponent.

"What did Whyvern know?"

Ivana grimaced. She didn't like admitting the fact that Pavel Mitkin had exposed some of her computer files to the world. "Very little. But whoever took him may know about our interest in *Napoleon's Diary*."

The discovery of the diary's potential sale a month ago, and the worry that it could lead to Napoleon's treasure, had nearly caused Golov to put off the Dynamo operation. But the plans had been in motion for nearly a year. They might not get another chance, especially if another party acquired the diary and the Jaffa Column and used them to find the spoils of war Napoleon had hauled away from Moscow more than two hundred years before.

His main adversaries in the hunt had been two Dutch brothers named Dijkstra, the owners of a shipping and industrial conglomerate. They had already conducted an operation to steal the Jaffa Column, and they had planned to outbid anyone else for the diary. They were the only others who knew that the diary had a value far outstripping its importance as an historical relic of Napoleon's captivity.

Thanks to the unique capabilities of Antonovich's *Achilles,* the Dijkstras were no longer a threat.

Antonovich had become increasingly paranoid as his wealth grew, and the *Achilles* was designed to be his unassailable bastion from which he could conduct all his business. As soon as the main construction of the superyacht was completed in an Italian shipyard, it sailed to the Primorskiy Kray Naval Base in Vladivostok. Among elite circles, it was known that, for the right price, the admiral in command would use the naval shipyard's resources to modify ships with new propulsion and weapons systems under the guise of building spy vessels for the Russian fleet. Antonovich opened his wallet and spared no expense on the project to refit his luxury catamaran.

The diesel engines were replaced with high-output turbines linked to a new propulsion system based on the Russian Shkval torpedo, which used a rocket to propel it through the water. The torpedo could reach velocities of 200 mph underwater because the nose emitted a string of bubbles and the torpedo flew through them.

Although it wasn't rocket-propelled, the *Achilles* itself used this technique to achieve straight-line speeds never before seen in a 400-foot-long vessel. Along the length of both catamaran pods were rings below the waterline that pumped out bubbles to surround the hull with air. Instead of mounting the propellers on the stern of the yacht where they would be fouled by the bubbles, they were placed on the front of each catamaran like the engines on a prop-driven airplane, pulling the *Achilles* to fantastical speeds.

To complement the ability to outpace any warship on the water, the *Achilles* was equipped with some of the most advanced weapons on the planet, courtesy of a newly revitalized Russian military-industrial complex that was rapidly devising new arms to keep up with the Chinese and Americans.

Defense of the vessel was paramount. To counter underwater threats, the *Achilles* could deploy mini-torpedoes designed to intercept incoming torpedoes fired from submarines and surface ships. To bring down aircraft and missiles, the yacht had something few other ships could boast: a high-energy laser.

Less costly to fire than million-dollar anti-aircraft missiles, and more accurate than Gatling guns, the 30,000-kilowatt solid-state laser had the power equivalent of six welding lasers used by the automobile industry. It could be fired in a lower-energy state to dazzle homing electronics or in a high-energy state to overheat warheads and fuel tanks of drones, missiles, and airplanes — just like it had when it caused the Dijkstras' private jet to explode during landing at Gibraltar.

No one would have suspected the *Achilles*'s role in the crash since the laser looked exactly like a telescope and was only visible for a short time while the protective white clamshell dome covering it was opened. Contrary to movie convention, no beam would have been visible during the essentially silent operation of the device.

Golov appreciated the defensive capabilities that rendered the *Achilles* virtually invulnerable to attack, but as a former navy captain, his preference was its offensive weaponry.

The onboard hangar held a Russian Ka-226 utility helicopter. Instead of a tail rotor, the chopper had twin rotors mounted one on top of the other that spun in opposite directions to provide stability. The rear fuselage consisted of a detachable pod that could be swapped in minutes. Normally, it held a passenger compartment for ferrying Antonovich when he needed to attend meetings on land. Another pod could be bolted on that carried four Switchblade anti-ship missiles.

But the *Achilles*'s deadliest weapon rose from doors concealed in the roof of the yacht so that it had a two-hundred-and-seventy-degree firing arc. Although it had a barrel like many warship cannons, this was no ordinary gun. It was a railgun.

Rather than using a chemical reaction to fire a shell with a high-explosive warhead, the railgun propelled its rounds electromagnetically, allowing it to shoot projectiles at incredible speeds, more than twice as fast as the round fired by an Abrams tank. The hypersonic rounds packed so much energy that an explosive warhead was unnecessary. The impact of its heavy tungsten shell at more than six thousand miles an hour could shatter the most heavily armored hull and cause steel to vaporize.

Ever since he took command of the *Achilles,* Golov had been eager to test out the railgun's firepower. The attack on the Dijkstra freighter *Narwhal* had given him that opportunity.

The *Narwhal* had been sent to Malta to

pick up the stolen Jaffa Column. Golov had a duplicate freighter painted to look just like it and take the *Narwhal*'s place when it picked up the massive stone obelisk, but he had to get rid of the original ship for the plan to work. The railgun provided the ideal solution and had performed perfectly. It took just seven rounds to send the *Narwhal* to the bottom.

Golov was sure his ultimate plan would work. But with the diary put back in play by whoever had rescued Erion Kula, he had more work to do.

"My dear," he said to Ivana as they walked, "let's go meet our host."

From the sun-dappled deck, Golov spotted the man from the Maltese Oceanic Museum, which was hosting both the gala tomorrow night and the auction the day after that. He wore a crisp beige suit and mirrored sunglasses and gave them a smart wave when he saw them.

The *Achilles* was docked in Valletta's Grand Harbour, with postcard-perfect views all around them and nearly as many high-end yachts as they'd seen in Monte Carlo. The sandy-colored capital city abutting the port was built like a fortress because it was one, with high limestone walls bordering nearly every shore. Situated at the strategic center of the Mediterranean, the island had been attacked dozens of times over the centuries, from the Greeks and Romans of antiquity to the Nazi bombers of World War II, though the battlements were now used by tourists as photo ops rather than for any defensive purpose.

Golov and Ivana walked down the gangplank and shook hands with Spadaro.

"Captain Sergey Golov and Ivana Semova, I presume," Spadaro said in English. "My name is Emvin Spadaro. How wonderful to meet you. Welcome to Malta. We hope you find it as beautiful as we do." Ivana went by her long-passed mother's surname so that she and her father wouldn't raise any questions about their relationship.

"Pleased to meet you, Mr. Spadaro," Golov said. "You will be showing us the sights?"

"It will be my pleasure. After we see the museum, I've arranged for a private tour of some of the locations visited by Napoleon himself during the French invasion of Malta. I think you will enjoy it. Will Mr. Antonovich be joining us today?"

"I'm afraid not. We will be his representatives on this outing."

"Before I forget," Spadaro said, reaching into his jacket and removing an envelope that he handed to Golov, "here are your tickets to the gala tomorrow night. Black tie, of course."

"We're looking forward to it."

They got into his Mercedes.

"The museum is only a five-minute ride away," Spadaro said as he pulled away. "As you probably saw in the news, we had a tragic situation at the museum yesterday, but I'm happy to say it's been resolved. A crane was used in an attack on the museum, damaging a corner of the façade. Some gunfire was also involved, and, sadly, we lost our curator, William Kensington, but the perpetrators have been caught. Our director decided that William would want us to go on with the gala and auction as planned, so there has been no change to the schedule."

Ivana and Golov exchanged glances.

"Yes, we did hear about that," Golov said. "Were any of the auction lots stolen?"

"Oh, no," Spadaro replied quickly. "No. All of the pieces are safely stored in our warehouse, which was not affected."

"We'd like to see the warehouse as well," Ivana said.

"Absolutely. It's on the way, not far from the museum. I will tell you, however, that we will not be able to go inside, for security reasons."

"The artifacts are kept there?"

"Yes. It is climate-controlled and guarded around the clock by the best security system on the island. In addition, we have numerous guards on staff to make sure the items will be safe until the auction. But rest assured, you will be able to see the items to bid on in a fantastic new way that I'm excited to show you."

As promised, they arrived at the warehouse after a short drive through the ancient city's winding streets. The modern steel construction stood out against the backdrop of classic stone buildings around it. Golov wondered if it had been converted from a shipping warehouse after the new container port had been built on the southeast side of the island. That's where the *Narwhal*'s double would be docking tomorrow to pick up the Jaffa Column.

They stopped next to a gate manned by two armed guards. An imposing chain-link fence topped with razor wire surrounded the building.

Another Mercedes pulled up to the gate.

"Oh, what luck!" Spadaro said cheerily. "That's Arturo Talavera, our museum director. Perhaps I can have him say hello before he goes in."

Spadaro honked his horn and waved as he

got out. Golov and Ivana followed him. The door on the other Mercedes opened and a portly gentleman with graying hair shuffled toward them with an outstretched hand.

Spadaro introduced them and said, "They will be our guests tomorrow night, representing Maxim Antonovich."

Talavera's eyes lit up at the mention of the billionaire's name. "We are hoping Mr. Antonovich finds some of the pieces intriguing. I wish I could show them to you now, but I have urgent business to attend to in the warehouse."

"Nothing unfortunate, I hope," Golov said with a smile.

"No, no. Of course, with the unfortunate incident yesterday and the passing of our curator, my responsibilities have doubled, so I have some last-minute items to take care of before the auction. We have over five hundred pieces to sell, and buyers are descending on the island from all over the world, so you can imagine how much there is to do."

"I saw how full the harbor is with yachts."

Talavera nodded. "The airport is just as packed with private jets. Mr. Antonovich will certainly have some competition when it comes to the bidding. Well, I must be off. I look forward to speaking with you more tomorrow night."

As they walked back to the car with Spadaro, Talavera sped through the gate and parked next to a door with a keypad on it. He inserted a card into the slot and entered when the door buzzed.

"I hope you are impressed with how we are safeguarding your future purchases," Spadaro said as they drove off. "Very impressed," Golov replied.

He leaned over and softly spoke Russian into Ivana's ear. "We're not waiting until the auction."

"When, then?"

"During the gala."

After watching Talavera, Golov now had a plan to assure they were the ones who would get *Napoleon's Diary.*

TWENTY-ONE

Juan ducked his head as he stepped out of the helicopter and then turned to help Gretchen exit. The slit of her black, floor-length gown fell to one side, revealing a toned leg, the one that hadn't been injured. During the past day and a half, her wound had healed enough for her to walk with a barely noticeable limp, but Julia Huxley had insisted she loan Gretchen flat shoes instead of the four-inch heels that would have been more appropriate for such an elegant dress.

When they were out of the chopper's rotor wash, Juan straightened his tuxedo and waved at Gomez, who took off and headed back to the *Oregon,* which was stationed twenty miles off the coast in international waters. Normally, her decrepit condition was an asset when coming into a port because Third World bureaucrats were often lazy or easily bribed, but Juan didn't want to risk a ship inspection by Malta's by-the-book harbormaster.

With Erion Kula and his family safely evacuated to Corfu and the waiting arms of Interpol, the *Oregon* had made good time to Malta. After analyzing Kula's information, they concluded that he really was Whyvern and had been framed by Shadow-Foe. Their only lead, however, was the hacker's intense interest in acquiring *Napoleon's Diary* and the treasure it would supposedly reveal. The link to the European electrical grid was still a mystery.

After a check at airport customs, Juan and Gretchen got into a BMW driven by Mike Trono, who had arrived earlier in the morning with MacD by boat to smuggle in the needed gear. The guys had spent the day casing the layout of the auction house and warehouse.

"Well, don't you two look spiffy," Trono said. "It's amazing what Kevin can whip up in the Magic Shop."

"Julia loaned me the gown," Gretchen said, omitting that Kevin Nixon had to adjust it to her more athletic frame. Juan always had his tux on hand for occasions like this.

Juan chuckled. "When she heard we were going to a fancy party, she nearly shot you up with a sedative so she could come in

245

your place." He could see glimpses of the harbor as it sparkled in the setting sun. "Where's MacD?"

"Securing alternate transportation in case we need it," Trono said. "He didn't think he'd have a problem."

"Good. Hopefully, the police will never know we're here, but better safe than sorry. Earpieces?"

Trono handed a small box over his shoulder. Juan opened it and gave one of the miniature transceivers to Gretchen, who fitted it deep in her ear canal. Juan inserted his own and said, "Does everyone read me?"

"Ah can hear you just fine," MacD replied in Juan's ear. "I'm done borrowing mah ride for the next couple of days. It's not stealing if Ah plan to give it back, right?"

"They won't miss it?"

"Ah left a nice note," MacD joked.

The tiny transmitters had a range of only a couple of miles, so the *Oregon* wasn't able to listen in, but the four of them would be able to communicate with one another while they were in the city.

"You want me to wait outside the party?" Trono asked.

Juan nodded. "Within a couple of blocks of the museum. We'll let you know when we're ready to leave. MacD, stay out of sight

246

unless we need you."

"Roger that," MacD said.

"And the auction tomorrow?" Trono asked.

"We can assume whoever overbids on the diary is the one ShadowFoe is connected to or might even be ShadowFoe herself," Gretchen said. "We'll follow them afterward to see where they go."

"We'll be there to drive up the bidding," Juan added. "Tonight, I want to get a sense of who else will be attending the auction. Should be an easy in-and-out recon mission." Through various contacts, the CIA had made him and Gretchen last-minute additions to the guest list under the pseudonyms they'd used during their final mission in Russia: Gabriel and Naomi Jackson.

Trono drove them to the entrance of the museum, where a red carpet flanked by two stone lions led inside. A corner of the museum's façade looked as if it had been knocked out with a sledgehammer — the result of an attack the day before involving a crane and some gunfire, according to the news — but the museum had insisted on going forward with the gala and auction anyway since the main hall didn't suffer any damage. Despite the attackers supposedly being caught, the security had been noticeably beefed up, with heavily armed teams of guards at every corner of the outdoor plaza.

As Juan and Gretchen walked the carpet, he noticed a tightening of her lips as she climbed the museum's front stairs.

"You okay?" he asked.

She smiled. "Never better. Let's get some champagne."

They each took a glass from the server at the entrance and strolled through the *glitterati* who had assembled for this unique occasion. Policemen guarded the front and rear of the hall, while numerous security staff in suits observed the guests. Juan thought he recognized a few billionaires and celebrities among the crowd, but he wasn't really up on the latest pop culture. Murph and Eric would have been slobbering over some of the starlets in attendance.

The grand central atrium of the Maltese Oceanic Museum served as the venue for the gala. Endowed in the last few years by a Maltese shipping mogul, the museum housed one of the world's finest collections of nautical artifacts and memorabilia. Marble columns supported a domed ceiling painted with famous sea battles. Juan recognized the British and French ships of the line at Trafalgar, the British and German dreadnoughts at Jutland, and the American and Japanese carriers at Midway as just a few of them.

Waiters in tuxedoes circulated around with trays of caviar and white truffles, and a chamber orchestra played classical music of Napoleon's era at the far end of the room. The most important pieces from the auction were displayed in kiosks set up throughout the hall.

When they stopped at the first item, marked as *Lot XXXI,* Juan looked for a moment at the stone tablet covered with ancient Egyptian art. He couldn't quite figure out what was odd about the scene depicting a tall green man seeming to levitate prone bodies while white-robed priests watched from the background. It wasn't until he moved sideways and saw the metal edge of the image that he realized what he was looking at.

"A hologram," a voice from behind them said. They turned to see the museum director, Arturo Talavera. "I don't believe we've had the pleasure."

Juan and Gretchen introduced themselves as owners of a New York–based hedge fund, billionaires looking for ways to spend their newfound wealth.

"Beautiful piece," Gretchen said. "But why are we looking at a hologram instead of the real item?"

"It was a condition of the sale," Talavera replied. "Besides, it really is the safest way to display the items. Most of them are fragile and we want to minimize any unnecessary transportation and handling for prospective buyers such as yourselves. As you can see, the high-definition, 3-D display is almost indistinguishable from the original."

"It took me a second to understand what I was looking at," Juan said. "It's a shame, though, that we can't see the real thing in person."

"You will be able to see them tomorrow at the auction, of course. And all of the holographic records are to be destroyed once the auction is complete, so this will be your only possibility to see most of the items at all. But this technology gives us a chance for us to show you some of the details that we wouldn't otherwise be able to show you. For example . . ." He walked toward the center of the atrium, coaxing them to follow.

They came to a stop in front of a display case marked *Lot XVI.* Two guests were already standing in front of it — a short, powerfully built man in his forties and a thin, attractive blonde half his age, a difference in years not uncommon in the party's couples. Talavera introduced them as Sergey Golov and Ivana Semova.

"I present *Napoleon's Diary*," Talavera said proudly. "The handwriting inside has been authenticated to be the emperor's. It is thought to have been stolen by one of the soldiers or servants upon the Little Corporal's death in 1821. Its existence had been legendary until it surfaced in this exquisite collection."

Juan and Gretchen leaned in and saw that the copy of *The Odyssey* was in excellent condition. The book was written in Greek, with French notations in a tight scrawl along the margins, and some of the printed text underlined or circled. After a moment, an animation flipped the page.

"You see," Talavera continued, "we couldn't have shown multiple pages of the book to our guests without risk of damage."

Juan frowned at the diary. "Mr. Talavera, it seems odd that Napoleon wouldn't have a French version of the story. Did he know Greek?"

"Not that we know of. That's one of the great mysteries of its existence. Some believe Napoleon was attempting to learn the language. Perhaps if you purchase the piece, you will be able to have someone study his notes."

"Have all the pages been scanned?" Gretchen asked. By this time, Golov and his companion had turned to join the discussion and watched Talavera intently for his answer.

Talavera shook his head. "Only a select few — again, to handle the document as little as possible. It will be up to the owner of this magnificent piece to decide how to display and catalog it."

Someone caught Talavera's eye. "If you'll excuse me, I hope you enjoy the rest of your evening." He glided away to welcome more guests.

"Are you collectors?" Juan asked the couple standing next to them, who had yet to say a word.

"My employer is," Golov said in accented English. "He particularly enjoys artifacts from the Napoleonic Wars. Do you intend to bid on the diary?" His smile was jovial, but his eyes shone with a barely contained intensity. He didn't carry himself with the ease of the wealthy but rather with a bearing that hinted at a military background. The blonde, however, watched them with amusement. And, a bit of disdain.

"I see a lot of items I'd like to buy," Juan said. "My wife and I are big history buffs. I understand there are a couple of old cannons for sale that I have my eye on."

"Oh, honey," Gretchen said, looping her arm through Juan's, "you know we couldn't even get those things into the elevator, let alone up to our penthouse."

"No, I was thinking of the Hamptons estate, dear."

Golov leaned over and muttered to Semova in Russian. She snickered in response.

He had assumed Juan wouldn't be able to understand, but Juan made it out perfectly, and Gretchen would have as well.

Perhaps we should call them Tsar and Tsarina since they have winter and summer palaces.

Gretchen playfully swiped at Golov's arm. "Now, that's not fair. What did he tell you?"

Semova gave them a Cheshire Cat grin. "He said that every house in America is armed like that. Is that true?"

"Not ours," Gretchen said. "I won't allow loaded guns in the home. Nonworking antiques only."

Juan nodded at the diary. "How about your boss? Is he bidding on it?"

"No," Golov said. "Old books are not of interest to him."

"And what is?"

"Perhaps we should simply acknowledge

that neither of us is going to reveal our intentions, Mr. and Mrs. Jackson. We both know that the art of bidding requires secrecy, wouldn't you agree?"

Juan raised his glass. "We do indeed."

"Shall we take a spin around the room, dear?" Gretchen cooed. She led Juan away by his elbow. As they moved out of earshot, she commented, "They're an odd couple."

"Not the friendliest, either. Something about them seemed off."

"You got that, too, then. But I can't put my finger on why."

"Let's hope we're not as obvious."

"We kept up a fake marriage for three weeks. I think we can handle one more night."

As they wandered around and chatted with other guests, Juan subtly kept an eye on Golov and Semova. After thirty minutes, Semova was teetering on her heels even though she'd only consumed one glass of bubbly. They were standing near Talavera when all of a sudden he wobbled, then stumbled and fell onto his back. Amid the surprised gasps from around the room, Golov, Semova, and several others bent down to aid the stricken museum director.

Golov yelled, "Someone call an ambulance!" Security guards swarmed over to them and began tending to Talavera.

"Did you see that?" Gretchen said.

Juan nodded. "Semova's good. I barely saw her slip something from his pocket."

"It was some kind of card. And she can't be tipsy. I've been counting her drinks."

"Talavera looks like he's been 'roofied.' They must have slipped it into his drink earlier tonight and have been hovering around him waiting for him to collapse."

Golov and Semova backed away and walked straight for the exit, Semova showing no signs of impairment at all now.

"Let's see where they're going with that card," Juan said. "Mike, meet us outside in thirty seconds."

"On my way," Trono replied.

Juan waited until the Russians were out the door, then took Gretchen's hand and started the pursuit.

TWENTY-TWO

Flashing lights of an ambulance passed them as they sped off from the museum. Trono did a masterful job staying back at a discreet distance while keeping Golov's car in sight.

Golov traveled only a few blocks before his car came to a stop next to a black SUV. He unrolled his window and handed the white card to someone.

"Who do I follow now?" Trono asked.

"The SUV," Juan said. "We need to know why they stole that card."

The SUV drove on and separated from Golov's car. It arrived at a gate outside a modern warehouse surrounded by a chain-link fence.

Trono turned the corner and pulled over so that the SUV was still in view.

The gate's barrier was already raised and the SUV drove through and stopped next to a door. After a minute, two large men, an

Indian and a redhead, got out, clad in black pants and sweaters, and pulled ski masks over their faces. The Indian swiped the card at the reader and they slipped through the door, which closed behind them.

"That's the museum's warehouse," Trono said.

"Now we know why they drugged Talavera," Gretchen said. "Do you think all these people are working with ShadowFoe? Or that this woman *is* ShadowFoe?"

"Only one way to find out," Juan said.

"Are we going to wait for them out here?"

"We can't. If they're after the diary and ShadowFoe realizes that Erion Kula was compromised, they may destroy it inside the warehouse after they get the info they need. Mike, we'll take those weapons now."

Trono reached under the front seat and removed two Glock 9mm semiautomatics, a pair of sound suppressors, and four spare magazines. Juan and Gretchen each took a pistol and spare ammo. Juan tucked his into his waistband and Gretchen put hers into her purse.

"MacD, do you read me?" Juan said.

"Five by five."

"Come pick up Mike. We may need you two for a quick evac from the warehouse, depending on what we find in there."

"Ah'll be there in fifteen seconds."

"We'll leave the car here," Juan told Trono. "Keys?"

Trono handed them over and they all got out of the car. "Radio the *Oregon* and tell Gomez to bring the chopper back now. I'm guessing we'll be needing to get off the island soon."

"Chairman, you sure you don't want me and MacD to go into the warehouse with you?" Trono asked.

"I'd rather have you watching our backs out here. But I'll push the panic button if I want you to come running."

A blue and white police car rounded the corner and came to a stop next to them. The driver rolled down the window.

"Am Ah going to have to arrest y'all for loitering?" MacD drawled. His uniform was an impeccable copy of Malta Police Force issue, thanks to Kevin Nixon's handiwork. His Maltese accent, however, needed a lot of work.

"You better worry about yourself," Juan said. "You'll get thrown in the pokey for grand theft auto."

"Nah. It was in the maintenance depot. They don't even know it's missing." He looked at Trono. "Ah've got your uniform in the backseat."

"We'll keep our ears open," Trono said before getting in the boosted police car. They drove away, and Juan and Gretchen walked toward the warehouse gate.

Juan peeked into the tiny gatehouse and confirmed that it was empty.

"Odd that it's unmanned," Gretchen said.

They tried the door the Indian used, but it was locked tight.

"Come on," Juan said. "Let's see if there's another way in."

They went around the side of the warehouse and found the loading dock door open. Next to it was a truck that had been backed up to it. No one was in sight.

Juan glanced at Gretchen. "We should have seen some guards by now."

They crept through the opening and took a moment to let their eyes adjust to the darkened interior of the warehouse. Deep shadows ruled where the few active lights couldn't reach in the cavernous space.

"This place is huge," Gretchen whispered. "How are we going to find them?"

"We find the diary, we find them."

The warehouse was packed with rows of crates, items covered with canvas, and exposed pieces. The row they were in seemed to hold items dating from the sixteenth to nineteenth century, including an iron anchor from a galleon that had sailed with the Spanish Armada and a ship's bell from Captain Cook's *Endeavour*. Most of the items were marked with serial numbers, but Juan couldn't make sense of the cataloging layout. He motioned for them to keep looking.

Gretchen stopped him when they were halfway down the aisle. She pointed at a silver placard mounted on a gray metal case. It read *Lot LXXII*. The placard listed it as a scimitar taken by Napoleon during his Egyptian campaign.

"At least the auction items are marked," Juan said.

"Yes, but they don't seem to be stored in any particular order." She pointed farther down the row. "See? There's another one."

They walked down the aisle and saw it was marked as *Lot XLI*.

"Any hunches where they put Lot Sixteen?" Juan asked.

"No. Maybe we should split up and —"

Voices ahead of them interrupted her. They crouched down behind a crate and peered over it. Flashlights bobbed as the voices approached, accompanied by the sound of wheels rolling along the concrete floor. When the group passed through the beam of an overhead light, Juan could see a man being propelled forward by four heavily armed thugs who reminded him of Nazari's terrorist cell. One of them was pushing a dolly.

"Now, who are *these* people?" Gretchen whispered. "Are they with Golov, too?"

"Can't tell," Juan replied. "They definitely aren't museum guards. Whoever's in charge of security here should be fired. It's like we're attending a convention for bad guys."

"Let's hope they don't check for our invitations."

Juan drew his Glock. Gretchen took hers out as well. They threaded the sound suppressors onto them.

The group turned the corner, and Juan and Gretchen followed behind them. At the next intersection, Juan peered around a crate, careful to stay in the shadows. The gunmen and their hostage turned down an aisle and out of sight. There was no sign of the Indian or the redhead.

"Here's another one," Gretchen said behind him. "But I can't read the placard. It's too dark."

Juan checked around them. "We're clear for the moment. Shade your cell phone light."

Twenty feet away, a pair of glass-walled water tanks reflected her light. Each of the tanks was the size of a small truck. One held various treasures on porcelain racks like a giant dishwasher. In the second tank, suspended by slings, were two large iron cannons that looked like they were in the process of being treated with distilled water to remove corrosion after centuries on the ocean floor.

"Not what we're looking for," Gretchen said in frustration.

"Let's move quickly. I'm not a fan of crowds."

With their pistols at the ready, they moved to the next aisle.

"Can you see where those men went?"

"Down and to the right. So we'll keep left."

While Gretchen checked every placard they found along the way, Juan kept watch. At one point, he saw two black-clad forms that he thought were the Indian and redhead, but they disappeared into the darkness before he could be sure.

Soon after, two of the gunmen who'd been escorting the hostage crept into view. Juan motioned for Gretchen to get down, but the gunmen weren't paying attention to them. Their eyes were focused on something above Juan and they raised their weapons.

He followed their gaze up until he saw a

man crawling along the scaffolding above. When the light caught him briefly, Juan was shocked to realize he recognized him. He'd met the man only once, but he never forgot a face, particularly one who worked for NUMA.

It was Joe Zavala, a colleague of Special Projects Director Kurt Austin.

And he was about to get killed.

Juan leaped up and fired four quick shots at the gunmen, taking them down before they could get a bead on Zavala.

That's when all hell broke loose.

Twenty-Three

Surprised by Juan's shooting, Gretchen whipped her head around and then brought her Glock up in a fluid motion.

"Behind you!" She popped off three quick shots. Juan turned to see a gunman dragging his injured comrade back behind some crates.

Footsteps pounded in their direction from where he'd taken down the two men aiming at Zavala. A head poked around the corner and Juan fired twice more to keep him back. A submachine gun stuck out and fired a wild volley, but none of the rounds were close to hitting them. A stack of clay amphorae shattered in a cloud of shards and dust.

They huddled at the intersection, Juan firing in one direction and Gretchen in the other.

"MacD, this is the Chairman," he said. "We're getting pounded in here. We need extraction pronto!"

"On our way," MacD said.

Automatic weapons fire chewed into the priceless artifacts around them.

Gretchen fired off a couple more rounds and slapped a new magazine into her Glock before letting off two more shots. "They're surrounding us, Juan! We need to move now!"

She was right. They'd be cut to ribbons if they stayed where they were.

Juan motioned for her to follow him down the only route open to them. He was about to sprint for it when a third set of gunmen rushed toward them. Juan dove to cover Gretchen.

He peered through a gap in the crates they were hiding behind. While the first two groups of men kept them pinned down, the third group was advancing and readying a block of C-4 to throw. Juan prepared himself to make a last stand before the C-4 blew them to bits.

The men with the C-4 were next to one of the water tanks when it was suddenly shattered by the cannon inside, sending down a wall of water that slammed the men into the shelves across from it.

A soaking wet man with a platinum shock of hair flowed out with the water and landed on top of one of the intruders. He punched the thug with a thunderous shot to the jaw and the man went limp. The man holding the C-4 was rising to his feet when a heavy object struck him in the head, thrown from the direction where Juan had seen Joe Zavala.

"Juan, this way!" the drenched man yelled.

Juan hesitated when he heard his named called. Gretchen peered around the crate in confusion.

The platinum-haired man pulled the electrical probes from the block of C-4 and turned in Juan's direction. "Hurry! You're getting surrounded."

Juan was stunned by the man's sudden appearance. He turned to Gretchen and said, "Go."

They fired several shots to give themselves cover and ran over to crouch beside their new ally. It was now a standoff.

"Kurt Austin," Juan said, shaking his head in disbelief at one of NUMA's finest coming to his rescue. "What brings you to this shindig?"

"Saving your hide, by the looks of it," Austin said, grabbing a pistol from the man he'd knocked cold. "And you?"

"Long story. It's related to the thing in Monaco."

By now, the intruders seemed less interested in getting to them. Perhaps they realized their numbers advantage had been whittled down. They could be spiriting away whatever they'd come for, maybe the same thing that he and Gretchen were after.

"Will someone please tell me what's going on here?" Gretchen blurted out.

"Old friend," Juan said.

Austin looked her over. "I don't suppose your name is Sophie?"

She stared at him, nonplussed, before saying, "Naomi."

Austin shrugged. "It was worth a shot."

Juan grinned at the exchange, then turned back to Austin. "What are you really doing here?"

Austin pointed toward the men they were fighting. "Those men. They have something to do with the disaster on Lampedusa."

"Is NUMA investigating that?"

"By way of another government," Austin said.

Juan nodded. "Sounds like we've both got our hands full. Anything I can do to help?"

Even though he'd been busy, Juan had heard of the tragedy at Lampedusa. For the past few days it had been competing with the destruction at the Monaco Grand Prix for airtime in the twenty-four-hour news cycle. Given the high-profile nature of the emergency, he couldn't be too surprised NUMA was on the case.

More shots came their way. All three of them pressed deeper into the recess under the lowest shelf. When they returned fire, the assailants pulled back once more.

"Not sure," Austin said. "It's all connected to some Egyptian artifacts I hoped to find here."

"Good luck finding anything in this place," Juan said. "We've been looking for a book Napoleon had on St. Helena."

Gretchen shot him a warning glare about sharing confidential info, but Juan ignored it.

"An old copy of *The Odyssey*?" Austin said. "With some handwritten notes in the margin?"

"That's the one. Have you seen it?"

Austin pointed toward their adversaries. "That way."

For now, the gunfire dwindled to the occasional random shot. Together with Austin, Juan and Gretchen crouched down on one end of the aisle, while their enemies guarded the two corners where the aisle intersected the next row. There was little hope for either side to gain any ground. "They seem intent on keeping us from heading *that way*," Juan noted.

"I've got a solution," Austin said. He looked up and whistled to Zavala.

Juan followed his eyes and saw Zavala, who had climbed all the way to the ceiling to reach what looked like a heat and smoke detector. He made it to the highest point on the upper shelf but couldn't reach the sensor. He moved a box out of the way and stretched, an effort that put him out in the open. One of the gunmen saw him and fired. Bullets began punching holes in the ceiling around him.

Juan turned and felled the shooter with a single round.

With the coast clear, Zavala reached for the sensor again and pressed a Taser against it. The heat of the snapping and sparking high-voltage electricity was instantly interpreted as a potential fire. Alarms screeched, strobes flashed, and jets of carbon dioxide blasted out into the open space of the warehouse.

The assailants waited only seconds before fleeing with whatever they'd been able to recover. Juan thought they had the right idea. Even though the carbon dioxide stopped pumping shortly after Zavala pulled the Taser away from the sensor, the authorities would be coming.

"Forty feet past that intersection," Austin

said. "First shelf on the left. I'd hurry, if I were you."

Juan offered a hand. " 'Til next time."

Austin shook it. "Over drinks instead of bullets."

With that, Juan and Gretchen sprinted toward the location Austin had indicated.

"We're outside the front door," MacD said in Juan's ear.

"Hold there," Juan replied. "We'll be out in a minute."

"I hope you're eventually going to explain what just happened," Gretchen said as they ran.

"Happy to," Juan said. "Let's just hope I'm not explaining it to the police as well."

They reached the aisle and saw the placard marked *Lot XVI.* Lying inside the container next to it was a fire-proof Nomex envelope. Juan unzipped it and saw *L'Odyssée.* They had originally planned to flip through it and take photos of each page, but they didn't have time for that now. He zipped the envelope back up and tucked it into his waistband.

"Let's get out of here," he said.

It was Juan's turn to be surprised when Gretchen fired twice down the aisle. He spun around to see Golov's men, still clad in black, duck for cover.

"Come on," Gretchen said. "The front door is right over here."

They raced toward the exit and dashed outside to the police car waiting for them.

"Hop in!" MacD yelled. "Gomez is at the airport."

Once they were in, MacD mashed the accelerator and drove off.

"Drop us at the car," Juan said.

"We're not headed to the helicopter?" Trono asked.

"Soon. We owe a favor to a couple of friends back there who might need a lift, Kurt Austin and Joe Zavala. You can't miss Austin and his platinum hair. They won't be at the loading dock. Too crowded. Look for them at a side door. We'll meet you two at the airport as soon as you drop them wherever they're staying and then ditch the police car."

By now, fire engines were approaching. Police cars and half the security team from the auction were not far behind. Juan and Gretchen got out of the stolen police car and into the BMW. MacD and Trono sped away back to the warehouse to pick up Austin and Zavala.

"The auction is sure to be canceled now," Gretchen said as Juan put the car into gear and slowly drove by the emergency vehicles heading for the warehouse.

Juan gave her the envelope holding the diary.

"It's good you speak French and Greek," he said, "because the only way we're going to find ShadowFoe and our money now is to beat them to Napoleon's treasure."

TWENTY-FOUR

Golov stood at the bridge's mahogany console, drumming his fingers, as he listened to Sirkal and O'Connor's report about the warehouse raid. Except for Ivana, the rest of the crew had been sent off the bridge. Now that he no longer needed the services of the harbor pilot and they were out of Valletta's harbor, Golov could steer the *Achilles* on his own. The task kept him from blowing up at his men and doing something he'd regret. Like killing them.

"Can you believe these guys?" Ivana said to her father. She was slumped in his captain's chair, twirling her tablet in her fingers. "We spend two hours at that snooty party to get the keycard, and they let the one thing we need get taken by a couple who looked like they walked out of the pages of *Vogue*."

"They were well trained," Sirkal said. He stood ramrod straight, with his hands clasped behind him. "And they had help."

"Bleedin' right," O'Connor said, leaning against the wall and munching on an apple. "Security guards, we could have taken care of easily. But how were we supposed to know they'd have a whole squad of soldiers in there? We were lucky to make it out without being hauled in by the police."

Sirkal nodded thoughtfully. "By the way they handled their weapons, I would guess they've had military or law enforcement training. They might have been the same people who rescued Kula."

"And you're sure the diary is gone?" Ivana asked pointedly.

"Yes," Sirkal said. "We saw them take it."

"So you've now put this whole operation at risk. One that we've been planning for over a year."

"What's the big deal?" O'Connor said. "So they have the diary? How can they possibly stop us?"

"Because if they discover Napoleon's treasure, they might find Alexei Polichev's formulas."

"You mean those mathematical equations you've been talking about? The ones that no one else has been able to duplicate in over two hundred years?"

"Exactly," Ivana said. "No one can decipher the cryptographic algorithms I developed based on Polichev's work. Antonovich found the only known documents with his formulas. But if the equations still exist in the treasure Napoleon took from Moscow and someone else finds them, our entire operation will be compromised. They could track down the money by rebuilding the encrypted databases."

O'Connor snorted. "It all sounds like a bunch of gibberish to me."

She rolled her eyes at him. "Of course it does. The red hair must be an alert that your brain cells are running low."

He bit another chunk of apple. "It's going to take more than a little insult like that to rile me, lass."

"At least you understood it was an insult."

"Enough," Golov said. "Up until the last day or so, we've had nothing but success. We were bound to run into problems sooner or later. The truly great are separated from the merely good by how they respond to setbacks. Sirkal, can you track down who those people really are? There's obviously more to them than meets the eye."

Sirkal nodded. "I'll tap my mercenary contacts and see if anyone knows them. I'd also request that Ivana put her computer skills to work."

Ivana waved one hand idly. "I can't do much without photos of them. But I can access Russian security archives and see if their names appear."

"Good," Golov said. "We can't let up now. It's not like we have an idea for the next big Internet company. We can't steal copper mines or oil refineries. This operation is our only chance at real wealth. We're a week away from being richer than any of us could have ever dreamed, and Mr. Antonovich made all of this possible. I'm not going to let anyone or anything keep us from the prize. Does anyone here disagree?"

All three of them shook their heads.

"Then I suggest we work together for one more week. After that, we will never see each other again, except for you and me, my dear."

Ivana blew him a kiss.

"When is the fake *Narwhal* expected to leave port?" he asked Sirkal.

"Tomorrow evening. That was the earliest they could reserve a slot in the port."

"Is the container ready for loading?"

"Yes, I saw it myself," Sirkal said. "The Jaffa Column is exactly where we expected it to be. Dijkstra's representative will have no way of knowing the *Narwhal* that he's delivering the container to isn't the real one.

Should I tell the captain to change the destination port now that the diary has been stolen?"

The original plan was to deliver the column to a shipyard in Marseilles and transport it by truck to a secret location in the south of France, where they could study it at their leisure once they had *Napoleon's Diary*. Golov would find the treasure and eliminate the threat to their plan once and for all. But now that the diary wasn't in their possession, the plan would have to change.

Golov shook his head. "The column is of no use to us anymore. In fact, it's a liability. We can't let it fall into the hands of whoever has the diary."

"What about blowing it up once it's delivered?" O'Connor suggested. It always came down to explosives with him.

"We could have the captain toss it overboard in the middle of the Mediterranean," Sirkal said. "He doesn't know what's inside the container."

"That's risky," Ivana said. "What if the captain remembers where he dumped it and squeals later?"

Golov patted her on the shoulder, proud of his daughter's insight. "Ivana's right. We can't take that chance. We'll have to repeat our sinking of the *Narwhal*. We'll give the

277

captain instructions to alter course. Once it's two hundred kilometers from Malta and out of the main shipping lanes, we'll put it on the bottom of the sea."

"I know I'm an idiot," O'Connor said, eyeing Ivana, "but if we can recover the diary, then maybe we can still find the treasure. I know we're all going to be rich, but, from what I hear, that treasure could be worth billions of euros."

"That's a lower priority," Golov said. "If these people get their hands on the column now that they have the diary, they can torpedo our entire plan and we'll have nothing. I won't let them jeopardize the Dynamo operation. Understood?"

Sirkal gave a smart nod. O'Connor shrugged and tossed the core of his apple into the wastebin.

"We need to stay on schedule," Golov continued. "We'll head to Sicily. The three of you will take the helicopter to Syracuse and catch airline flights from there. Sirkal and O'Connor will head to Frankfurt and take care of the substation there. Ivana will head to Paris and put the fear of God into the authorities with the next bank shutdown. I'll stay with the *Achilles* and intercept the *Narwhal.* Any questions?"

"Just one," O'Connor said with a smile.

"Did anyone choose Australia yet for their retirement place? Because I've got my eye on a thirty-acre estate in Sydney."

Sirkal glared at him, because the agreement was that none of them would reveal their destinations after the operation was over. Golov suspected that the Indian would choose somewhere on the subcontinent, while Ivana had designs on Southeast Asia, maybe Thailand or Bali.

Golov turned back to the view of the sea afforded by the expansive windows and the quarter moon reflected on the calm waters. He had no desire to retire to a private island or exotic locale. He was more interested in the power that the newfound fortune would give him. He'd always chafed at serving at the whim of the rich and powerful, and being drummed out of the Ukrainian Navy convinced him that nationalism was a fool's game. Money was the only true lever of power in the world, and he would soon have enough to decide the fate of entire nations, should he choose.

No matter what he decided to do, he had no doubt that he'd continue to maintain a presence on the high seas, even if it wasn't on the *Achilles.* The ocean was too ingrained in his blood to stay away for long.

He would certainly have a vessel to rival

the features of the *Achilles.* He was now spoiled for anything less extraordinary than the high-tech yacht. He shuddered at the thought of being stuck captaining a ship as dilapidated and pathetic as the one they were cruising past.

Still, he did feel a twinge of empathy for the master consigned to that rusty cargo ship, a tramp freighter, whose stern read *Nogero.*

TWENTY-FIVE

Juan brought Gretchen another cup of coffee from the Gulfstream's rear galley. Eddie napped on the sofa, Linc lounged while he thumbed through a catalog of motorcycle parts, and Tiny was in the cockpit of the Corporation's private jet halfway through their flight to Vladivostok. Now that they had more leads in the search for Shadow-Foe, the next step was finding out who they were up against. If the hacker was part of a team that had its ship modified at the same naval base where the *Oregon* was refitted, Juan wanted to know its identity and capabilities. Only by gaining access to the Primorskiy Kray shipyard could they get the answers.

The plan was to introduce Eddie to the current base commander, Admiral Nestor Zakharin, as the son of a Hong Kong communications billionaire wanting his yacht upgraded with the latest armaments. When the *Oregon* was being refitted, Juan had presented himself as a representative of the "real owner" and had met Zakharin briefly, although the admiral had been just a captain at the time. Gretchen would play Eddie's aide, and Linc would undertake the role of bodyguard.

Juan handed Gretchen the coffee and sat down across from her. She set the mug on the table and barely looked up from *Napoleon's Diary*. For the last twelve hours, she had immersed herself in reading it, translating the emperor's notations and jotting down references in *The Odyssey* that might be relevant. Knowing that they were only borrowing the delicate book and planned to give it back to the museum when they were done with it, she turned each page with care.

Of course, the book was already damaged by Napoleon himself. He had torn three pages from it. One was from the scene in which Odysseus escapes from the Cyclops, one was from his passing the island of the Sirens while lashed to the mast so that he could safely hear their beckoning song, and the final page was taken from the perilous passage between the sea monsters Scylla and Charybdis. Without knowing what notations were on those pages, Gretchen had to piece together any other clues to determine whether the diary really would lead to the Russian treasure that he'd been forced to abandon before it could be taken to France.

"It's strange that Napoleon would have left such a valuable item behind when he was taken off St. Helena," she said idly. "If he thought it would lead to the treasure, why not take it with him? Or at least destroy it?"

"If there's any truth to this story, they went to a lot of trouble to leave a double behind. Napoleon might have been worried that the missing diary would be suspicious and took only a few key pages with him during his abduction."

"But he left some clues behind, although I'm sure no one would guess they led to a treasure. We wouldn't have either if it hadn't been for Delacroix's letter. Look here." Juan sat next to her, leaning close to read the diary. A faint whiff of her perfume suddenly brought back their days spent as a married couple.

She pointed to a page with handwriting that looked like the ink scribbles of a seismograph during a magnitude 7 earthquake. The page before it had been torn out.

"How can you read those chicken scratches?" he said.

"It's taken a while to get used to, but I can now understand most of it in context." She traced the right-hand margin with her index finger. "This says that the 'items' have been stored for safekeeping. I think we can assume that the items he means refers to the treasure. It implies that whatever was on the page before this one is the key for decoding the location of the items, using a system based on the page numbers in this diary. The key is some object that Napoleon encountered in his travels. According to his notes, whatever the object is has writing on it."

"Then it could have been in the warehouse with the other Napoleon artifacts."

"That's possible."

"But without that page, how are we supposed to figure out what it is?"

"I think I may have a way to narrow it down. Back in Napoleon's day, they used quills dipped in ink to write. It could be messy if you weren't careful." She picked up the magnifying glass next to her and showed Juan the faint outline of ink on the page opposing the missing one. "He must have closed the book before the ink dried."

Juan could barely make out the reverse image of the word *Clé* and, next to it, *CJ.*

"*Clé* means 'key' in French," she continued. "That's why he tore out the page, and probably the others as well. Those pages listed the key for deciphering the code. He may have been trying to smuggle the treasure location off St. Helena but never got the chance."

"But what's *CJ*?"

"Maybe we can search the auction database to see if there's a match," Gretchen suggested.

"It's worth a shot." He rang up the *Oregon* on his laptop with the jet's satellite linkup. After two rings, Murph's face appeared onscreen.

"I was just about to call you," he said. "We got some intel on your party crashers."

"Who are they?"

"We don't have anything on Ivana Semova, but Sergey Golov lit up the CIA's database. He's a former Ukrainian frigate captain who got canned when the Russians took over his ship during the Crimea incident. According to the Maltese Oceanic Museum, he and Semova were there representing Maxim Antonovich."

"Antonovich?" Gretchen said, surprised. "The Russian mining tycoon?"

"The same one. The museum's rep said that he saw them get off his yacht."

"Then either Antonovich is behind the

warehouse attack," Juan said, "or Golov and Semova are running some kind of rogue operation in secret."

"Oh, wait," Murph said with glee. "It gets better."

"Spill."

"Antonovich's yacht is called the *Achilles.*"

Why did that name sound familiar to Juan? Then he realized where he'd heard it recently.

"Monaco," he said.

Gretchen looked at Juan with wide eyes. "That's the yacht where the president of Credit Condamine was last seen before his wild ride."

"Right on both counts," Murph said.

"Is the yacht still docked at Malta?" Juan asked.

"Negative. It set sail soon after the warehouse mess. Must have passed right by us. And, so far, the Malta police have no suspects, which is great for you guys, but doesn't help us finger Golov for the break-in. Apparently, you were the only ones to see his girlfriend take the director's keycard."

"That means that Interpol doesn't have enough even to question Antonovich and his crew," Gretchen said, "let alone pin the bank heist on him."

"Then we have to track down the yacht ourselves and do a little covert investigation."

"Now that we think the *Achilles* is the boat we're looking for," Murph said, "are you guys going to abort the Vladivostok mission?"

Juan shook his head. "I want to know exactly how the *Achilles* was modified before we attempt to infiltrate it. If we can find the plans, it might tell us the best way in." Max was in command of the *Oregon* until he returned.

"Murph," Gretchen said, "we have another question for you."

"Shoot."

"Do you have access to the list of items being sold in the auction?"

He tapped on his keyboard. "Pulling it up now."

"We're looking for something listed as *CJ.*"

"There can't be too many of those," he replied, and typed again. After a pause, he said, "Actually, there are none of those."

"What about abbreviations or acronyms?" Juan asked.

"Nope. Nothing that even comes close."

"Wait a minute," Gretchen said. "Weren't

287

there some items given to the museum by the donor that weren't included in the auction?"

"You're right," Juan said. "Murph, check any references to new pieces the museum acquired."

"My fingers are flying." He took a little longer this time, then said, "Oh."

"What?"

"There is one piece that comes close. But it's called the Jaffa Column. *JC,* not *CJ.*"

"*Colonne Jaffa,*" Gretchen said. "That's how it would be written in French. We found it!"

Murph scratched his head and grimaced. "Well, we almost found it."

Juan knew that expression and it wasn't good. "Why?"

"Because the museum just reported that it's gone missing."

TWENTY-SIX

PARIS

Ivana pretended to be asleep while Marcel Blanc rose from the bed and went into the bathroom. The lovemaking session had been blessedly short as usual. She had played the role of occasional mistress of the cybersecurity firm's director for the last six months in anticipation of this night. The luxury apartment in the Neuilly suburb had been rented under a pseudonym specifically for these trysts.

As soon as Blanc closed the door, she slipped from under the covers and darted over to his briefcase. She waited for him to turn on the shower and then removed the laptop and authentication token from the case.

Blanc's company, Relvat Security, provided computer protection software for some of the biggest banks in Europe. Ivana logged into Relvat's virtual private network and referred to the authentication token. Its digital readout changed every sixty seconds so that no one could log in with just Blanc's password, which she had obtained weeks ago. With a few keystrokes, she was into Relvat's system.

Now it was time to initiate the second stage of Operation Dynamo. As anticipated, banking security protocols had been changed in the aftermath of the Credit Condamine bank heist, playing right into her hands. She plugged her USB memory stick into the laptop and began uploading her custom-built virus into Relvat's server.

She was only a few seconds into the process when light spilled from the bathroom. Her breath caught when she realized she could see Blanc reflected in the laptop's screen, his doughy physique wrapped in a towel.

"Oh, you're awake," he said in English. "I can't find the toothpaste . . ." He suddenly noticed what she was doing and froze. "Why do you have my laptop?"

Ivana tried to place her body between him and the screen, leaning seductively over the chair. Her hand hovered by her purse. "I was just checking my email. Why don't you forget the shower and come back to bed? I'll be done in a minute."

"If you're checking your email, why is my security token on the desk?" He strode toward her and roughly pushed her aside, his eyes widening when he saw the screen. "That's Relvat's network!"

Ivana plunged her hand into her purse and drew the tiny .22 caliber Beretta. Blanc stopped when he saw the gun pointed at him.

Ivana shook her head. "Why couldn't you have just taken a shower and then gone home to your wife like a good boy?"

"Darling, what are you doing?"

"What does it look like I'm doing?"

"It looks like you're using my security codes to break into Relvat's system."

"Right. So asking what I'm doing now seems like a stupid question, doesn't it?"

"But why?"

"Now, *that's* a smart question. It should have been your first." She continued to monitor the download progress of her virus while keeping an eye on her duped paramour.

"I don't understand. Why would you do this to me?"

"Well, it's not really about you. This is about me. Specifically, about money that I intend to take."

"You're stealing from Relvat?"

"No, *you* are," she said coyly. "No one knows about me, do they?" She rose from the chair, aiming the pistol at his head. "Do they?"

Blanc shook his head vigorously. "No! No!"

"That's good. And it will stay that way?"

He nodded just as vehemently. "Of course! I'll tell no one."

She smiled. "That's what I wanted to hear." She pulled the gun back, though she continued to keep it trained on him. He relaxed a bit but remained wary. "Sit on the bed and turn on the TV. I want to hear the news."

He did as he was told and tuned the TV to the BBC evening report.

"I don't know how much you think you can take," Blanc said. "Most of our assets are in stock value and property."

"Do you really think I care about the two million euros I could take from your little company?"

"But you said —"

"That *you* are stealing from Relvat. It's a pittance compared to what I'm going to net. Turn it up louder," she said. When he hesitated, she motioned with the gun and he pressed the VOLUME button until the newscasters seemed to be yelling. "Now, just stay quiet until I'm finished."

It took two more minutes for the virus to upload. When it was complete, she wiped the security token with a tissue and stuck it back in the briefcase but kept the laptop out.

"Now I'm going to tie you up," she said. "Turn over so that you're lying facedown, hands behind your back, face toward the drapes."

"But I —"

"Do it!"

He did as instructed. With his face turned, he couldn't see her.

She went to the sofa and picked up a throw pillow. This was going to be the hardest part, but she steeled herself. She walked over to the bed with the pistol up against the pillow, placed it against Blanc's head, and pulled the trigger. The TV drowned out the muffled shot.

Blanc's body went limp.

Ivana pulled the pillow away and appraised the small hole in the back of his head. There wasn't even much blood.

She shrugged. That didn't seem so hard after all.

She dressed quickly and wiped down every surface she had touched. Then she took Blanc's wallet and laptop to make it look like a burglary gone wrong. By the time they connected Blanc with the bank theft to come, any leads would be ice-cold.

She mentally retraced her steps and confirmed that she had left nothing incriminating behind. With a satisfied nod, she headed to the door. Even though it hadn't gone as she'd expected, it wasn't a bad night's work. She didn't know a single soul who wouldn't kill for thirty billion euros.

As she walked out of the apartment, she could hear the BBC announcer going to a special bulletin. The computer system of France's largest bank just went down.

TWENTY-SEVEN

FRANKFURT

Sirkal lay on a hill on the outskirts of the city, a .50 caliber Barrett sniper rifle firm against his shoulder. O'Connor was prone next to him, observing Frankfurt's biggest electrical substation through binoculars. Between them was a map of the substation, with twenty-five high-voltage transformers highlighted.

The brightly lit facility was situated in the middle of a farming region split by an autobahn, where headlights sped by in the distance. No one was within a mile of their hiding spot on the edge of a forested park.

The substation was monitored remotely, so nobody currently occupied the twelve-acre property surrounded by chain-link fences topped with barbed wire. Security cameras had a good view of the facility itself, but none of them were pointed outside the fence.

O'Connor snapped gum as he surveyed the target, a habit that had helped him quit smoking. The sound irked Sirkal, but it didn't pose a threat in their isolated position. The Irishman was a good operative and a trusted partner in a fight, but he could be a pain in the butt.

"What idiots," O'Connor said with another snap. "Not a soul around and lit up like a roman candle. They might as well have painted a bull's-eye on it."

"Their vulnerability is our advantage. 'He who is prudent and lies in wait for an enemy who is not, will be victorious.' "

"Do you always have to sound like a Buddhist monk with those sayings?"

"That's Sun Tzu, from *The Art of War.* You should read it sometime. And I'm a Hindu." While that was technically true, he didn't follow the teachings of the Hindu scriptures any more than O'Connor adhered to the tenets of Catholicism.

They'd already received confirmation from Ivana that her portion of the operation was complete. The banking system was in a panic because of the new breach. Steps were being taken to secure data that had previously seemed protected. Now it was time to set in motion the other part of the plan.

The idea for this mission actually came

from a little-known attack on an electrical substation outside of San Jose, California, in 2013. Unknown assailants pumped more than two hundred rounds into a key Silicon Valley power hub. Because the substation was unmanned, it seemed at first to be nothing more than an equipment malfunction on the remote maintenance screens, and it took authorities nineteen minutes to respond. By the time the police arrived, the attackers had disappeared without a trace, leaving no clues as to their identities or motivation. The bill for the damage totaled over fifteen million dollars.

Seeing how easy it had been to take out an entire unguarded substation in the United States, Sirkal thought the same kind of attack would work in Europe. He had been an electrical engineer in college before gaining his mercenary experience in the Indian Army, so his expertise was critical for planning Operation Dynamo. After a careful study of the European Continental Synchronous Power Grid, he had pinpointed this one in Frankfurt as the prime target. He and O'Connor had scouted out the location over a month ago, picking this very spot for its unobstructed view of the facility.

As part of the reconnaissance for the mission, they had set off some fireworks in the area and timed how long it took the *Polizei* to respond. The Germans had done much better than the Americans, arriving at the remote spot in only eight minutes.

"Ready on the timer?" Sirkal said.

"Ready. Do you have the first transformer lined up?"

Sirkal looked through the scope and placed the crosshairs on the word *Siemens* stenciled on the side of the transformer. That would put the shot right through the tank of the transformer's oil-filled cooling system.

"Got it." He had the progression of targets memorized.

O'Connor checked his wind gauge and the binoculars' laser range finder. "Wind is three knots due east. Distance to target is 1,085 meters."

Sirkal adjusted the scope to compensate for the conditions and distance. "Ready."

"Starting the timer." O'Connor's phone beeped.

Sirkal let out his breath, waited for the lull between his heartbeats, and squeezed the trigger. The rifle butt slammed against his shoulder, and the gun fired with an ear-shattering roar. His earplugs were the only thing preventing permanent hearing impairment.

"Dead on target," O'Connor said. "Oil is spewing from the transformer."

Sirkal adjusted the Barrett to the next transformer and fired again. He got into a rhythm, stopping only to slap in another magazine. By the time he was done, all twenty-five transformers were leaking critical coolant. Eventually, they'd overheat and have to be shut down.

He wasn't going to wait for that to happen.

"Time?" Sirkal asked.

"Five minutes left."

"Then let's give the oil time to pool," Sirkal said, his voice betraying some of the enjoyment he felt at a job well done.

"That's some good shooting," O'Connor said. "The farthest shot I've ever made is a thousand yards. It was a moving target, but still . . . Looks like you've got some experience with this."

"Fifteen kills on special operations in Kashmir."

"Nice." O'Connor raised the binoculars again. "We've got a long pool from one end of the substation to the other, and oil is still flowing."

"Now you will see a real roman candle,"

Sirkal said.

This time, he targeted the junction box on the centermost transformer.

He fired. Instead of simply putting another hole in the equipment, the .50 caliber round tore through the transformer's main hub and shorted it out instantaneously. The sudden overload caused a detonation, sending sparks shooting across the facility.

The pooled oil went up in flames. As soon as the fire hit the tanks in the other transformers, they blew apart in a chain reaction like exploding dominos.

In seconds, the entire substation was a fireball visible for miles.

O'Connor checked the timer. "We need to go."

Sirkal stood and picked up the rifle. He and O'Connor collected the shell casings and covered up their impressions in the ground to clear the scene of any evidence.

O'Connor made a move to go back to the car, but Sirkal held up his hand to wait. It took only a few more seconds to see what he was waiting for.

The high-powered lights surrounding the substation winked out, followed in close succession by the streetlights, and then the lights of the houses and towns in the distance. In a matter of moments, the glow in the sky above Frankfurt was virtually extinguished. Except for the fire and the headlights on the autobahn, the night was pitch-black, likely for the first time since World War II.

One additional light source intruded on the perfect darkness. Blue and red lights flashed as police cars and fire engines raced to the substation.

"Now it's time to go," Sirkal said, and they disappeared into the forest.

Twenty-Eight

MALTA

In the waiting area outside the harbormaster's office, Linda Ross watched the bustling activity of cranes off-loading containers from three giant ships. Even at six in the morning, Manwel Alessi made her and Eric Stone cool their heels while he took care of port matters.

Under the guise of the fake IDs they'd used in Monaco, she had explained that they were insurance investigators looking into the theft at the museum warehouse. Alessi had readily agreed to meet with them, as curious about the normally tranquil island's unusual events as he was eager to assist the investigation.

He swung the door open and waved them inside. "I'm sorry to keep you waiting." He was a trim man in his fifties, wearing horn-rimmed glasses.

"Not at all," Linda said. "Thank you for

meeting with us. We know how busy you must be."

"Sit, please. Of course, when I heard that you needed information, I was happy to help. The museum director and I are old friends."

"Then you'll be glad to know he's made a full recovery," Eric said.

"That's good to hear. Strange what happened. Did they catch anyone?"

Linda shook her head. "No suspects as yet. And some items were stolen, which is why we're here."

"Yes, I heard about it. Such a tragedy. Have you tracked any of the pieces down?"

"That's what we're trying to do. One of the items was something called the Jaffa Column. It's a stone obelisk from Syria taken by Napoleon during his Egyptian campaign."

Alessi leaned back as soon as he understood the implication. "You think someone's trying to smuggle it out of the Freeport."

"That's a possibility," Eric said. "The Maltese police are following leads on the island in case it's being stored somewhere here. Smuggling is the other option."

"The problem is its size," Linda said. "The column weighs thirty tons. It's unlikely they would have attempted to fly it off

303

the island. Besides, we checked into that prospect and no cargo planes large enough to carry it have taken off in the last three days, which is the last time anyone saw it."

"Well, I'm afraid it may be long gone by now," Alessi said. "We've had eight ships leave in that time. Almost all of them were as big as those." He pointed at the gigantic ships framed in the window overlooking the harbor. Each of them was large enough to carry more than five thousand containers.

"I know that we're sailing into the wind here, Mr. Alessi," Linda said. "But we need to follow any possible leads. The museum is desperate to recover what could be a cornerstone of their collection."

"I'm happy to give you a list of the ships that have already sailed and the ones that are scheduled to leave in the next two weeks, but you'll have to contact each of the lines yourselves to request an inspection of their cargo. Of course, any containers that originated in Malta we will check before they leave."

He printed out the list and handed it to Linda. The ships were listed, along with the name of their operators, the number of containers off-loaded and loaded at the port, and the arrival and departure dates. Before Linda had a chance to scan the complete tally, Eric pointed at one odd item.

"The *Narwhal* loaded only one container?" he asked Alessi.

"Oh, yes. That was a strange one. We don't often get small feeder vessels. As I said, the giant containerships are what normally dock here, and they're getting bigger by the day. This one off-loaded thirty-five containers and loaded a single one for the trip out."

"Did the container originate here?"

Alessi checked his computer. "As a matter of fact, it did. According to my records, it was carrying machine parts."

"Was it inspected?"

"Yes. Two days ago."

Linda didn't put much stock in that. Dockworkers could always be bribed for the right price.

The printout said the *Narwhal* sailed last night. No destination was listed.

"Do you know where the *Narwhal* was headed?" Eric asked, reading Linda's mind.

Alessi shrugged as he looked at his screen. "They claimed they were bound for Marseilles, but that could easily be changed en route, which they likely would do if you think they came for stolen cargo. They could even off-load it to another ship at sea. We would have no way to know."

Suddenly, a strange look crossed his face.

"What is it?" Linda said.

"Well, you said you were looking into anything odd, and I did hear something strange recently."

"About the *Narwhal*?"

"Yes. Two days ago, a couple of men were plucked from the sea by a fishing trawler in the middle of a storm east of Spain. One of the men has recovered enough to talk about what happened to him, but he was thought to be crazed by the ordeal."

Eric leaned forward. "What did he say?"

"He said that he was a sailor on the *Narwhal* and that it blew up and sank. He and his friend jumped overboard and were lucky to find a floating container to climb aboard until they were rescued."

"But you said the *Narwhal* was here. It left last night."

"That's exactly why they thought this man was raving mad. He told this fantastical story that the ship had been replaced with a replica that sailed right by him. Does that make any sense to you?"

Linda stood abruptly and Eric followed suit. "We'll look into all the possibilities, of course, Mr. Alessi," she said. "We thank you for your time."

When they were out of earshot, Eric said, "You think that's the one?"

"I wouldn't bet against it. Whoever stole the column wouldn't want to take the chance that it would get lost among a thousand other containers. They'd want to know exactly where it was."

"Or they'd even want to control the ship itself. If the *Narwhal* is the one with the column on board, they already have an eight-hour head start. They could be more than a hundred miles away from Malta by now."

"Then we better get back to the *Oregon* and begin our search. We'll just have to hope they haven't already dumped it overboard."

The only problem was where to start looking.

TWENTY-NINE

VLADIVOSTOK

A polished black limousine pulled up to the luxurious Villa Arte Hotel at eight o'clock at night, ready to take Juan, Gretchen, Eddie, and Linc to the Primorskiy Kray Naval Base. Admiral Zakharin thought it would be best to show them the facilities in the evening when fewer sailors would be around to ask questions about the guests. Juan agreed that the timing was prudent.

His phone rang as they were getting ready to leave the lobby. It was Max. Juan told the rest of them to get in the limo and he'd be out in a minute.

"I hope you're bringing me back some pirozhkis," Max said. He had fallen in love with the meat pies when he'd visited the city during the *Oregon*'s refit. "Is that little place still there? What was it called?"

"Vostok," Juan said. "We stopped there on the way from the airport. I got you two fish and two mushroom."

"Only four?"

"I got more, but we ate the rest. I had to fight Linc to save the last ones from him. What's the news on the *Narwhal*?" Max had emailed him about Linda's investigation a few hours ago.

"We're fairly confident it's the ship we're looking for. The owners of the shipping line, two brothers named Dijkstra, were killed in a plane crash on Gibraltar just a few days ago."

"You know how I love coincidences."

"About as much as I love my ex-wives' divorce lawyers."

"How's the search going?"

"Thanks to the bank debacle in France last night, the CIA made our request top priority. They retasked a satellite just like we asked and scanned a hundred-and-fifty-mile radius around Malta for any ships fitting the *Narwhal*'s description. Jackpot."

"You found it?"

"Steaming northwest at twelve knots. Looks like they're heading toward Barcelona. They've been in the main shipping lanes for a while, then veered away about an hour ago. Maybe hoping to dump the cargo once they're sure no one will see them. We're on a pursuit course now. Should be in sight within the hour."

"Nice work."

"The port interview was Linda's idea. I'm just steering the ship."

"When you catch up, keep them under surveillance until they reach port. We'll have Spanish customs confiscate the container, provided they haven't ditched it already. I'm sure Interpol will give us a chance to examine the column as thanks for finding it."

They could easily stop the *Narwhal* and seize the container themselves, but high-seas piracy was frowned upon by the maritime authorities. And if it turned out the column wasn't aboard, they'd be in even deeper trouble.

Gretchen was waving to Juan.

"Max, I gotta go. I'll give you a call when we've got info on the *Achilles.*"

"And I'll text you when we have visual contact with the *Narwhal.*"

Juan hung up and got in the limo, adjusting his suit and tie as he sat. The others had already assumed their roles. Eddie was dressed in a two-thousand-dollar Armani suit and held his phone with one hand as his thumb idly slid across the screen. Linc, wearing a gray T-shirt under a plain black jacket, sat across from him, staring stoically backward. Gretchen, in a white silk blouse, tailored slacks, and black heels, jotted notes on a pad, giving the appearance of being Eddie's dutiful assistant.

Twenty minutes later, they were waved through the gates of the Primorskiy Kray Naval Base. Two guided missile cruisers were tied up at the docks, next to three immense sheds sheltering dry docks. One of them was open, revealing the huge gantry cranes that were sturdy enough to carry whole ship sections.

The limo came to a stop in front of a Soviet-era office building, notable for its heavy use of concrete and for thorough lack of charm. Two armed sailors and a lieutenant met them at the door. The sailors frisked them and searched their cases, finding no weapons. The only thing that gave them pause was Juan's artificial leg, but, after a brief inspection, they let him pass.

The lieutenant led them through halls that brought back memories for Juan. He could almost hear Yuri Borodin's booming voice echoing off the cinder block walls and linoleum floor. The late base commander, who had died in a prison rescue attempt by the *Oregon* crew, had been a friend of Juan's.

They were escorted into the office of

311

Admiral Zakharin, who stood and greeted them warmly, hugging Juan before the introductions and a round of handshaking, while his underlings left. To commemorate the meeting, the admiral poured shots of Stolichnaya Gold vodka for all of them, as was the custom.

The generously rotund admiral toasted the group in a deep basso while Juan translated into English for his guest from Hong Kong. "As my old boss and dear late friend Yuri Borodin told me: One man said to the stranger, 'I have the most delicious bread but no friend to eat it with.' And the stranger said, 'I have the finest wine but no friend to drink it with.' And, with that, they were no longer strangers. So let us drink to making new friends. To our meeting!"

They downed the vodka and sat on the same nineteenth-century furniture that had been here when Borodin was the commander. Like a good bodyguard, Linc remained standing.

"Thank you for meeting us on such short notice, Admiral," Juan said.

Zakharin grinned. "For an old friend who proposes to bring me even more business, how could I say no? Now, before I give you a tour of our facilities, what kind of ship do you want us to modify?"

"Yachts are what we're interested in," Juan said as he rose and poured two more vodkas for him and the admiral. "Have you ever refitted a mega-yacht before?"

Zakharin tossed back the vodka with Juan and said, "Of course! You know we can handle any ship up to three hundred meters in length. And we have the latest technology at our disposal from all over the world."

"I'm sure you do. For example, what did you put on a yacht called the *Achilles*?"

The admiral flinched, then stared at him for a moment.

"So you *did* do work on it?" Juan said.

"You know I can't share confidential information about our clients. I'm sure you, of all people, would appreciate that."

"I do, but we suspect the owner of the *Achilles*, Maxim Antonovich, has stolen our money and, understandably, we'd like it back."

"That is not my concern," Zakharin said, standing. "It's time for you to leave."

"Actually, it *is* your concern," Juan said. He had opened his combat leg and drew his .45 ACP Colt Defender, as well as a small vial of clear liquid, which he opened and gave to Eddie.

"I wouldn't call for help," Juan said. "That

313

vial contains the second half of a binary toxin."

Zakharin was nonplussed for a moment, then looked down at his vodka glass in dawning comprehension.

"You poisoned me?"

"Not really. Not yet. The two halves of the binary poison only work in combination. If my friend here sprays you with the liquid in that vial, it will trigger a massive cardiac seizure. Your aides will rush in and think, quite understandably, given your less-than-healthy lifestyle, that you've suffered a sudden heart attack. And we will walk out of here without any suspicion cast upon us."

Zakharin gawked at him, while Gretchen went over to his file cabinet and began rifling through the contents.

"But if you cooperate with us," Juan continued, "the binary half that you just drank will pass out of your system in twenty-four hours without ill effect."

The admiral sank into his chair.

Gretchen pulled a file from the cabinet. "I found something about the *Achilles.*"

"What is it?" Juan asked.

"Payments related to the refit. But they're all coded entries, acronyms, and abbreviations. They don't make much sense without the detailed accounting ledger."

314

"No engineering specs?"

"Doesn't look like it."

Juan sighed and looked at Zakharin.

"What do you want to know?" the admiral whimpered.

"Unfortunately, I wouldn't believe a word you told me," Juan said. "See, I know you were instrumental in getting my old friend Yuri Borodin sent to that Siberian prison. You'd tell me a bunch of lies and send me on my way."

"So what should I do? Do you have truth serum as well?"

"No. I need you to sit right here and be quiet until we get back. These two gentlemen will keep you company."

Juan walked over to the secret door hidden in the wall. The latch was exactly where it had been when he'd last used it. It popped open, and he motioned to Gretchen. "After you." She disappeared into the opening.

"Where are you going?" Zakharin demanded.

"You can either find out when I get back," Juan said, "or you'll never know."

He looked pointedly at the vial in Eddie's hand and then followed Gretchen into the dimly lit corridor.

THIRTY

Golov was conducting a routine inspection of the *Achilles*'s engine room when the call came down that the *Narwhal* had been spotted. The yacht had raced ahead of the cargo ship so that Golov could pick out an isolated spot to sink it. The nearly thousand-foot depth in this part of the Mediterranean meant the *Narwhal* and the Jaffa Column it was carrying would never be found.

He was in no hurry to get to the bridge. He stopped at the galley to grab a snack of rolled blinis, the best he'd ever tasted. Then he checked on the assault team preparing its equipment for the upcoming raid in a few days. He was pleased to see that everything was progressing as planned.

Mitkin's betrayal in Gibraltar and his subsequent punishment had been a rude awakening for the crew who had agreed to join him in Operation Dynamo. Just as Stalin had done, Golov had purged a third of Antonovich's original crew after presenting them with the plan that he and Ivana had put together. Despite the rich rewards that were promised, some of the crew had balked, as he knew they would. They'd be allowed to leave, no harm done, as long as they vowed to remain silent.

Of course, that had been a lie to keep them from rebelling. The dissenters were rounded up, killed, and thrown overboard, vanishing into the ocean as Mitkin had. Curious family and friends were told that the crew members had resigned and taken jobs on other yachts. There had been some follow-up inquiries, but by the time any authorities could get involved, the operation would be over and the rest of them would disperse.

Mr. Antonovich protested about the deaths, but Golov assured him that there was no other choice. Since that day, Antonovich hadn't left his plush cabin, and he got daily updates from Golov on the situation.

The remaining crew, and the new crew he'd had to recruit, were in all the way. With the number of crimes they could be convicted of for aiding and abetting, there was no going back. From the squad of mercenaries that Sirkal had handpicked down to the yacht's cook, all of them knew what was at stake. If Dynamo went according to plan, they'd each be set with a fortune that they otherwise wouldn't have been able to acquire in a hundred lifetimes. The payday was worth whatever risk presented itself. And if some of them didn't make it out alive, even more would be available for the survivors.

Thirty billion euros, distributed proportionally to the crew — thirty-five billion U.S. dollars, at the current exchange rate — that was the amount Ivana estimated that they'd swindle from the European banks, in the end. It was a sum that dwarfed any known heist. Four million dollars in gold from an armored car robbery? A hundred million euros in diamonds stolen from a Belgian vault? Those thefts seemed laughably petty compared to the ambitious scheme they were undertaking.

"Status," Golov barked, and took a seat in his chair, which had a commanding three-hundred-and-sixty-degree view through the three-inch-thick polycarbonate windows surrounding him.

His faithful XO, Dmitri Kravchuk, who'd served with him in the Ukrainian Navy, pointed toward the bow. "We have confirmation it's the false *Narwhal,* Captain. Twenty miles off the port bow."

Golov flipped up the high-definition screen embedded in his armrest to see the feed from one of the digital zoom cameras mounted on the hull. He increased magnification until he could clearly see the *Narwhal*'s familiar shape.

"Didn't I already kill you?" he mumbled to himself.

"They're continuing, straight and true, at a steady twelve knots," Kravchuk said.

"Any other ships in the vicinity?"

"No, sir. Nothing on radar, and we're monitoring the transponders on all cargo vessels in the area. None are within eighty miles."

"Excellent. Power up the railgun."

"Aye, sir. Powering up railgun."

Kravchuk flipped a switch on his console and the entire yacht hummed with the vibration of the capacitors building the charges they would need to fling tungsten projectiles at hypersonic speeds.

Golov pressed the button for the shipwide intercom.

"Attention. This is the captain. The railgun has been activated and is preparing to fire. Secure all breakables and clear the exterior decks. This is not a drill."

After one minute, Kravchuk announced, "The capacitors are fully charged."

319

"Very well. Open the roof."

"Aye, sir. Opening the roof."

Fifty feet of the white deck in front of them drew apart. When the doors were fully retracted, a sinister-looking, steel-gray barrel rose from the depths of the *Achilles,* riding atop a four-sided turret. Unlike the round barrel of a cannon, the railgun's barrel was octagonal and lined with heat-dissipating fins to keep it from melting due to the fantastic temperatures generated by projectiles moving through it at eight thousand miles an hour.

When it had risen completely from its hidden chamber, the turret rotated around its full two-hundred-and-seventy-degree range of motion.

"Railgun ready to fire," Kravchuk announced.

"Same firing profile we used on the real *Narwhal,*" Golov said. "I want to see that ship underwater in five minutes."

"Aye, sir. Targeting profile entered and locked in."

"Contact!" the radar operator shouted. "Thirty miles at bearing three four five."

"What?"

"I'm sorry, sir. It just appeared on the screen."

"You didn't see its transponder?"

"No, sir. It must not have one."

That ruled out a cargo ship. Any ship larger than three hundred tons was required by international convention to carry a satellite-tracked automatic identification system.

"What's its course and speed?"

"Same course as the *Narwhal,* sir. Speed twelve knots."

"How big is it? A fishing vessel maybe?"

"No, much larger than that," the radar operator said. "I'd say over five hundred feet long."

Kravchuk frowned at him. "Naval warship?"

"Can't be," Golov said, but he had a bad feeling that's exactly what it was. If some nation had sent out a destroyer to intercept the *Narwhal,* he'd have to come up with a new plan quickly.

He moved the exterior camera around and focused it on the ship that had intruded on their perfect, isolated location. He zoomed in until he had a good look at the ship's profile.

He gaped when he recognized the outline. It was the wretched tramp steamer they'd passed when they were leaving Malta. The *Nogero,* as he recalled.

Did it follow the *Achilles* here?

"You said it's running steady at twelve knots?" Golov asked the radar operator.

"Aye, sir. Almost perfectly in the wake of the *Narwhal.*"

So it was following the cargo ship with the Jaffa Column on it. But why?

He sat back to think for a moment. If he were trailing the ship, he'd be doing it to see where the next destination would be and then he'd take the container when the ship docked.

Therefore, ordering the *Narwhal* to come to a stop wouldn't help. The *Nogero* would either do the same and wait or board the ship when they realized something was wrong.

"We're going to sink them both," he said to Kravchuk.

"Aye, sir," the XO responded without hesitation. "Which should we target first?"

"Stay on the *Narwhal,* but we'll wait until it's closer. Five miles should do it. Then that rusty excuse for a freighter will only be fifteen miles away when we destroy her."

THIRTY-ONE

"Was this built as an escape route in case of attack?" Gretchen asked Juan as they crept down the admiral's hidden passageway.

"I guess it was originally," Juan said, keeping his ears alert for any indication that someone else was up ahead around the next corner. "But I think it's more often used now to smuggle mistresses into the office."

She rolled her eyes. "I should have known. Of course a man would use it for that."

"In Russia, it's considered a perk of command."

"And on the *Oregon*?"

"Come on. Give me *some* credit."

"So, offshore dating only?"

"When I have time."

"Anything lately?"

Juan thought back to a torrid week with a U.S. Navy commander in Okinawa, but that was a long time ago.

He simply shrugged. "You?"

She shrugged in reply. "Been busy since my divorce."

They locked eyes for a moment.

Before anything more could happen, Juan heard the sound of voices coming from beyond the passageway exit. He grabbed Gretchen's hand and pulled her to the door to listen.

There was a peephole in the door. He looked out and saw two sailors ambling down a hallway, gabbing about which bar to visit later that night. Their voices faded as they turned the corner. When it was quiet, he eased open the door and looked out.

The corridor was empty. When the door was closed behind them, it disappeared into the wall, invisible to the naked eye. A clock cleverly placed over the peephole marked its location.

A set of stairs was directly across from the door. They went down two flights, carrying themselves like military investigators. A couple of sailors passed them on the way up but didn't give them a second glance. Juan knew that once you gain access to a secure facility, everyone thinks you're supposed to be there.

They went down eight flights to the basement, where they found the room marked *Records.*

They entered and found a young sailor posted at a desk, a sidearm on his hip. He adjusted himself from a slouch and looked up at them with mild interest.

"Da?" he said, bored with the duty.

Juan and Gretchen flashed the identifications that Kevin Nixon had prepared for them.

"I am Agent Bukir of the Far Eastern Military Investigation Directorate," Juan said in fluent Russian, "and this is Agent Kamarova. We require access to your records vault."

"May I ask what this is regarding?"

Juan leaned on the desk and glared at the sailor. "If you must satisfy your curiosity, seaman, we are investigating a serious breach of security here at Primorskiy Kray. That is all you need to know."

"I . . . I understand, Agent Bukir," he stammered, "but I am under strict orders from the admiral himself not to let anyone who has not been preauthorized to access the vault."

Juan stood up and smiled. "Excellent, sailor. Although I don't need your permission to enter the vault, I admire your dedication and willingness to put your prospects for promotion on the line."

"But . . . But . . ."

"Why don't you call the admiral's office?" Gretchen said. "I'm sure he will confirm our identities."

Juan nodded. "Very well. Put him on speaker when you get him on the line." Since Eddie and Linc didn't speak Russian, he wanted to be sure Zakharin didn't try to sneak a coded message through.

The sailor nodded and punched the buttons on the phone so hard that Juan thought he might break a finger.

"I need to speak to the admiral," he said into the handset. "Yes, now! It's urgent." Then he nodded and pressed the SPEAKER button before hanging up the handset.

Zakharin answered in a distinctly gruff tone. "What is it?"

"Admiral, sir, I have two agents here who want access to the records vault, and I told them —"

"What? You know your orders! Who are they?"

"It's me, Admiral Zakharin," Juan said. "Agent Bukir. We spoke in your office just a few minutes ago."

The phone was silent for a few seconds.

"Admiral, are you still feeling well?" Juan could picture Eddie threatening him with the vial.

"Oh . . . Oh, yes," Zakharin said reluctantly. "Now I recall. Seaman, you are to give every courtesy to the agents."

"Aye, sir," he said smartly, but the admiral was already off the line. He stood and said, "Come this way."

He walked over to a heavy steel door and fumbled around with a set of keys. He swung open the door and let them in.

"Do you need any assistance?" he said, groveling now that he'd been chastened.

"No, we can handle it from here," Gretchen said.

"We'll need some privacy," Juan said, "so make sure no one else enters while we're conducting our assessment."

He snapped his heels. "Yes, sir." The door closed quietly behind them. It was thick enough that there was no chance of being overheard.

Rows of old filing cabinets filled the musty room. It would have been easier to find what they were looking for if everything had been computerized, but infrastructure upgrades were a low priority for a base so far from Moscow.

"Where should we start searching?" Gretchen said.

"I'll take the engineering files. You look through the finances."

After a minute of scanning the cabinets,

Juan found one marked *Commercial Operations.* He yanked it open and confirmed that the files contained information about all of the naval base's extracurricular activities. No wonder the admiral kept access so tightly controlled. Unfortunately, the files were in chronological instead of alphabetical order, so he started with three years ago and worked forward.

Halfway through, Gretchen, who was two rows away, called out, "I found it!"

"The *Achilles*?"

She nodded, her face buried in a file. "It's the official accounting ledger. Wow, Antonovich opened up his wallet on this job and made it rain. You would not believe how much money is flowing through this base."

Juan thought back to how much it had cost to refit the *Oregon* and said, "Actually, I think I would."

"Zakharin is raking in millions a year."

"Why do you think he wanted the job badly enough to send Borodin to prison?"

"Well, I don't think his bosses back at headquarters know it's this much."

"Greed is never sated," Juan said as he kept riffling through the files.

"Oh, the admiral has been much naughtier than he was letting on. It looks like Zakharin's been keeping a separate account on the *Achilles* job. Probably does it with all the work here. It looks like the figures he reports get cut by twenty percent when they go to his bosses."

"They wouldn't be happy to find that out. Corrupt officers hate getting fleeced out of their fair shares. Does the ledger detail what the money was spent on?"

She shook her head. "It has the same coded entries. For example, this item is referred to as *LaWS.*" She spelled out the acronym in the Latin alphabet.

"It's not written in Cyrillic?"

"Most of them are, but not this one."

It sounded familiar to Juan, but he couldn't place it without context. She whistled. "I hope they got their money's worth. They could have built another yacht, for what it cost."

He was about to ask her to read out more when he came across the engineering specs for the *Achilles.*

"Bingo!" Juan said, pulling out the thick file.

Gretchen joined him by the cabinet. Juan flipped through the file, feeling the blood drain from his face as he read.

"Does it say what LaWS is?" she asked.

"Yes, it does. Now I remember what it stands for."

"What?"

"Laser weapon system."

Gretchen laughed. "You're kidding." When she saw his ashen face, she stopped. "You're not kidding."

"It gets worse," Juan said as he kept reading. "Much worse."

He pulled out his phone. No signal.

"We've got to warn Max. Now!"

Juan grabbed the file and raced for the door, but something in the pit of his stomach told him that he was already too late.

THIRTY-TWO

After pushing the engines to the limit so that the *Oregon* could catch up to the *Narwhal,* Max had been content to have the ship dawdle behind the Dutch cargo freighter as if it were heading for the same destination.

Then, out of nowhere, the *Achilles* appeared as if it had been waiting for them. It was still fifteen miles away, but the unique outline was unmistakable. Max had Linda put it on the main view screen, with the *Narwhal* inset beside it.

"What's Antonovich doing?"

"You think he's planning to take the column off the *Narwhal* before it reaches port?" Linda asked from her position at the radar and sonar.

"He can't," said Eric, who manned the helm. "No cranes on either ship."

Murph, sitting at the weapons station, chimed in, "Looks like there's a helicopter deck, but no way they've got a chopper that can lift thirty tons."

"Maybe he just wants to board to get a look at the column," Linda said.

Hali said, "But that wouldn't keep us from taking a look at it once it reaches port."

"Any radio communications between them?" Max asked.

Hali checked the radio for chatter, then shook his head. "Nada."

"I don't like this. Something's wrong with this scenario."

Max peered at the screen and saw an odd protuberance on the *Achilles*'s deck.

"Linda, zoom in on the yacht as much as you can."

Because the yacht was so far away, the picture was blurry, but there was definitely a gray object on top of the yacht that didn't fit in.

Then to Max's surprise, it rotated.

A turret. And now the gun barrel was obvious.

"What the . . ."

A flash of light erupted from the barrel.

By the time he finished yelling, "Battle stations!" the *Narwhal*'s superstructure had blown apart in a fiery explosion.

The timing didn't make sense. The explosion on the cargo ship happened much too fast after the shot was taken.

"Murph, how long from shot to explosion?"

"A little more than two seconds, by my calcs."

"The projectile traveled five miles in just over two seconds," repeated Max. "That's impossible!"

The muzzle velocity of a typical shipboard gun was 2,600 feet per second. The round should have taken ten seconds to cross that distance.

The *Achilles*'s gun fired again. This time, he counted to himself. Two seconds later, another fireball erupted from the *Narwhal.*

There was only one type of weapon that could launch rounds at that speed.

Murph beat him to it. "My God, they have a railgun."

The *Narwhal* was being systematically taken apart. Most likely the crew was already dead. Another few rounds and the ship would be in pieces.

The *Oregon*'s gun would be useless at this range.

"Mr. Murphy, ready an Exocet."

The ship-to-ship missile was one of the deadliest in the world. A single one fired by the Argentine Navy during the Falklands

War sank the Royal Navy destroyer *Shef-field.*

"Exocet ready!"

The *Achilles* launched another round.

"Fire!"

"Missile away!" The Exocet rocketed from its tube.

At the same time, the railgun shell tore at the foundering *Narwhal,* which was awash in flames.

The missile skimmed across the water at seven hundred miles an hour. At that speed, it would cover the fifteen miles in a minute.

It would be too late for the *Narwhal,* but seeing how the railgun was systematically dismantling the cargo ship, Max was now more worried about the *Oregon.*

"Mr. Stone," Max said, "put us bow on to the *Achilles.* I want us to present as small a target as we can."

"Coming around," Eric said. With the two magnetohydrodynamic engines thrusting at full power in opposite directions, the *Oregon* could practically rotate on its own axis. The camera focused on the yacht compensated for the turn.

The *Narwhal* was already sinking at the stern. The Jaffa Column would be at the bottom of the Mediterranean in minutes. Now all Max could do was watch the flaming tail of the Exocet as it streaked toward the *Achilles.*

As with its namesake, the replica *Narwhal* didn't stand a chance against the railgun, and Golov was finding the attack somewhat routine. Next, he'd turn his attention to the *Nogero.* It was larger than the feeder ship, but he'd sink it all the same.

"We have a missile launch!" the radar operator shouted.

"What? From where?"

"From that tramp freighter. One minute to impact."

"You must be mistaken. Is there a warship behind it?"

"No, sir."

"Aircraft in the region?"

"None detected, Captain."

Golov felt his adrenaline surge. Now he had a challenge. He put the image of the missile on his console. Smoke trailed it as the missile he now recognized as an Exocet raced toward him.

"Activate the LaWS."

"Activating LaWS."

The dome over the laser weapon system retracted, exposing the telescope-like laser.

"Forty seconds to impact!"

"Target the missile."

"Targeting missile." Red crosshairs lined up on the missile.

"Fire!"

Unlike the recoil from the railgun, the laser functioned with little more than a faint whine.

The nose of the missile glowed red for a fraction of a second. Then, without warning, the missile shattered as its warhead and fuel detonated.

"Another missile launched, Captain! Now two torpedoes in the water!"

"So our adversary has a few surprises," Golov said. "Ready the mini-torpedoes. Target the second missile with the laser."

Sirkal liked to quote Sun Tzu's *The Art of War.* So did Golov, and one of his favorite lines was "What the ancients called a clever fighter is one who not only wins but excels in winning with ease."

"Turn the railgun on the *Nogero,*" he ordered, and then smiled at his cleverness.

Golov was going to win this battle with ease.

THIRTY-THREE

Juan raced through the secret passageway, leaving Gretchen to close the hidden door behind him. The thick concrete of the old Soviet building made getting a cell phone signal tricky, but he finally had a connection. The *Oregon*'s line was ringing.

As soon as Hali picked up, Juan said, "Put me through to Max, Hali."

"Aye, Chairman." There was a pause before Hali came back. "Max wants to know if it can wait."

It wasn't like Max to blow him off. "What's happening?"

"We're in the middle of a fight with the *Achilles.*"

It's just what Juan had feared. "Put Max on right now."

"Aye, sir." Another pause.

Max came on the line.

"You picked a doozy of a time to call, my friend." Even though Max sounded calm,

Juan could detect the strain of battle in his voice. "The *Achilles* has a railgun."

"I know," Juan said. "We found the engineering specs. Any damage to the *Oregon*?"

"Not yet. But they did a number on the *Narwhal.*"

"You have to get out of there if you can."

"Too late for that. I've already fired two Exocets, and Golov swatted them out of the sky like they were gnats. We can't tell how he's doing it. He didn't use missiles of his own, and there are no tracers from a Gatling gun."

"He has a solid-state laser weapon system."

Max whistled. "That explains it."

"And don't bother with torpedoes, either. The *Achilles* is equipped with mini-torpedoes that can intercept our heavy torpedoes."

"Also too late. Sonar shows the two I launched exploding two thousand yards from the target. We're pretty much screwed, aren't we?"

Juan burst into Zakharin's office.

"Maybe not," he said, and grabbed the admiral by the lapel, dragging him to the desk. He threw the folder down and tossed his phone to Eddie. "Show me where the disarming code is."

Gretchen closed the entrance to the passageway, and Linc stood by the office door.

"What? I don't know what you're —"

"Yes, you do. For every weapon you mount on these clients' ships, you install hidden disarming codes into the software that can be received by a radio signal so these specially outfitted ships won't be used against the Russian Navy. I know because we found the code you planted on the *Oregon*. Now, I'm sure you hid one in the *Achilles* software, too. Tell me where it is in this pile of papers."

"I can't . . ."

"I don't have time to mess around with this." Juan yanked the Colt Defender from Linc's hand and pushed the barrel against Zakharin's temple. "After you're dead, they can come take me away. But either you tell me what the code is in the next ten seconds or I put a bullet in your brain."

Zakharin sneered. "You're bluffing."

Juan cocked the hammer. "My ship is about to be sunk. If that happens, you're a dead man . . . One!"

Zakharin began to nervously flip through the file.

"Two!"

"I can't remember where —"

"Three!"

"Chairman," Eddie said.

"Four! What?"

"Hali says they're being fired upon."

"Hard aport!" Max yelled. "Full power astern!"

The *Achilles* had fired its railgun two seconds ago. Now that the *Oregon* was only twelve miles away, it would take the shell just six seconds to hit.

He counted down in his head as the ship slewed around. Four seconds later, the *Oregon* was rocked by a sonic boom that blew out the windows on the bridge as the projectile buzzed past them. Like he had with the *Narwhal,* the captain of the distant yacht had targeted the superstructure to take out all the controls and crew simultaneously.

Max had bet on the tactic. The main disadvantage of the railgun was that its round was a dumb weapon. It was essentially a cannon shell and couldn't adjust course in flight, unlike a guided missile. The unique agility and speed of the *Oregon* was the only thing that kept it from being struck.

But Max knew Golov wouldn't make the same mistake twice. He'd aim for the hull next time. The Gatling guns and Metal Storm array were useless against such a high-velocity weapon.

"Eric, full speed ahead. Random evasive maneuvers."

The *Oregon*'s hull was armor-plated, but it couldn't repel rounds of that energy. If one of them pierced an ammo magazine, the entire ship would go up in a blast that would break it in two. And if it hit the engine room, they'd be dead in the water.

"Another shot!" Linda shouted.

"All back! Hard astarboard!"

Eric masterfully swung the ship again.

Max counted.

This time, they weren't so lucky. Although the round missed the hull, it sliced right through the amidships crane, one of the two that were operational. The base blew apart and the steel rigging fell onto the deck, leaving a gash in the steel, before tumbling over the side.

Max looked at Hali, huddling with Murph. They had Juan on the line. Max had heard him demanding the disarming code from the Russian admiral, the same kind of code Murph himself had removed from the *Oregon*'s software.

"Tell me Juan's got some magic trick up his sleeve," Max said.

"Working on it" was all Murph would say.

"Shot's away!" Linda called out.

"Full speed ahead!"

Max braced himself as the *Oregon* lurched forward.

Six seconds later, the ship was jolted by an explosion that nearly threw Max out of his chair.

"Damage report!"

Linda checked the closed-circuit cameras. "Looks like they got us in the forward hold. It's above the waterline, so we don't have flooding, but the missile battery is off-line."

"Permanently?"

"Can't say yet."

"We can't take much more pounding like this," Max said. "Murph, give me some good news."

"The admiral spilled his guts," Hali said as Murph furiously tapped at his keyboard. "He's broadcasting the disarming signal now."

Max held his breath to see if it worked. He knew ShadowFoe's reputation as a programmer, so it was possible she had removed the disarming code.

They'd know soon enough. Because the next round from the *Achilles* would be the kill shot.

THIRTY-FOUR

Golov had to admit it. He was impressed. He thought the intriguing warship disguised as a rusty old cargo vessel would go down with two shots, but her commander was doing a fine job dodging the *Achilles*'s automated targeting system. In the end, though, his efforts would be useless. The ships were getting close enough to each other that evasion would soon be impossible. The end was near.

He smiled as he took control of the firing solution. This was just like hunting ducks as a child, back in Ukraine, when he learned to lead the target. He centered the crosshairs on the center of the ship. No matter which way the *Nogero* turned, it would suffer catastrophic damage.

"Fire at will," he ordered.

"Firing," came the reply.

But nothing happened. The hypersonic railgun remained silent. The weapons operator stabbed futilely at his console several times, then turned to Golov with a puzzled look.

"The railgun is off-line, Captain!"

Golov jumped from his seat. "What?"

The officer frantically worked the controls. "I . . . I don't know. According to all of the readouts, the weapon status is nominal. It should be firing."

"Is there a jam in the gun?"

"No, sir. The round loaded correctly."

"Did the barrel overheat?"

"Temperature gauge shows normal heat dissipation. The barrel is cool and true."

If it wasn't a mechanical issue, then it had to be a problem with the software. Without Ivana here, diagnosing the error could take hours.

"How long to reboot the system?" Golov demanded.

The weapons officer shook his head. "At least thirty minutes. Captain, I thought I saw . . ." He hesitated.

"You saw what?"

"For a moment, just as I was about to fire, there seemed to be a signal interrupt as if the system were receiving new commands. Then it went back to normal."

"A signal? From where?"

"I don't know."

Golov blanched. Could it be sabotage? Did he have another traitor on board? It would be the most opportune moment for someone to disable his offensive weapons . . .

Then he had an even worse thought. If someone had deactivated the railgun, then they could have shut down all of the weapons simultaneously, including the defensive systems.

"What's the status of the laser?"

"Nominal, Captain."

"Fire it."

"What's the target?"

"I think we're the target. Fire it at the water, starboard side. Make it boil."

The officer shrugged. "Aye, sir. Firing."

Again, nothing happened.

Golov's stomach went cold. Now he was the duck. And he was firmly on his seat.

"Get us out of here!" he yelled. "Turn one hundred and eighty degrees!"

"Turning, aye!"

"Full speed! I want everything we've got out of the engines."

The *Achilles* slewed around and raced away in the opposite direction.

Golov slammed his palms on the wood console in frustration. Despite a worthy adversary, certain victory had been at hand.

But instead of savoring the taste of winning a hard-fought battle, he was fleeing with his tail between his legs and readying himself for the announcement of another incoming missile, one that he would have no way to shoot down this time.

He loathed being on the other side of the crosshairs.

"It worked!" Murph cried out as they watched the *Achilles* come about. "The weapons must be off-line. She's making a run for it."

"Not so fast," Max said. "They're not slinking away that easily. Murph, can you get the missile launcher back up?"

"No can do. It'll need some serious attention from welders."

"What about our guns?"

"Ready to go, but we're way out of range."

"Then let's get closer. Eric, full speed ahead. We're not letting him get away."

"Power at one hundred percent," Eric replied.

Max felt himself pushed back in his chair as the *Oregon* leaped forward. Soon the ship was pushing forty-five knots.

The stern of the *Achilles* was solidly in their sights. All they needed was to close the gap.

After a few minutes, the *Achilles* didn't seem any closer. In fact, it looked like it was getting smaller on the screen.

"My eyesight must finally be going on me," Max said. "Linda, what's our distance to target?"

"I don't believe it," she blurted. "Distance is fourteen miles — and increasing. She's outpacing us by at least ten knots, maybe fifteen."

Max couldn't contain his shock. "That's impossible!" He took pride in the *Oregon*'s speed. No other ship her size could even come close to her pace. Yet here was the exception receding into the distance on-screen.

"Think she's got magnetohydrodynamic engines like we do?" Murph said.

"No," Linda said with a headset pressed to her ear. "I can hear screws on the sonar. But they seem to be muffled somehow."

Eric looked at her. "Muffled?"

"Like they're covered in Styrofoam."

He thought for a moment, then turned to Max. "Remember the Shkval torpedoes we stole from the Iranians? Could the *Achilles* have that kind of propulsion?"

Max shook his head. "Those were rocket torpedoes. Incredibly high-speed, but short-range."

"Right, but they also pumped out air bubbles for supercavitation to reduce drag in the water. We could be seeing the same thing here, but with screws doing the job instead of rockets."

"I've heard of it in experimental ships, but nothing of that size. The bubbles would have to encase the entire hull."

"Well, they're getting away from us somehow," Murph said. "Eric may have pegged it."

"I'm reading a pressure loss in our cooling system," Eric said. "We'll have to check it, but it's likely that one of the pipes was punctured when they took out our missile launcher."

"How bad?" Max asked.

"If we keep running at full power, we might do irreparable damage to the engines."

Max grimaced. He hated to let the *Achilles* get away, but following them farther would be futile at this point. And if the *Achilles* figured out how to get the weapons back online quickly and turned around to attack again, the *Oregon* obviously couldn't outrun her.

He sighed and said, "Let them go. Reduce to half speed and put us on a heading to Naples. I know a guy there who owes me a favor. If we need any additional equipment to make repairs, he'll get it for us."

As the ship came about, the looks of worry on the faces of the rest of the op center crew mirrored Max's own concern. It was an unfamiliar sensation, contemplating a scenario that had been to this point unthinkable. If they ever again had to battle the *Achilles,* a ship that was faster and more powerfully armed than the state-of-the-art *Oregon,* how could they possibly win?

THIRTY-FIVE

Once Juan was certain the *Oregon* was out of danger, he hung up the phone and stared at Admiral Zakharin with a steely gaze.

"You're lucky no one on my ship was injured," he said.

"What about the *Oregon*?" Eddie asked.

"Some damage, but Max thinks we can get everything back in working order within a day or two at a maintenance facility. He's sending the destination to Tiny so we can meet up with them." Juan didn't say that their destination was Naples so that the admiral wouldn't overhear it.

"Why did you think ShadowFoe hadn't disabled the disarming codes like you did?" Gretchen asked.

"I'm sure when Zakharin's predecessor found out we'd discovered ours, they began to do a much more thorough job of hiding it. Besides, ShadowFoe thinks like a hacker. She might not have specifically looked for something like a kill code. I, on the other hand, think like a spy."

Linc nodded at the admiral. "What do we do with him?"

"Well, I was going to have him escort us back to the airport," Juan said. "But I don't think that's necessary now." He looked pointedly at Gretchen, who was huddled over the accounting ledger with her phone, snapping photos.

"Just about done here," she said, then trained her eyes on Zakharin. "This is a lot of incriminating evidence you have here. I've just uploaded it to the servers at Interpol. We'll keep the information to ourselves, unless, of course, there's reason for us to release it to — I don't know — the Kremlin?"

Juan smiled mirthlessly. "I don't think the current leadership in Moscow would forgive reading in the news about a Russian admiral turning his naval base into a personal piggy bank, especially when he isn't sharing all the profits."

Zakharin glared at them. "What do you want now?"

"You've probably built up substantial savings from your activities here — enough to fund a generous retirement at a very nice beach resort, I imagine. So this is where it ends. No more ships will be refitted here."

Zakharin's eyes bugged from his head. "What? You want me to give up a multimillion-dollar business?"

"That's about the size of it."

"Or what? You'll kill me?" Zakharin focused on the vial of clear liquid in Eddie's hand.

"No, we'll share your illicit moneymaking with the public and expose what really goes on here."

"And expose yourselves at the same time." The admiral grinned. He obviously thought he held the ace.

Juan walked over to Gretchen and picked up two file folders that were under the one she was using.

"You mean these?" He slammed the files on the desk. Each of them said OREGON on the cover. He had removed them from the vault when he took the *Achilles* files. "No sense in leaving these lying around here." Juan had noticed the one piece of up-to-date equipment in the admiral's office was a high-capacity-level P7 paper shredder, the kind the CIA used to destroy classified documents.

He dropped each file on the *Oregon* into the shredder. The machine whined as it tore the paper into particles smaller than a grain of sand.

"*I* still know."

"All you know is the name of a ship that can be easily altered. And I don't think you'll be able to share the information if Moscow decides to send you to the same Siberian prison that the previous base commander went to."

Zakharin slumped back in his chair, knowing he'd been beaten. He nodded at Eddie's vial. "Can you at least put that away?"

"This?" Juan said, taking the vial from Eddie. He approached the admiral, who cringed back in his chair. Juan raised it over Zakharin, then tipped the contents into his own mouth.

Zakharin let out a gasp.

"What?" Juan said in feigned confusion. "It's just water."

The admiral gaped. "You tricked me?"

"Although I'm sure the Russian security services would love to get their hands on a binary poison, none exist, as far as I know." He looked around at Eddie, Linc, and Gretchen. "You guys ever heard of one?"

They all shrugged and shook their heads, much to their amusement and Zakharin's chagrin.

"Come on," Juan said, urging the admiral to his feet. "I'm sure you want to escort us safely off the base personally. Remember, while the binary poison might not work, my gun still does."

As expected from the weaselly admiral, he didn't put up any resistance to letting them go peacefully. Just in case, though, Juan had Tiny get the wheels up on the plane and fly out of Russian airspace as soon as they were aboard.

The first person he called, once they were in the air, was Langston Overholt at the CIA. Juan told him about the *Achilles*'s sinking of the *Narwhal* and the attack on the *Oregon.*

"Max said he got it all recorded. Apparently, it's a bit fuzzy because of the distances involved, but it was definitely the *Achilles.*"

"Can you see the ship's name in the video?" Overholt asked.

"At fifteen miles? I doubt it."

"Then we can't do anything."

"Are you kidding?"

"See it from my perspective, Juan. You want me to inform Europe's navies that Maxim Antonovich, one of the richest men in Russia, sank a Dutch cargo vessel in the middle of the Mediterranean with a railgun hidden on his luxury yacht? They'd laugh so hard, they'd drool their wine on their shirts."

"What about the video?"

"With special effects these days? Easily doctored. You know that. And we can't exactly explain where the video came from, can we?"

"What about an inspection of some kind?"

"To look for what? Weapons that pop up out of the decks? They'd have to tear the ship apart to find them. They'd risk being made fools of and angering one of the richest men in the world. Imagine if Germany called me up and told me that Paul Allen's *Octopus* sank a fishing trawler with a phaser. I'd want incontrovertible proof before I even considered asking to take a look at the yacht. The investigation alone could take months before we moved on it."

Juan fumed. "So we do nothing? Antonovich gets away with murder, not to mention taking our money?"

He looked at the photo of Antonovich that Murph had found on the Internet. The billionaire hadn't been seen in public for years, so it wasn't a recent picture. He was in his sixties, with a bit of a stomach, salt-and-pepper hair, and a crescent-shaped port-wine stain on his left cheek. According to the CIA, his patronage and loyalty to the

Kremlin had come under suspicion recently, leading to his reclusive and paranoid behavior.

Now he was funding a more sinister operation. Perhaps he got frustrated with his progress in changing Russia and was on to other ambitions. Whatever was going on, Juan was sure of one thing. Antonovich and his people were behind it.

"*I* do nothing," Overholt said. "*You* keep going. Personally, I think you're right that something bigger is going on here. It's bad enough that Antonovich seems to have built his anti-*Oregon* and assembled his own crew of mercenaries that can take on the same types of missions that you can. Now we've found out that there was an attack on an electrical substation outside Frankfurt last night, so there just might be a connection between the bank heist and the European electrical grid, like you thought. I'll send you the details. And we'll keep sifting for evidence about the threat to the financial system, including the latest bank failure in France. We haven't received any ransom demands as of yet, so unless we crack the virus that was installed at Credit Condamine, we don't have much to go on. What's your next step?"

Juan thought about it and texted a question to Max. Then, without waiting for a reply, he answered his old mentor.

"Well, with the *Achilles* vanished and the Jaffa Column at the bottom of the Med, it looks like we're fresh out of leads right now. There's no way to complete Napoleon's message without it."

Overholt cleared his throat. "It's not like you to give up so easily."

Juan's phone buzzed and he glanced at Max's response.

~800 feet

Close to the limit but manageable.

"I said we're out of leads *right now*. That should change in the next couple of days."

"Why?"

Juan texted back Start prepping Nomad, then answered Overholt.

"Because we're going to dive on the wreck of the *Narwhal* and raise the column."

Thirty-Six

MELILLA, MOROCCO

Instead of going to France as they'd originally planned, Golov thought it would be wise to use the more out-of-the-way Moroccan port to pick up Ivana, Sirkal, and O'Connor after their missions. Within minutes of arrival, the *Achilles* was back at sea and headed toward the Strait of Gibraltar.

While Ivana got to work on diagnosing the software malfunction, Sirkal and O'Connor debriefed Golov in his quarters about the Frankfurt operation. The office adjoining his cabin was as lavishly appointed as the rest of the yacht, with the finest woods and marble from around the world. The top-notch furnishings made the cramped yet comfortable accommodations aboard the frigate he'd commanded seem like the interior of a garbage scow. Still, a small part of him missed the naval camaraderie and sense of purpose.

Of course, he realized those feelings had all been a phantom the moment his ship and career were stolen away from him by the Russians. The luxury that now surrounded him didn't just symbolize wealth. They were the trappings of power. And he intended to take some for himself.

"From what I saw on the news," Golov said, sitting in his leather chair behind his imposing mahogany desk, "I understand that the mission was a success."

"The whole transformer substation was blazing away by the time the *Polizei* arrived," O'Connor said as he munched on an apple and lounged on the sofa. "The papers said it took the fire department two days to put it out."

"It's completely out of commission?" Golov asked.

Sirkal, who stood ramrod straight during the report, nodded. "A total loss. They'll have to replace all of the equipment. It could take months."

"What about the power redistribution?"

"According to our sources, the power outages were limited to the Frankfurt region. But that's only because of quick work to shunt the electricity to other major substations. The remaining transformers can handle the load, but only barely. The adjustments required balancing power across the twenty-four countries connected to the grid. Any further transformer outages and they'd have to shut down some of the power plants to compensate."

Golov smiled. "Perfect."

For Operation Dynamo to work, central Europe's power plants had to be operating at full capacity. The power grid, also known as the Continental Europe Synchronous Area, formed the largest interconnected electric system in the world, supplying over seven hundred gigawatts of electricity on a daily basis from nuclear, coal, gas, solar, and wind power plants. High-tension lines crossed borders freely so that power could be distributed efficiently to where it was needed most. But with the key Frankfurt substation destroyed, the grid now had little protection if there was a power surge in the system. All it would take to overload the grid would be a push in the right direction and Dynamo was designed to do just that.

When that happened, the blackout would span the entire continent, from the Atlantic coast to the Ukrainian border, and from the North Sea to the Mediterranean. Over four hundred million people would be plunged into darkness. Transport would grind to a standstill, as petrol station pumps no longer operated, city traffic lights were extinguished, airports shut down, and rail switching operations went off-line. Banks would be unable to make any transactions and businesses would be paralyzed, causing an economic crisis. The euro would plummet in value instantly. And the best part was that Golov would make sure the Russian government took the fall for all of it, paying them back for invading his homeland and taking his ship from him.

He had always liked the symmetry of the plan. Napoleon's invasion of Russia was the beginning of his downfall, as the European powers rose against him, and now the treasure he was forced to leave behind was the catalyst for Dynamo. From the grave, the French emperor would finally get his revenge on the continent that exiled him not once, but twice.

"Excellent work," Golov said with a gleam in his eye. "I will have to let Mr. Antonovich know about our progress. Get your men prepared for the final phase of Dynamo. I want them to be drilled and ready in four days."

"They will be," Sirkal said confidently.

"For their cut of thirty billion euros, I'd hope so," O'Connor said with a laugh, but neither Sirkal nor Golov joined in. He continued. "What? You think they're doing this for free?"

"You know they're never going to see that money," Sirkal said. It just wasn't possible. Too many potential witnesses after the fact.

O'Connor smirked. "Right, but *they* don't know that."

Golov stared at him for a moment, then said, "Dismissed." Some naval habits died hard.

They left Golov to contemplate doing away with the crew that had performed so well. He didn't take the prospect lightly, but he felt no loyalty or responsibility to the men and women that he'd inherited or hired. They were motivated by money, just as he was, and likely would do the same if their roles were reversed. Once Golov had left behind his sense of duty and acquired a taste for wealth, there had been no turning back. He was willing to do whatever it took to accomplish his goals.

He wasn't sure how long he'd been sitting when there was a light rap on the door and Ivana entered.

She cocked her head at him. "Anything wrong, Papa?"

He shook himself out of his dark reverie. "No, dear, come in."

She came and sat on the desk, patting his arm like the concerned daughter she was. "Are you sure you're all right? You look like you need some sleep."

"I'll be fine. There'll be plenty of time to sleep when this is over. Did you find out what went wrong with the weapons systems?"

"Yes, and I was not happy when I found it. The Russians left a little present in our code."

"A present?"

"A disarming code. It was triggered by radio signal. That's why all the weapons went down without warning. The other ship must have broadcast it. Don't worry, I've stripped it out of the operating system, and I'll make sure there are no more surprises like that."

Golov leaned back and looked at the ceiling in thought. "How did the crew of that fake tramp steamer know . . ." He snapped his head around. "Zakharin told them."

Ivana pursed her lips. "That's one possible explanation."

"Then the question is whether he's partnering with them somehow, perhaps paid off . . ."

"Or he was blackmailed or forced into it."

He smiled. Just like her mother, she could

complete his sentences for him.

"I think we need to talk to him."

"Already checked. His personal transport filed a flight plan for Barcelona this morning. Apparently, he has a villa on the Costa Brava."

He didn't need to ask how she knew all that. Her skill at finding information about people was unparalleled.

Golov calculated how much of a detour it would take to go to northern Spain. With an adjustment in cruising speed, they'd have plenty of time.

He called up to the bridge. "New course. Set a heading for Barcelona, three-quarters speed."

"Aye, Captain."

Almost immediately, he felt the yacht turning.

"It's time we find out who we're up against and take the offensive."

"I may have a little more info about that." She took out her phone and showed him a photo. He recognized the building in the background as the Credit Condamine bank in Monaco. Five people stood in front of it. Three of them he'd never seen before, two younger men and a tiny woman with her hair cut in a shaggy silver bob.

But he was very familiar with the other

two. He'd just met them a couple of nights ago at the Malta museum gala.

"I'm guessing their real names aren't Naomi and Gabriel Jackson," he said.

"And they're not billionaires from New York. This photo is from a security camera the day after our bank heist. She's an Interpol agent named Gretchen Wagner. The rest of the people with her, including the man calling himself Gabriel Jackson, presented themselves as insurance investigators. I doubt that's true, either."

"Then who are they?"

Ivana shrugged. "I can't find anything about them. Which, actually, says a lot about them. Not many organizations could hide that kind of information from me."

"All the more reason to chat with Admiral Zakharin. I think this will provide a good training exercise for Sirkal's men." Golov stood. "And speaking of a chat, it's time I went to see Mr. Antonovich."

Ivana escorted him to the door. "Is he still requesting that the air filters in his room be changed three times a day?"

"Four."

Ivana rolled her eyes and kissed Golov on the cheek before she turned and walked off in the other direction.

Golov took the stairs down to Antonovich's palatial suite and nodded to the personal guard who was stationed outside the door. He knocked and entered without waiting for a response.

He found Maxim Antonovich seated at his desk, wearing only a pair of silk shorts and black socks. His bristly hair, transformed in the last six months from salt-and-pepper to completely gray, sprouted in all directions, and his distended belly scraped against the front edge of the desk as he scribbled away on a notepad. He didn't look up when Golov entered.

"My air filters haven't been changed in two hours," he grumbled. "I can taste the buildup of dust."

Golov couldn't help but chuckle at the man's eccentricities. "I'll make sure it's taken care of, Mr. Antonovich."

He walked over to the expansive windows that displayed a superb view of the ocean. During port visits, the windows, which were impregnated with LCD panels, would darken so that no one could see in while still providing a dim view out. Through the bulletproof glass, the sun glistened off the placid seas stretching to the horizon in front of the *Achilles*.

"What do you want?" Antonovich said, still writing furiously.

"I thought you'd like to know that our operation in Frankfurt was a success, which means we will need you to join our team for a land excursion in a few days."

Antonovich stopped writing and looked at Golov. The port-wine stain on his cheek was dotted with stubble. His face looked more drawn and tired than Golov had ever seen it. Maybe that's what Ivana saw in his own face.

"Do you really think this will work?" the billionaire asked.

"I know it will. As long as you perform your part of the mission, that is. What are you writing?"

"My memoirs. Not that anyone will ever see them. I wrote a new last will and testament earlier this morning, but I assume that will be fruitless as well. My cousins will squabble over the corpse of my businesses until they're scraps and sold off piecemeal."

Golov nodded silently.

"Did you find out who forced your retreat yesterday?" Antonovich asked with mild amusement.

"We're in the act of finding out."

"I had this yacht designed to take on anything on the high seas and you were beaten by a rusty cargo ship?"

Golov scowled at Antonovich. He must

have been watching the battle.

"Believe me, if we run into them again, the results will be different."

"We'll see," Antonovich said. "And what's going to happen to the *Achilles* when this is all over?"

"I'm afraid she won't survive the operation, beauty that she is."

Golov thought he could spot the glistening of tears in Antonovich's eyes. The billionaire had no children, and his ex-wife claimed a huge chunk of his wealth long ago. The *Achilles* was his baby.

"No one has asked about me?"

"Oh, we've had inquiries from various business partners, but your accountant is handling those requests. He's quite good at your signature."

Golov walked over to the door to leave.

"And if I cooperate with your plan, you'll let me go?" Antonovich asked plaintively.

"Of course," Golov said with a smile. "That's the deal."

He closed and locked the door behind him, leaving the guard at his post outside.

It really wasn't the deal. Maxim Antonovich, his former patron and now prisoner, would face the same fate as the rest of the crew. No witnesses.

THIRTY-SEVEN

The damage to the *Oregon* was not as serious as originally feared and repairs were made in record time to get the missile launchers and engines back in operational order. The holes in the ship were patched up with metal sheeting, which didn't look out of place on the hull's dilapidated façade. A more thorough overhaul would have to wait, but Juan was confident in Max's assessment that the ship was ready to sail again, only twenty-four hours after it had arrived in Naples. By the next evening, the *Oregon* neared the site of the *Narwhal*'s sinking west of Sicily.

While the technicians in the moon pool prepped the underwater vehicles for deployment, Juan sat in the conference room as Gretchen, Murph, and Eric briefed him on their analysis of the computer data she had received about the bank heist. As usual, the two eager software experts were throwing around jargon he'd never heard before.

"What's a *multipartite virus?*" Juan asked.

Murph, who was dressed in a black T-shirt that read *I'm just here to establish an alibi,* said, "It's really impressive work. Most computer viruses infect the system in only one way. But a multipartite, also called a hybrid virus, infects along a variety of vectors, allowing it to propagate very easily and quickly. We think that's what ShadowFoe installed when she got access to the Credit Condamine system."

"And there's no way to use a backup to reinstall the system?"

Eric shook his head. "That's the insidious part of a multipartite virus. It installs itself in the root sector of a computer system, which means that even if you wipe it from memory, it'll reinfect the computer as soon as the system starts up. It's incredibly hard to get rid of completely unless you know what to look for."

"So our money is lost?"

"Whoa, whoa, whoa!" said Murph, putting his hands up in a defensive posture. "No one said that. I'm not letting a virus eat up my money."

"The one good thing about these hybrid viruses," Eric said, "is that they install themselves in a lot of places in the system, so there are lots of opportunities for us to find it. Once we can crack the underlying code, we should be able to dig it out."

"Have they detected this virus on any other bank's system?" Juan asked Gretchen.

She shrugged. "There's no way to know without finding the algorithm used to design the virus. But Credit Condamine was closely connected to a number of other banks on a secure network. It's possible that once ShadowFoe had penetrated the bank's external security by kidnapping the president and using his biometric log-in, she had access to banks throughout Europe."

"Do you think the failure of the bank in Paris is the one she warned us about?"

"Has to be. It's too coincidental to be unrelated."

"So what's the ultimate goal? To bring down the financial system one bank at a time unless they get some ransom?"

"I doubt it. There are easier ways for hackers to take large sums of money from financial institutions. Just last year, we discovered that malware had been introduced in some of the biggest banks in the world through phishing emails. JPMorgan Chase and the Agricultural Bank of China were just a couple of them. The criminals observed banking operations for two years, directly siphoning off money to ATMs and phony accounts across the globe."

"How much was stolen?"

"Banks aren't exactly eager to share the news that their systems have been penetrated. Not good for the trust of depositors. But the estimates range as high as nine hundred million dollars."

Murph whistled, and Eric said, "Not bad, for two years of work."

"What I can't understand," Murph said, "is why Antonovich would be doing this. He's already a billionaire. Now he has to get money by stealing it? Doesn't make sense."

"There has to be a larger agenda at work," Gretchen said. "My superiors at Interpol think that Antonovich could be trying to work his way back into the Kremlin's good graces by helping the Russian government destabilize the West. If he brings down the financial system, even for a short time, it could enhance Russia's negotiating power in the region."

"Or start a war," Juan added. "If lasting damage is done, we could return to the days before the Berlin Wall fell. The embargo against Russia for the Ukraine incursion tanked the ruble and the markets in Moscow. If there's evidence that Russia launched an all-out cyberattack on the European financial system, trading between the two blocs could shut down completely."

"I know some of our former colleagues wouldn't mind that," Gretchen said. "The CIA would love another showdown with the big bad Russians. The problem is that we have no proof that Antonovich was involved in the Credit Condamine heist. His yacht was in Monaco at the time, but it's all circumstantial evidence."

"The *Achilles* sinking the *Narwhal* isn't circumstantial," Eric said. "I watched it happen."

Gretchen replied, "But the only link between the sinking and the banking infiltration is the *Achilles*'s presence in both places."

"Another question, then," Murph said. "Why would ShadowFoe leave us a message if she never intended to collect a ransom?"

"Because she knew what the response from banks would be," Gretchen said. "The threat in her message would trigger an update in their cybersecurity software as soon as possible. Yesterday, a man was found dead in a Paris apartment, killed during a supposed robbery. He happened to be the chief of computer security for a firm that most European banks use. We think that

ShadowFoe, or one of her accomplices, forced him to give them access to the updated software. Now the bank shutdown virus could be spreading throughout the entire industry and we'd never know it."

"The real mystery is how all of this is connected," Juan said, ticking off the items on his fingers. "We've got a bank heist, to possibly bring down the European financial system; an attack on the electrical grid, which, so far, hasn't had any major repercussions; a cryptic diary written by Napoleon Bonaparte before he was supposedly abducted from exile on St. Helena; and a billionaire so desperate to keep anyone from finding the treasure that was stolen during the invasion of Russia that he sinks a ship carrying a three-thousand-year-old stone column. Am I missing anything?"

Murph smirked. "Well, when you put it that way, it sounds like those things should have nothing to do with each other."

"The only way we'll figure it out," Eric said, "is if we locate the treasure and find whatever Antonovich is trying to keep secret."

"And I know how you love to solve Russian mysteries," Gretchen said, an inside joke about their Moscow mission together. Her accompanying smile didn't escape the notice of Murph and Eric.

Juan kept himself from blushing, otherwise he'd never hear the end of it. He pointed at the two coding experts. "If we retrieve the column, can you two decipher the clues that Napoleon left?"

Eric and Murph exchanged a glance, then nodded confidently in unison.

"Absolutely," Murph said. "No problem."

"With enough time, of course," Eric said.

The two of them took their computers and left.

"Do you think they really can do it?" Gretchen asked when they were alone.

"They're the best in the business," Juan said. "If they can't do it, no one can."

She leaned over and looked him in the eye. "You really trust your people, don't you?"

He returned her gaze. "I wouldn't have hired them if I didn't."

"That's admirable. Not every boss is like that."

"This isn't your typical company."

"I've noticed." She paused, and then a smile curled at the corners of her mouth. "I forgot what you were like."

"I never forgot what you were like."

"Do you wonder how things could have been back at the CIA if we hadn't been married? To other people, I mean."

Juan had often wondered the same thing over the last few days, but before he had a chance to answer, the intercom on the table buzzed.

Gretchen sighed. "The captain's work is never done."

Juan stabbed the button.

"Your timing is impeccable," he said into the microphone.

"I do have a knack for that sort of thing," Max replied, thinking he was getting a compliment.

"Are we ready for the dive?"

"The equipment's prepped, but we have a bit of an issue with the dive site."

"You can't locate the container?"

"No, we found it on the side-scan sonar. The problem is with the *Narwhal.*"

"What about it?"

"She settled on her side. On a slope. With the container holding the Jaffa Column still partially attached."

"I'm assuming that's not what you were expecting," Gretchen said.

Juan slowly shook his head. He had hoped the *Narwhal* had settled on the sea bottom in an upright position, making the container recovery relatively easy. With her hull in an awkward position, the degree of difficulty had increased by a factor of ten.

"Got it, Max," Juan said with an eyebrow raised at Gretchen. "Not great."

"It could have been worse," Max said, and Juan could picture his sarcastic grin. "At least she's not upside down."

"*Always the optimist* is not something I would ever say to you. I'll be down in a minute."

He closed the connection.

"You're going down in that sub?" Gretchen asked.

"No, Max is driving Nomad today. I'm going to dive separately."

"Didn't you say the wreck is at a depth of eight hundred feet?"

"That I did."

"How can you do that? It's way too deep for scuba gear, isn't it?"

"Four hundred feet is the limit for scuba; and to get down that far, you need to breathe a helium-oxygen mixture."

Gretchen put on a fake thoughtful expression. "Don't tell me. You're Aquaman."

Juan got up. "More like the Michelin Man."

She followed him out the door. "Now, this I have to see."

THIRTY-EIGHT

Juan and Gretchen arrived at the moon pool to find Nomad already lowered into the water. Because the pool was even with sea level outside, opening the keel doors didn't cause the ocean to rush into the chamber. The salty tang of seawater filled the cavernous space, which bustled with noise and activity from techs getting their gear in order. Max's head poked out of the sixty-five-foot-long sub's hatch. Linda was visible inside the transparent nose, doing a last predive check. Each of the manipulator arms reached out momentarily and clasped air like a crab snapping its claws. She would operate them while Max piloted the craft.

Although Nomad could function untethered, when necessary, radio frequencies didn't work underwater, and the backup acoustic communication was slow and unreliable. For this operation, the submersible was to be attached to the *Oregon* by an umbilical that allowed it to communicate with the ship.

"How are you getting down there?" Gretchen asked.

Juan pointed above her head, where what looked like a giant metal spacesuit hung from the gantry. A clear helmet sat on top of a stout orange torso that sprouted bulbous limbs with articulated joints. The arms ended in silver pincers for grasping objects. A huge backpack was mounted on the body, and twin thrusters were attached to each side that let it maneuver in the water just like a submarine.

"Allow me to introduce you to Jim," he said.

Gretchen laughed. "He looks more like Waldo, if you ask me."

Juan waved for the technicians to begin lowering Jim to the deck. "It's called an atmospheric diving suit. The first one was named Jim, after the inventor's chief diver, back in the sixties. This model has been updated significantly since then, but I liked the name, so we kept it."

"It looks like the offspring of the Michelin Man and a pumpkin."

"The traffic cone coloring is for both visibility and style. This kind of rig is used by ocean drilling operations for maintenance, and most of the world's biggest navies have them in their inventories."

"How do you walk in that thing? It looks like it weighs a ton."

"Only about six hundred pounds, since it's made of wrought aluminum. But I don't intend to be walking in Jim. There's a pedal, which I operate with my good foot, for lateral and vertical movements, using thrusters."

When Jim was steady on the deck, technicians swung the backpack away from the suit on hinges.

"This is where I get in," Juan said.

"I hope you and Jim have a fun time together. Good —"

Juan interrupted her with his hand. He could tell she was about to say *Good luck,* which they never said aboard the *Oregon* before a dangerous mission. Although Juan wasn't superstitious, the rest of the crew considered the phrase bad luck.

"We don't say that here. How about 'I'll see you when you get back'?"

Gretchen grinned at the request. "My horoscope today said that's acceptable. See you when you get back."

Juan climbed into his suit and went through the pre-dive check. Once everything was in order and Nomad had launched,

Juan was sealed inside the Jim suit and lowered into the moon pool.

"Do you copy, Max?" he said as water lapped at his helmet. Jim was tethered to the *Oregon* like Nomad was, so they could speak to each other directly.

"Loud and clear, Juan," Max replied. "Linda's got the cable and we're ready to dive."

He was talking about the thick steel cable from the deck crane that would be used to haul the container aboard.

"I'm coming down."

The suit was released from the *Oregon*, and Juan adjusted the buoyancy so that he would descend at a slow and steady rate. The setting sun barely penetrated the gloom under the ship. In seconds, Juan was clear of the enormous doors along the keel.

Max stayed by him in Nomad as they went down. By the time they reached a depth of a hundred feet, their powerful LED lamps provided the only illumination. The routine descent meant they had a few minutes before the real work got under way.

Linda's high-pitched voice came through the suit's speakers. "Chairman, I've been reading up on Napoleon's retreat from Moscow to see if we can narrow down where the treasure might be stashed."

"Self-storage unit?" Juan joked.

"Unlikely," she countered without missing a beat. "He started missing the monthly payments about two hundred years ago. The contents would have been auctioned off by now."

"Then I'd say it's either underwater or underground."

"Most of the speculation says it's underwater. With Napoleon's horses dying left and right from the cold, they wouldn't have had time to scout for caves. Sir Walter Scott's nine-volume biography of Napoleon claims that the loot from Moscow was dumped into Semlev Lake, which is outside Smolensk."

"Could it still be there?"

"I doubt it. The Communists conducted an exhaustive search of that lake, looking for the treasure, and came up empty."

"What do they think the treasure is?"

"All the usual stuff. Silver and gold bullion, gold coins, precious gems, ancient weaponry. My favorite is the gold-plated cross that used to top Ivan the Great's bell tower. To find it, we'll have a lot of ground to cover. There are hundreds of lakes on the route Napoleon's men took during their retreat."

"I have a hard time believing the treasure

is in a lake."

"Why?" Linda asked.

"For two reasons. The lakes would have been frozen at the time Napoleon was retreating. It would have been difficult for his men to dump the treasure in the water. They would have had to cut away the thick ice."

"And the second reason?"

"How would he have gotten the treasure out of the lake, assuming he ever returned to Russia to retrieve it? If the lake was deep, it would have been difficult to recover the treasure with the technology of the time. And if it was that shallow, the lake would have been frozen solid."

"Which leaves us where?" Linda asked.

"If it's in the water, it would have to be in a river. One that was fast moving enough so that it wouldn't be frozen over by the time of the retreat. But it would have to be small enough so that it could be dammed and rerouted."

"Letting them collect it easily. You may be onto something."

Juan added, "If someone kidnapped Napoleon to help them find the treasure, all he'd have to do was point out where it was and they could do the rest. But since the loot has never resurfaced, we have to assume that their mission was unsuccessful."

"Then it's still there," Linda said.

Max piped up. "If that's true, what we're looking at now may give us the answer."

Max must have seen the outline of the sunken ship seconds before it came into view for Juan, who could now see that the stern of the *Narwhal* was turned at an unnatural angle. Only the rear half of the ship's name had survived the railgun's tremendous blows.

Just how tough this job would be didn't sink in until Juan panned across deck, turned at more than ninety degrees with the cargo ship lying on its side.

Most of the superstructure had been destroyed in the opening salvo and what was left of it was the only thing propping up the ship on the sloped seafloor. If it tipped over, the entire ship would go belly up, crushing the container underneath it and destroying any chance of salvaging the column.

THIRTY-NINE

As Juan glided along the sunken 300-foot-long ship, the awesome power of the railgun was evident in the catastrophic holes that had been torn in the *Narwhal*'s hull and deck. No wonder the ship had gone down so quickly. Some of the chasms were twenty feet across, with jagged metal protruding from the edges like the serrated teeth of a buzz saw. When he saw the extensive damage, he felt even more relieved that the *Oregon* had come out of the battle with the *Achilles* relatively unscathed.

"I have a better appreciation for your boat-driving skills, Max," he said.

"It was all Eric," Max said. "He was at the helm, dodging and weaving. I was just making lucky guesses about where to go."

Juan knew better. It was his crew's training and teamwork that saved them.

"Hold on. There it is."

Nomad's lights focused on the only container attached to the deck. The forty-foot-long blue box was tied down amidships, halfway between the port and starboard sides.

Juan activated the pedals so that he did a circumnavigation of the container. The doors were closed, and there were no holes in the corrugated metal.

"It's intact," Juan said. "I assume the column is still in there."

That didn't mean it remained secured inside the container. The column may have come loose from the chains tying it down. That could make the container very unwieldy if the thirty-ton granite column shifted while they were moving it. It could even slam through the doors and fall to the seabed below, making it more difficult to recover.

Juan took the Jim suit in for a closer look at the fasteners holding the container to the deck. Modern containers were secured with a relatively simple mechanism called a twistlock. Three of the twistlock couplings were undamaged, but the fourth, which was now at the upper corner of the rotated container, had been severed during the attack. That corner leaned out noticeably from the deck.

"I think this might work," Juan said.

"You always think everything might work," Max replied.

"I told you. Of the two of us, I'm the optimist."

The plan was simple in conception, difficult in execution. Juan would connect four lines from the main cable to the four corner castings on the container's normal top side. Then he would free the container from the deck and, when it swung loose, the *Oregon*'s crane would reel it in.

The water provided enough drag that the container would sink slowly, if at all, buoyed by balloons that he would attach to the four top corners, the ones farthest from the *Narwhal*'s deck.

Juan took uninflated balloons from No-mad's tool tray, which was situated under its nose. One at a time, he tied the balloons to the container. Each was equipped with a light so that the container would be visible in the darkness. When the balloons were all secured, he backed away and radioed Max.

"They're ready to go. Give them some air."

"Inflating now."

Max keyed the signal that ordered the air cartridges to inflate the balloons. The yellow rubber spheres expanded until each was the size of an SUV.

The next step was attaching the crane cables. While Linda held the main cable with Nomad's manipulator, Juan latched each of the four ends to the same corners where the balloons were connected. Once they were secure, Linda released the cable, and Juan radioed the crane operator to take up the slack.

Juan tried manually disengaging the twistlocks to free the container, but two of them were jammed.

"They aren't budging," he radioed Max.

"Looks like it's time to break out the fireworks," Max said.

They'd anticipated this problem. The Nomad's tool tray held four shaped charges to blow the locks.

Juan motored over to Nomad and took one of the charges from the tray. He then carefully attached it to the stuck joint, making sure that the explosive force would be focused toward the lock and away from the container. He repeated the task with the second explosive. After triple-checking the setup, he pulled back to a safe distance.

"Fire in the hole," Linda said calmly.

Two bright flashes lit up the entire ship like a strobe, followed by muffled thumps a moment later. They waited expectantly for the container to swing away.

For a second, it seemed to separate from the deck, then nothing. It remained lodged in place. They waited another minute to see if the container would work itself free, but it remained stubbornly attached.

"I'll check it out," Juan said.

"Be careful," Max said. "Stay on top of it in case it decides to break loose."

Juan used his thrusters to get a close look at the problem. He checked both twistlocks and saw that the explosives had worked perfectly. The locks were sliced away without damaging the container.

What Juan hadn't been able to see before was the damage to the ship under the container, which had pulled away enough to expose the underside.

An explosion from one of the railgun rounds had driven a metal girder into the container, possibly destroying part of the column.

"It's hung up on a structural beam," he said.

"Can we pull the container loose?" Max asked. "I can have the crane operator reel the cable in."

"No, that might peel the container open and spill the column out. I think the beam is narrow enough that another shaped charge will cut it in half. The only problem will be wedging myself in there to attach it."

"I don't like the idea of you wedging yourself in anywhere. Why don't we give it a try?"

"I appreciate the thought, but even with its longer arms, Nomad won't be able to get close enough. And we can't lose this opportunity to retrieve the column."

"Your call."

Juan retrieved a third explosive and went back to the container. It seemed to have shifted again by the time he returned. Then he realized it wasn't the container that had moved, it was the entire ship. The *Narwhal* was now leaning over even farther.

"We've got a problem here," Juan said. "The *Narwhal* has tilted by another few degrees. We can't wait much longer. Get ready to set off the explosive on my mark."

"Not until you're back here," Linda said.

"I'll get to a safe distance. But don't delay because of me. If the ship falls onto the container, we may not be able to dig it out."

Juan inched himself into the small space that had opened up between the deck and container, coming up from underneath to reach the girder. He could just barely touch it. With a mighty push, he stuck the charge on the girder and was starting to back out when he heard the shriek of tearing metal.

The *Narwhal* was keeling over.

The container shifted suddenly, crushing the Jim suit's thruster pack and holding it fast. Juan pushed the thruster to maximum power, but he couldn't move.

He was about to go down with the ship and it wasn't even his ship.

"Linda! Blow it!"

"Wait, where are you?" Max protested. "We can't see you."

"I'm stuck and the *Narwhal* is collapsing! Linda, do it now!"

Linda followed his order without question. "Fire in the hole," she said.

The shaped charge went off, blasting away from him and cutting through the beam, but the explosion packed a wallop. The concussion caused an impact that Juan felt through his whole body, rattling him like he was in a cement mixer. The Jim suit's helmet cracked but held. At this depth, he'd be dead in seconds if it leaked.

But the explosive worked. The beam broke in two, wrenching the container away from the deck and taking his communication umbilical with it.

The container swung out from the falling ship, and Juan tried to follow it, but his lateral thrusters must have been damaged when the container crushed him because he was moving at a fraction of his normal speed.

His vertical thrusters, however, seemed to be fully operational. The problem was that the ship was capsizing too fast. He knew he wouldn't make it to safety before the ship's deck crashed down and flattened him. Then he remembered his earlier survey of the ship.

The railgun, ironically, provided the only possibility for his survival.

With only seconds to react, Juan resorted to the only option he had left.

He went down.

FORTY

Admiral Nestor Zakharin awoke to find himself soaked in sweat. Waves pounded the rocky coastline outside the open window of his villa, and the shine of the moon reflected off the sea. For a moment, he thought a sound had jolted him from sleep, but more likely it was just a nightmare. He couldn't remember what it was about, but an image of Juan Cabrillo's face popped into his mind and then faded.

After the run-in with the *Oregon* captain, he'd had leave coming, so he left Vladivostok as soon as he could to regroup and plan his next steps. Certainly Maxim Antonovich would be very unhappy if he ever found out that Zakharin had betrayed him. But more importantly, the admiral had to ensure that Moscow would never learn the real reason why he was shutting down the refitting operation.

Zakharin's stomach rumbled. Perhaps a midnight snack was what he needed to get back to sleep. That and a couple of shots of vodka.

He threw off the damp sheets and pushed himself out of bed. After donning a silk robe, he padded barefoot down the moonlit hall on the newly installed marble tile.

He was halfway to the kitchen when his foot slipped on a dark puddle. He backed up, wiping his sole on the tile to dry it. He thought his remodeled villa had already sprung a leak until he realized that the liquid was warm and sticky. Then the coppery tang hit his nostrils.

It was a puddle of blood.

Terror gripped him. He squinted to see in the faint light and could barely make out the body of a dead guard, lying in the front foyer of the house. His throat was slit.

Zakharin's heart raced at the realization that he had an intruder. The perspiration that had awakened him came back even stronger.

He stopped himself from yelling for help or from turning on any lights. If the intruder — possibly, several of them — had already gotten past the guards outside, the rest of Zakharin's men might also be dead. He'd only be telling his enemy where he was. The intruder might think he was still asleep in bed. His nightmare possibly saved his life.

Without him knowing what was going on outside, making a run for it was risky. The police were his best option in this situation.

He made his way cautiously to the nearest landline phone in his den and picked it up. No dial tone. The intruders must have cut the wires.

Zakharin's mobile phone was back in the bedroom, but that would be the last place he could go now. He needed another one. He crept back to the foyer, avoiding the spreading pool of blood, and searched the dead guard's pockets.

He found the guard's phone in his coat pocket. With trembling fingers, he pressed the button to unlock it, but the passcode was set. However, there was an emergency dial feature. He swiped, brought up the numeric keypad, and dialed 112, the European emergency number.

Instead of connecting Zakharin with the police, the phone displayed a screen that read *No signal.* The mobile service had always been so reliable in this area that Zakharin hadn't even thought to check. But there it was. No bars.

The intruders had to be using a cell phone jamming device, which confirmed that he wasn't dealing with an ordinary burglar.

Two doors down was the security room. Zakharin pressed himself against the wall and inched toward it, paying attention for any sound that would indicate he was being stalked. He made it safely to the room and ducked inside, closing the door behind him.

The guard here was dead, too. He was still in his chair, his neck twisted at an unnatural angle.

Zakharin rolled the chair aside and peered at the six monitors that showed the exterior of the house.

Two more guards were dead on the lawn at the front of the house. The front gate was closed. There was no sign of anyone guarding the lone exit. Situated on a peninsula, the estate was protected on three sides by high cliffs.

There was only one way to escape. If he could make it to the garage, he could take the Mercedes G-Wagen and ram through the gate even if the electronics had been disabled. He knew exactly where he'd left the keys in the kitchen.

The security guard's pistol was still in its shoulder holster. Zakharin took it.

With a little more courage that the firearm gave him, he went back out into the hall and continued on the path toward the kitchen, keeping the gun in front of him.

He had reached the living room when a voice to his left startled him.

"Where are you going, Admiral?" the man asked in Russian.

Zakharin whipped around to fire, but an arm behind him came down on his wrist with immense force and knocked the pistol from his hand. Zakharin collapsed to his knees and held his wrist in agony. He tried to move his fingers, but all that did was send a shock of pain up his arm.

"Bring him over here," the voice said.

The same hand that shattered his wrist squeezed his biceps and pulled him to his feet. The living room lights snapped on. The man holding him up was a huge Indian man, who dragged him to one of his hand-picked antique Rococo chairs and tossed him into it as easily as a child would a stuffed toy.

Zakharin looked up at the man sitting on his sofa. He was much shorter than the Indian, with thinning, close-cropped hair and a scar on the left side of his neck. A red-haired man with the hardened eyes of a soldier stood behind him with an amused grin. A submachine gun with an attached sound suppressor hung from the soldier's shoulder.

"Who are you?" Zakharin asked through gritted teeth.

"I'm a navy man, just like you," the seated man said.

He recognized the Ukrainian accent. "Kiev?"

"Very good. Of course, you know that your navy has decimated my country's navy."

"I had nothing to do with that. My posting is nine thousand kilometers away."

"Are you saying you disagree with your country's policy toward Ukraine?"

Zakharin knew that to answer was a trap. He remained silent.

"No matter. That's not why I'm here. My name is Sergey Golov and I would like to know why you gave someone the code to disable the weapons on a ship under my command."

Zakharin sat up. "You're the captain of the *Achilles*?" Immediately, he realized he'd made a terrible mistake in revealing any information about the yacht.

Golov's eyes lit up. "Ah, so it *was* you."

"My naval base was compromised," Zakharin quickly sputtered. "I didn't tell them anything. They accessed our files."

"So you know who did this?"

"Yes, and I was trying to contact Mr. Antonovich to warn him, but he's so reclusive, I couldn't reach him."

"No, you didn't. If you don't want to die right here, you're going to have to stop lying to me. My ship was nearly destroyed because of your incompetence."

Zakharin silently cursed himself. Being at the mercy of yet another ship captain was humiliating. As an admiral, he should be on the other side of this kind of interrogation.

"Fine," he said. "I don't know the real name of the man who took that code, but he has his own ship, one that we modified in the same shipyard where Mr. Antonovich refitted the *Achilles*. It's called the *Oregon*."

"Was he a tall blond man?"

"Yes."

Golov's eyes flicked to the Indian and then back to Zakharin. "Do you have the files on this ship?"

"No, they were destroyed."

"But you know the specifications, don't you?"

Zakharin nodded. "What do you want to know?"

Golov's eyes gleamed as if he were peering at the world's largest diamond. He set down a phone on the coffee table and

pressed the button to start a voice recording.

"Tell me everything."

FORTY-ONE

Max would never forget the sight of the Jim suit's light being snuffed out by the collapsing ship. He had frantically radioed Juan, but his calls went unanswered. He and Linda watched helplessly as Juan valiantly tried to follow the swinging container to safety, but something must have been wrong with his thrusters and he sunk instead. Their last view of the Jim suit was when the *Narwhal*'s hull came crashing down on the seabed in a cloud of silt, its black keel pointing toward the surface.

They circled the *Narwhal* in Nomad while the crane hoisted the container on board the *Oregon*. News came down that the container had made it in one piece, and the column, though marred and cracked, was intact. Max told Eric to take charge of examining it, while he continued scouring the shipwreck for any signs that Juan might still be alive.

"Do you think there's any chance the suit survived the impact?" Linda asked. "Maybe under the wreckage?"

"The Jim suit was already under a lot of pressure at this depth," Max said. "With a thousand tons of steel on top of him . . ." He didn't complete the sentence, letting the implications hang in the air.

Their best hope was that Juan had been pushed clear of the wreckage. Max goosed the thrusters, and Nomad edged along the side of the *Narwhal* with a soft whine of the impellers. All of their lights were focused on the seafloor.

With the emergency buoyancy system, the Jim suit should have floated to the surface by now.

Linda called up to Hali. "*Oregon,* has the Chairman been spotted?"

"Nothing on the radio beacon, Nomad. We've got people on all sides of the ship looking for his light. It's pretty dark up here, but no one has seen it yet. We did haul in his umbilical. It was sheared off. That must mean he's still down there. What's his oxygen situation?"

"He's got two redundant breathing systems, including a carbon dioxide scrubber that should give him fifty hours of air."

"Roger that, Nomad. We'll let you know if

402

we find him."

"Same here. Have Mark Murphy send down *Little Geek* to expand the search," Linda said. *Little Geek* was a remotely operated underwater vehicle. Murph named it after a similar design in the movie *The Abyss.*

"He's already got it in the moon pool. It should be on-site in ten minutes."

"Glad to have the help. Keep in touch."

Max did a quick survey of the ocean floor for any trace of Juan.

"If any of his lights were working, we would have seen them by now," Linda said.

"And with the umbilical cut," Max said, "we have no way to contact him. He could be unconscious."

"That's what worries me," Linda said. "If he's not capable of activating any of his emergency devices, either he was knocked out, which means his suit took extensive damage . . ."

"Or his suit is bleeding air, which caused him to black out," Max finished. "The longer we can't find him, the more likely that his life support gives out."

Linda checked Nomad's air and battery gauges. "Batteries look good. We've got four more hours before we have to surface to refill the O_2 tanks."

"Good. We're not going up a second earlier."

They spent tedious hours in the pitch-black water sweeping Nomad's lights inch by inch over the ocean floor around the *Narwhal*, looking for any sign of the Jim suit, but the search was fruitless. Not even a glint of the pumpkin-orange suit to give them hope, although if they found any pieces of Jim, it would be an awful sign that Juan had probably not lived through the accident.

"We're getting close to Bingo! on our air," Linda said as they did one more pass on the opposite side of the *Narwhal*. Her voice was weary with regret. "We're going to have to head for the surface in a few minutes."

"Tell the moon pool to be ready. I want to come back down as soon as we're able." With a set jaw, he looked at Linda. "In the meantime, have Hali contact our salvage firm."

While Linda radioed to the surface, Max kept his eyes glued outside, hoping that the salvage team would be unnecessary. The *Oregon* didn't have the capability to raise the *Narwhal*, so they'd need to hire specialized contractors to raise the ship if this became a mission to recover Juan's body.

As Linda made preparations to ascend, Max stopped Nomad one last time and looked at the wreck that might have taken his best friend. He was about to order Linda to empty the ballast tanks when he heard the distant clang of metal. At first, he thought it was a mechanical problem with the sub, so he removed his headset to listen. The sound had an odd cadence to it, arrhythmic and intermittent, and it definitely wasn't coming from Nomad.

Linda, who was still on her headset, said, "The moon pool's ready for us. They —"

Max put his finger up to quiet her, and she slid down her headset. The weak clanging continued.

Max edged Nomad closer to the sunken ship, then shut down the thrusters and every other nonessential system. The sub became deathly silent.

The clanging returned. Max was sure of it now. It was distant and tinny, but unmistakable.

"Do you hear that?" Max said with a growing smile.

Linda slowly nodded, her eyes widening in shock when she understood what she was listening to.

"That's Morse code."

Max pointed at the *Narwhal.* "Juan's in there somewhere and he's still alive."

FORTY-TWO

With the *Achilles* on a course away from the mainland of Spain toward the island of Ibiza, Golov went in search of Ivana, since she wasn't answering his texts and she wasn't in her cabin. He was proud of her work ethic, but her immersion in her coding was infuriating when it led to her ignoring him.

He finally found her sitting on a sofa in the luxurious main drawing room where he'd first met with Henri Munier. A half-eaten plate of pita and assorted dips had been pushed out of the way of the twin laptops that were arranged on the table in front of her.

He was about to say her name when he realized that she wouldn't be able to hear him. She wore a pair of virtual reality goggles and headphones that covered her ears. She made minute movements with the mouse as her lips silently formed the words to some song that Golov couldn't hear.

He walked over and sat heavily on the sofa next to her.

She tugged the goggles off in a surprised motion, ready to swear at the idiot who had interrupted her. When she saw it was her father, her expression changed to one of exasperation.

"I hate it when you do that," she said, pulling the headphones down around her neck. Before she hit the MUTE button, Golov heard the thumping beat of electronic dance music popular in Europe.

"If you answered my texts, I wouldn't have to."

"I was working on that research you wanted me to do. I think I've found a spot."

She handed him the goggles. Golov wasn't a fan of these 3-D gadgets, so when he looked at it in distaste, she said, "Go on. It won't kill you."

He put them on, and instead of nighttime, it was suddenly a sunny daytime on the French Riviera. The pebbled beach stretched for miles ahead of him along a road lined with hotels, apartments, and restaurants.

"Go ahead and turn around," Ivana said.

Golov did, and the scenery rotated with the motion of his head. He could see in every direction as if he were standing on the shore.

"Do you see that gray and white building?"

He swiveled his head until he saw the structure she was talking about. It was an eight-story building with balconies.

"I see it," he said.

"That's the Radisson Blu Hotel."

"Why do you think this is the perfect location?"

"I haven't shown you the rooftop deck yet," she said with obvious delight.

Golov experienced a moment of disorientation as the view instantly switched. He was now standing atop the hotel. On one side was a restaurant with tables shaded by umbrellas. In the other direction was a pool surrounded on all sides by deck chairs.

He then focused on the surrounding buildings and saw why Ivana had chosen this location. A tall apartment building to the northeast was framed by the distant mountains.

"You're right," he said, taking off the goggles. "It's perfect."

"Did you find out the information you were looking for from Zakharin?" she asked as she nibbled on a triangle of pita.

"Yes. I got it all on a voice recording

before the admiral tragically came to his end. The ship is called the *Oregon*."

"Then he did modify another ship with weapons like ours."

"Several others, but only the *Oregon* comes close to our capabilities. His predecessor did the work, but he knew enough of the specifications to be useful."

He played the recording for her. Zakharin went into excruciating detail about the *Oregon*'s armaments, defensive capabilities, and special features, such as the moon pool from which she could launch submarines.

When the recording ended, Ivana said, "They've certainly disabled their own disarming code by now, if they hadn't already."

"If their captain is as good as Zakharin implied, he probably removed it years ago." The image of his counterpart from the museum party in Malta came to mind. Golov had described him to Zakharin, who confirmed that he was the commander of the *Oregon*.

"Do you think they could raise the column from where the *Narwhal* sank?"

"Clever girl," Golov replied. "That was my first thought as well. I'd say it's easily within the realm of possibility, which means they could be there right now."

"If they find the column, they could

decipher the clues Napoleon left and find the treasure before we're able to complete Dynamo, putting the whole operation in jeopardy."

"Which is why we need to make sure they don't find it before we can get to it."

"Do you really think it's still there? The treasure?"

"It has to be. We know Napoleon didn't lead his abductors to it."

"Then we should go back to the shipwreck and intercept —"

Golov shook his head. "They could be gone by the time we arrive. Or we might wait there for days before they return, and we don't have time for that in our schedule. No, the best plan is to make them come to us."

Antonovich's private jet would meet them in Ibiza. The *Achilles* would only be in port long enough for the transfer to the plane.

"What lure do we have?" Ivana asked.

"Money. They showed up in Monaco claiming to be insurance investigators. That means they care about what happened to the deposits, and I don't think it was because they were hired to look into the heist. Assuming they operate as mercenaries, like the admiral thinks they do, then I'd say we made a big hit on their finances."

Ivana nodded. "Then they'll want it back."

"I know I would. This is yet another occasion when having someone on the Monaco police force has been useful."

"What are you thinking?"

After Golov was done outlining the plan for her, he said, "We need to get a message to the captain of the *Oregon.* One that he can't ignore."

Ivana smiled. "I think I can take care of that."

"Send him a pleasant invitation."

"Do you think he'll come?" she asked as her fingers danced across the keyboard. "He'll suspect it's a trap."

Golov kissed his daughter on the forehead and stood to go back to his cabin and get a good night's sleep. "That, my dear, is exactly what I'm hoping."

FORTY-THREE

When the *Narwhal* had collapsed, Juan's only option had been to head for the biggest railgun hole in the deck that he could see close by, which was below him. He'd made it just before the ship slammed into the seabed, but the jagged edge caught his thruster pack, pinning him to the bottom. It took him a couple of hours to wriggle free enough to jettison the pack. He could now move freely, but he was limited to the hobbling walk similar to the ones seen in the films of moonwalking astronauts.

His light was strong enough to show the jumble of metal and equipment that lay on what was now the floor of the upside-down ship. The cracked visor seemed to be holding, and since there was nothing he could do about it, he tried to ignore the star pattern staring him in the face. He explored the interior of the expansive open hold, hoping to find a hole big enough for him to squeeze through, but he couldn't even locate an opening big enough to see through.

His acoustic backup communication system was useless because it would be blocked by the steel hull. He chose a spot closest to the outer hull and began tapping out the famous • • • — — — • • •, representing the universal call for help, SOS. Several times during the hour that he'd clinked the mechanical claw against the steel frame of the ship he'd heard the faint whirr of Nomad passing close by. He'd tapped as hard as he could, but the sub kept on going without stopping.

He had lost track of time when he heard the sound that he'd expected to come many hours later. It was a warning beep, signaling that his battery power was fading fast, another casualty of one of the impacts the suit had withstood. Not only did the battery power his light but also the carbon dioxide scrubber that was keeping him alive. If it failed, there was only enough oxygen in the suit to last for five minutes before he passed out.

The beep indicated that it would fail in twenty minutes.

He kept tapping the monotonous rhythm of the SOS. Nomad passed by yet again, and he amped up the volume as much as he could. The whine of the impellers stopped for a minute, giving Juan hope that he'd been heard. Then they started up again, and Juan was prepared to hear the motors fade into the distance.

But this time, the sound came toward him.

He clanged away with both claws so they could home in on his location. The motors came to a stop again, quite close.

He stopped tapping and listened.

A slow, methodical set of bangs against the outer hull gave him a renewed hope. It had to be Nomad's less responsive robotic manipulator, tapping its own message on the ship. It was the sweetest sound he'd ever heard.

We are here, Juan, Linda tapped with Nomad's arm.

Thought you left, Juan replied.

Not a chance. We will get you out. Are you hurt?

No. 15 min of air left.

There was a pause, probably because they realized there wasn't enough time to bring down a cutting torch to get him out.

Got one explosive left, Linda finally tapped. *Will blow you out.*

Won't work. Too small.

Linda replied, *Can't cut you out in 15 min.*

414

Much as Juan didn't like to admit it, there was only one way to make a big enough hole for him to go through in the time he had remaining.

Juan tapped, *Use torp.*

Another pause, this one even longer as they contemplated the notion of firing a torpedo at the *Narwhal.*

Finally, Linda tapped, *Max sez you crazy.*

Got a better idea?

No.

Then do it. Pick a spot toward the bow. I have a clear path. This part of the cargo hold was a huge open space that had likely been used to transport vehicles. He was at least half the length of the ship away from the bow, a hundred and fifty feet. The water hammer effect would be powerful, but being blown up trying to get out was better than suffocating inside a dead ship. If he wasn't crushed in the explosion, he could shuffle his way to the hole and inflate his emergency buoyancy device to get back to the surface.

Linda responded, *Okay. Try to find cover. Countdown is 2 min.*

Juan tapped, *Roger that.*

He retreated behind a thick bulkhead that was the farthest from the anticipated impact point and waited. He now had less than ten minutes of power. Walking through the ship without a light would be virtually impossible. If Juan didn't make it out before his battery died, so would he.

Crouching was impossible in the ungainly suit, so he stood three feet from the bulkhead. Trying to stand next to it and steady himself by grasping the frame might rip the arms from the suit during the explosion.

Except for his breathing, there was total silence. Then he heard the high-pitched whine of the torpedo propeller revving up to top speed. It grew quieter as the torpedo sped away to get the proper angle before turning and whizzing back toward the *Narwhal.*

The ocean seemed to erupt like a volcano, pummeling him with a giant shock wave that threw him backward against the next bulkhead. His head slammed against the padding inside the helmet, and his vision tunneled, threatening to black out completely. His organs felt as if they'd been pureed.

He teetered on the edge of consciousness before coming back to his senses.

That's when he noticed the battery warning chirping at him insistently. His battery life was almost gone.

He pushed himself past the bulkhead and

focused his light ahead of him. In the gloom, he thought he could make out a hole in the bow.

Juan stumbled ahead, clumsily clambering over piles of metal when he had to. He was three-quarters of the way to the bow when his battery died. There was a complicated pile of destroyed equipment he had to navigate around and he didn't know if he could do it with the five minutes of air he had left in the suit.

He pictured what he'd seen in his memory and began to pick his way across. The laborious process seemed to pay dividends and he thought he was in the clear, when his arm snagged on something. Without tactile feedback and visual cues, it was impossible to tell what had caught him.

He knew he was close to the hole blown in the side of the ship. But until he got out, he couldn't inflate his buoyancy device. If he did that inside the hull, he'd simply pin himself up against the keel of the ship.

A faint ray of light pierced the darkness. It grew stronger by the moment until an intense beam of white shot through the opening in the ship and illuminated the hold.

It was Nomad. Max was showing him the way home.

He was starting to get light-headed from the excess carbon dioxide in his suit. His extremities growing cold and numb, and he began to get dizzy and lose his concentration.

With the light, he could see that the claw had become lodged in a jagged piece of metal. He wrenched it free and started a slow-motion dash to the beckoning glow.

Juan seemed to be on autopilot as he struggled to put one leg in front of the other as if he were making a final ascent of Everest. The light grew so strong that it was blinding, and he could no longer tell if he was inside the *Narwhal.*

But it didn't matter. He was about to pass out. There wouldn't be time to send in *Little Geek* to pull him out before he asphyxiated. He had to activate the emergency float and either he'd rush to the surface or he'd die inside the shipwreck.

With his final ounce of strength, he flipped the switch and heard the CO_2 cartridge inflate the buoy.

It was the last thing he sensed before darkness enveloped him.

FORTY-FOUR

The ascent to the surface seemed to take an eternity. Gretchen kept looking from her watch to the water outside the *Oregon*'s boat garage, where she was waiting for Nomad to surface. According to Max, the sub and Jim suit would be topside in two minutes.

On Max's orders, the *Oregon* had moved away from the dive site so that it wouldn't be directly above the torpedo explosion, which also meant there was no way they could surface in the moon pool. Gretchen, who had been watching the search from the op center, dashed down to the boat garage as soon as Hali told her that's where they'd be pulling Juan in.

Julia Huxley stood ready next to her with her medical crash kit.

"Is he breathing?" Gretchen asked her.

"I think so," Julia replied without conviction. "Max says he doesn't think the suit's leaking."

Suddenly, a balloon broke the surface, followed by the Jim suit. Half of the pack holding the environmental systems was crushed.

"Now we know why he was low on air," Julia said. "We need to get him out of that suit."

It was an agonizing wait as Max motored over to the suit and the mechanical arms grasped the handle on its front.

Max turned Nomad and sped toward the lights of the *Oregon*'s boat garage. Technicians attached a line to the Jim suit and winched it aboard. They laid it down on its front, but the latches were jammed shut by the crush damage.

Gretchen didn't wait for them to act. She took a heavy wrench that one of them was holding and fiercely bashed two latches until they sprung free. The clamshell back snapped open and they hoisted Juan's limp body out. His lips were bright blue and his skin was ashen.

As soon as they had him lying on his back on the deck, Julia took over. Gretchen stood back and watched as the doctor felt for a pulse. She put a mask on his face and turned the tank's valve.

"He's still got a heartbeat," she said. "He's also got a nasty bump on the back of his head." She jostled him lightly. "Juan, wake up."

Julia rubbed his sternum with her fist to get a response. He remained motionless. The other crewmen watched in concerned silence.

Suddenly, Juan took a huge breath and his eyelids fluttered. Then they opened wide as if he were startled and he tried to sit up, but Julia held him down.

"Juan, you're on the *Oregon.* There's a mask on your face giving you oxygen. I want you to relax for a minute and take deep breaths. Do you understand?"

He nodded slightly. "Who . . . What happened?" he mumbled. His groggy voice was muffled by the mask.

Gretchen felt a wave of relief wash over her when she heard him speak. She knelt next to him and took his hand. "Your stupid idea about the torpedo worked. You got out of the wreckage just in time."

"My insides feel like jelly."

"That's the concussion effect of the torpedo," Julia said. "We need to do a CAT scan to make sure there's no internal bleeding."

"Don't bother. I'm all right."

Gretchen squeezed his hand. "Are you going to disobey doctor's orders?"

He looked at both of them. And then seeing that he was going to lose the argument, he said, "You two would make good professional arm-twisters."

"It doesn't pay enough," said Gretchen.

"And I already have a job keeping this ship's sorry lot in one piece," Julia added.

Juan removed the mask and tried getting to his feet. "Okay. Let's get this over with."

Julia pushed him back down. "No you don't. I have to clear you with the CT before you're allowed to walk. I don't want you passing out on me from blood loss on the way to the medical bay."

Despite his protestations, they loaded Juan onto a stretcher. Gretchen walked beside him as he was wheeled to get his scan.

"Did we get the container?" he asked.

"Max said they got it on board. Eric and Murph are examining it now."

"Tell them I want to know the minute they have anything to report."

She grinned at him. "What, am I part of your crew now?"

"Maybe you should be."

"You definitely live interesting lives around here. It's been fun doing some fieldwork again."

"I'll take that as a job application."

"I'll think about it," she said, but the idea

intrigued her more than she let on.

The CAT scan didn't take long, and Julia pronounced him free of any internal injuries, although he'd probably be sore for a few days. The concussion assessment protocol similarly came up negative. She gave him some pain meds, but he simply pocketed them.

They went up to the deck and found Eric and Murph inside the open container, poring over the engravings etched into the surface of the white granite column.

There were three rows of writing, in Latin, Hebrew, and Greek. According to their analysis of *Napoleon's Diary,* specific letters in his copy of *The Odyssey* referred to Greek letters on the column, and the corresponding Latin letters would spell out some kind of clue. Napoleon must have had a drawing of the Jaffa Column with him on St. Helena in order to be able to create the clues, but the drawings were lost or destroyed after the report of the emperor's death.

Eric looked up from the tablet computer he was using to take photos of the etchings. "How are you feeling?"

"Nothing that a snifter of Rémy Martin won't take care of," Juan said. "Have you made any progress?"

"It's very cool stuff," Murph said without looking up from his own tablet computer. "The markings are exactly the kind we expected to find based on the clues in the diary. We think we've already narrowed down the location to Vilnius, Lithuania. Got a problem, though."

"What's that?"

"It's something you need to solve with logic, deduction, and creativity, but that's not important right now."

Gretchen chuckled at Murph's reference to the movie *Airplane!* "You did walk right into that one."

Juan smirked. "My mind must still be fuzzy. I mean, what's the problem?"

"The damage to the container," Eric said. "The metal gouged the column on the underside. It destroyed some of the markings, which could make it difficult to find the exact location of the treasure. We won't know until we get a chance to remove it and stand it up. Max said he'd rig up something in the hold."

"What's the time frame?"

"We should have it removed from the container and standing by morning."

Murph's phone buzzed. He answered, then said, "Really?"

He tapped on his tablet and handed it to

Juan. "It's for you. A video call." He looked at Gretchen. "I think you'll want to see this, too."

Juan took the tablet from Murph. Gretchen crowded in as well, intrigued as to who could be calling.

Juan answered the call, and Gretchen immediately recognized the face staring back at them. She had first met him a few nights ago.

It was Whyvern, the Albanian hacker. Now she was doubly curious as to why he would contact them.

"Hello, sir," Erion Kula said. They had never revealed their real names to him, but they'd left an untraceable number for him to use if he remembered anything else about his break-in to ShadowFoe's computer. "You look like you've had a long day."

"I feel fine," Juan answered reflexively. "Do you have some more information for us?"

"In a way. I have a message for you. It's from ShadowFoe. Somehow, she knew I could contact you. Speaking of which, I'm not supposed to know this, but I found out that the message was routed to me through the computers at Monaco police headquarters."

Gretchen whispered into Juan's ear, "Rivard?"

He turned to her and under his breath said, "It would explain why the chief inspector of the Sûreté was such a thorn in our sides during the investigation."

Juan faced the screen again. "What's the message?"

"ShadowFoe says to meet her on the rooftop of the Radisson Blu Hotel in Nice tomorrow at five p.m. The note said she specifically wants to see Gabriel and Naomi Jackson."

ShadowFoe must have made the connection between them and the diary. "Did she say why?" Gretchen asked.

"Yes," Whyvern said. "She wants to give you your money back."

FORTY-FIVE

NICE, FRANCE

Juan returned to the top-floor room they'd reserved in the Radisson Blu triumphantly holding a hanger encased in a black wardrobe bag.

"We've got thirty minutes until the rendezvous," Gretchen said. "Does that fit?"

"It might be a bit snug," he said, "but it'll do."

"Are you sure you're up to this? You were dead yesterday."

"*Mostly* dead," he corrected her. "And if you can hobble around on a wounded leg during a firefight in that Maltese warehouse, then going to a meet and greet on top of this hotel should be a snap."

"Do you think Rivard will be with them?"

"It's possible. Even though it would be out of his jurisdiction, having a respected police detective from a neighboring country as an eyewitness might help their plan."

"I wonder how much he's getting paid for his services," Gretchen said.

"It would have to be enough to set him up for life. But now we know why and how Monaco was chosen for the heist. Having someone inside the Sûreté would make covering their tracks that much easier."

"We need to get proof that he's involved."

"First things first. We have a date with ShadowFoe. Supposedly."

"Then we should get changed," she said. "Do you mind if I take the bathroom?"

"Be my guest."

Linc and Eddie returned to the room before she could get started.

"How'd the reconnaissance go?" Juan asked. Since Eddie and Linc hadn't been seen in Malta, they were the best choices to scout out the location. They were both dressed in shorts and T-shirts, like many of the other tourists strolling on the beachside drive below their window.

"Multiple exits, so a quick getaway should be easy," Eddie said. "And there's an apartment building with a great view of the terrace. We didn't see anyone on the terrace who looked suspicious."

"Any trouble getting the photos?"

Linc attached the camera he was carrying to a tablet computer. "Nope. Just two guys taking some pictures of the scenery."

He and Gretchen scanned through the pictures. Golov and Semova were nowhere to be seen. They went through a second time, and Gretchen stopped on a photo that focused on one side of the pool's deck chairs and zoomed in.

"Well, that's not who I was expecting to see here," Juan said. He looked at Gretchen with a raised eyebrow. "I suddenly get the feeling that Chief Inspector Rivard won't be coming."

"Do you think they'll show up?" O'Connor asked.

The bedroom window of the apartment they'd broken into had a perfect view of the hotel's pool area, where the meeting was to take place. The late-afternoon sun cast shadows on the rooftop terrace, but it wasn't anything Sirkal couldn't compensate for.

He adjusted the scope on the Barrett sniper rifle. Zero wind today. Three hundred meters. The dining area, with its tables and umbrellas, was off to the left, while the swimming pool was centered on the roof. Dozens of guests sunbathed in lounge chairs surrounding the water, but they got up and moved around sporadically. It would be an easy shot.

"These people want their money, don't they?" Sirkal said.

"I wouldn't show up. It's obviously a trap."

"Yes, but the bait is too appealing to resist."

O'Connor took a long, annoying slurp from a can of Diet Coke. "I still think this is a risky plan. If they've figured out the location of Napoleon's treasure from the clues in the diary and column, they might be about to go there to get it. Then we're screwed."

"Which is why this is the best option. If it works like Mr. Golov thinks it will, it should throw them off the track for days, plenty of time to complete Dynamo and get rid of the evidence."

O'Connor shrugged. "I just work here, mate. Golov's the brains behind this. Well, him and his smoking-hot daughter. Who'd guess that someone with a body like that could be a computer whiz?"

"That's because you base people's worth on what they look like, not what they accomplish. It's why I keep you around despite your face."

O'Connor choked on his drink. "Is that a joke, Sirkal? Did I actually hear you make a funny?"

Sirkal didn't crack a smile. "I would stay away from her. There's nothing he values more than his daughter."

"No worries about that," O'Connor said with a chuckle. He put the binoculars back up. "She's radioactive to me. I don't want to end up like the rest of the crew after . . . Wait, we've got movement toward our bait."

Sirkal looked through the scope and saw an auburn-haired woman in a bikini top, a sarong, wide-brimmed hat, and huge sunglasses walk along the row of deck chairs nearest to him. A hotel employee with a towel draped over his arm followed her, carrying a standing umbrella that shielded his face. She pointed to the sun, and then at a chair she had chosen, and he began to set it up for her.

"My mistake," O'Connor said. "Just some tourist trying to save her spray tan skin from UV rays. Speaking of smoking-hot, though."

"Be ready," Sirkal said. "They should be here any minute."

He kept his eye on the umbrella, primarily because it was now blocking his shot.

Juan, who was wearing a dark wig to cover his blond hair, and, to complete the disguise, the borrowed hotel uniform, set down the large umbrella. He made sure that it

431

was between them and the apartment building, and he continued to fiddle with it as though he were adjusting its position just so. The feeling that he almost certainly had a rifle trained on him made his skin crawl.

Gretchen took the chair next to a young blond woman in a white bikini. The woman's horn-rimmed spectacles had been replaced by expensive sunglasses, but the pixie cut that Juan remembered hadn't changed.

"Hello, Ms. Marceau," he said, continuing to shield his face with the umbrella while he pretended to take drink orders. He had never suspected the involvement of Marie Marceau, the forensic analyst Murph and Eric had been crushing on back at Credit Condamine when they were deciphering the message left in the code. Of course, now it made complete sense. Who better for a hacker like ShadowFoe to recruit than the Monaco police's top computer expert?

"No wonder you had trouble accessing the code that ShadowFoe left for us," Gretchen said while she flipped through a magazine. "I'm sure you would have 'found' it eventually, but our people were just too efficient and discovered it early."

Marceau gaped at the two of them for a moment.

Juan smiled. "You didn't expect us to show up as ourselves, did you?"

"Why did you do it?" Gretchen asked.

Marceau put on her most innocent expression. "Do what? I'm just here on holiday. I'm simply surprised to see you."

"Are you ShadowFoe?"

"Who?"

"We know the request for us to meet here was sent through the Sûreté's servers," Juan said. "And now you're here. You don't have to be a genius or a mathematician to add one and one."

By now, her face had lost its golden tan and gone as pale as her bikini. Her eyes kept darting to the umbrella.

"Your friends can't help you," Gretchen said. "Why don't you come with us to Interpol? I'm sure they will be willing to strike a deal with you."

"You don't know who you're dealing with."

"Actually, we do," Juan said. "But we need you to help us prove it."

Marceau's grin dripped with contempt. "I think you've got nothing, which is why I'm going to be leaving now."

She stood and started gathering her things.

"You're making a mistake," Gretchen said.

"We will find the evidence that you've been helping ShadowFoe."

"No you won't," Marceau said, tossing her tote bag over her shoulder, and then she threw herself at the umbrella, pulling it down despite Juan's efforts. It exposed them for just a moment, but that was enough time for one shot.

Juan dived for cover, and the round hit Marceau in the upper chest, spinning her around in a fountain of blood. The crack of the rifle came immediately after. Screams of panicking tourists erupted around the pool as they ran for safety.

Juan held the umbrella steady again, shielding them with it as he and Gretchen dragged Marceau's limp body toward the protection of the restaurant. Once they were out of danger, they laid her down, and Gretchen put pressure on the wound.

Marceau's eyes were fading fast.

"They . . . betrayed me."

"Who?" Juan said.

"Shadow . . . Foe. Plans."

"What plans?"

"The formula . . . is in the treasure. Polichev. It's . . . the code." She swallowed hard to get the words out. "They're going . . . *zings.* Germany. *Lightning grid.*" Her hand reached for her tote bag before dropping to the floor.

Gretchen checked for a pulse, then shook her head.

Juan searched the tote bag. Besides Marceau's wallet, the only thing it held was her phone. That's what she was reaching for.

He tried to access the smartphone, but it was password-protected. He took Marceau's still-warm thumb and placed it on the fingerprint reader. The screen unlocked. He switched the auto-lock setting to *Never* so the phone would remain open.

"Come on," Juan said. "We don't want to stick around." He took out his phone and called Eddie as they made their way to the stairs to evacuate along with everyone else.

"We heard a shot," Eddie said. "Are you all right?"

"We're fine. Meet us at the back exit."

Juan looked down at Marceau's phone. If there was anything on there that could lead them to ShadowFoe, Eric and Murph would find it.

O'Connor packed up their gear so they could make their getaway before the police could figure out where the shot came from, while Sirkal called Golov and put him on speaker.

"Tell me you have good news," Golov

said. "Did you get the target?"

"Yes, sir," Sirkal said, looking at the red dot blinking on his phone's map of Nice. "Marceau is dead, and her phone is on the move. The mission is a success."

FORTY-SIX

After disabling the location feature on Marie Marceau's phone and ensuring that it was not equipped with any kind of tracking device, Juan and the others went back to the *Oregon* to see if there was any actionable intelligence on it. Within an hour of handing Marceau's phone over to Eric and Murph, the two computer experts called a meeting to report their findings.

The *Oregon*'s senior staff assembled in the conference room along with Gretchen. Maurice unobtrusively set out a spread of smoked duck, Brie and Camembert cheeses, and French bread for them to eat while they talked. Juan didn't realize how hungry he was until he took his first bite. He and the others munched happily while Eric began the talk.

"As you suspected, Marie Marceau has been working with ShadowFoe for quite a while. We've found emails on her phone dating back six months."

Murph shook his head in disappointment. "A crying shame. And I was planning to ask her out, too. Eventually."

"Sure you were," Eric teased. "Of course, you would have been dating the accomplice of a murderer."

"So procrastination worked for me yet again."

"Anyway," Eric continued, "there was enough incriminating evidence in those emails to send her away for life, if she had lived."

"She even had a cool hacker alias," Murph said. "MasqueBleu, or Blue Mask. She was flaunting her double life, as a police employee and as a criminal, while keeping it hidden. Almost worked until she tried to get the two of you shot and took the bullet instead."

"Did you find anything about *zings* or *lightning grid*?" Juan asked.

Eric shook his head. "We did a cursory search for both, but nothing jumped out. We'll keep working on it."

"Make sure you include *Germany* in your search terms," Gretchen said. "I got the impression that whatever they're planning will happen in Germany somewhere."

"Could be," Murph said. "The attack on

that Frankfurt power station already gives us a link to Deutschland. We'll look into it."

"Marceau also mentioned something about a formula," Juan recalled. "She said, 'The formula is in the treasure. Polichev. It's the code.' Did you find anything related to those terms?"

Eric shook his head again. "Nothing."

"Why would a formula be in the treasure?" Max asked.

"We probably won't know until we find it," Murph said. "And we have no clue who Polichev is or was. But we do know that it's a Russian surname, so it could be linked somehow to the treasure Napoleon took from Moscow."

"Okay," Juan said. "Keep searching."

"Chairman," Eric said, "we did find one email that I think you'll find interesting. It was sent from Marceau to ShadowFoe two weeks before the bank heist."

"Is it about how to get into the bank's system?" They knew ShadowFoe's offer to return their money had been a ruse, but Juan still wanted it back.

"Unfortunately, no. But, *fortunately,* it *is* about where the treasure can be found."

Juan chewed on a piece of bread slathered with Brie. "You're right. I'm interested."

Murph turned on the large display screen

at the end of the table and linked it to his laptop. "It seems that our cute computer traitor was doing some extracurricular work for ShadowFoe. The original email from ShadowFoe asked Marceau to use the Monaco Sûreté's forensic lab to analyze the writing on both sides of the three missing pages from *Napoleon's Diary*. Even though a university lab would have better equipment, they didn't want to risk using one."

Eric jumped in. "Apparently, the pages had been stored poorly and faded quite a bit in the two hundred years since Napoleon's death. They'd also suffered some damage and tearing, so the emperor's handwritten margin notes were illegible to the naked eye."

"Go ahead, Murph," Juan said. "I can see you're dying to get to the kicker."

Murph rubbed his hands together in glee. "I give you the missing diary pages." He punched a key on his laptop and six book pages appeared on the display. They were frayed and worm-eaten, but Juan recognized them as having the same typography as the copy of *The Odyssey* he and Gretchen had taken from Malta.

Juan leaned forward. "Are we sure these are authentic?"

"One hundred percent," Eric said. "The

torn edges match up precisely with the missing pages in the diary. Marceau must have used their lab equipment to enhance the images artificially."

"So Antonovich had the pages all along," Gretchen said.

"Which is why he needed the diary," Murph said. "These pages tell where the treasure is, but they're incomplete."

"You see those missing spots?" Eric said, pointing at the parts that had been chewed away over the years by pests. "They included some of the details that would help us find it. But it does confirm there is a treasure to be found."

"Do the notes tell us anything about the location?" Max asked.

"Yes," Gretchen said, getting to her feet. She traced one of Napoleon's notes with her finger and translated the French. "Here it talks about a river that they followed on the retreat from Moscow. It's called the Neris."

Linda looked at Juan with a grin. "You called it, Chairman. They dumped the treasure in a river."

"Where's the Neris?" Juan asked.

"In Lithuania," Eric said. "It fits the path that Napoleon took, back out of Russia."

Max frowned. "Did he get any more

specific than a whole river?"

Gretchen went to another page. "It says here that they unloaded it somewhere between Vilnius and Grigiškės."

"That does seem to narrow it down," Juan said. "Stoney, show us the river."

Eric put the map up on the screen. Grigiškės was practically a suburb of Lithuania's capital, Vilnius. The town was only five miles from Vilnius's city center, but the winding river's route doubled the distance.

"How long would it take us to search ten miles of river using a metal detector?" Juan asked.

Murph's eyes jittered as he did the calculation in his head. "Maybe only three or four days, but it depends how much mud and silt has covered the objects in the last two hundred years."

"Whatever Antonovich has planned," Juan said, "it's going down soon, so we need to get moving. Linda, tell Tiny to get the plane ready to take us to Lithuania. We need to begin the search as soon as we can. Linda, Gretchen, Trono, MacD, and I will go. Eric and Murph will stay here and continue working on the diary and column clues to see if they can narrow down the search grid."

"We'll also keep nosing around with those

other items that Marceau mentioned before she died," Eric said. *"Polichev, zings, and lightning grid."*

Murph said, "They sound like an antidepressant, a Hostess snack, and a game show round."

"Whatever they are," Juan said, "I want to know why Marceau thought they were important enough to use her dying breath to get them out. In the meantime, Max, I want you to take the *Oregon* up to Hamburg. My gut tells me that the *Achilles* is part of the plan — as is something in Germany, according to Marceau — and I want to be ready to intercept that yacht if we need to."

"And if we meet her again," Max said, "how do we defeat them?"

Juan paused as all eyes were on him. "I'm working on that."

"One more thing, Chairman," Linda said. "We're going to require a boat and scanning equipment in Lithuania. I'll have to find a supplier. It may take a while to procure exactly what we need."

"We may be able to get NUMA's help on that one," Juan said as he gave a knowing look to Gretchen. "Kurt Austin and I owe each other a favor."

Forty-Seven

VILNIUS, LITHUANIA

As their SUV crawled through the center of Lithuania's largest city, Golov could barely contain his excitement at the possibility of seeing the fabled treasure Napoleon had spirited out of Moscow during his retreat. Normally, he wouldn't come along on a shore mission like this, but he wanted to lay eyes on the Russian hoard before it was destroyed forever.

Much of the seven-hundred-year-old city was a winding jumble of cobblestone streets flanked by quaint row houses that were topped with red tiles, but the area where they drove teemed with modern skyscrapers and smooth asphalt roads. It was nearly the end of the workday, and traffic was at its worst. But even if they were late, Golov was quite sure that the person they were meeting would wait.

He, Sirkal, O'Connor, and two of their

former Special Forces mercenaries had arrived in Vilnius just a day after the assassination of Marie Marceau. The deception had been conceived by his daughter.

They'd had the three missing pages from *Napoleon's Diary* for over a month, thanks to Maxim Antonovich's purchase from an underground rare-documents dealer, the same one who'd sold them Polichev's mathematical formulas a year ago that had set the Dynamo plan in motion. They'd known about the treasure and Napoleon's St. Helena kidnapping from Delacroix's letter, but the location of the loot had been a mystery until the pages showed up. By then, the operation to steal the diary and column from the auction in Malta were well under way, so Golov, at the time, thought that finding the treasure himself just to get rid of it was superfluous and would expose them to unnecessary risk.

He did, however, know where it was, courtesy of those three pages Napoleon had taken with him when he escaped exile. He pictured them in his mind, completely intact and pristine.

The images Ivana had loaded onto Marceau's phone had been digitally altered with the information they wanted the *Oregon* crew to have. Although most of the emails were, in fact, unaltered messages that Ivana and Marceau had actually exchanged, the message about the missing pages was a complete fabrication. The elaborate ruse to convince them that the data was real counted on them thinking the assassination attempt was intended for their captain, not Marceau. Of course, Sirkal had been instructed to make it look like he missed his target. Marceau, who knew how good a shot he was, wouldn't have realized until it was too late that she had been used.

The deception gave them time to get to Lithuania and carry out their mission to wipe out the treasure and the evidence of the formula that it held. As a side benefit, Golov got another chance to strike at the country that had ruined his career. Russia would never be reunited with the precious items that had been taken from it.

The SUV arrived at the prearranged meeting place, a coffee shop two blocks away from the glass-clad offices of the local natural gas utility, Metanas Energija. Golov, Sirkal, and O'Connor entered the shop, while the two other men stayed with the vehicle.

They all ordered drinks and sat down. Two minutes later, Robertas Kulpa entered, surveying the other customers before letting his eyes settle on Golov. He was a burly man in his forties with long sideburns and an aquiline nose that looked like it had been broken several times. He took a seat at their table without ordering.

"This is not a good place for me to meet," Kulpa said in a low voice. "People I know from Metanas may come in."

"That is your problem, not mine," said Golov. "You've been paid well enough to take the risk. I assume you received the deposit?"

He nodded as he kept an eye on the front door. "Thirty thousand euros, just as you promised. And the other half?"

"On completion of our project."

Kulpa's eyes glittered at the thought of the next payment. The avarice fairly radiated from Metanas's most senior operations foreman, and Golov was sure they'd picked the right man. Ivana had identified Kulpa as the person at the company most likely to be compromised because of massive gambling debts he'd accrued.

"We sent you a list of equipment that we'll need," Golov said. "Is it ready for tomorrow?"

Kulpa nodded eagerly. "I've signed out a van and it's loaded with all of the gear you asked for."

"And the location I specified?"

"It shouldn't be a problem —"

"Shouldn't be?" Golov interrupted.

Kulpa corrected himself quickly. "I mean, it *won't be* a problem to evacuate the building as you wanted. I have the authority to declare an emergency. Our company's men will be told it's a drill and instructed to stay away. We'll even have police officers stationed outside to keep the building secure."

"Good."

"How long will you need?"

"Three days. Perhaps five, if we are unlucky in our search."

Kulpa was shocked. "Five days?"

"Is that a problem? If it is, then give us our money back and we'll go." He stood up as if he were about to leave.

Kulpa's hands went up in supplication. "No!" He looked around again after his outburst and lowered his voice again. "No, five days will be fine, if you need it."

"Good. We'll meet you at seven tomorrow morning. I'd better be satisfied with your preparations."

Kulpa swallowed and nodded.

Without another word, Golov strode out of the coffee shop, flanked by Sirkal and O'Connor. They had another supplier to see before they turned in for the night.

As he got in the SUV, Golov imagined his American counterpart from the *Oregon* also beginning a search at the same time tomorrow. The news of the discovery and simultaneous loss of the cache hidden for two centuries would certainly make international headlines. He wished he could see the look on the *Oregon* captain's face when he realized just how close he'd come to finding the treasure.

As Juan had expected, by the time he and his people had flown into Vilnius, NUMA had come through with a thirty-foot Sea Ray powerboat and scanning equipment borrowed from the Lithuanian Maritime Academy. The boat and gear were being trailered from the coastal city of Klaipėda and would arrive in Vilnius by dawn.

With the equipment acquired, Linda, Gretchen, Trono, and MacD planned the Neris River search grid in Juan's hotel room after dinner. Linda and Gretchen would operate the metal-sensor array while Juan drove the boat, and Trono and MacD would use their scuba equipment if the sensors picked up anything worthy of inspecting more closely in the river. They decided to start on the far side of Grigiškės and work their way back toward Vilnius.

They wrapped up at ten o'clock. In the morning, they'd head out as soon as the boat arrived.

Gretchen lagged behind as the others said their good-nights and went to their rooms.

"I've been wondering about Marie Marceau," she said.

"About why she got involved with ShadowFoe?" Juan poured himself a scotch from the mini-bar. "Want one?"

"Please. No, I was wondering why she said she was betrayed."

Juan emptied another small bottle and handed her the glass. He took a seat on the room's sofa. "It does seem odd for her to make that switch so quickly. One minute she's planted there as bait to get us sniped and, the next, she's saying she was betrayed and giving us information about their plans."

Gretchen put two cubes of ice in her glass and sat down next to Juan. "If what she told us *is* useful information. Maybe it was all phony. Maybe it was her last act to protect ShadowFoe."

Juan shook his head. "I was looking into her eyes when she spoke. She really did think they double-crossed her."

"Or she knew she was dying and wanted to atone for her sins."

Juan shrugged. "Could be. Either way, it's been good getting back into the spy game with you for a little while."

"Do you miss it?"

"The CIA? No. The *Oregon* is where I belong." He put his drink on the table and looked up to see Gretchen staring at him. He returned her gaze just as intensely. "But I'd forgotten what a good team we were."

"Yes, we were." Her hand grazed his softly. "If the last week has proven anything, we still are."

When he'd worked with Gretchen before, Juan had resisted the attraction between them because of his marriage. But now there was no reason to hold back and he gave in to their mutual chemistry.

As if pulled by a magnet, he leaned toward her. She came to him at the same time, and their lips met, tentatively at first, then building in intensity until they were locked in a passionate embrace.

It was clear to both of them that Gretchen wouldn't be leaving the room until morning.

FORTY-EIGHT

At eight a.m. the full-sized Metanas Energija van crossed the bridge over the Neris River, Robertas Kulpa in the driver's seat and Sergey Golov sitting next to him. Sirkal, O'Connor, and the two other men — Jablonski and Monroe — were nearly finished changing into uniforms in the back. Thick clouds portended the heavy rain that was forecast for later in the day. Two more blocks and they reached their destination.

"There it is," Kulpa said, nodding at an imposing white neoclassical church.

The Vilnius Cathedral, built over the remains of a pagan temple, was fronted by a row of six huge columns, an homage to ancient Greek architecture. The dominant feature of the vast plaza outside the church was a freestanding bell tower. It seemed to be leaning, like the famous tower in Pisa, but Golov couldn't decide whether it was an optical illusion or not.

"I've seen the church already," he said. "We came here yesterday to take the tour."

Kulpa gaped at him. "Are you crazy? Then they will recognize you!"

"Relax. The guide was the only one who saw us, and the tours don't start until eleven. She won't be here."

Kulpa shook his head but kept driving. He slowed to a stop in front of the entrance next to two white and green police cars.

"I called ahead to get the evacuation started," he said.

The few tourists visiting the cathedral at this early hour were being ushered out of the building calmly but urgently. The cover story given to the church leaders was that a gas line running under the church had ruptured, detected by a drop in pressure at the central monitoring facility. Kulpa and his "workers" were there to determine if there really was a leak and where it was coming from inside the structure.

"Did the archbishop have any objections?" Golov asked.

Kulpa shook his head. "Once I explained the danger of a possible explosion, he seemed happy to have us come for the inspection, even if it takes a few days."

The cathedral had been rebuilt several times over the centuries due to wars and fires. It had been turned into a warehouse by the Soviets after World War II and returned to its role as a fully functional cathedral only in 1989. It was understandable that the archbishop should not want to see it destroyed yet again.

They unloaded the van, each carrying a bag of equipment. O'Connor stacked several boxes onto a handcart and they all headed to the main door. There they met the policeman in charge of the evacuation as he escorted a couple out through the main entrance.

"Is the building clear?" Kulpa asked in Russian. Although Lithuanian was the official language, most residents were also fluent in their neighboring country's tongue.

The uniformed officer nodded. "We have made a thorough sweep of the building. No one else is left inside. The archbishop has confirmed it and returned home. Two officers will remain outside to ensure that no one else goes in. All of the other doors have been locked."

"Good. Make sure your men stay out here as well. I don't want them causing an explosion by striking a careless spark. Absolutely no smoking."

"I'll inform the men."

Kulpa turned to Golov. "Masks on from here."

They all donned gas masks purely for show. When they were kitted up, they entered the church.

The central nave was lined with square pillars and painted a pristine white. Elaborate designs adorned the arched ceiling. Large oil paintings were the only other decorations. Row upon row of wooden pews stretched to the altar at the far end, which was buttressed by green marble columns.

"This way," Golov said, who was more familiar with the cathedral's interior than Kulpa was thanks to the tour the previous day.

They made their way to the far end of the room and went through a door that led to a set of descending stairs.

Golov nodded, and they all removed their masks.

He pointed at Kulpa. "You wait here. Make sure we are left alone. I'll station a man up here with you to keep you company."

Kulpa's eyes wandered to the staircase. Golov could tell that the utility foreman desperately wanted to know what they were up to, but he was either smart enough or scared enough not to ask.

"Of course," Kulpa said. He looked around and, seeing no chairs, plopped down on the floor.

"Stay with him," Golov said to Monroe, who nodded and took up a post standing next to the door.

The rest of them went down the stairs, carrying the boxes that had been on the handcart. As they entered the lower part of the church, the walls changed to exposed brick held in place by crude mortar. A musty smell pervaded the air.

They were in the cathedral's age-old catacombs. For the benefit of tourists, the ancient floor had been covered over by modern material, and soft lights at the base of the vaulted walls cast a moody glow. Although there was a maze of passages, clues Napoleon left in the diary pages would allow them to narrow down the search area considerably.

"Where do we start?" O'Connor asked as he set his box down.

Golov oriented himself so that he was facing north. "The pages from *Napoleon's Diary* indicated the treasure would be somewhere in that direction."

Finding valuables hidden away inside the cathedral wouldn't be unprecedented. Twenty years ago in the same cathedral, workers installing electrical cables discovered a cache of pre–World War II antiques secreted behind a wall. They had been sealed up as the Nazi invasion began, and then remained there after those who'd hidden the treasure were killed in the war, taking the knowledge of the secret stash with them.

Golov was certain Napoleon's men had similarly hid the treasure from Moscow. They had stowed it in a large chamber and then sealed it up so that the barrier looked like any of the other walls in the catacombs. After the men who did the work succumbed to the bitter cold during the remainder of the retreat, the emperor was left as the sole remaining person who knew exactly where the treasure was hidden. That information had died with him. Given the thickness of the walls, attempting to penetrate them with any type of sensing device would be useless. Brute force was the only way the riches would be unearthed.

Golov nodded to Sirkal, who unzipped his bag. He took out a handheld electric demolition hammer and a loop of heavy-duty extension cord.

"Find somewhere to plug that in," Golov said. "Let's start digging."

Forty-Nine

Rain had been pelting the river for an hour and it didn't show any signs of letting up. The fabric cover kept Juan dry as he piloted the Sea Ray during the monotonous search pattern up and down the river, three hundred yards in one direction and three hundred yards in the other, until they'd exhausted a grid and moved on to the next section. They'd been able to rig up covers for the metal detecting equipment, but Linda and Gretchen had to monitor the displays with only their rain jackets to shield them from the weather. Trono and MacD kept out of the way inside the cabin, playing cards.

The tedious operation had been going on for six hours now without a peep from the sensors. They ate sandwiches as they worked, and the boat had a small head, so there was no need to stop until they ran out of fuel. Their supply would last them until it was dark, at their current slow trolling speed.

The routine left Juan a lot of time alone with his thoughts. Gretchen had said little to him when they'd all met for breakfast to finalize their plans. His bed was empty when his alarm went off that morning.

Juan had set a rule for himself that he'd never get involved with a member of his crew, but Gretchen wasn't part of the crew. At least, not yet. His comments about her joining the *Oregon* were serious, but now he wasn't sure that was a good idea. The spark between them had always been there. It's just that they'd never acted on it while they were both married.

"Chairman," Trono called from inside the cabin, "I've got Eric on the line. Says it's urgent."

"All right," Juan said. "Take the wheel for me."

"I thought you'd never ask. It's been a while since I've been powerboat racing."

"Restrain yourself. Three knots is all we need."

They switched places. Juan took the mobile phone from him and ducked into the cabin. Raindrops hammered against the roof so loudly that Juan put his finger in his free ear.

"What have you got for me, Stoney?"

"Chairman, Murph and I have made some discoveries you need to know about."

"On the diary code or the words that Marie Marceau told us?"

"Both. We don't think Marceau said *zings,* like you thought. It's more likely that she said *Zingst,* which is a town along the Baltic coast — Zingst, Germany."

That certainly made more sense than anything else Juan had come up with. "What's the significance?"

"There's a huge transformer station there. One that feeds all of the power from the largest offshore wind farm in the world to the European electrical grid."

"That fits with our intel that ShadowFoe was looking into the power system. Do you think they're targeting that station like the one they did in Frankfurt?"

"It's possible, especially since we've deciphered what Marceau meant by *lightning grid.*"

"Don't keep me in suspense," Juan said.

"When I was doing my Internet search, the Dutch translation of *lightning grid* popped up. It's *bliksem raster.* The reason it came up is that Bliksem Raster is also the name of one of the largest suppliers of industrial-grade electrical equipment to the

European Union."

"Any connection to Antonovich?"

"Just that he owns half of it as part of a joint venture."

Juan shook his head in amazement.

"It gets better," Eric continued. "The other half of Bliksem Raster was owned by Lars and Oskar Dijkstra."

"Why is that important?"

"Because Lars and Oskar are currently dead. Their private jet went down in Gibraltar last week on their way to the auction in Malta. Authorities still have no theory why the plane crashed, but one witness said the wing was glowing red before it caught fire."

"Sounds like the work of a high-powered laser."

"That's what we thought."

"Wait a minute. I know the Dijkstra name. They own a shipping line, don't they?"

"You stole my thunder. Guess what shipping line owned the *Narwhal.*"

Now it was all coming into focus. The Dijkstras must have gone into business with Antonovich and then something went wrong. Perhaps they had learned about the treasure and planned to acquire the Jaffa Column and *Napoleon's Diary* out from under him to find it themselves, but Antonovich killed them before they had the chance.

"What's the connection between Bliksem Raster and the transformer station in Zingst?" Juan asked. "Why would Marceau think those two pieces of information were important enough to tell us while she was dying?"

"We're still working on that one. Now Murph wants to talk to you."

Juan heard the phone shuffling and then Murph spoke.

"Chairman, I just got done with my analysis of the column. I wanted to make sure I had it right before I sent you on a wild-goose chase."

Juan frowned. "What do you mean?"

"I was able to reconstruct the etchings on the part of the Jaffa Column that was damaged and compare it to the notes in the diary. It took a bit of massaging, but I think I teased out the location of the treasure."

"You've got an exact spot on the river where we should look?"

"Not exactly. I don't think it's in the river at all."

"What are you talking about? The diary pages were clear."

"I think they were forged. Impressive job, if you ask me," Murph said.

"How do you know?"

"Because of what I found in the part of

the diary we have. See, ShadowFoe must have known we'd be able to narrow down the location of the treasure to Vilnius, so they couldn't just direct us to somewhere in, I don't know, Belarus. They had to make the location of the treasure believable but not where it really is. So they came up with this alternative."

"Then where *is* the treasure?"

"The code in the diary comes down to a fairly simple cipher that refers to specific letters in the diary itself. Then we transferred those letters to Greek inscriptions on the column, which referred to corresponding Latin characters underneath them. The damage obliterated some of the markings, but the ones that remained helped me partially spell out a particular location."

"Which is?" Juan asked impatiently.

"I'm texting it to you now."

Moments later, the phone dinged with the message.

Cata_om__s Cath__r_l_ Vi__ius.

"It's the best I could do. I think it's supposed to spell out 'Catacombes Cathédrale Vilnius.' The Vilnius Cathedral is in the center of the city, practically right next to the Neris River, and there's extensive catacombs underneath it."

Juan grimaced at being deceived. Marceau was just a pawn. She was killed simply as a diversion, to make him believe the information that had been planted on her phone. And he had been manipulated into wasting his time looking in the wrong place.

"We're on our way there," Juan said, then yelled up to Trono, "Mike! You're going to test your power racing skills after all."

"Really?" Trono called back with glee.

"I want to be in Vilnius as soon as you can get us there. Gun it."

Fifty

Piles of bricks littered the floor in three different locations where Golov and his men had removed them to reveal nothing more than the stone that formed the bedrock beneath the cathedral. But in the fourth spot he had chosen the demolition hammer punched through three layers of brick and mortar into a hollow space behind the wall. It had taken them another hour to pull enough bricks down to open a hole large enough for them to walk through and now Golov took the first step inside.

His flashlight illuminated a vault at least sixty feet long and forty feet wide. It was stacked six feet high with objects. Only a central aisle the width of a car remained accessible.

O'Connor passed him two high-powered work lights mounted on stands and Golov placed them so that they flanked either side of the aisle. When he turned them on, he gasped at the magnificent treasure that lay before him.

The entire wealth of nineteenth-century Moscow that hadn't been taken or burned by the Russians in their frantic retreat before Napoleon's army was crammed into this one room. The first item Golov noticed near the entrance was the gilded cross from the Ivan the Great Bell Tower, the tallest building in the Kremlin. It was the most famous item thought to be part of the treasure hoard and yet it lay on its side as if it were tossed there in haste. The gold leaf was just as bright as it had been over two hundred years ago when it was sealed in its hiding place.

The heaviest objects lay closest to the front, including at least a dozen ancient cannons, crates brimming with tarnished silver housewares, and iron boxes. He used a crowbar to open one and found it full of antique weapons dating back to the Gothic period. The next box he opened was only half full, but that's because it was filled with gold jewelry that outweighed the steel weapons.

Golov imagined the soldiers hiding this hoard, exhausted from their retreat through the frigid Russian winter, many having survived on nothing more than moldy bread and horsemeat they could scavenge from fallen animals. They would have carried the heaviest items only as far as they needed to, putting the lighter objects to the rear, before completing the arduous task of bricking up the entrance so that it would be virtually indistinguishable from the rest of the catacombs.

Now Golov had his chance to make sure that none of Alexei Polichev's formulas had survived and fallen into Napoleon's hands. If they were still here, he had to either retrieve them or destroy them.

Sirkal was the next into the room and surveyed the cache stoically. He walked with a measured pace behind Golov. He understood that the treasure in this chamber was nothing more than a stepping-stone to their true objective.

O'Connor and Jablonski, however, whooped it up as they came through and saw the riches before them. O'Connor scooped up a handful of gold jewelry to stuff in his pocket when Golov barked, "Put that back."

"Nobody's going to miss it," O'Connor protested.

"You can buy all the gold you want when we're done with Dynamo. I don't want this to turn into a scavenging free-for-all. We're here for a purpose."

"Fine," O'Connor grumbled. He tossed the jewelry back in the box.

Golov walked to the end of the aisle, scanning the crates and boxes for any sign of something from Moscow State University. He got to the dim end of the chamber without seeing anything that stood out. Relieved, he turned on his heel and walked past Sirkal, who had paused three-quarters of the way in.

Golov stopped next to him. "What is it?"

Sirkal pointed at something near the wall. "There's an illustration that looks like the one Ivana showed us. It seems to be a seal or a logo."

Golov never would have seen what the taller Indian had spotted. He climbed onto a crate and shined his flashlight in the direction Sirkal was pointing.

There it was. The old seal of Moscow State University. It was blackened at the edges but readable. The seal was affixed to the side of a leather trunk, which was also charred but intact.

"Bring it out here," Golov instructed. Sirkal and O'Connor hauled the trunk back to the aisle, where they set it down in front of Golov. The trunk was latched but unlocked.

Golov knelt and worked to unclasp the latches. The brass fittings had corroded shut over the centuries, so it took several strikes of his hammer to free them.

He raised the lid. There, in perfect condition, was a trove of papers dating from the time of Napoleon. His researchers at the Academy of Sciences had specifically requested that he bring back any noteworthy papers recovered during the invasion. He had done the same when he had conquered Egypt, bringing back discoveries identified there by his science adviser, Joseph Fourier, whose advanced differential equations are still taught to physics students.

Golov riffled through the papers until he saw a familiar name. He lifted a file out. The title was laden with mathematical jargon about encryption and codes that Golov didn't understand, but he definitely recognized the author's name: *Alexei Polichev.* He looked at several more papers by Polichev and they all seemed to be related to cryptography and the unique formulas that had formed the basis for Ivana's virus programs.

Now he had a decision to make. Should he take the trunk with him or destroy it with the rest of the treasure? The plan had been to destroy everything and let the recovery team take weeks to sort it all out. The files would be forever lost.

But he also wondered if there might be further use for Polichev's work. If Ivana could make sense of these papers, perhaps there was more they could accomplish in the future using his theories.

In the end, it was his curiosity that won out. He wanted to know what was in these documents.

Golov slammed the lid shut and closed the latches.

"We're bringing the trunk with us," he said to Sirkal and O'Connor. "Let's move it to the van. Carrying this out will look suspicious, so we'll have to take care of the police."

"And the rest of it?" Sirkal asked.

Golov took one last look at the vast treasure.

"Have your men set the charges."

"Ten minutes?"

Golov nodded. "That should give us plenty of time to get away."

Sirkal pointed to where they should place the explosives to produce the maximum damage to the treasure. They had enough C-4 to reduce the hoard to fragments. O'Connor and Jablonski grumbled about destroying that much gold, but they did as they were told.

Not only would the Russians fail to get their lost treasure back but the devastation would seem to be the result of the natural gas explosion they'd been sent here to prevent. By the time anyone suspected differently, Golov and his men would be long gone.

FIFTY-ONE

When Trono brought the boat to a halt under the bridge closest to the Vilnius Cathedral, water was falling from the sky in sheets, making the late-afternoon light even more dim. According to the forecast, it wouldn't let up for another hour. Juan, in his rain jacket, leaped out of the boat with a line, looping it around the bridge support and tying it off.

A wide concrete path, with grass growing in its crevices, bordered the river for those who wanted to stroll along the Neris or drop in a fishing line on a lazy afternoon. Today, the heavy downpour kept the path empty. A large tour boat docked farther up the river was also dark.

"I don't think anyone will mess with the boat on a day like today," Trono said as he hopped off. Linda, MacD, and Gretchen followed him.

"We won't be gone long," Juan said. "I'll

meet with whoever is in charge of the church and find out if anyone has been interested in the catacombs recently. Or, worse, if the catacombs have already been ransacked. Gretchen, we may need to bring Interpol's weight down on this one."

She nodded. "Assuming that the catacombs are still undisturbed, we can request that the Lithuanian authorities have them inspected for any possible hidden cavities."

"The other possibility is that they are in the cathedral right now," Juan said. "Without any intel, going in there will be risky, but we may also be able to catch them by surprise since they think we're still scouring the river for the treasure. We'll have to improvise. Anyone who thinks we should hold off speak now."

They were lightly armed with pistols only. However, Juan wasn't surprised when everyone remained silent.

"If Ah catch any of them myself, Chairman," MacD said, checking his weapon before replacing it in his waistband under his jacket, "Ah will make sure they give us our money back, unless they want firsthand knowledge of what happens to a gelding."

Trono winced. "I saw it done once. It's not pretty."

"I'm just glad you're on my side," Juan

said to MacD. "Let's go."

They climbed the stairs leading up through the steep, grassy embankment separating the riverside path from the city street level above.

Linda pointed down the street. "The church is a hundred yards that way."

A thick stand of trees made it impossible to see the cathedral from this distance. They started walking, and when they were within half a block, Juan could see an ornate white church with a circular tower out front.

He also saw a utility van parked in the square near a police car. Two officers were posted outside the entrance.

They stopped walking.

"What do you think that's about?" Linda wondered aloud.

"It can't be a coincidence," Juan replied.

"Only one way to find out," Gretchen said, putting her arm through Juan's. "Let's ask."

Juan shrugged. "Tourists?"

"That's what I had in mind."

"All right." He turned to Linda, Trono, and MacD. "The three of you, wait here."

"Wait a sec," Trono said. "That might not be the real police."

"Mike's right," MacD said. "They could be pulling off the same trick he and Ah did in Malta."

"If that's the case," Linda said, "they might recognize the two of you."

Juan frowned. They had a point. With all of their rain hoods pulled down, no ID was possible from this distance. But up close, Juan and Gretchen would be readily identifiable. "You have another idea?"

"No," Linda said, grabbing Trono's hand. "Same idea, different people. Be back in a minute."

Trono smiled at MacD before Linda led him away. Soon they were talking and laughing like a newlywed couple.

MacD looked at Juan with a sardonic grin. "She picked him instead of me? Ah will never hear the end of it."

Linda wasn't as experienced as the Chairman in deceptive practices, but she thought this would be an easy task. She was just worried about Trono. She'd chosen him because MacD might lay it on too thick, especially with that accent of his. Trono seemed more like a normal, unassuming boyfriend.

But now that they were walking, she was having second thoughts.

"What should I say?" Trono worried even as he was fake-laughing like she told him to. "I can parachute out of helicopters. I can dive down to three hundred feet. Acting isn't really my thing, although I make a good fake drunk on occasion."

"We'll work on that when we get back to the *Oregon,*" she said, patting his arm. "For now, just stay sober and follow my lead." He sounded more concerned than she was. Besides, it was too late to turn around. The police officers had already spotted them. It wasn't hard, since the downpour ensured they were the only tourists on the plaza.

The officers, who'd been chatting and laughing, turned to the obvious foreigners when Linda and Trono reached the dry portico.

"Church closed," one of the policeman said in halting English.

"We just want to take a look inside for a minute," Linda said. "We've heard a lot about this cathedral."

Trono smiled awkwardly and nodded but said nothing.

"Gas leak," the officer said. "Very dangerous."

Trono cleared his throat. "How long will it be closed?"

"Closed all day. Maybe tomorrow."

Linda took out her phone. "There's no way we could just get a few pictures?"

The officer was unmoved by her plea. His face remained a paragon of stoicism. "Maybe tomorrow," he repeated.

"So I'm thinking we need to come back tomorrow," Trono said to Linda.

"I'm getting that as well," she replied. To the officers she said, "Well, thanks anyway."

The officer nodded, tacitly sending them on their way.

"Come on," Linda said to Trono, leading him away and pointing to the bell tower. "I have an idea."

"We're not going back to the others to tell them what's going on?"

"In a minute."

Linda stopped near the utility van, which was parked next to the tower.

"Do you really think there's a gas leak in there?" she asked him.

"Not a chance," he said.

"I agree." She pulled Trono close to her and held up the phone like she was taking a selfie. "Smile, Mike. Remember, we're a happy couple."

They took a few photos, and then Linda said, "Stay here. Pretend like I'm going to take your picture in front of the tower."

As she backed up, Trono said, "Pretend how?"

"I don't know," she said as she put the

van between her and the policemen. "Strike different poses. Wow me."

While Trono chose ridiculous body positions like the world's worst supermodel, Linda bent down, unscrewed the cap on the front tire's inflation valve, and used a pen to press on the valve's stem. When the tire was completely flat, she screwed the cap on and went back to Trono.

"How was that?" he asked as they walked back toward the rest of the team.

"David Beckham has nothing to worry about."

They walked casually back to where the Chairman, Gretchen, and MacD were waiting out of view.

"They seemed like real police to me," Linda said.

"Why are they posted out front?" Gretchen asked.

"They told us there's a gas leak inside."

The Chairman nodded in appreciation. "I would have done something similar. Keeps everybody out of the building while they're doing the 'inspection.' How long have they been in there?"

"All day," Trono said. "And they might still be here tomorrow."

"Good. Then maybe they haven't found the treasure yet. Linda, wait here and keep the front entrance under observation."

Trono smiled at Linda. "If anyone comes out, it'll take them a while to get anywhere. Linda had the bright idea to flatten one of the van tires."

"Nice work," the Chairman said to her.

"Where are you going?" she asked.

"We'll find another way in," he said. "Churches aren't exactly known for their high security. I want to see if there's a way to ambush them inside. Outside, there's too much distance to cover before they'd see us, not to mention that they may have the cops in their pockets. Give me a call if you see anything that needs attention."

Linda didn't like being left out, but she had to admit that she was the one with the least combat training. "I'll keep you on speed dial."

The three of them left to circle around to the back of the church while Linda crept farther forward until she could see the front entrance from behind one of the trees.

Three minutes later, the police turned in unison toward the door of the church as if someone were speaking to them. The Chairman and the others could have made it inside by now, but certainly they wouldn't have called over to the police. Someone else had to have gotten their attention.

On further prompting, the officers strolled through the door and disappeared. For a few moments, there was no movement at all. Linda quickly texted the Chairman.

Be aware. Police coming inside.

As soon as she finished sending the message, three different men came out of the cathedral. The three uniformed utility workers were hauling an antique trunk.

FIFTY-TWO

After leaving Linda and finding a side door that was easily jimmied, Juan and the others were inside the Vilnius Cathedral, looking at the dead body of a beefy man sporting sideburns down to his jaw. He was lying at the top of the stairs leading down to the catacombs.

Juan searched the corpse and found a card identifying him as Robertas Kulpa, an employee of the local energy utility. He found Kulpa's phone, but this one didn't have a thumbprint reader, like Marie Marceau's did, so he couldn't unlock it. They'd have to try to crack it for clues later.

"Now we know how they staged this," Gretchen said in a low voice.

Juan's phone vibrated. He quickly pocketed Kulpa's phone before he read the text from Linda on his own that said Police coming inside. Another came only seconds later: Three men carrying trunk coming out. One fits your description of Golov.

So the captain of the *Achilles* himself was here. Juan realized this might be the perfect opportunity to stop their scheme in one shot. And with the van crippled with a flat, now would be the time to strike. Juan peeked into the cathedral nave, where he saw two more bodies lying on the floor at the far end. Both were wearing police uniforms, and blood was pooling on the marble tile.

The sound of two sets of footsteps approached from the catacombs below. Juan motioned for Gretchen, MacD, and Trono to press themselves against the wall opposite Kulpa's corpse, their pistols at the ready.

One of the men coming from the catacombs was speaking into a radio. "Jablonski and I are done setting the charges," he said in English. "Nine minutes, and counting, before the treasure is toast. What should we do with Kulpa?"

A voice Juan recognized as Golov's replied, "Put him in the chamber. We'll take the policemen down there, too. It'll look like an accident long enough for us to get away."

"Got it. How long to fix the flat?"

"Sirkal and O'Connor are changing the

tire now. We'll be back inside in two minutes."

Their radio conversation ended, Jablonski and his comrade marched up the stairs, discussing what they were going to have for dinner as if they were on any ordinary job. Juan couldn't believe his luck. With a pair of ambushes, they could capture Golov and his men in one fell swoop, quietly and bloodlessly.

That plan lasted all of six seconds. Just one ding ruined it.

While reading Linda's text, Juan had forgotten to turn off the ringer on Kulpa's phone. He didn't know if the utility worker's cell had received a text or just announced a calendar reminder, but it didn't matter. The problem was that the phone — the only one that should have been there — was no longer on the same side of the room as its owner's body. One of the men coming up the stairs must have realized that because he stopped dead.

"What is it?" Jablonski asked.

"Something's wrong," the radio guy replied.

"What do you mean . . . Wait, wasn't Kulpa on —"

The surprise was gone. Juan couldn't wait. He dived to the floor at the top of the stairs, his pistol aimed where he'd heard the closer voice.

Two athletic ex-military types were side by side on the stairs. The man on the right held a radio in one hand and already had his gun raised in the other. Juan's sudden appearance on the floor caused him to snap off a shot before he could adjust his aim. Juan put a round through his forehead and the man dropped like a rag doll.

The blond man to the left had to be Jablonski. He was pulling his own weapon from its holster when Juan's barrel shifted to point at his face. Jablonski froze mid-draw.

"Drop it!" Juan yelled.

Jablonski complied and the gun clattered as it tumbled down the stairs.

Juan kept his gun on the man as MacD brought him up the steps and Trono retrieved the dropped weapon.

"Golov had to have heard those shots," Gretchen said.

"And it won't take long for them to figure out what happened," Juan said. "These two might not be important enough to wait for."

His phone buzzed. Linda was calling. At the same time, the radio came to life.

"Monroe, are you there? What happened?"

Juan picked up the radio, gave it to

Jablonski, and pointed his pistol at the blond's temple. "Tell him that one of the policemen wasn't dead. He shot Monroe and you need help carrying him out."

Jablonski stared at Juan for a moment, then nodded and spoke into the radio. "This is Jablonski. One of the cops was still alive. He got Monroe, but I killed him. Monroe's still breathing, but I need help bringing him out."

"Okay, give us a minute."

"I doubt that," Juan said under his breath before answering Linda's call. "We're okay. What's Golov doing?"

"Those shots kicked them into high gear. They're scrambling to get the spare on. They'll be done in a minute or two."

"Can you hit them?"

"It'd be luck from this distance in the rain."

"Get ready to shoot anyway," Juan said. "We're coming out." He hung up and turned to Jablonski. "What's in the trunk?"

"Papers."

"What kind of papers?"

Jablonski shrugged. "I just work here, man."

"And you just love your job, don't you?" MacD said sarcastically, nodding at Kulpa's body. "What about the explosives, Chairman?"

"Make Jablonski show you where they are and disarm them. Gretchen, Trono — you're with me. Golov is here because of us. We can't let him get away."

"If they drive off, we can't follow them," Gretchen said. "We don't have a car."

"No," Juan said, "but the policemen do."

FIFTY-THREE

Sitting in the driver's seat, Golov kept his pistol trained on the cathedral's front door while Sirkal and O'Connor flung the flat tire aside and slammed the spare onto the hub. He knew that neither of the gunshots could have come from the policemen inside. No one survives a slit throat.

The square was deserted. It was unlikely that any passersby had heard the muffled shots or knew they represented gunfire. Still, whoever was inside with Jablonski could have called the police, meaning their window for escape could be growing narrower by the second.

"What's taking so long?" Golov shouted.

"It took us a while to get the flat tire off!" O'Connor yelled back. "Some of the lugs were screwed on too tight!"

"Well, hurry up!"

"Two on, three to go!" Sirkal called out with a grunt as he spun the wrench.

As Golov expected, someone pulled the church's large wooden door back. Golov aimed down the sight, ready to nail anyone who came through.

But at that moment, Golov was distracted by motion out of the corner of his eye by the side of the church. Rapid gunshots rang out as bullets burst through the van's windshield.

More shots blasted from the trees near the park, peppering the rear quarter of the van, where Sirkal and O'Connor were hunched over. They dropped their tools and dived inside the utility vehicle for cover.

Golov started the van, threw it into gear, and mashed the accelerator. Even more shots came from the front of the church, causing Golov to slew the van around and head in the direction of the river.

He could already tell that the spare tire was poorly attached to the van. The steering wheel threatened to tear itself from his hand as the tire wobbled on its hub. All he had to do was get a mile away, where they could ditch the van and steal another car so they could make their escape out of the country with the trunk of papers.

In the rearview mirror, he saw a police car gaining on them fast.

O'Connor saw them, too. "The cops are

coming!"

"That's not the police," Golov said. "Kill them."

Sirkal threw the rear door open, trying to take aim at the driver. He got off three shots before the police car was able to overtake them and pull alongside as they approached the Mindaugas Bridge.

Golov glanced over and couldn't believe his eyes when he saw the driver.

It was the same man who'd been at the gala in Malta. The captain of the *Oregon.* He was in the car with his fake wife and another man.

The captain smiled as he yanked the police car's steering wheel over and crashed into the side of the van.

With the hobbled wheel, Golov couldn't keep the van on a straight track. It veered to the right, aiming straight at the bridge's steel railing.

By instinct, Golov jerked the steering wheel right to avoid a collision with the railing. He realized too late that it was the wrong choice. He stood on the brakes, but the van was already on the wet grass alongside the Neris River. The wheel carved muddy ruts in the ground as the van slid toward the embankment. It flew over the edge and down the soggy slope toward the water. The van smacked, nose first, into the concrete path, bounced up, and splashed into the river.

The air bag saved Golov's life, but it didn't leave him unscathed. Blood coursed down his face. His forehead had struck the wheel as the van hit the water. That was nothing compared to the agony of his three fingers, which were dislocated when he had tried to brace himself on the dashboard.

With water swirling around his knees, he turned to see Sirkal and O'Connor in the back. O'Connor was up, but holding his head in both hands.

A screwdriver had impaled Sirkal in the shoulder. He stood and pulled it out without a word. He pressed his hand against the wound to stanch the flow of blood. The two of them left the trunk behind and leaped through the rear of the sinking van.

Golov jumped through the driver's door into the river, ready to swim to the shore and use the last of his bullets to fight his way up to the bridge. With any luck, they could hijack a car there.

Then he saw the boat moored under the bridge and he knew Providence was smiling on him. He yelled to the others and swam over to it, clenching his jaw from the intense pain of each stroke.

Sirkal was the one to reach it first. Using his powerful, uninjured arm, he pulled himself in, then reached down and heaved O'Connor and Golov inside with him.

Gunshots punched through the boat's fiberglass hull. O'Connor returned fire while Sirkal pried open the dashboard so that Golov could hot-wire the ignition. His dislocated fingers screamed as he manipulated the wires with his thumb and index finger until the connection was made. With a spark, the engine roared to life.

Sirkal sliced through the lines tying the boat to the bridge, and Golov hammered the throttle forward. He looked back in frustration at leaving Polichev's formulas to sink in the river. The van's rear end slid beneath the surface with barely a splash.

He expected the police car to parallel their course along the river. Instead, the man who'd been in the car with the captain was racing down the stairs toward where the van had gone down, stripping off his jacket as he ran. The Oregon's captain was hot on his heels.

They must have been trying to save the contents of the submerged trunk. Surely the ink and paper would turn into a sodden mess, but if it were saved quickly, the formulas might still be legible.

Golov slowed and spun the wheel, bringing the Sea Ray around in a U-turn.

"What are you doing?" O'Connor yelled, incredulous. "We've got to get out of here!"

Golov ignored him and jammed the throttle to its stops, determined that this operation wouldn't be a complete failure.

FIFTY-FOUR

Juan chased Trono down the steps of the embankment to the river, yelling for him to wait. As Trono had seen the van sinking with the trunk that might hold the clues to what Golov was after, he pulled a length of rope and a flashlight from the police car's supplies and raced down the stairs in an attempt to save it. Over his shoulder, he had called for Juan and Gretchen to chase the boat and come back for him later. He was so fixated on the sunken van that he didn't notice Golov swinging the boat around downriver.

But Juan had noticed. He leaped down the steps two at a time, but he couldn't stop Trono from plunging into the river. An experienced diver, Trono would have no trouble swimming down to the van and attaching the rope to the trunk so they could haul it up.

With his gun still in hand, Juan dived into

the water and kicked his way down to the van. Trono was already inside the cargo space, tying the rope to the trunk's handle. Juan grabbed his arm and motioned for him to get out of there. Confused by Juan's presence, Trono nodded and followed him out of the van, still holding the free end of the rope.

The roar of the Sea Ray's engine announced that it was fast approaching. Trono's eyes went wide with understanding that they were in danger. They both dolphin-kicked underwater all the way to the river's bank. When they reached the concrete lip, Juan surfaced and saw the boat coming even with the bridge and slowing down. Golov was driving, and his lip curled in satisfaction when their eyes met. He had Juan just where he wanted.

What happened next took only seconds, but, for Juan, they would always play back in his mind in slow motion.

A red-haired man behind Golov had his pistol pointed at Juan. There was a third man in the boat, a huge Indian, but he was unarmed.

Out of breath, Trono came up for air next to Juan, who shoved Trono aside, using the momentum to push himself in the other direction.

As he did so, a bullet whizzed past Juan's head. He raised his own gun from the water and fired three quick shots at the redhead. Two of Juan's shots hit home, one in the chest and one in the temple. The redhead fell forward, firing as he dropped. Rounds plunked into the water beside Juan.

Shots came from behind Juan and stitched a line across the boat's hull. Golov ducked, turned the boat around, and revved it up to full throttle. He glanced back in fury as he took the Sea Ray downriver at full speed. Not only had they missed their target but Golov was now down another man.

Juan spun around and saw Linda on the pathway nearby. With her pistol down by her side and a look of horror on her face, she turned and called up to Gretchen.

"He's been shot!"

Juan started to correct her, to say it had just been a close shave, when he realized Linda wasn't looking at him.

Juan whipped around and saw that the water had turned crimson with Trono's blood. Trono gasped as he tried to stay afloat with only one good arm. His left arm was rendered useless by the gunshot wound in his chest.

Juan swam over and wrapped his arm around Trono to keep him from sinking.

"I dropped the line," Trono sputtered.

"Don't worry about that," Juan said as he dragged Trono to the bank of the river so that Linda could grab his hand. "Hold on to him."

"You're going to be okay, Mike," Linda said.

Juan scrambled out of the water and then pulled Trono out by his shoulders. The motion should have been agonizing, but the former pararescue jumper did little more than grunt.

Juan lay Trono down on the concrete, and Linda put pressure on the wound.

"We need to get him to a hospital," she said. "I mean, right now."

"I know," Juan replied. "He's losing blood fast. We can't wait for an ambulance. We need to get him up to the police car."

He was about to pick up Trono and carry him up the stairs when he saw the police car nose over the hill and skate down the slick grass. Gretchen expertly guided the car onto the concrete, stopping before it could tumble into the river. She jumped out and ran over to them.

"There's a sloping cement pathway about a quarter mile from here where I can drive out," she said. "I've already mapped the route to the hospital on my phone."

They put Trono in the backseat with his head on Linda's lap so she could keep applying pressure. Gretchen handed Juan her phone with the map instructions on it and put the car in gear. As she accelerated along the river, Juan hit the sirens and lights before twisting around to see Trono. His face was bone-white, but he was still conscious.

"We'll be there in a few minutes, Mike," Juan said. "Hang on."

Trono looked up at Linda, who stroked his hair with one hand while the other stayed firmly against his chest. Despite the pressure, blood continued to ooze between her fingers.

"No hurry," he croaked with a faint, lopsided grin. "This isn't so bad."

"Is that all of them?" MacD asked Jablonski, the catacomb vault echoing with his words.

He kept his pistol trained on his captive and picked up the last of twenty blocks of plastic explosives that Jablonski and his friend had scattered throughout the vast Russian treasure. The countdown timer had less than two minutes left. The rest of the blocks were piled near the entrance, their detonators removed and timers disengaged.

"That's it," Jablonski said.

"Good," MacD said, walking toward the entrance to the chamber and motioning for Jablonski to follow him. "Because if you're lying, Ah will not appreciate it."

"I guess you'll have to take my word for it."

"No, Ah won't. We're going back to the front to turn off all the lights. If Ah see the glow of another timer in the darkness, your pants will be on fire in more ways than one."

When MacD got close to the entrance, his phone began to buzz insistently. It was only this close to the stairs that his phone could get a signal.

He put up a hand to Jablonski for him to stop. He pulled the detonator out of the explosive and set it down on one of the antique cannons, keeping his eye on the timer as it continued to count down.

The phone showed the Chairman's number.

"MacD here."

"Get out of there as soon as you can," the Chairman said in a clipped voice, the tension in it palpable.

"What happened?"

"Mike's been shot. We're heading to the hospital. The police are going to be swarming around the church any minute now, so you need to leave."

MacD had never heard that amount of tension in the Chairman's voice. It had to mean Trono was in bad shape. MacD's grip tightened on the phone.

"Meet Tiny at the airport," the Chairman said. "We'll join you there if and when we can."

"But I have —"

MacD had become distracted by the Chairman's news and didn't notice that Jablonski had edged over to the cache of weapons beside him and put his hand on the hilt of an antique sword. He had only a fraction of a second to react to Jablonski's lightning-quick slash. The blade barely missed chopping MacD's arm off, but it struck the SIG Sauer he was carrying, sending the pistol skidding along the floor.

He tumbled backward to avoid a lethal thrust aimed at his chest. He didn't stand much of a chance in the small space of the vault without a weapon. He plucked the plastic explosive from atop the cannon, jabbing the detonator back into the block.

The timer was down to thirty seconds and he waved it in front of him so Jablonski could see. The mercenary halted his advance but stayed balanced on the balls of his feet.

"Drop that sword or we both die," MacD said.

Jablonski sneered. "You don't have the guts, man."

"You're wrong about that. What about you?"

Fifteen seconds left.

"After this, I'm dead anyway. So, I think I'll call your bluff."

Ten seconds.

"Fine," MacD said. "Here you go." He held out the block of explosives as if he were handing it over.

Five seconds.

Jablonski reached out to yank the detonator from the explosive, but MacD pulled the block of C-4 away at the last moment. He crammed it down the barrel of the ancient cannon, dropped to the floor, and covered his ears.

Jablonski was standing right in front of the cannon. The thick iron barrel focused the massive detonation just like the gunpowder that used to fire its shells.

The shock wave hurled Jablonski across the chamber. His smoking corpse came to rest atop the gilded Ivan the Great cross.

The concussion knocked the wind from MacD's lungs. The ringing in his ears muffled the sound of his own footsteps as he got to his feet.

He retrieved his gun and phone. The cell's

screen had been shattered by the explosion.

MacD staggered up the stairs, still dazed not only by the blast but also by the news of Trono's serious injury. And now he had no way to contact the Chairman for an update until he returned to the airport.

He eased open the cathedral's side door to the approaching wail of police sirens. He stepped out and walked away as casually as he could past the police cars pulling up to the front of the cathedral. He tried to look like a curious tourist giving them space.

It was only by force of will that he made himself wait two blocks before taking off at a sprint to look for a cab that could get him back to the airport.

Gretchen had her full concentration on the road as she weaved around cars in the race against time toward Vilnius University Hospital. The siren and lights were doing their job getting people out of her way as she ran every red light, but several times she had to slow down for a semi that was too slow to get out of the way, unleashing a string of curses from her as she blasted the horn for them to move.

"We're a mile out," Juan said, trying to keep his voice calm. Trono's breathing had become ragged. "How are you doing, Mike?"

"Getting . . . cold," he rasped. "Got a blanket?"

"We'll get you patched up in no time," Linda said in her most soothing tone, but a quick glance at Juan betrayed her fear for Trono's condition. Despite the pressure she was putting on his chest, she hadn't been able to completely stop the flow of blood pouring from him.

"Not sure . . . I'll make it . . . there."

"Sure you will."

"You better, mister," Juan said. "We need you back at work."

With every ounce of remaining strength, Trono lifted his arm up and extended a trembling hand to Juan, who reached over the seat and took it. It felt cold and clammy and had none of the vigor and vitality Trono was known for among the crew. He lifted his head and fixed Juan with a melancholy gaze.

"Thank you," Trono said, barely able to breathe out the words.

Juan's voice choked up. "For what?"

"For the . . . best job I've ever . . . had . . ."

Juan shook his head. "No, Mike. Thank you."

Trono's head fell back and he looked up

at Linda, whose eyes welled with tears.

"Such a nice face," Trono said. Then he hissed out one final breath and his eyes glazed over, the pupils dilated. His hand went limp in Juan's.

Juan gently placed Trono's hand down on his chest. Linda, sobbing unabashedly, closed his eyes and continued to stroke his hair.

Juan turned off the lights and siren. Gretchen was about to ask what he was doing when she looked in the rearview mirror and saw Linda crying. She bashed her hand against the wheel with a shout of pure rage.

At this point, Juan was simply drained. His rage would come later.

"Where do you want me to go?" Gretchen asked.

"We need to find another car."

"I'll look for an empty parking lot where we can borrow one. Then to the airport?"

Juan nodded slowly, swallowing the grief that threatened to overwhelm him. "Back to the *Oregon.* We're taking Mike home."

FIFTY-FIVE

COPENHAGEN

It wasn't until the next morning that Golov and Sirkal were able to rendezvous with the *Achilles.* They weighted O'Connor's body with some of the expensive sensing equipment on board the Sea Ray and unceremoniously dumped it overboard in a more remote section of the Neris River before abandoning the boat. They stole a car to drive to the Lithuanian border, where they used false passports to cross into Belarus. During the entire flight from Minsk to Copenhagen on Antonovich's private jet, Golov fumed at the near-total failure of the operation in Vilnius.

He went straight to Ivana's cabin when he boarded the yacht, sending Sirkal to get his arm sutured properly to replace Golov's makeshift sewing job. When Sirkal was done, he'd revise his upcoming mission, since they were now down three men.

"How are your plans coming?" Golov said abruptly when he opened her door and quickly closed it behind him.

Ivana's quarters weren't quite as spacious as Antonovich's suite, but they were far larger than all but the most lavish accommodations aboard a cruise ship. Most of the space was taken up by a vast array of computer equipment whose purpose Golov had no interest in understanding. Half a dozen monitors displayed software code or videos in small windows. European electropop blared from huge floor speakers. It was all connected to the yacht's high-speed satellite Internet feed.

Unlike the disgusting hives of hackers Golov had seen on TV shows and in movies, Ivana's desk was tidy and clean. All of her empty protein bar wrappers and Red Bull cans had found their appropriate place in her wastebasket, and the only papers on the desk were piled in a stack as if aligned by a T square.

She was startled by the sudden entrance. When she saw who it was, she muted the music and tossed a plastic bag away as she shoved the last couple of almonds into her mouth. She leaped to her feet and gave her father a big hug.

"I'm so glad you made it back in one

piece." She inspected his bandaged nose and fingers, which Sirkal taped up after snapping them back into place.

"O'Connor didn't," Golov said. "And neither did Monroe and Jablonski. Even worse, the Russians will now get their hands on everything Napoleon stole from Moscow."

There was nonstop television coverage about the bizarre and violent discovery of "Napoleon's treasure," as all the news outlets were now calling it. Reports of the trove's immensity were coming to light in slow drips as the investigators and bomb removal experts inspected the uncovered vault, but it was already being compared to King Tut's tomb in intrinsic and historical value. The consensus was that although the treasure had been found in Lithuania, the government there would ultimately return the items to Russia, either by virtue of a lawsuit or as a goodwill gesture.

The thought of the Russians celebrating their good luck turned Golov's stomach. But soon they would forget all about that when they were blamed for one of the world's greatest manmade disasters.

Ivana nodded. "The news from Vilnius has been on every network. They found five bodies in the cathedral, including our guys,

Kulpa, and the two policemen."

"No mention of anyone else?"

"They did mention a shoot-out at the river. They've sent divers into the water, looking for bodies. No one is attempting to recover the van or its contents yet. Do you think there's anything in Lithuania that can lead back to us?"

"No, there's no record of Monroe or Jablonski being in Antonovich's employ, and they won't find O'Connor for a long time. At least we were able to destroy Polichev's work. Even if they recover the trunk now, it'll take them weeks or months to properly dry and separate the papers. Depending on the extent of the water damage, they may never find out what's in them."

"By then, we'll be home free," Ivana said.

"Except we weren't able to eliminate the *Oregon* crew. I saw O'Connor hit one of them, but not their captain."

"You think they're still a threat?"

"I don't think their captain is the type who gives up when he's been smacked in the face. He'll come back at us even harder now. That's why I'm moving up our time line."

"To when?"

"The weather should be favorable for the next few days," Golov said. "I'll check to see when Sirkal can be ready. Which leads back to my original question. How are your plans coming?"

She nodded at her computer setup. "The banking code is all ready to go, thanks to Alexei Polichev. So is the circuit breaker virus."

Golov's chest expanded with pride at his daughter's ingenuity. Her latest masterpiece was a virus that would close all of the transformer circuit breakers designed by Antonovich and Dijkstra's joint venture. These were the critical components of the grid's industrial-sized substations. The vulnerability she'd be exploiting was actually built into the system to allow for centralized management of the power grid. When the breakers were closed and locked, there would be no way to keep a power surge from frying the entire grid. All it would take would be a single event to cause a cascading failure.

"After I activate the banking virus," Ivana continued, "it will take about five minutes to transmit and verify the receipt of thirty billion euros in the accounts we've set up in the Caymans, Panama, Singapore, and the Seychelles. Once the transfer is complete, I'll upload my other virus to the power grid and I'll shut down the circuit breakers. Then it's up to you to give the electrical system its push over the edge. After that, there will be no way to track the funds."

"And Antonovich?"

"He understands his part. He still thinks he'll live through this."

"He will," Golov said. "For a little while."

Once the transfers were complete and Europe was in chaos, the *Achilles* would make its way to Brazil, where it would be sunk in sight of the coast and plenty of witnesses, seemingly with all hands on board. Any remnants of their trail would go cold in a fiery cataclysm.

And if the *Oregon* made its way into their path, so much the better. They would blow it out of the water as well.

Ivana smiled at him.

"What?"

"I thought of one benefit of your trip to Vilnius."

Golov frowned at her. "Which is?"

"With O'Connor dead, we have another seven and a half billion euros to split between us and Sirkal."

Golov returned her smile and shook his head at the naïveté she still hung on to in spite of her brilliance. Her took her hands in his and said, "My dear, we were never going to give that money to him."

She furrowed her brow and said, "And Sirkal?"

Golov shook his head. "Did you really think I was going to share thirty billion euros with anyone but you?"

FIFTY-SIX

THE NORTH SEA

It wasn't often that the entire crew of the *Oregon* assembled on deck, but no one was going to miss Mike Trono's funeral. The notoriously vicious weather this area off the coast of Norway was known for had given way to a cloudless sky, allowing the ship to maintain its position on the placid sea. The peaks flanking a fjord in the distance lent the ceremony a majesty that complemented its solemn mood.

Before speaking, Juan took a moment to look at his people one by one. He caught the eye of some of them. Others couldn't look at him for fear of breaking down. Some wore dark suits and dresses — even Murph had foregone his normal T-shirt for a formal suit and tie borrowed from Eric Stone. Many of the military veterans, including Linc, Linda, Eric, and MacD, were in their dress uniforms. Gretchen, who didn't know

Mike the way the rest of them did, respectfully stood in the back. Few of the eyes were dry, and every face choked back emotions at losing one of their own.

Mike's body lay inside a metal casket atop a platform draped with an American flag. The death certificate and necessary permit for transporting his remains into Oslo had been created by Kevin Nixon in the Magic Shop.

Because they knew how dangerous this job was, every crew member had filed a last will and testament with the Corporation. Mike's directive had been for Juan to notify his mother, father, and sister in Vermont, where they would arrange a memorial service. The conversation with his family had been just as heart-wrenching as Juan had anticipated. Mike's final wish was for the *Oregon* crew to commit his body to the sea.

This wasn't the first time that a member of the crew had been killed in action, but that didn't make the occasion any easier to endure. In Mike's sealed letter to Juan, he asked that remarks during his burial be brief. He'd rather the crew spend their time drinking and laughing as they remembered him. Juan did his best to grant that request.

"We've lost a great friend and co-worker

in Michael James Trono," he said, "but, more than that, we've lost a part of our family. Mike died the way he lived, putting his life on the line to ensure our success without ever thinking of himself. He was a man of action and honor, and he made the world a better place just by being in it."

Juan cleared his throat and went on. "Mike wanted us to send him off with a celebration of his life. Sharing a drink. Sharing some laughs. Sharing war stories. And we'll do all of that when we can. But he also would have wanted us to finish our mission first. There was no place Mike would rather be than on this ship and with this crew and he will be here as long as we remember him."

Juan stepped aside for Julia Huxley, who worked hard to keep her voice steady as she read a prayer. Then Juan commanded, "Firing party, present arms!" Linc, Linda, and MacD stepped forward, weapons at the ready. The pallbearers tilted the platform holding the casket, sending it into the sea during a three-gun salute. There was no bugle on board, so Max started a playback of Taps over the *Oregon*'s external speakers. They stood rigid for the mournful dirge, while two of the pallbearers folded the flag and handed it to Juan. He would send it to

Mike's parents along with their son's other effects.

Still in his suit, he went down to the conference room, where his senior staff gathered along with Gretchen.

"I'm sorry we have to get right back into this," he said, "but I don't think we have much time to act. Gretchen, before the funeral you told me that you got a tip about Antonovich's upcoming whereabouts."

"Yes, Interpol has been in contact with the two sons of Lars and Oskar Dijkstra, the brothers killed in the Gibraltar plane crash. We've been investigating it as a possible act of terrorism, and their family has given their full cooperation. They told us that their fathers had been scheduled to attend a private opening of the new European Continental Control Hub outside of Maastricht, the Netherlands, in a few days."

Juan sat forward. "Is that related to the electrical grid?"

"Yes. Bliksem Raster, the Dijkstra-Antonovich joint venture, was responsible for a good portion of the control architecture. It came online last week, and the CEOs are scheduled to get a private tour of the facility."

"When?"

"It was supposed to be day after tomorrow at four p.m."

"I'll bet Antonovich asked to move it up, didn't he?"

Gretchen nodded. "He asked to shift it to tomorrow at the same time."

"They're pushing their time line forward because they're jumpy about what happened in Vilnius. The question is, what's their endgame?"

"Eric and I have an idea about that," Murph said.

"The Control Hub was designed to manage all of the European grid's transformer stations from one central location," Eric said. "It would be the perfect spot to attack the power system."

"You think they're trying to take down the continent's whole electrical grid?" Juan asked.

"We're already past the ten days that was warned about in the message ShadowFoe left at Credit Condamine for us," Murph said, "and there hasn't been a financial meltdown, so the banks have breathed a sigh of relief, right? Well, what if that threat was empty? Maybe they never planned to take down the banking system. We suspect that the bank security code was compromised as a result of the Credit Condamine heist, so what if their plan all along was to hack into the banks for money?"

Gretchen shook her head. "But we've been monitoring the banks very carefully since then. There have been no large discrepancies in trading or deposits."

Eric raised a finger. "They'd know you'd be watching. But what would happen if the trades were transacted right before a major power outage?"

Her face clouded at the implications of the question. "The banks would be scrambling just to get the system back online. Any extended disruption would cause a financial meltdown. Tracking any bogus trades would be a low priority until we got everything up and running again. In fact, it might be impossible to trace them even after the system was functional again."

"I think ShadowFoe knows that," Murph said. "They could get away with billions."

Juan asked, "What does the transformer station at Zingst have to do with this?"

Eric answered, "The destruction of the Frankfurt transformer station has minimized the ways power can be redistributed. Suddenly, losing the Zingst station would be catastrophic."

"We're talking a continent-wide blackout," Murph said. "Transportation would grind to a halt. Gas pumps wouldn't work. Airports would shut down. Computers and communication networks would be inoperable. No phones. No Internet. The economy would go into a free fall."

"How long would it take to get the power back up if most of Europe's transformers went off-line?" Juan asked.

"Three months, if we're lucky."

"Three *months*?"

"When we say the transformers would melt down," Eric said, "we mean that literally. They would be totally destroyed. And industrial-sized transformers aren't exactly available at the local hardware store. They'd have to be built from scratch, transported, and installed after the damaged ones were ripped out."

Murph added, "Without power, how do factories in Europe make new ones? They'd have to come from overseas, which would take even longer."

"It would be complete anarchy," Juan said with grim understanding. "Millions could be starving within weeks without food shipments."

"I have to warn my superiors at Interpol," Gretchen said. "Get them to stop the tour."

"You can try. But based on what evidence? This is all a hunch, though it's one I happen to believe."

"Then postpone it at least."

"Give it a shot," Juan said. "But I'm not putting my eggs all in that basket. Billionaires are hard to say no to."

"You want to stop them ourselves."

"I'm not going to sit on my hands while Antonovich and Golov bring Europe to its knees. If there are two prongs to their attack on the electrical grid — the Control Hub and the transformer station — then we have to take on both prongs. Eddie, take Linc and Murph to the Netherlands and meet with the relatives of the Dijkstras. I want you on that tour with them in case ShadowFoe tries anything."

"Sure," Eddie said, "but how do we convince them to take us along?"

"I'm going to send them the video of the *Achilles* destroying the *Narwhal.* That should be enough to give them doubts about their fathers' business partner."

"Where will I be?" Gretchen asked.

"With me right here on the *Oregon,* " he said. "I don't think a coastal transformer station was chosen randomly. I bet Golov is going to use Antonovich's yacht to destroy it and I want you there with the full force of Interpol when we capture the *Achilles.*"

FIFTY-SEVEN

At nine a.m. the next morning, Eddie, Linc, and Murph checked in at the reception desk of Dijkstra Industries, headquartered in a stately Gothic stone building in the center of town. As they were escorted to the CEO's office, Eddie noticed that the Dijkstras had spared no expense on the antiques lining the halls. It was decorated like an elegant royal palace and, as far as Eddie knew, it might have been one.

The CEO's office was even more ornately furnished. A reed-thin man in his late twenties leaned on the desk, talking on his phone. He waved them in with two fingers. The three of them stood as they waited for his call to finish. After a few more words in Dutch, the man hung up the phone.

"Gustaaf Dijkstra," he said in a regal tone as he stood and shook their hands. "Oskar Dijkstra was my father. You are Edward

Seng, Franklin Lincoln, and Mark Murphy, is that correct?"

"Yes, sir," Eddie said. "We're very sorry for your loss."

"Yes, it's been difficult for all of us. My cousin Niels is sorry he couldn't be here, but he's in Singapore negotiating a large shipping contract. He threw himself back into work after the funeral of my uncle Lars." Gustaaf paused to shake his head slowly. "So, you think Maxim Antonovich had my father killed?"

"We don't have any conclusive evidence that he was responsible," Murph said, "but we're sure his people did it."

"What makes you so sure?"

"According to the forensic team analyzing the wreckage," Linc said, "there's evidence that the plane's wing was heated from the outside before it caught fire. A high-powered laser would leave that exact signature."

Gustaaf frowned. "I thought the crash was suspicious, but a laser?"

"You saw the video we sent of the *Achilles,*" Eddie said. "I'm guessing we wouldn't be here if you hadn't. Antonovich's yacht brought down your father's plane with the same laser that was used in the video of the *Narwhal*'s sinking."

"I don't know where you got that video,

but all I saw were missiles exploding in midair. I couldn't tell why."

"Then why are you helping us?" asked Linc.

"Because I very clearly saw the *Achilles* destroy the *Narwhal.* I have no idea why Antonovich would want to kill my father and sink one of our ships. Ownership of the joint venture remains fifty-fifty even with my father's and uncle's deaths, so assassination makes no sense for Antonovich. However, I do know that I don't trust him."

"But you trust us?"

"As your chairman suggested, I called the Kuwaiti emir, who is a friend of our family. He was very impressed with the job your company did for him and recommended your services very highly. If he trusts you, I trust you. And if Antonovich *is* behind my father's death, he might be coming after me and Niels next. I'm not about to sit back and wait for that to happen."

There was a knock at the office door and a young woman entered, carrying a roll of blueprints.

"Thank you, Yvonne," Gustaaf said, taking the plans from her. "Please close the door behind you on the way out."

He spread the papers on his desk and invited the rest of them closer.

521

"As you requested, these are the floor plans of the European Continental Control Hub. It's a high-security facility, with fingerprint and retinal scan access pads at all the doors. No one gets in if they're not in the system."

"Unless you're on a tour," Murph corrected.

"Yes. The tour will show off the main features of the Control Hub. If you're suspicious that Antonovich and this ShadowFoe hacker intend to hack the electrical grid, they'd have to do it from the command center."

The command center, located at the heart of the facility, was a large room containing over three dozen monitoring stations and a wall-sized screen mapping out the entire European grid.

"Are you sure we can't get this tour canceled or postponed?" Eddie asked.

As their Chairman had guessed, the warnings fell on deaf ears. The European electrical authorities weren't going to tick off one of their biggest suppliers on the basis of rumors and hearsay.

"I can cancel my participation in the tour," Gustaaf said, "but if Antonovich wants to go forward with it this afternoon, I'm sure they won't say no."

"Then it's important that you don't cancel. We need to be there when he and ShadowFoe are. We'll have to be ready for anything."

"But what could they do? Even Antonovich, and anyone he's with, couldn't get inside without being screened. They can't possibly be armed, and there are guards everywhere."

"Believe us, they'll have a plan to account for that," Linc said.

"They'll need access to the computers," Murph said, "which means they'll have to subdue the workers inside the command center somehow. No way ShadowFoe could hack into the system without anyone noticing."

"This all sounds so absurd," Gustaaf said, "but I'm willing to take you with me if it means we can stop them."

"That's all we ask," Eddie said. "We'd like to take some time to go over these plans so we can come up with some possible scenarios they might use and develop our countermeasures. Will it be any trouble getting us in with you?

Gustaaf shook his head. "I've already arranged for employee IDs for all of you, so —" He was interrupted by his phone. "It's my contact at the Control Hub."

Eddie couldn't understand what Gustaaf was saying in rapid-fire Dutch, but when the young businessman's eyes went wide, he knew it couldn't be good.

"Antonovich is on his way to the Control Hub," Gustaaf told them. "He asked them to push up the tour to this morning as a last-minute request."

"Right now?" Murph said.

Gustaaf nodded. "His helicopter is about to take off from the airport to fly to the Control Hub."

"Please tell me you have a chopper, too," Linc said.

"Of course. It's at the airport. But the Control Hub is in the other direction, near a small town called Terlinden."

"How far is that?" Eddie asked.

"Twenty kilometers," Gustaaf said. "We can be there in about twenty minutes."

"Have your car brought around. We need to go."

"I bet I can get us there faster than twenty minutes," Linc said.

Murph was already rolling up the building plans to look at in the car. As they hurried out of the office, Eddie called the *Oregon.*

The Chairman asked, "Did you get in to see Gustaaf?"

"We did, but we're just leaving. At this

moment, Antonovich is on his way to the Control Hub. We are, too."

"So he moved up the timetable even more. Smart. Luckily, so did we."

"You've caught up to the *Achilles*?"

"We've got them on the screen, right in the crosshairs." Eddie could hear the satisfaction in the Chairman's voice. "And Golov has no idea we can see them."

FIFTY-EIGHT

TWENTY MILES OFF THE COAST OF ZINGST, GERMANY

Sergey Golov watched the *Achilles*'s Russian flag whipping in the brisk wind and thought the morning couldn't be more perfect. Although the sun was shining, the Baltic Sea was churned into frothy white-caps by the steady breeze that caused the windmills in the far distance to spin at a furious pace. Over two hundred of the propellers, broader than the wingspan of a 747, fed their awesome power to the sprawling transformer station perched on the German coast.

The *Achilles* was actually closer to Denmark than Germany, which would aid in its escape once the transformers were destroyed. The yacht would simply disappear into the maze of islands that made up a good portion of the Danish land area. Then they'd swing around into the North Sea and rendezvous with Ivana's helicopter near Rotterdam before setting flank speed for Brazilian waters.

The sunny day helped as well. Solar power was making up a larger and larger portion of Europe's electricity supply, and because it was difficult to ratchet back solar cells during the daytime, the constant output made power regulation a challenge. The grid would be struggling to juggle the distribution from its maxed-out wind and solar farms while modulating the traditional gas, coal, and nuclear capacity. All it needed now was a nudge to throw it off balance and the system would collapse completely.

Golov was happy to see that traffic on the sea was relatively light today in these often heavily traveled waters. A containership had passed a few minutes before, and was nearly out of sight around the headlands of Falster Island, while a massive white cruise ship approached from the east, likely on a Scandinavian tour coming from Helsinki or Stockholm.

"Any other ships on the scope?" Golov asked the radar operator.

"No, sir, but I'm reading a small contact bearing three five zero."

Something was coming at them from the north, almost directly behind them, over the island.

The XO, Kravchuk, went over to the radar and leaned over the operator's shoulder. "Speed?"

"Eighty knots. It's in the air."

"Range?"

"Ten kilometers and closing."

Golov sat straighter in his chair. The *Oregon*. It had to be. "Is it a helicopter?"

"No," the radar operator replied. "Too small. It must be a drone. Probably not much larger than three meters wide."

"What are you up to?" Golov said under his breath. He eyed Kravchuk and ordered, "All hands to battle stations. Bring the laser and railgun online."

"Aye, sir," the XO replied, and the klaxon sounded throughout the ship.

Both the laser and railgun rose out of their hidden compartments.

The *Oregon* had to be out of sight somewhere, concealed by Falster Island's mass.

Golov called Ivana.

She answered on the first ring. "We're just landing outside the Control Hub."

"Good," he said. "I need you to send me a number."

Juan was inside the op center aboard the *Oregon*. Eric guided the ship through the narrow channels separating the islands in this part of the chain, a position that made her undetectable to the *Achilles.* The yacht was exactly where he thought it would be to give Golov a clear shot at Zingst's transformer station.

The image of the *Achilles* on the main view screen came courtesy of an observation drone operated by Gomez Adams. The size of an albatross, it flew in a circular pattern above the island far enough from the yacht that it wouldn't be recognized for what it was. Gomez's expert flying skills were being put to the test by keeping multiple drones on course.

At the same time, the large supply drone was now on a collision course with the *Achilles.* Golov had seen it by now, which was the reason that Juan could see the menacing railgun and telescope-like laser system rise from the yacht's deck.

"They're getting ready to shoot it down," Gomez said.

"I'd say it's a small price to pay," Juan replied. He turned to Max. "I'm sorry we're going to lose your baby."

"Hey, it was my idea to use it. I just wish we could shove it down Golov's throat."

"Linda, are you ready?" Juan asked her. She was sitting at Murph's normal position on weapons control.

She gave him a smile. "I've been ready for days."

"Chairman, I've got a call for you," Hali said. He was holding a cell phone. "It came in on Marie Marceau's phone. I've been monitoring the traffic on it. The caller says it's Sergey Golov."

"Put it on speaker." Hali nodded, and Juan said, "Why didn't you stick around in Vilnius, Golov? I had more to say to you."

"Why do you think I'm calling now? I've always enjoyed our interactions. And given how close we've become over the last week, don't you think I should know your real name, Captain?"

"I'm happy to let you know who beat you. My name is Juan Cabrillo."

"Captain Cabrillo, a pleasure to meet a challenger who's up to the task. But you have to know that an aerial attack against me is futile. You were threatening an admiral in Vladivostok during our two ships' last engagement, but I'm sure you heard what happened. And don't bother trying to disengage our weapons again. We've taken care of that issue."

"I wouldn't expect any less," Juan said. The supply drone was now only two miles from the *Achilles.* "By the way, thanks for leading us to Napoleon's treasure. You've made the Russians very happy."

He knew Golov's military history. The dig had to sting just a little.

"Yes, you got me there," Golov said. "But you won't get me here. Watch."

The supply drone began to glow red. In a few seconds, its lithium-ion batteries overheated and exploded, ripping the drone apart and sending it fluttering in pieces into the sea below.

Golov came back on the line. He was laughing.

"By all means, keep them coming, Captain Cabrillo. We could use the target practice. I'm enjoying it so much, I could do this all day."

"Actually," Juan said, "I don't think you can."

"Really? Why's that?"

"Watch." Juan nodded at Gomez, who was flying a third drone, a quadcopter called a Wasp. It approached the *Achilles* from an angle perpendicular to the supply drone's route. Because it was no larger than a gull, the radar signature was too small for it to be detected as it skimmed the waves under Gomez's sure-handed piloting skills.

At that moment, the Wasp hovered next to the *Achilles*'s white hull. The supply drone had been a decoy to get Golov to expose the laser, bringing it out of its protective covering. The Wasp rose until it was even with the yacht's deck. The laser's highly polished lens was the target.

Gomez flew the Wasp up to the laser as it madly spun, searching for a new target. He lowered the drone until it was only inches from the lens. When it was in position, he detonated the two pounds of C-4 it carried.

The Wasp's video feed went dark, but shouts Juan could hear over the phone told him all he needed to know. The drone had done its job.

"Having problems with your laser, Golov?" Juan casually asked. That brought a few smiles from his crew.

Golov came back on the line, fury in his voice. "Cabrillo, I will hunt you down and make sure that disgraceful pile of rusting metal you call a ship is reduced to fragments scattered across the bottom of the ocean."

"I think you'd better worry about your own ship, Golov. Linda, fire one."

"With pleasure, Chairman," Linda said.

With the press of a button, an Exocet anti-ship missile blasted from its launcher and rocketed toward the *Achilles.*

FIFTY-NINE

"Flank speed!" Golov shouted, when the radar operator announced that an Exocet was on the way, and hung up on Cabrillo. "Evasive maneuvers!"

The *Achilles* shot forward like a drag racer. But with no way to focus its deadly beam, the laser was a total loss. And Golov couldn't use the railgun if he didn't know where to aim it.

He ran over to the radar station and yelled into the operator's ear, "Find me a target!"

"I can't see them!"

"Where did the missile come from?"

"Over the top of Falster Island. Impact in ten seconds."

Golov spun on the XO. "Kravchuk, fire the railgun back along the missile's trajectory."

"Captain, we can't know where it was launched from or —"

"I said do it!" Golov screamed.

Kravchuk nodded grimly. "Aye, Captain." He gave the order to aim the weapon along the missile's flight path.

The railgun spun on its turret, compensating for the *Achilles*'s movements.

"Target locked."

"Fire!"

A hypersonic round shot from the railgun, but Golov had his eye fixed on the flaming tail of the missile coming toward them.

The radar operator yelled, "Brace for impact!"

For a moment, Golov was certain the Exocet would blow apart the yacht's bridge, but the missile hit the *Achilles* dead amidships in a fiery blast. The entire bridge crew was thrown to the deck, but the polycarbonate windows deflected the shrapnel from the explosion.

As Golov scrambled back to his feet, he shouted for a damage report.

Kravchuk peered at a monitor that was flashing red. "Fire suppression systems have activated. The fire is out, but the railgun turret was damaged. We have elevation control of the weapon, but the turntable is off-line. We can't rotate it to aim it anymore."

"Can it still fire?"

Kravchuk frantically typed into the computer. "Yes, but we've got a fault in the capacitor system. We might blow the whole ship apart if we continue firing."

"We'll have to risk it."

"But shooting at them is futile!"

"That's for me to decide!"

Golov's phone, which he finally realized was still in his hand, rang with a jingle that was completely discordant with the chaos on the bridge.

The *Oregon* was calling back.

"Is there another missile coming?" Golov asked the radar operator.

"No, sir."

"Get the helicopter in the air now." He had ordered the Ka-226 fully fueled and armed with Russian Switchblade anti-ship missiles just in case he ran into a coast guard vessel that got too curious.

The phone rang insistently. He gritted his teeth and answered the call, if only to buy some time.

"What?" he growled.

"Why'd you hang up on me, Golov?" Cabrillo asked in a mocking tone. "You guys busy over there or something? By the way, you missed us. It wasn't even close."

"Calling to gloat over your victory?"

"I'm calling to see if you want to surrender. Personally, I'm hoping the answer is no, but I have someone from Interpol here who wants to take you into custody and deliver you to any number of countries that would love to interrogate you and your crew about your activities over the last few weeks."

Golov slammed his hand on the chair. He wasn't going to give up when he was so close to completing the operation. Not when Ivana was about to fulfill her part.

But he couldn't fire on the transformer station until she had deactivated the circuit breakers. If he destroyed it early, the cascade effect on the electrical grid wouldn't work. It had to happen after she had uploaded her software.

While Golov was contemplating his options, the helicopter took off. As he watched it swoop away toward the island, he locked his gaze on the cruise ship behind it in the distance.

"Since you launched an attack chopper," Cabrillo said, "I'm going to interpret your stunned silence as a big fat no to surrendering. Linda, fire two. Bye, Golov."

"Wait," Golov said into the phone.

"Too late. Missile's away."

"Don't you want to hear my counterproposal?" As he was talking, he pointed at the immense white cruise ship ten miles off their port bow and motioned for the helmsman to bring the *Achilles* around. Maybe the railgun couldn't turn, but the yacht could.

Cabrillo laughed. "Counterproposal? You're joking, right?"

"Missile incoming!" the panicked radar operator shouted. "Twenty seconds to impact!"

"In ten seconds, I'm going to start firing on that cruise ship," Golov said to Cabrillo with no bluff in his caustic delivery of the line. "And if you don't kill me with this next missile, I'm going to keep firing until all five thousand people on that ship are dead."

Juan and the rest of the crew inside the op center watched as the *Achilles* slewed around until the barrel of the railgun was pointed at the cruise ship. He knew Golov would fire. He could only imagine the devastation that the railgun's round would cause if it struck a crowded part of the passenger decks.

He didn't have time to think about it further. The missile was too close to the *Achilles.*

"Abort the missile," he told Linda.

"Aborting, aye," she replied, and the Exocet detonated halfway to the target.

"All right, Golov. Looks like we've got ourselves a Mexican standoff."

"That's just the way it seems," Golov said. "Don't bother trying to warn the cruise ship. We're monitoring the same radio frequencies they are."

"We'll pull back," Juan said.

"Not good enough. As soon as that ship is out of range, I'll be at your mercy again."

"Then what's your counterproposal?"

"Bring your ship out of hiding. I want it right next to the *Achilles.*"

"Why?"

"Because *you're* the one who's going to surrender. I estimate the cruise ship will be in range for another fifteen minutes. You have ten minutes to bring the *Oregon* to me."

Juan signaled Hali with the finger-across-the-throat gesture so that he'd mute the call. Hali nodded that they were clear.

Max erupted. "We can't surrender to that madman!"

"Golov won't hesitate to blow that ship apart," Gretchen said. "Since he thinks he can still win, prison isn't an option for him, or anyone else on the *Achilles.* He has nothing to lose."

"I'm not inclined to give up any more easily than he is," Juan said. "Is there any other way to take his railgun out?"

Max shook his head. "Not before he could get off three or four shots. Even a ship as big as that one might not be able to survive that kind of barrage."

"Anyone else have an idea of how to take the gun out?"

Silence was his only reply.

"Then I don't see any alternative," Juan said. "We have to do what he says. Hali, put us back on."

Hali nodded again.

Juan sighed for effect. "I've considered your tempting proposal. We're on our way."

"Wise choice," Golov said. "If you launch a single missile, or if there are any weapons visible on that wonder ship of yours, I will fire."

"I don't doubt you're a man of your word. But if you fire, I will destroy you."

"Two men of our word, then. I expect to see you out on deck with the rest of your crew when you get here."

"I understand."

"I can't wait to see you again," Golov said, and hung up.

"Stoney," Juan said. "Set a course for the *Achilles*."

"Aye, Chairman," Eric said. The *Oregon* began to move.

A deathly quiet filled the op center.

"He'll kill us all, you know," Linda finally said. "You've seen what he's capable of."

"I know," Juan said as he set the timer on his watch. "So we've got ten minutes to come up with a way to keep Golov from sinking that cruise ship while also stopping him from causing a continent-wide disaster. Any ideas?"

More silence, excruciating in its totality. It was broken when Eric cleared his throat.

"You've got something, Stoney?" Juan asked.

"Remember those Jetlev-Flyers Murph and I were playing around with a few weeks ago before we started that job in Algeria?"

"Murph liked those more than his beloved skateboard," Max said. "He even convinced me to buy four for the ship to use for R and R."

Eric nodded. "Well, Golov said he wanted to see you on deck."

Juan sat forward, intrigued. "Where are you going with this?"

Eric had just the hint of a smile, and Juan knew he was onto something. "He didn't say whose deck."

SIXTY

Ivana got a good look at the Continental Control Hub as the Airbus Eurocopter circled high above it before touching down. Just as she'd seen in satellite photos, it was designed with a distinctive lightning bolt shape as an homage to its purpose. The silver exterior sparkled in the sun.

Antonovich sat across from her, watching her with glazed eyes. He'd been given a mild sedative to keep him compliant while still being able to function.

Sirkal sat beside him, holding a large professional video camera. Behind him were five mercenaries that made up his assault force. Two of them were dressed in suits like Sirkal and Antonovich, while the rest wore black windbreakers and pants.

As the chopper began its descent, Ivana's phone rang. It was her father.

"We are almost there," she answered.

"Good," Golov said. "Because we've had

trouble up here." He gave her a brief recap of the attack by the *Oregon.* "They'll be here in nine minutes. How long until you can get the virus uploaded?"

"It'll be operational a few minutes after we are able to secure the command center."

"And the transactions?"

"I'll start them right now." She tapped on her phone and the downloads began. Banks across Europe would start noticing unusual activity in just a few minutes, but it would take them some time to realize the extent of the problem. By then, the financial system would be frozen, along with the rest of the continent.

"I've started the downloads," she said. "Remember, don't take down the transformer station until I've confirmed the virus is active."

"I know. We'll be ready."

"Be careful, Father. Don't trust that man."

"I don't. Right now, he has no choice but to do as I say."

"Love you."

"I love you, too, dear. The next time we see each other, we'll be billionaires."

"See you in Rotterdam." She hung up and turned to Antonovich.

"We're not going to have any trouble with you, are we?"

Antonovich shook his head in defeat. The assertive businessman of the past was long gone. He was now a shell of his former self, transformed by paranoia, drugs, and almost a year of captivity.

"I'm glad to know that," she said. "I wouldn't want to have Sirkal kill you just before you earned your freedom."

They landed on an empty part of the parking lot outside the Control Hub and were met by a stocky woman in her late thirties, dressed in a skirt and jacket. With her dark hair pinned up in a bun and frameless glasses, she carried herself with authority. She stood between two men, both of whom looked like they were part of the security team.

When the helicopter's main rotor had spun down sufficiently, Ivana exited, holding her briefcase, while Sirkal helped Antonovich out. Two of the other men in suits carried the camera and microphone. The three wearing windbreakers got out but stayed by the helicopter.

Ivana took Antonovich by the arm as if he were unsteady on his feet and led him to the waiting woman, who gave them a bright smile.

"Mr. Antonovich," she said in English, "it's such a pleasure to finally meet you. My name is Beatrix Dräger, manager of the Continental Control Hub."

As they shook hands, Ivana translated for Antonovich, who asked Dräger hopefully, "Do you speak Russian?"

Dräger kept on smiling, waiting for the translation.

Ivana said in Russian, "No one here speaks Russian, and you don't speak English, Mr. Antonovich, so remember to do what I say."

She returned Dräger's smile and said, "Mr. Antonovich is delighted to be here and see the fruits of his joint venture. He doesn't speak English, so I will be his interpreter during the tour. My name is Ivana Semova."

"And your companions?"

"Mr. Sirkal is documenting Mr. Antonovich's visit, if that's all right. We'd also like to do an interview with you when the tour is over."

"Of course," Dräger said. "I'd be happy to do a short interview. The only place where you are not allowed to film is in the command center. For security reasons. I'm sure you understand."

"Certainly. These other men are Mr. Antonovich's assistants, and the three gentlemen by the helicopter are part of Mr. Antonovich's security team. They will remain outside with the helicopter."

"By all means."

"Shall we begin the tour?" Ivana asked, trying not to sound too anxious. "Mr. Antonovich is particularly eager to see the command center."

"We can start there, if you'd like," Dräger said as she began to walk around the building to the Control Hub's main entrance. On the way, Ivana noted an emergency exit that opened into the parking lot not far from the helicopter.

"Thank you," Ivana said. "That would be wonderful. Will the Dijkstras be joining us?"

"We heard from Gustaaf Dijkstra that he's on his way. Would you like to wait for him?"

"That won't be possible. Unfortunately, Mr. Antonovich has other engagements today, so we can't stay very long. We appreciate you moving the tour up at the last minute."

"Not at all," Dräger said. "We're very proud of the facility, so we're thrilled to show it off."

While they walked, Dräger rattled off statistics about the building and its role in controlling the flow of electricity for over three hundred million people. Ivana dutifully interpreted the information while observing the security measures. The grounds were surrounded by a ten-foot-high wrought-iron fence topped with spikes. A ditch inside the fence line was meant to stop trucks carrying explosives, as were the thick metal columns at the front gate that had to be lowered below grade by the armed guards to allow cars to enter.

They went through metal detectors at the entrance, and their bags and equipment were searched, but there was no X-ray machine, just as they expected.

They walked down the sleek tiled halls to the rear of the building, where the command center was located. As they went, Sirkal backpedaled while he focused the camera on Antonovich, who didn't crack a smile or speak. Dräger's patter continued nonstop.

When they reached the door to the command center, Dräger asked Sirkal to turn the camera off and he complied. At the same time, he subtly opened the camera's body, while the two other men removed stilettos from the audio equipment they were carrying.

After Dräger scanned her palm on the reader and typed in a passcode, the door buzzed open.

There was a marked contrast between the silence outside the door and the bustling noise and activity inside the command center as they stepped in. Over thirty analysts and technicians were stationed at three tiers of computer desks facing a giant wall of screens with all sorts of maps and status displays showing the current state of the continent's electricity grid. A row of glass-enclosed offices lined one side of the room. The only other door was the emergency exit at the far side of the room.

Sirkal nodded at his companions and they plunged their stilettos into the necks of the two security men, who collapsed in a gush of blood. Beatrix Dräger shrank back against the nearest console, dumbstruck with horror.

Before anyone else had a chance to react, Sirkal handed out pistol magazines he had hidden within the camera body to Ivana and the two mercenaries. They all loaded them into small semi-automatics they had tucked into the back of their belts.

Steel pistols would have set off the metal detectors, which they had known would be in place. Instead, they'd fashioned non-metallic pistols based on firearm designs found on the Internet that were meant to be used with 3-D printers. The black bodies of the guns were constructed out of polymer, the springs plastic, and the barrels a high-strength ceramic. They looked just like ordinary pistols.

The downside of the homemade pistols was that their life span was very short. They could fire the entire ten-round magazine of .22 caliber ammunition, but the barrels would crack and become useless after that.

Ivana racked the slide and fired a single bullet into the ceiling. The crack of the gunshot made everyone inside the command center turn in unison.

Shouts and screams erupted from the workers when they saw the men bleeding out on the carpet.

Ivana leveled the pistol at the workers while keeping one hand on Antonovich. If he made any move to escape or resist, she would have no problem killing him, although that would ruin the illusion that he was behind the whole attack.

"Everyone put your hands up now or die," she demanded.

Half the room's occupants raised their arms in the air, but the other half were either confused or hesitant. Ivana picked the nearest noncompliant person and put a bullet through his head.

"Now!"

All of the other hands shot up.

"Now, stand up. My friends here will

come around and empty your pockets of phones. If I see anyone make an attempt to call or text someone, that person will be the next to die."

Phones were quickly collected without incident.

"What we do now," she said in as pompous a voice as she could muster, "we do for our Mother Russia. No longer will our country be subjugated to the whims of Europe's illegal and immoral sanctions. It's your turn to suffer."

After the offices' landline phones, computers, and panic buttons were disabled, all of the workers, including Dräger, were herded into them and locked inside.

Ivana attached her laptop to an Ethernet cable connected to the command center's network. In a few minutes, the entire network was infected and she could now control all of the remote circuit breakers from the application on her laptop.

She instructed all of the breakers to lock in the closed position. One by one, the lights on the big board turned red to indicate the dangerous condition each location had been put in.

When the whole continent was a beautiful scarlet, Ivana checked the sum of the accounts where the money had been transferred. The number of zeroes blew her away. The total read just over thirty billion euros. She grinned and texted her father.

Money is transferred and Dynamo is active. You are a go.

Golov replied seconds later.

Understood. Commencing attack once we have Oregon under control. Get out of there. Good work, my girl.

Ivana smiled at that. Soon, whole nations would go dark, and she'd get to see it happen from the air. She detached her laptop and put it back in the briefcase.

"Time to get back to the *Achilles* and pop some bubbly," she said to Sirkal.

The Indian didn't smile, but he gave her a satisfied nod. The other men whooped in excitement at becoming multimillionaires.

"What about me?" Antonovich pleaded.

"What *about* you?" Ivana shot back.

"Do I go free now?"

"Not until we get to Rotterdam. Let's go."

She wanted to make sure they were in the air before any other Control Hub security guards realized something was wrong. As she shoved the visibly dispirited Antonovich toward the emergency exit, she called the helicopter pilot.

"Spin up the engine," she said. "We're leaving."

Sixty-One

Eddie cupped the phone in his hand. "Murph says there's no answer from Beatrix Dräger," he said to Linc, who was driving their rented SUV.

"I'm going to go out on a limb and guess it's not because her phone battery died," Linc said as he followed Gustaaf Dijkstra's Mercedes sedan through the front gate of the Continental Control Hub. By breaking every speed limit in the Netherlands and weaving through traffic like they were on an obstacle course, the two-vehicle convoy made it to the facility in record time.

"There's no way she'd ignore a call from Gustaaf Dijkstra." He took his hand off the phone and spoke to Murph, who was in the Mercedes's backseat with Gustaaf. "Go through the front entrance with Dijkstra to the command center. Make sure you take plenty of armed security guards with you, just in case."

The throb of rotor blades picking up speed vibrated the windows.

"It sounds like the helicopter is getting ready to take off," Murph said.

"We hear it. We'll circle around the building and make sure they don't leave."

"Roger that."

Eddie drew his pistol and now wished he'd brought a more substantial weapon.

They rounded the point of the building's lightning bolt shape and saw the Eurocopter's rotors spinning at full speed.

A door at the back of the building opened and two athletic men sprinted toward the helicopter. They were followed by a tall Indian, a young woman, and Maxim Antonovich, who was practically being dragged by the woman. She had to be Ivana Semova. They weaved their way through the cars in the parking lot.

"There they are," Eddie said.

"Timing is everything," Linc said.

"We also have three men by the helicopter. They've got automatic weapons."

Antonovich was the first one to spot their approaching SUV. He wrested himself away from Ivana and dived behind a car. Eddie was amazed to see her shoot at the billionaire. If he was in charge of this whole operation, why was one of his underlings trying to kill him?

He popped off three quick shots at Ivana. None of them hit, but the sudden shots made her rethink going after Antonovich. She turned and ran for the helicopter with the Indian.

The three men guarding the helicopter sprayed the front of the SUV with fire, splattering the windshield with holes, as Eddie and Linc ducked. Eddie popped up to take down one of the guards, but the other two retreated into the helicopter as soon as Ivana and the Indian arrived.

The pitch of the chopper engine increased.

"They're about to take off!"

Linc tightened his grip on the steering wheel and spun the SUV one hundred and eighty degrees. "Feel like doing something crazy?" He mashed the accelerator down as he kept his eye on the backup camera.

They were pointed directly at the helicopter and picking up speed.

"Let's go nuts," Eddie said, cinching up his seat belt.

They roared through the parking lot as bullets punched into the SUV's rear, exploding the back window. The helicopter's wheels rose off the asphalt as the SUV's back roof smashed into the tail section.

The SUV bounced off and rolled onto its

side, skidding across the pavement and popping the windshield out as it slid to a stop. Eddie shook the cobwebs out and then swatted the deployed air bags out of the way to watch the helicopter.

At first, it didn't seem as if the helicopter had been significantly damaged, just knocked off its initial flight path. Because the tail rotor was encased inside a protective housing, the blades didn't snap off instantly. But the aluminum housing was bent enough that the rotors began to wobble and then hit the frame.

As pieces of the rotor started to fly off, Eddie knew the helicopter wasn't going to get very far.

Ivana hadn't had time to strap herself in and she knew the helicopter wasn't going to make it. The warning alarm signaled a major malfunction caused by the impact with the SUV.

Smoke poured from under the rotors, filling the cabin with noxious fumes. The door on her side of the chopper was still open. The men behind her were shouting in panic.

The helicopter spun in a lazy circle as it crossed over the Control Hub's roof. For a moment, it seemed as though they'd crash on top of the building itself, but they cleared it, with only a few feet to spare, as they began their final descent onto the facility's front lawn.

The spin violently increased as they plummeted. Ivana let go of the briefcase holding her laptop and it flew out the door. Not wanting to be trapped inside the helicopter when it crashed, she jumped free when it was still twenty feet above the ground. She curled herself into a ball, taking the brunt of the impact with her shoulder. The jarring blow knocked the wind out of her as she rolled to a stop.

Sirkal tensed to jump, too, but he made the mistake of leaping out at the same time that the pilot tried to bank the helicopter in a corrective maneuver.

Sirkal threw his hands up and screamed as he saw the massive main rotor churning toward him. It caught him in midflight, chopping him to pieces in a spray of blood and gore. Nothing larger than a hand made it to the ground.

The fragile rotor came apart and the Eurocopter slammed into the ground. The fuel tank ruptured as the fuselage collapsed from the crushing impact. The entire chopper exploded, taking the rest of the occupants with it.

Despite the pain in her shoulder, Ivana

looked around for any way to escape. Then she saw her one chance.

A Mercedes was idling by the Control Hub's entrance.

After Eddie and Linc crawled from the SUV's remains with little more than scratches and bruises from the crash, they ran toward the smoke that was billowing up over the Control Hub building.

Eddie came around the corner to see Ivana pick up a briefcase and throw it into the burning hulk of the helicopter. She held one arm close to her body as if it were injured while she ran toward Gustaaf Dijkstra's Mercedes, which was idling at the front entrance. Its driver, who had gotten out after the helicopter crashed, fled toward the building's entrance when he saw Ivana waving a pistol at him.

Eddie sprinted toward her with Linc hot on his heels, but she climbed into the car and slammed the door. The Mercedes screeched away toward the facility's gate.

"Close the gate!" he yelled at the guards.

One of them pressed the button to raise the cylindrical truck barriers.

Instead of slowing, the powerful Mercedes, which had already reached highway speeds, continued to accelerate in an attempt to make it across the top of the cylinders before they were fully raised.

But the top of the cylinders had risen just enough to catch the front of the chassis. The Mercedes catapulted over the cylinders and somersaulted in the air.

The air bags deployed, but the car continued to tumble over the pavement. Ivana, who hadn't been wearing a seat belt, was slingshotted from the car and bounced across the pavement like a rag doll before the Mercedes came to rest as a jumble of nearly unrecognizable metal.

Eddie and Linc were the first ones to reach her. She stared up at them with unseeing eyes, her neck broken from the impact.

Eddie's phone dinged. It was Murph.

"Eddie, are you and Linc okay? We heard an explosion."

"We're fine. The helicopter went down in front of the building."

"Did Ivana Semova make it out? Because the electrical grid is about to melt down and we need her alive to stop it. And see if you can find that laptop she was carrying."

"I've got bad news and worse news," Eddie said as he looked at Ivana's corpse. "Ivana survived the crash, but the bad news is that she threw her briefcase into the fire.

I assume her laptop was inside. The worse news is that she's no longer in a position to help us restore the grid. Her next destination is the morgue."

"Then we are supremely hosed if Golov hits that transformer station."

"Actually, there is one survivor," Linc offered. "Antonovich might be able to help."

Now that Beatrix Dräger and her team were freed from the offices, they assessed the damage that Ivana Semova had done to the grid. As Murph continued to see nothing but red lights on the big board, the shouts that echoed around the room were panicked, some in English, most in Dutch.

"I'm still locked out!"

"I can't access the breaker subroutines!"

"What did she do?"

Gustaaf Dijkstra watched helplessly as Dräger begged Murph to help them.

"If you have any idea what that woman did to our system, we need to know right now."

"There's one possibility outside," Murph said, hustling to the emergency exit. "I'll be right back. Keep the door open for me."

"Where is he?" he asked Eddie, who was still on the line.

"The last I saw, he was near a blue Audi."

"You sure Semova was trying to kill him?"

"Sure looked that way to me."

Murph spotted the billionaire, who was still huddled behind the car. "I guess I'll ask him."

"Linc's on his way to give you a hand."

Murph hung up and ran over to Antonovich, who was holding his left leg. Blood oozed through his fingers and down his pant leg. When he saw Murph, Antonovich spoke at him in rapid-fire Russian.

Murph didn't speak the language, so he tapped on the same language translation application he'd used at the Albanian Mafia castle. He spoke into the phone as it interpreted his words.

"Mr. Antonovich, my name is Mark Murphy. Speak slowly and clearly."

Antonovich nodded and said, "They made me do this. I'm innocent."

"They who?"

"Golov and his daughter."

"Ivana Semova was his daughter? Was she also a hacker named ShadowFoe?"

Antonovich nodded and winced from the pain as he moved his leg. "They've been holding me captive for nearly a year. My whole crew mutinied and took over the *Achilles* under Golov's direction. He's the one behind this attack."

Linc rushed up and knelt beside them. He rolled up Antonovich's pant leg to reveal a bullet hole in his calf.

"He says he's completely innocent," Murph said as Linc took off his jacket and put pressure on the wound.

"Sounds like a convenient story," Linc replied.

"Then why did Semova shoot him? And Dräger said he didn't seem to be directing her inside. If anything, he seemed to be at her mercy."

"Then he won't mind helping us, will he?"

"Good point," Murph said, and turned the translation app back on. "Mr. Antonovich, if you're telling the truth, then how do we reactivate the continental grid's circuit breakers?"

Antonovich shook his head. "I don't know. Ivana had a program on her laptop. It let her lock out access from the Control Hub's systems. Her program is the only way to control the breakers."

"Her laptop is destroyed and Ivana is dead. There must be some other way."

"There isn't. You would have to get another copy of her program."

"How can we do that? Do you know someplace online where we can find it?"

"No," Antonovich said. "You won't be

able to get it. There's only one place she would keep a backup of that file."

Murph wanted to shake the answer out of him. "Where?"

Antonovich shook his head in hopelessness. "In her cabin on the *Achilles*."

SIXTY-TWO

Juan had his phone on speaker while he quickly donned his wetsuit and slung a Heckler & Koch MP5 over his shoulder. Next to the *Oregon*'s moon pool, Eric, MacD, and Gretchen were doing the same.

"I've got the *Achilles* in sight," Max said over the phone. "We're two minutes out."

"Take your time," Juan said.

"Not up to me. Hali's got Murph on the line for you."

"Chairman, we've got a big problem," Murph said. "The Control Hub's system is locked up. Ivana Semova, aka ShadowFoe, designed a program that is the only way to unlock it quickly, but her laptop with the program was destroyed. They've got calls in to reset the breakers manually at each station, but that could take hours."

"Where is she?"

"Dead, along with the rest of her accomplices. And here's something we didn't know. She's Sergey Golov's daughter."

That information might be useful, Juan thought. "Tell Max to share that news with Golov when the time is right. He'll know the moment. What about Antonovich? Is he dead, too?"

"No, he's alive and mostly well. According to him, he's a victim in all this. We're inclined to believe him because Ivana tried to kill him. He says the only other existing copy of the program we need is on his yacht in Ivana's cabin."

Juan shot a look at Gretchen. "We might be able to help you out, then. We're about to board the *Achilles.* Which one is her cabin?" He had memorized the layout of the *Achilles,* thanks to the blueprints they'd obtained in Vladivostok.

There was a pause before Murph responded. "He says it's on deck four, the same level as the main lounge. Third door on the right as you exit the lounge toward the bow."

Eric, who'd been listening to the conversation, said, "But even if we get there, she'll have it password-protected, won't she? I'm good, but I can't crack it that fast."

"You don't need to," Murph said. "Eddie retrieved her phone and unlocked it with her thumbprint. It has a password manager on it. It's got to be one of those passwords. If you can get into her computer and send the program to me, I can load it onto a computer here and reactivate the circuit breakers."

"We'll call you when we've got it," Juan said.

"Okay." Murph was gone.

Juan could feel the *Oregon* slowing as it approached the *Achilles*. Eric had just a minute to instruct Juan, MacD, and Gretchen on the use of the Jetlev-Flyers. If they were going to get onto the *Achilles* to find ShadowFoe's circuit breaker program and disable its railgun, they'd have to be fast. Climbing up a conventional rope ladder wouldn't work. They'd be picked off long before they could get aboard. The water-powered jetpacks gave them their only chance.

Like the gas-powered jetpack Juan had used once on a mission in China, the Jetlev-Flyers were mounted on a backpack with two nozzles pointed downward. Arm braces controlled the angle of the water jets, and a motorcycle-style throttle at the right hand determined how much pressure shot from the nozzles.

For recreational use, the pressurized water for the jets was supplied by a small surface vessel with a four-stroke marine engine, which would follow them around while they performed aerial maneuvers. But for this mission, technicians had linked together as much fire hose as they could so that the water could be pumped directly from inside the moon pool chamber.

They put on the jetpacks and climbed into the pool. Each of them did a brief test to make sure they could propel themselves both in and above the water.

There was no room to wear scuba tanks along with the jetpacks, so they had to use miniature tanks connected to regulator mouthpieces, rigs that were normally used in emergencies by divers and kayakers.

"Remember," Juan said to the others, "we'll only get about thirty breaths once we go under, which gives us three minutes at most."

They all nodded. Gretchen was the least experienced diver among them, but Juan detected no apprehension in her face, only nervous energy.

They donned their masks as they bobbed in the moon pool waiting for the signal from Max that the ship was in position. After a short delay, a technician said, "We're a go."

Juan clamped his teeth over the mouthpiece and submerged, making sure that his hose, which was now fully pressurized, didn't get fouled in the massive doors in the *Oregon*'s keel. Once he was in the open, he could see the white double hull of the *Achilles.*

He checked with Eric, MacD, and Gretchen and they all gave him the OK sign. He oriented himself into a horizontal position, throttled up his jetpack, and shot toward the massive yacht.

Golov was pleased to see that the *Oregon* had eased to a stop next to the *Achilles* on her starboard side. Still, he made sure that the yacht kept yawing in place to maintain a railgun lock on the cruise ship, which was still ten miles away. The *Oregon* matched his turn so that it remained parallel.

The faux cargo ship's deck was deserted and no weapons were visible. The Ka-226 helicopter hovered above them with its missiles trained on the *Oregon.*

Golov called Marie Marceau's phone again.

"Very good seamanship, Captain Cabrillo. Now we will discuss your method of surrendering your ship to me."

"This isn't Cabrillo," another voice said. "My name is Max Hanley."

"Where is Cabrillo?"

567

"He's on his way up to the deck, just like you asked. But first, we want assurances that no one will be harmed."

"I only want your ship. Once we have attached a towline, you will abandon ship in your lifeboats."

"How do we know you won't kill us, once we're in the water?"

"Remember, Mr. Hanley, I know the specifications on those lifeboats. They're armed, armored, and fast. You'll be out of range of the *Achilles* in minutes, once you find the shelter of the islands."

Of course, he was lying. He had no intention of letting them get that far. The helicopter would track them and take out both lifeboats before they reached the islands.

Hanley sighed. "I suppose we don't have any choice."

"You don't."

"We'll move the *Oregon* close enough for you to shoot over a towline."

"Slowly, Mr. Hanley."

Golov ordered some men onto the *Achilles* deck with a towline as the *Oregon* nudged into range to receive it.

"Now show me Mr. Cabrillo," he said.

"Actually, Mr. Cabrillo just received a phone call. He said it relates to you."

"What do you mean?"

"Look at your phone."

Look at my phone? What kind of message was that?

His phone rang. It was Ivana's number.

"Better get that," Hanley said.

Confused, Golov switched over to her call.

"Ivana? Where are you, my dear? On your way to Rotterdam, I hope."

He was stunned to hear a man reply and it wasn't Sirkal.

"Captain Golov, this is Eddie Seng. I'm a crew member on the *Oregon,* and Juan Cabrillo asked me to give a message to you. Your daughter is dead."

Then four things happened simultaneously.

On Golov's phone, a photo appeared in his text messages. He started shaking in rage and grief when he saw an image of his lifeless daughter, lying in the grass.

On the port side of the *Achilles,* four people shot up out of the water, each balanced on a pair of water jets shooting from contraptions on their backs, before each of them landed on the deck. They unlatched their jetpacks, spit tiny air tanks from their mouths, and disappeared into the yacht's interior.

On the deck of the *Oregon,* an air-to-air missile rocketed from a hidden canister toward the stationary Ka-226 helicopter. The chopper pilot banked abruptly but couldn't escape the warhead. The helicopter and its anti-ship missiles exploded in a huge fireball.

And on the starboard side, the *Oregon* suddenly lurched sideways toward the *Achilles.*

Thrown off by the anguishing news about his beloved daughter and distracted by the sudden appearance of the odd commando raiders, Golov hesitated before he realized what he had to do. He yelled, "Fire!" just as the *Oregon* smacked into the *Achilles*'s starboard hull.

The entire bridge crew was knocked off their feet. The weapons officer recovered first and punched the button to fire the railgun.

A round blasted from the barrel. Golov got to his feet and watched the cruise ship as he shouted for them to load another shell.

He counted down the seconds until the cruise ship erupted in fire.

Instead, the hypersonic round plunged into the water a hundred feet off the big liner's stern, spewing a gigantic fountain of water into the air.

The *Oregon* continued to push, preventing them from turning to aim the railgun.

They had no shot at the cruise ship now.

If they could get free of the *Oregon,* they could once again target the transformer station and finish the mission that he and his daughter had started.

"All engines full speed ahead!" he commanded, before wheeling on Kravchuk.

He pierced his XO with a venomous glare. "Secure the bridge and all critical areas of the ship. I want every available person searching for that boarding party. If they aren't dead in the next five minutes, I will personally see to it that no one gets off the *Achilles* alive."

SIXTY-THREE

As the *Achilles* surged forward, Juan, Eric, MacD, and Gretchen proceeded with caution through the interior. Juan thought there was still a chance that Antonovich was lying and leading them into a trap.

They reached the main lounge and crept through it, keeping their eyes on all of the doors. Through the panoramic windows, Juan could see the bulk of the *Oregon* pressed against the yacht's hull, trying to drive her sideways and keep her from getting in position to fire on either the cruise ship or transformer station. The .30 caliber machine guns hidden in the rusty barrels aboard the *Oregon* had popped up and were firing at unseen targets on the deck above. Max could stop any boarding party Golov tried to send over.

Juan was sure Golov had a shipwide search going on for them. When they got to the bow end of the lounge, Juan took point and moved down the hall.

At the third cabin on the right, Juan tried the door handle, but it was locked.

With everyone ready, he kicked the door in. He rushed inside with his submachine gun prepared to fire, but the room was deserted.

"Hurry up, Eric," Juan said. "We don't have much time." Gretchen kept watch at the door, and MacD prepped the C-4 they'd brought with them to sabotage the railgun.

"On it," Eric said, taking a seat at the keyboard. The array of monitors came alive with a tap on the space bar. He input several passwords from the list Murph had sent over. The fourth one worked and he was in.

All of the file names were written in English, the universal language of hackers. Eric looked up which files had been copied most recently.

"I think this is it!" he announced triumphantly. He pointed at a file called *Dynamo Break Config*. He opened it to display a control panel for operating the circuit breakers remotely. "I can use the *Achilles*'s network to get this to Murph."

Gretchen snapped her fingers and whispered, "We've got company. Main lounge."

"Send it," Juan said quietly.

"Already on its way," Eric replied. "One more thing to do." His fingers flew across the keyboard.

"You're done," Juan said, pulling him up. Eric resisted for a moment and tapped the ENTER key before he was yanked from the chair. A window popped up on the screen, but Juan didn't take the time to see what it said.

Gretchen fired her MP5 in three controlled bursts at the main lounge. They were answered by screams of those hit and shouts of the remaining survivors.

"Move!" she yelled, and unleashed an extended barrage of suppressing fire.

MacD and Eric shot as they retreated in cover formation while Juan ran down the hall to clear their path. By now, he could see that the *Achilles* was beginning to pull away from the *Oregon.* They didn't have much time before she would be free to maneuver into a firing position on the transformer station.

Juan was met by three men attempting to flank them by coming down from the deck above. Juan got the first one in the chest as he was coming down the stairs, but the other two retreated upstairs, sporadically firing to cut off escape in that direction.

Juan led MacD, Eric, and Gretchen down

the stairs. Their destination was the rail-gun's main power supply.

"These guys don't seem as well trained as the other mercs we've run into," MacD said, barely breaking a sweat as they ran down the stairs.

"Golov probably sent his best people on the raid in the Netherlands," Gretchen said.

"They still have us outnumbered," Juan reminded them. "It won't take them long to figure out where we went."

They sprinted through the corridor to the room housing the railgun power supply. Two men inside raised pistols as the team rushed in, but Juan put them down before they could fire.

The large room, filled with electrical panels, consoles, computer terminals, and wiring conduits, hummed from generators charging the massive capacitors. It had doors on either end, one toward the bow and the other toward the stern, making defense of the space particularly difficult.

"Gretchen, Eric, take the doors while MacD and I plant the explosives. MacD, set them for sixty seconds."

Juan worked as quickly as he could to mash the C-4 against the control panel.

Max had the *Oregon*'s engines at full throttle, but they still couldn't keep up with the *Achilles*'s fantastic speed. Despite Linda's expert helm control, the yacht was pulling away.

Their hulls continued to grind together, but the armored plating of both ships withstood the enormous pressure. The *Achilles*'s stern was now almost even with the *Oregon*'s bow.

Max forced a last few drops of power from the magnetohydrodynamic engines and ordered, "Hard aport!"

Linda slewed the *Oregon* around and it mashed even harder against the *Achilles*'s stern in a shriek of metal.

But it was no use. The *Achilles* was free.

Max tried to open the panel to expose the 120mm cannon, but the impact had crushed the doors and jammed them shut. They were out of operational Exocet missiles, and the *Oregon*'s torpedoes were useless against the *Achilles*'s mini-torpedoes.

He brought the Gatling guns to bear on the yacht. The angry buzz-saw sound of the rotating six-barreled guns was accompanied by the chunks of the *Achilles* flying away as the tungsten rounds chewed into her stern, but they did nothing to slow her down. In seconds, she'd be in position to fire on the transformers.

Juan and his team were now the only ones who could take out the railgun.

SIXTY-FOUR

On the *Achilles*'s bridge, four of the monitors were showing live street webcam feeds from Paris, Amsterdam, Frankfurt, and Brussels. When the screens went black, Golov would have confirmation that Europe's power system had been fried.

It was a struggle to keep his mind off Ivana's death, but he did his best by focusing on the havoc he was about to wreak, a bittersweet revenge for his devastating loss.

The *Oregon* was in pursuit but falling behind quickly. Her rotary cannons relentlessly hammered away at the *Achilles*.

"Bring us around, Mr. Kravchuk," Golov said, standing defiantly in the middle of the bridge to show that he would not succumb to the worst that Cabrillo could dish out. "Take aim on the main transformer housing."

"Aye, Captain."

The *Achilles* swung around, continuing at

flank speed. The railgun's elevation lowered. The targeting reticle on the screen was coming into focus on the transformer station.

Juan was planting the last explosive charge in the railgun's power supply room when he heard Max in his earpiece.

"Juan, you're out of time. They're lining up to fire."

"Got it." Juan turned to MacD. "Okay, you heard him. Let's cut down the time to fifteen seconds and hope that we —"

A barrage of bullets from the aft door cut him short. MacD was hit in the shoulder and fell back. Juan dragged him out of the line of fire, while Gretchen took down the first of half a dozen attackers. Eric shot two men trying to box them in from the bow side. More rounds ricocheted around them, forcing them to retreat behind an equipment panel before they could arm the bombs.

They all returned fire, but they were at a stalemate. Neither side could advance.

"We're stuck," Gretchen said. "They'd cut us down before we could arm the explosives."

Juan reported the situation to Max while he pictured the layout of the *Achilles* in his mind. There was a corridor one flight up that would allow him to circle around and ambush the gunmen from the rear, if they remained where they were.

"You two stay here and distract them," Juan said to Eric and MacD.

Without another word, he looked at Gretchen and tilted his head toward the door. She understood and nodded.

Under cover of a withering fusillade from Eric and MacD, Juan and Gretchen crawled out of the room.

As soon as they were out of sight, they sprinted up the closest set of stairs.

The command center personnel at the Continental Control Hub silently watched Murph as he waited in frustration for the program Eric sent him to install on his laptop. They all wanted to crowd around to see what was going on, but Linc and Eddie kept them back to give him breathing space. Although Murph was used to working under pressure, this was a whole new level. He was essentially trying to deactivate a nuke that was going to take out the entire grid for hundreds of millions of people, and the clock was ticking.

Antonovich, who stood off to the side under the guard of the facility's security team, had shown him the exact cable Ivana had connected her own computer to. The little blue progress bar on Murph's screen filled in with excruciating sluggishness.

Max was on a speakerphone, calling a play-by-play on the *Achilles*'s attempt to line up a shot on the transformer station.

"He's turning now," Max said. "It's allowing us to make up some of the distance."

"How much?" Eddie asked.

"Not enough. They'll be able to fire in less than a minute."

Linc leaned over the speaker. "Is there any way you can stall them?"

"I've done everything I can. And Juan has his own problems. It's up to you now."

Murph's fingers hovered over the mouse and keyboard as the last five percent of the progress bar counted down.

When it reached one hundred percent, the application opened. Several of the command center employees cheered, but Murph knew that they weren't out of the woods yet.

The app confirmed that he was connected to the Control Hub's system. He swiftly scanned ShadowFoe's user interface, searching for the command to deactivate the lock on the circuit breakers.

He found the proper menu item and a command window popped up: DEACTIVATE

BREAKER LOCK. He clicked on it.

A pop-up window helpfully asked, *Are you sure?*

"What am I, an idiot?" Murph said, and clicked *OK*.

Every eye turned to the big board. After an agonizing wait, one of the red lights turned to green. Then a second light switched to green. Dozens more remained red, but the program seemed to be working as a third red light converted to green.

"The *Achilles* is in firing position," Max announced.

Murph held his breath. This was going to be close.

SIXTY-FIVE

Juan and Gretchen reached the stairwell behind the crew attacking the power supply room.

"What's your sitrep, Stoney?" Juan whispered into his throat mic.

"Still here," Eric replied. "We got three of them. Three left, but I'm almost out of ammo."

"One mag for me," MacD grunted.

"Okay," Juan said. "We're in position. As soon as you start shooting, we'll rush them. On my mark. Three . . . two . . . one . . . Now!"

Two sustained volleys of fire came from below. Juan and Gretchen ran down the stairs and saw the backs of two men, crouching behind the doorjambs. The inexperienced crew members raised their assault rifles to fire, but Juan and Gretchen took them out with a couple of short bursts.

The one remaining man, who had advanced into the power supply room, whirled around at the shots behind him, exposing his position. MacD and Eric brought him down before Juan and Gretchen could finish the job.

They rushed in and found all but one of the bombs intact. Its timer had been damaged in the hail of gunfire. In spite of that, Juan thought enough explosives had been planted to take out the system.

"Remember, fifteen seconds," Juan said to Eric, while Gretchen helped MacD up and covered their path out.

Juan entered the new time into the first detonator, but a high-pitched whine froze him before he could get to the next one. The eerie sound was followed immediately by a mammoth bang that shook the whole room.

They were too late. The railgun had fired.

The superheated air and smoke around the railgun's barrel cleared almost instantly in the strong wind. Golov raised binoculars to watch the results of all his and Ivana's hard work come to fruition. He silently mouthed the seconds to impact.

The vast station's main transformer housing was unguarded except for a chain-link fence and barbed wire. Because it was unmanned, there would be no casualties — not that Golov cared. The building was shielded from the weather by a steel wall. The hypersonic round would drill through it as easily as it knifed through the air.

When Golov mouthed, "One," a huge explosion engulfed the housing. Sparks flew from the transformers as they short-circuited, their oil-cooling systems blowing apart in succession like dominos. The spectacular chain reaction was even better than what he'd hoped for.

He dropped the binoculars and eagerly watched the TV monitors.

For a moment, there was no change, but Golov knew that it would take a few seconds for the cascade effect to ripple through the electrical system.

Then the first monitor went black. Amsterdam was dark. There was an elated cheer of victory from the bridge crew. They knew that meant their stolen money could no longer be tracked by investigators. By the time the grid came back online, the trail would be ice-cold.

Golov smiled wistfully and imagined Ivana's pride at their accomplishment. He watched expectantly for the other screens to go dark.

But none of them did. The feeds remained

up and running. The traffic lights remained functional. Vehicles continued to move.

His smile faded.

Then the live feed from Amsterdam came back online. The electrical grid was still intact. Golov stood staring in disbelief.

"No, no, no," he muttered, hoping that there was just a delay, but after another few seconds, it was clear that there would be no cascading grid failure.

His mission had failed. Now there would be nowhere he could run without being tracked down.

His phone rang. It was Marie Marceau's number.

He answered. "I'll get you for this."

"And my little dog, too?" Cabrillo replied, his voice masked by the sound of machinery in the background. "Give it up, Golov. Ivana's program was deactivated. You're done. If I were you —"

Golov hurled the phone against the bulkhead, shattering it.

He yelled at his XO, "Turn so we can fire on the *Oregon*!"

"But Captain, the railgun is overheating," Kravchuk said. "It's only a matter of time before the liquid-cooled capacitors explode, unless we shut it down."

Golov grabbed him by the lapel. "Don't

you see that our only chance to get away now is to keep them from following us?"

"Sir, we risk destroying the *Achilles* if we fire a damaged gun."

"I don't care!" Golov shouted, practically spitting the words. "Destroy that ship!"

He stared down the helmsman, who finally set a new course. The *Achilles* began its turn. Kravchuk reluctantly ordered a new shell loaded into the railgun.

"Now they're turning on us," Max told Juan.

"Don't worry," Juan said. "We're about to take care of that."

He pulled MacD to his feet and nodded to Eric. The timers were set at fifteen seconds. Eric flicked them on and they ran out of the power supply room. Leading the way and watching for any further gunmen, Juan sprinted up the stairs as Eric and Gretchen helped MacD behind him. They were two decks up, and moving down the hall toward daylight, when the detonators went off.

The blasts tore through the power room, spewing a jet of fire out through the corridor and licking at the bottom of the stairwell. The railgun wouldn't be firing again. The detonation worked just as they'd hoped.

It was the next explosion that Juan wasn't expecting.

Their C-4 must have damaged some system they weren't aware of, setting off a secondary reaction, because a huge blast threw him down the hall.

Juan's vision blacked out for a moment and then returned as he, strangely, found himself lying on the floor. He shook his head to regain his senses.

Down the hall, Eric writhed on the ground, holding his leg. Juan crawled over to him.

"Stoney, are you hurt?"

"My leg," Eric said, grimacing. "I think it's broken."

"Hold on. We'll get you out of here." Flames crept up the walls on the other side of the yacht. The automated fire suppression system had been knocked out in the blast.

Juan looked around and saw MacD propped up in a seated position, regarding him with a ragged smile.

"Ah expected better amenities on a yacht like this."

"Where's Gretchen?"

MacD turned his head in surprise as if

he'd forgotten she was with them.

They both spotted her at the same time. She was motionless, with her hip pinned under a beam that had fallen from the ceiling.

Juan ran to her and leaned down to check her breathing. She was still alive but unconscious.

Eric was in no condition to help Juan, and MacD wasn't much better, but at least he was mobile.

"MacD, grab her arm and pull her out when I lift the beam."

Using his good hand, MacD got hold of her arm. Juan thrust his titanium-framed combat leg under the beam and pried it up. He got just enough leverage for MacD to drag Gretchen out. When she was clear, Juan lowered the beam and picked her up very carefully, not knowing the extent of her injuries.

"Help Eric," Juan said, then nodded toward the door leading out onto the deck. "There should be a life raft outside that exit. Come on. I don't think the *Achilles* is going to be afloat much longer."

Outside, Juan put Gretchen down for a moment, opened a hatch, and withdrew a life raft canister. There were also several life vests, which he handed to MacD and Eric, before fitting one on Gretchen.

The *Achilles* had slowed to half speed but was still traveling faster than most other ships could. It didn't matter. They had to risk jumping overboard.

"This is going to hurt, Stoney," he said.

Eric nodded in understanding. "I know."

Movement caught Juan's eye. He looked up, past the ruined railgun, to a man dashing out onto the flying wing outside the bridge. Golov glared down at him from the railing, yelling something that Juan couldn't understand.

Juan gave Golov a mocking salute. Then with a nod to MacD, who was balanced on the railing alongside Eric, he threw the raft canister overboard at the same time that they jumped. The life raft inflated automatically when it hit the water. Juan gently lifted Gretchen's limp body over the side and dropped with her into the Baltic Sea.

Golov watched as Cabrillo and the others with him were swept into the *Achilles*'s frothing wake.

"Captain, I must insist that we go," Kravchuk said as he joined him on the bridge wing. "The *Achilles* is doomed." The XO waved his hand at the fire raging through half the vessel.

Kravchuk was right. It was only a matter of time before the unchecked fire reached the fuel tanks.

Golov tore himself away from the sight of Cabrillo and the raft receding behind them, no doubt thinking they had successfully escaped.

But for Golov, this wasn't over yet. He had one more card to play. An ace.

"We're abandoning ship," he told the XO. "Ready the submarine for launch."

Sixty-Six

Large wind-driven swells made it a challenge for Juan to reach Gretchen. With powerful strokes, he finally made it to her, latched her vest to his, and swam toward the large yellow life raft, bobbing on the sea, twenty yards away.

As he swam, he saw the *Achilles* slow to a crawl. Several figures jumped overboard, but no lifeboats or additional rafts were launched. He thought he saw a splash in the dark space between the yacht's twin catamaran hulls. He couldn't be sure.

He scanned the water and spotted two orange life vests ahead of him near the raft. Those had to be Eric and MacD. Juan swam toward them harder, knowing that neither of them would have the strength to pull themselves into the raft once they reached it. He knew the *Oregon* was behind him and had to have seen the raft deployed. Max would be racing to pick them up.

The fire aboard the *Achilles* reached its apex. Huge geysers of flame shot into the sky, throwing off thick clouds of black smoke. The fuel tanks finally succumbed to the heat and exploded, annihilating the stern of the majestic yacht and blasting away shards of steel, fiberglass, gold, mahogany, and crystal. The bow, still on fire, settled into the water at a steep angle and seconds later disappeared from view. Except for an oil slick and floating bits of debris, the *Achilles* was gone.

Juan reached the raft. "How is everyone?" he asked MacD and Eric. He could see now that it was octagonal, with a weatherproof canopy to shield occupants from the sun and rain.

"Going swimmingly," MacD said with a forced grin.

Eric coughed up some water. "I could sleep for about three days."

Both of them looked ashen but in good spirits.

"I think shore leave for the entire crew has been well earned," Juan said as he untied Gretchen's line. He hauled himself into the raft, pausing to catch his breath before pulling Gretchen in with him. Then he pulled up MacD and, finally, Eric, who cried out when a wave hit them and caused his leg to bang against the lip of the raft.

Juan checked Gretchen. She was still unconscious. He brushed the hair from her face and swaddled a reflective blanket around her to keep her warm. Frustrated that he couldn't do more for her, he lay back in exhaustion and triggered his mic. "Max, can you read me?"

Max's voice came back garbled and indistinct, the result of damage to Juan's comm system.

"Juan . . . you seen . . . coming to . . . sonar . . ."

"Max, if you can hear, tell Julia to get the medical team ready. We've got casualties."

"Juan . . . it's coming toward you . . ." He could now hear that Max's voice had an urgency that he wasn't expecting.

He peered out of the canopy's opening, expecting to see the *Oregon* coming toward them. Instead, he saw a disturbance in the water, like the wake of a ghost ship. Moments after that, a black fin pierced the surface as it rose.

No, not a fin. A conning tower.

It was the *Achilles*'s submarine. And it was charging straight toward them.

The conning tower hatch flew open and there was Golov, maniacally grinning at Juan as he brandished an assault rifle.

Juan momentarily thought about dumping everyone overboard and diving under the water, but there wasn't enough time and he didn't think the others would make it back to the surface. All of their weapons had been discarded when they jumped into the water, but he still had the .45 ACP Colt Defender in his combat leg. He drew it and found the raft's flare gun, which he wielded with his other hand. Neither was a match for a high-powered assault rifle at this distance.

Golov seemed to agree with his assessment and waggled a finger at Juan when they were a hundred yards away, well out of effective range of his pistol. He raised the rifle to his shoulder and waved good-bye to Juan.

Before he could fire, someone from inside the sub grabbed Golov's attention. He yanked the rifle away from his shoulder, called down into the sub, then looked to his left in horror.

Juan looked right to see the familiar rusty bow that he knew so well racing toward the submarine.

Golov yelled for the sub to dive, but it was too late. The kinetic energy of eleven thousand tons of armored steel bore down on the relatively puny eight-man submarine.

Golov screamed in terror and defeat as the bow of the *Oregon* hit the sub dead center.

It split in two as if it were cleaved by a butcher's knife. The conning tower was crushed, pinning Golov inside the hatch. Water surged into the broken front half of the sub, pulling it down. Juan's last sight of the Ukrainian ship captain was him flailing desperately as he was sucked down beneath the sea's surface to a watery grave.

Max reestablished comms. "Juan . . . you there?"

"Still here, Max. Thanks for riding to the rescue."

"Our pleasure. The old girl took a licking, but she came through it all right. Did we lose anyone?"

"Not yet, but some are in bad shape. Come and get us as soon as you can."

"Hux is waiting in the boat garage with stretchers. We'll be there in a minute."

Juan felt a hand grasp his arm. He looked down and saw Gretchen's eyes open, searching and confused.

"What's happening?" she asked. "Where am I?"

Juan took her hand gently and knelt beside her. "We're on a life raft. How are you feeling?"

"I can't move my right leg."

"You've been injured in an explosion, but Julia is on her way to take care of you."

"Doesn't hurt too much."

Juan knew that wouldn't last long. She was still in shock. The pain hadn't hit her yet, but it soon would.

She looked at Eric, then MacD, before returning her gaze to Juan. "Did we . . . Did we stop them?"

"We sure did. You missed all the fun."

Gretchen wheezed a hoarse laugh. "You call this fun?"

Juan shook his head and smiled at her. "I call this a typical day at the office."

Epilogue

SIX WEEKS LATER
BORNHOLM ISLAND, BALTIC SEA
This kind of view must be why tourists flock to the island, Juan thought as he stood alone on the aft deck of the *Oregon.* The late-afternoon sun perfectly framed the scenic rocky coastline of the Danish island, situated halfway between Sweden and Poland. Gossamer wisps of clouds daubed the azure sky, and a light breeze lifted a pleasant salty tang from the sea. A lone gull noiselessly hovering over the fantail was his only company.

Soon the sound of the waves crashing against the nearby shoreline was punctured by the throb of helicopter blades pulsing in the air. The seagull banked away, making room for the *Oregon*'s MD 520N helicopter as it flared out over the ship's landing pad. Gomez Adams grinned at him as he smoothly landed the unusual chopper, with its rotorless tail. The skids had barely kissed the deck when he killed the engine.

Juan walked over and opened the helicopter's passenger door. Gretchen greeted him with a warm smile.

"Nice of you to send this first-class ride for me," she said as she gingerly climbed down with Juan's assistance. "Breathing outdoor air is a nice change after being cooped up in a hospital room for a month."

When she had both feet firmly planted on the deck, she removed a brass-tipped cane from beside the seat while Juan grabbed her small suitcase.

"No more walker for you, I see," he said, holding her arm as she hobbled off with him.

"My first full day with a cane. I felt like an old lady riding in those courtesy carts at the airport on the way here, but they do get you around fast."

"I like it. Very sophisticated."

"Oh, I'm sure the rehab nurses at Bethesda thought the same thing when they taught me how to use it. By the way, I'm supposed to pass compliments on to Julia Huxley from the surgeons there. They commented several times on what an excellent job she did realigning my fractured pelvis."

That was high praise coming from doctors at Bethesda Naval Hospital, one of the best in the world. Juan had taken Gretchen there personally after her injury and spent several days with her before returning to the *Oregon.*

"You can tell her yourself tonight over dinner," Juan said. "Chef has put together a banquet fit for a queen."

"I just wish I could have been there for Mike Trono's wake. I imagine it was quite the party."

"You will definitely hear stories about it. Ask MacD about his impromptu karaoke serenade."

"Can't wait. How are he and Eric doing?"

"Eric's still in a cast, but he loves whizzing down the halls on his scooter. MacD's shoulder didn't sustain any structural damage, and he's already bragged about showing off his nice new scar to the ladies."

"As if he needs more help in that department." Instead of going inside, Gretchen steered them toward the railing. "I want to take in this view."

They leaned against the railing for a few silent moments. Gretchen's eyes reflected the sunlight as she inhaled the sea breeze.

Maurice appeared seemingly out of nowhere, carrying a tray holding two glasses.

"A refreshment after your trip, Ms. Wagner. It's an elderflower cordial, a local Danish concoction."

"Thank you, Maurice."

"I'll take your luggage to your cabin." The octogenarian steward retreated with her bag just as quietly as he had arrived.

"How does he do that?" she asked Juan as she sipped her drink.

"My theory is that he was trained by ninjas." He paused to take a sip, then said, "I'm sorry I couldn't have stayed longer with you at the hospital."

She waved off the apology. "Don't worry about it. I know you had a lot to do back here. The ship looks as awful as usual, by the way."

Juan smiled. "Why, thank you. We do make an effort."

"Did it take long to fix?"

"A couple of weeks in port after we returned the Jaffa Column to the Maltese Oceanic Museum. Of course, we couldn't return to Vladivostok after what happened there, but we have a few other options around the world for repairs."

"The less I know, the better."

"It sounds like the *Oregon* isn't in your future."

"According to the doctors, fieldwork isn't in my future after this." She pointed at her hip. "But the CIA has given me a promotion, heading up a new financial analysis department. I start as soon as I get back."

Juan clinked glasses with her. "I'm happy for you. But they didn't give it to you. You earned it."

Neither had brought up their night together in Lithuania, and Juan didn't think there was any point now, despite how he felt about her. It was clear their paths had intersected only briefly and were now diverging again. Their time with each other would have to remain a wonderful memory.

To avoid the subject, Juan filled her in about the aftermath of the attack on the electrical grid and banking system. Although Gretchen had seen news updates from her hospital bed, she hadn't yet heard some of the most important details.

Before Juan could tear Eric away from ShadowFoe's computer, Eric had initiated an upload of all its contents to the *Oregon*'s servers. Most of the files were transferred before the *Achilles* was destroyed and they provided a wealth of knowledge about Ivana Semova's hacking activities.

Using the data that Eric and Murph gleaned, they were able to unlock the Credit Condamine computer system and restore all of the funds, including the Corporation's.

In addition, they learned about Shadow-Foe's unusual coding technique, which had its roots in a radical mathematical concept previously hidden for two hundred years.

Maxim Antonovich — whose captivity and innocence in the entire affair had been confirmed by three crewmen who confessed after being saved from the wreckage of the *Achilles* — had purchased several rare documents, most of which had been in the yacht's safe when it went down. But prior to that, they'd all been scanned into ShadowFoe's computer. One of those documents was a centuries-old mathematical treatise by a Russian named Alexei Polichev, who was an instructor at Moscow State University at the time of Napoleon's invasion. His revolutionary algorithms were lost during the war — or so it was thought. But two copies had survived, the one that Antonovich ended up buying and a second set whisked away by Napoleon's soldiers, along with the rest of the treasure. That copy was damaged beyond repair when it went into the Neris River inside the trunk that Trono tried to save. ShadowFoe had based her unique computer viruses on Polichev's formulas.

After reverse engineering Ivana's programs, Eric and Murph consulted with the banks to recover the stolen funds, collecting a tidy reward in the process, enough to not only refit and rearm the *Oregon* but also to install a few upgrades. The Corporation then turned Polichev's equations over to the CIA for use in the government's various counter-cyberwarfare operations.

"In addition to electronic copies of the torn-out pages from *Napoleon's Diary,* we also found an interesting letter on Shadow-Foe's computer," Juan said. "Remember Pierre Delacroix?"

"You mean the naval lieutenant who wrote about kidnapping Napoleon from St. Helena?"

"That's him. Antonovich never told us about a second letter Delacroix had written."

He took a folded sheet of paper from his pocket and handed it to Gretchen.

"It was addressed to a wealthy businessman named Jacques Aubuchon, although we don't know if the letter actually made it to him. Aubuchon, apparently, funded the operation to kidnap Napoleon in the hopes of finding the treasure he stole from Moscow."

She unfolded the printout and began to read.